In Treachery Forged

In Treachery Forged

David A. Tatum

Fennec Fox Press

In Treachery Forged

Printed in the United States of America
First Trade Edition, 2014

ISBN-13 978-0-9912844-2-9

Fennec Fox Press
Ashburn, Va 20147
http://www.FennecFoxPress.com

Cover art by Alex Kolesar (http://www.nn4b.com)

Dedication and Acknowledgements

To Andrew "Mageohki" Norris, whose chats regarding fantasy tropes influenced my magic system and my dwarven culture, and without whom those elements would have been a lot more generic.

To Sarah Myer, whose concept art helped me flesh out Euleilla's character greatly. I wish we hadn't lost touch.

To Alex Kolesar, for providing some wonderful cover art.

To my brother, Jonathan Ken Tatum, without whom this would never have been possible.

To my mother, Betty Jo Tatum, without whose financial and logistic support I wouldn't have had the time to write.

And finally to my late father, librarian extraordinaire and book expert George Marvin Tatum, who instilled a great love for writing throughout our whole family before he passed away. I miss you, dad.

Prologue

The young girl concentrated with all her might, using all of the meditation techniques her father had taught her. Today she would control the boundless magic inside of her and not allow herself to be distracted by her long, messy hair or the drafts let in by her threadbare cotton frock.

At first, only one grain of the magic powder made from fine iron sand moved, but moving that one grain told her just what to do. It wasn't long before the magic powder flew to attention around her. "Look, papa, look!" she cried, gesturing with her hands. She always loved spirals and swirls, and by twirling around she managed to make it dance in those patterns. She only wished she had the more expensive nickel bead "powder" to make it all sparkle. "I'm doing it!"

Her father had often told her that he couldn't always watch her practice when he was working. Until the formula he had been working on could be sold, they would never have the money to replace her worn clothing or to let her use fancy magic powder.

As busy as he was, though, he always had some time for her. Even as a failed mage, he always knew when she was practicing even when he couldn't watch her. "I'm proud of you, honey," he said, glancing up at her but not breaking his own concentration. She was a gifted student, and it showed. "But I've got to work."

"You might as well stop and watch your daughter's little show," a gravelly voice said from behind the counter of their shop. "Because if you keep working we'll be forced to stop you."

Her father glanced up at the person he had assumed was a normal, everyday customer and stiffened. "Daughter, maybe you should go out and play."

The girl glanced up at her father curiously. She recognized that tone, and she hated it. Every other time she'd heard him speak like that, they had to move in a hurry and she would have to start her life all over again. She missed the lessons in magic that her father's friend, Cawnpore, had provided, and the mountain snows of her native Sycanth. Every time she was getting used to a place, it seemed, they had to move again.

"No, stay," the stranger sneered, unleashing a wave of magical force that shattered many of the glass jars full of metallic powders that stocked the store's shelves. "Until your father and I complete our business, I want you here."

The girl covered her face to avoid the flying glass. This stranger was confusing and scaring her, but she had been through this sort of thing before. She looked up to her father for answers once the glass shards had settled. He looked down at her, first, then up at the stranger. "I guess, if they're sending a real mage this time, they're getting serious. What do I need to do for you to let her go?" he asked.

"Your notes are ours," the stranger demanded. "And you will need to be... silenced."

"Your predecessor gave me better terms," her father snorted. Moving quickly, he lifted a cudgel hidden behind his counter and swung as quickly as he could.

The stranger ducked, and with a flash of magic threw some sort of blunt object at her father. It was an iron candle-holder, the candle in it still lit. The girl's father ducked and the candle flew into the broken vials of chemicals. A thick senbon needle with an oily sheen – an assassin's tool – flew in its wake, stabbing into her father, as the candle started a fire amidst the chemicals of their alchemist shop.

There was a brief spark, and then a large flash as the chemicals exploded. Half the room was taken with them. The stranger was consumed by the fire and parts of the store collapsed around the girl and her father. As she tried to run out of the house, a large, burning splinter went flying at her head. She screamed, and then was consumed by darkness.

Chapter 1

Sword Prince Maelgyn was in trouble again, returning late from a ride to visit his mother's grave on the anniversary of her death. He wasn't exactly in the best of moods, and he wasn't looking forward to the tongue-lashing Troubuxet was sure to dish out if he was late to his lessons again. Turning his chestnut roan over to the grooming hand at the stables, he hurried on without stopping for his customary pleasantries with the horse-master. Nor did he even stop to change out of the dragonhide armor he wore whenever he left the castle.

For the past three years, Maelgyn had attended lessons on history, etiquette, and protocol at the insistence of his father, Sword Prince Nattiel, Duke of Rubick, brother to the King, and third in line of succession to the throne of Svieda.

Maelgyn – who was the presumptive Duke of Sopan Province and fourth in the line of succession, himself – had turned eighteen two months before. Normally, that birthday would have been the end of his sessions with the tutor, but Nattiel had insisted they continue until he made the trip to Sopan and formally took up the title of Duke. The winds were such that it was too perilous to travel by sea until the season changed, and there was no land route that didn't require crossing into one of the neighboring kingdoms, so it would still be some months until he could make the journey. He'd been anticipating the trip hungrily, frustrated with the demands of an increasingly strict father, a tutor who played favorites, and the whims of a spoiled ambassador's child.

In his earlier years, Maelgyn's training had concentrated on swordplay and magic, and he missed the physical and mental exercise they offered. He knew that a Duke needed to know history and protocol, but he still argued with his father over his previous instructors' dismissals. Fortunately, he also enjoyed the scholarly lessons his father did permit, if not the tutor.

Or rather, he had enjoyed them until Prince Mussack of Sho'Curlas, nephew of High King Fitz IV and son of the High King's Ambassador to Svieda, arrived at the castle with his father.

For months, the High King of Sho'Curlas had been pressuring Sword King Gilbereth to renegotiate the terms of their tenuous alliance. Tense negotiations still ongoing, King Gilbereth couldn't afford to argue when the Ambassador, Prince Hussack, made a simple request for his ill-mannered son to share the same tutor as Maelgyn and his two cousins: Sword Prince Brode, the Duke of Glorest, and Sword Prince Arnach, the Duke of Happaso.

Maelgyn knew it was the right decision for the Kingdom, but it still grated on him. Mussack had never gotten along with the people of Svieda, particularly Maelgyn and his cousins. Mussack looked down on them, and demanded more rights than his station was supposed to allow. He had even been known to give the tutor bribes, most recently an iron-chained necklace with a golden medallion, to secure preferential treatment during instruction. Troubuxet now focused his lectures only on things of interest to Mussack, to the exclusion of subjects the Sviedan princes desired to hear about.

Maelgyn sighed as he reached the entrance to Svieda castle. The guards' smart salute did little to improve his mood as he hurried through past the walls and through courtyard, seeking the West tower. He wouldn't have time to change out of his armor before the lesson without making himself late. He just hoped that wouldn't cause him more problems.

Fortunately, Troubuxet was the last to arrive at the tutoring session, much to Maelgyn's relief. A moment later Maelgyn realized why; he could vaguely hear Troubuxet and Prince Hussack chatting quietly as they walked toward the chamber.

Mussack, of course, used the delay to throw jibes at Maelgyn.

"Fancy suit of armor, Maelgyn," he sneered. "I thought only the nobles of real kingdoms could afford dragonhide, but I suppose it matches those pretty swords all of you 'sword princesses' always wear. Afraid to leave your quarters without them? Do the cooks and chambermaids really hate you that much?"

"That sword is the symbol of the royal family of Svieda," Troubuxet noted from the doorway, walking in.

Mussack's father, Hussack, followed Troubuxet into the room as if to speak, but only nodded curtly to his son before departing. Maelgyn raised an eyebrow, his curiosity piqued. Mussack had seemed to stiffen at his father's gesture, biting his lip in an expression Maelgyn could only interpret as... fear?

For once, at least, Mussack's sarcasm seemed to have offended Troubuxet, who launched into a lecture with his sternest voice, "The royal swords are katana, which can only be forged by a properly trained master blacksmith. By patiently folding and hammering different types of steel together, the smith creates layers and layers of laminated steel that can hold a keen edge without becoming brittle. If Master Maelgyn were to draw the sword – not that I advise it, mind you – you would see the pattern of those layers in the blade. The forging requires both skill and experience; slight errors in heating, cooling, or handling the steel will make a blade inferior, which might cause it to break in battle.

"Centuries ago, around the time Svieda was founded, a powerful mage named Tasai took up the blacksmith's craft. He was a master among masters, refining his steel to a degree no normal blacksmith could manage, using his magic and his exceptional skill to forge blades the likes of which no-one since has achieved. King Greyholden I, founder of our kingdom, commissioned ten blades from Tasai at the peak of his skill. These would become the royal heirlooms of our nation and symbols to be worn only by the highest of our royalty, the Swords.

"The king is always to hold the best of them, which is why the kings of Svieda are known as Sword Kings, Master Mussack. One of the royal swords was lost during the Borden Island Rebellions over a hundred years ago, but the remaining eight are still divided among the eight members of the royal family closest in line to succession. Each Sword is a symbol of leadership over a particular duchy or province of the kingdom, attested to by the design on the hilt. When the king dies, the Swords change hands as the line of succession demands.

"The Law of the Swords is complex, however. If, for example, the king were to die through war, misadventure, or assassination, and his Sword then lost, any of the eight remaining Swords may restore the throne to the kingdom of Svieda, regardless of his normal place in succession."

"Fascinating," Mussack said, staring at Maelgyn's sword. "Is the sword magic?

"Magic?" Maelgyn scoffed. "Of course not. Magic is simply the ability some people have to control forces that affect certain metals such as iron and nickel. There are quite a few stories you'll hear about magic spells which turn people into frogs or some silly thing like that, but it doesn't really work that way."

"What do you know about magic, anyway?" said Mussack. "Magic affects people, not just metal."

Sword Prince Brode stared at Mussack. "You do realize Maelgyn spent the first fifteen years of his life training as a mage, don't you?"

"Master Maelgyn is correct," Troubuxet interrupted, taking a step toward the students to intervene. "Have you ever bit your lip and tasted your own blood? There's metal in all kinds of things you wouldn't think of – sea water, dirt, rocks, some fruits and vegetables. When you're talking about how slight the trace of iron is in human blood, though, it takes quite a bit of power and concentration to affect people. This is why even the weak magical field of a lodestone can offer protection against your average mage. But know this – a truly skilled mage is more powerful than a whole array of lodestones, and can force his magic through the protection they provide with little effort. The only real defense against magic is dragonhide."

"Forget this jabbering about magic," Mussack grumbled in frustration. "We were talking about the Swords of Svieda." He paused, biting his lip again.

There was an awkward silence. Once more, Maelgyn felt that Mussack seemed unusually tense and hesitant.

"Well then," Mussack finally went on, clearing his throat. "It's clear I'll have to have one of my own."

"Well, that's not likely unless you were to marry into the royal line," Troubuxet replied.

"Oh, that's no problem," Mussack said crisply, turning to Maelgyn. He stepped forward and stood straight up, his eyes narrowing maliciously as he found his resolve. "This runt will just have to give me his."

Maelgyn couldn't believe his ears for a moment, but then stood up in anger. "Excuse me, but did you just tell me to give you my Sword?"

"Yes," Mussack agreed. "It's much too valuable of a bauble to be wasted on a whelp like yourself."

Maelgyn stared at Mussack, his expression calm but deadly. Childish pranks were one thing; hostile demands by a foreign royal were quite another. "Such demands are not those of an ally, Prince Mussack. My Sword leaves me only if I die or leave the line of succession, and not before."

"Exactly. I will take your place in the line of succession, and you will relinquish it," Mussack explained, reaching out his hand. "So, give it here!"

Everyone was still for a few moments before Mussack impatiently jumped for Maelgyn's sword. Without a second's thought, all three Sword Princes had their weapons drawn and pointed at the Sho'Curlas prince.

"W-wait," Troubuxet stuttered. "I don't think we should all be so hasty. Master Mussack is just playing with you all, I'm sure..."

"Of course," said Maelgyn, his tone dangerously quiet and obliging. "If Mussack backs down, I will be glad to assume that he wasn't aware that the penalty for intentionally touching a Sword without permission or right is the death of the offender. Or that it is occasionally among my functions as Sword Prince to dispense justice in all capital crimes in the name of the King."

"Oh, but I have the right," Mussack said, now not even hiding his arrogance, even to Troubuxet. "I am a royal of the Sho'Curlas line. I supersede all other authorities wherever I go, save my father's or uncle's. By my authority and right as a Prince of Sho'Curlas, I demand that sword."

Troubuxet, shaking visibly, stepped in to defuse the situation and reassert his control of the class. "Now see here, Master Mussack. This is enough – if you do not desist, I will not only have you thrown out of my class, I'll have the king throw you out of Svieda as well!"

"Hmm," came a slick voice from behind him. Prince Hussack of Sho'Curlas had returned, and was now approaching his son. "We will see about that. Why don't we head over to King Gilbereth's throne room and ask him who is in the right? And get that stupid Maelgyn boy's father, too, will you? He should be there when his son is so rightly punished for his defiance."

Troubuxet swallowed hard.   Hussack was known as the most powerful man in the world aside from the High King of Sho'Curlas himself, and defying him was likely to cost him more than just his job as the Royal Tutor of Svieda.

"Yes, perhaps that would be wise."

The throne room of the Sword King of Svieda in Castle Svieda was not constructed like the typical royal court. Ten tapestries lined the walls, representing the ten duchies and provinces over which the Swords ruled. Behind each tapestry was a small chamber holding a glass covered pedestal to display the main contribution of that province or duchy to the nation.

The case of the Royal Province of Svieda, the kingdom's namesake, was situated behind the throne, and displayed a model of the crown. The Sopan province's case displayed foreign coins from the various bordering kingdoms, representing the tolls they levied on passage out of the mouth of the Orful River. Sycanth's chamber held a translucent, gold-flecked piece of quartz to represent their many gold mines. Rubick's held a woodblock print of a wheat field in honor of their large farmlands.   In Happaso's chamber lay a single log of mahogany to represent the timber industry. Glorest was represented by a sword to honor the manufacturing sector, Leyland a chunk of polished granite for its stone mines, Stanget a large leather bound book for its world renowned library, and Largo a scale model of a trireme for its naval construction.

One final tapestry, however, was concealed by a veil, and its chamber's pedestal was covered by black veils instead of the usual clear glass. It represented the Borden Islands, whose still ongoing revolt nearly a century before – during the reign of Sword King Nargle IV – ultimately led to the decision for Svieda to enter the Sho'Curlas Alliance.

On those few occasions when all or most of the Swords were present for a formal council, each Sword would ceremonially step forth from their province's chamber to begin the meeting. That afternoon, however, only Arnach, Brode, Nattiel, and Maelgyn were able to represent their respective provinces for the meeting Hussack had demanded. The four present Swords disappeared to their respective chambers, emerging when court etiquette dictated and standing ceremonially in each doorway, while Hussack – as petitioner of the King – walked to the center of the court. This positioned Hussack between the three Sword Princes and their King.

The room was, in fact, extraordinarily empty. Hussack was so frequent a visitor to the throne room – always with complaints – that, for expediencies' sake, only a token guard was ever summoned, any more. Maelgyn, his cousins, and Troubuxet were soon joined by Maelgyn's grim-faced father. They stood in front of the throne, heads bowed, awaiting Sword King Gilbereth's entrance. Hussack and Mussack were also present, but they clearly had no intention of showing the proper respect to the throne.

Finally, Gilbereth arrived. He wasn't properly dressed for a meeting, wearing neither his royal regalia nor the dragonhide armor he typically wore even at informal meetings. He was partially protected from magic, nevertheless, by his two guards, each wearing large lodestone plates in their armor. Gilbereth took his seat on the throne, further protected by two massive pillars of lodestone on either side. Between the armed guards and the massive lodestones, the royalty of Svieda could be kept fairly safe from either conventional or magical attack. Even that seemed unnecessary, as the only two people in the room who weren't entirely trusted had no record of magic talent and neither was armed.

"Well?" Gilbereth demanded, not looking too happy to anyone. "I am not accustomed to being 'summoned' to my own throne room without warning. Certainly not by someone who is not even a member of my court."

"Ah," Hussack said sardonically. "I see. Well, of course I did not intend to offend you, Your Majesty, but there is an issue we must discuss regarding young Maelgyn, here."

The king sighed. He had been dealing with these complaints – most of which were unjustified – since Hussack and his son had arrived in the Sviedan court. "And why the urgency? Couldn't you wait until the hour the Royal Court of Svieda usually listens to complaints?"

"Why, because of the seriousness of the matter," Hussack explained, feigning surprise at the need for such a question. "It may result in a major shift in our mutual relations."

The younger Sword Princes looked at one another grimly. To them, the shift had already occurred.

"And what is this... serious matter?" the king bristled, gritting his teeth.

"A matter of protocol, your Majesty. You see, young Maelgyn fails to recognize his betters. My son wishes to take his place as the Sword Prince of Sopan Province, but Maelgyn refuses to surrender the position."

Silence reigned over the throne room as that declaration was made. Everyone inside – even, apparently, the same Prince Mussack who started the mess – seemed shocked that the man would be that blunt or speak in that tone in the Sword King's own court.

Gilbereth's hand tightened on the wooden arm rest of his throne, and a faint crack could be heard as the wood split underneath it. "So this is how it begins," he muttered, almost to himself. He shook himself and turned to address Hussack directly, the gleam of royal rage in his eyes.

"First of all, I should emphasize that it was not only the right, but the duty of Our kin, the Sword Prince Maelgyn, to refuse such a demand. Indeed, I have every right to order Mussack's execution and reward Maelgyn a great bounty from your very testimony just now. Your son's crime is extremely serious, Hussack. But before I pronounce judgment – not on Maelgyn, but on your son – I will give you one single chance to explain just why you believe I should not have Prince Mussack shortened by a head."

"Why," Hussack countered, defiantly stepping forward. "Isn't it obvious? Mussack is my son, and a Prince in line for the throne of the High King of Sho'Curlas. Our royal line is older, our armies are stronger, and we are wealthier than you could ever hope to be. Svieda is little more than a protectorate of ours. We are your superiors in every way, and so any one of us has the right to expect an appropriate tribute from you when we ask it."

"The right, you say?" Gilbereth repeated slowly, drawing the phrase out while he reined in his temper and restrained himself from killing the man instantly. "If that is your answer, then this alliance is at an end!"

"A petty threat," Hussack snorted dismissively. "We both

know that Svieda needs our alliance. However, we do not need Svieda."

"You know, Prince Hussack, none of the Swords ever wanted this alliance. My Great Grandfather, Gilbereth I, only agreed to it to forestall a greater conflict. In truth, he should have listened to his last six predecessors, all of whom rejected you."

"Sho'Curlas grew for many years, often demanding we join your alliance, but we were strong enough not to fear your demands. Then Abindol Province unexpectedly rebelled against us. We lost the resources to support our military, and we feared we would be forced to ally with a greater power, either Sho'Curlas or the Imperial Republic of Oregal. To our surprise, as we were about to surrender to the inevitable and join your alliance, Oregal offered to cede Sopan to us. They knew we had to remain independent to preserve the balance of power. They had no thirst for war and conquest, but they knew war would be inevitable if your borders ever met.

"Oregal's strategy worked. With us acting as a buffer, there were no conflicts between the two great powers for many years... but then another disaster befell our kingdom – the Sword of Borden also betrayed us, and led yet another province into rebellion. Many of our resources were drained fighting that still ongoing war, while Borden seemed to have no end to the number of ships and soldiers they could bring into the conflict. Somehow it has been able to sustain itself indefinitely against the collected might of nine other provinces, many of which were even larger.

"When Sho'Curlas sent its ambassadors to us a few years into the war, we gained our first glimpse of the forces at work. My great grandfather and namesake, Sword King Gilbereth I, came to realize he had but two choices: To prepare our bankrupt nation to fight a war with you, or to join you. He joined, but used the threat of an alliance with Oregal – as well as our large and experienced armies – to force your nation into accepting our terms. Terms which grant us more power than most of the other 'allies' you obtained. And now, apparently, those terms are no longer satisfactory to you."

Gilbereth rose to his feet, pointing accusingly at the ambassador. "We are not fools, Hussack! You slipped up. We now know why Abindol and Borden abandoned us – you subverted them. You turned them against us and funded their rebellions to force us into alliance with you.

"I had hoped to choose my own time to address this, but your actions tonight – and those of your nation – cannot go unanswered. As of this moment, the Kingdom of Svieda withdraws from the Sho'Curlas Alliance. Our armies will stand ready to meet you whenever they're needed."

Hussack didn't even flinch. If anything, he looked amused at the revelation, smiling coldly. "I see. Well, sire, I'm afraid it's a bit too late for that. Your spies missed one rather important detail: We already had an army stationed north of here, along the border of your Province of Sycanth. According to a message I received this morning, that army began the invasion yesterday. Given the lack of any organized defense along that border, they should be arriving here..." he paused, considering. "Perhaps as early as tomorrow.

"Your armies are scattered and cannot be marshaled in time to defend this city. Your people may be able to put up a token resistance, but it will take some time before you can amass a proper army to match us. Your kingdom will fall, and the men and women of your royal line will become the subservient little pissants they should have been since the time of our great grandfathers."

With an arrogant grin, Hussack raised an arm towards Troubuxet, who was standing behind him, well outside of the protection of any of the guards or lodestones. With a single thought. the iron-chained medallion Mussack had recently gifted their tutor was torn off, snapping the tutor's neck in the process.

"He's a mage!," Maelgyn cried out. He hurried to bring up the mindset needed to counter a magical attack. "Watch yourselves!"

Troubuxet fell to the ground, dead, as the chain was bent, warped, and melted to form several seven-inch long senbon needles, landing safely into Hussack's outstretched palm. Before anyone could react, he threw those needles into the throats and eyes of several guards around the room.

Maelgyn barely managed to raise a magical defense against the improvised weapons, shielding himself, his cousins and his father from the deadly needles mere moments before they would all have been struck.

Hussack didn't even notice Maelgyn's feat as he had moved on to a new target. With the guards disposed of, he had the time to punch his magic through the disruptive barrier provided by the lodestones, and ripped the Royal Sword right out of its sheath, still in its belt at King Gilbereth's side.

"Hmm, not bad," Hussack mused absently, testing the sword's weight. "I suppose I might grow to like a weapon like this... but I need to test its sharpness, first." Gilbereth tried to dive for one of the downed guard's weapons, but he was cut off by Mussack, who had already taken one and was moving to help his father. A white-hot line of pain across the back of his neck was the final sensation Gilbereth felt, as Hussack turned the old King's sword against him.

"I'm sorry, Your Majesty," Hussack taunted the dying king. "But I must inform you that it is too late to withdraw your kingdom from the alliance. And, well, I'm afraid that the chances of your armies 'meeting us when they are needed' are not as good as you think."

Chapter 2

Nattiel was the first person to recover from the shock of Gilbereth's assassination. Grabbing the three younger princes, he shoved them behind him. Hussack hardly noticed, his attention occupied fighting off the dozens of royal guards streaming into the room as cries of alarm drew them in. Hussack was now wielding two swords recovered from the dead bodies of his victims, while a third was handed off to his son. Even Mussack, who obviously knew of the plot beforehand, seemed a little shocked, but he nevertheless was fighting alongside his father, and it was obvious that they were better swordsmen than anyone in the castle had suspected.

Had Hussack not also been an extraordinary mage the guards may have stood a chance, but guards trained and equipped to fight mages as powerful as Hussack were rare. The Sho'Curlas nobleman-turned-assassin had even less trouble magicking through the lodestone protection the guards wore than he had overcoming the more powerful lodestones used to protect the throne. Maelgyn might stand a chance of protecting himself with his dragonhide armor and his own magical abilities, but that was chancy, at best – he'd never seen anyone as magically powerful as Hussack.

"Get out of here," Nattiel whispered fiercely. "Send word to the other Swords, then split up and take charge of your own provinces. If they've already hit Sycanth, chances are they'll be here soon, and will move on to the other provinces shortly – you need to prepare your forces to meet them. And don't worry about Hussack and his brat. I'll keep him from following you."

"How, father?" Maelgyn asked, worried.

"Well, I may not be a mage," he replied, snorting in disgust. "But I'm wearing dragonhide armor, and I'm fairly skilled with a sword. I don't have to beat him. I just have to stop him from following you, and then barricade him in the throne room while you all make your escape."

"But... father, what about you?"

He grimaced. "Someone has to be here to lead the castle through the siege. The longer the castle holds, the more time you three will have to organize Svieda's defense, and I know this old castle's defenses better than anyone – I can hold the castle for some time. If I don't... well, let's not think about that. I'll try to get away before the city falls, but in the meantime I'm needed here. You three are needed elsewhere, and quickly. Now, go! Get out of here before you can't."

"Father, I... "

"I know, son," he said. "But there's no time. *Go!*"

"But I can help you fight!" Maelgyn exclaimed furiously. "I know both the way of the sword and magic! I may not be good enough in either to match this man, but together, we can defeat him!"

Nattiel started to turn back to the men fighting at the other end of the throne room. "Brode, Arnach? Help him leave, please."

Brode and Arnach grabbed one of Maelgyn's arms each, and started dragging him away. "Come on, 'gyn," Arnach said. "He's right. I know it hurts. We've already lost our father, and yes, you might yet lose yours, as well. But he's right, we have to go."

Maelgyn tensed. With the strength of his magic, there was no way his cousins could force him away. He could stay, and no-one would be able to stop him.

"Very well," Maelgyn said, shrugging off their grips. He would honor his father's sacrifice. "But I shall return."

The three young men mounted their horses soberly. They had passed the word for castle defenses to be prepared, but in the chaos of Gilbereth's death and the on-going battle in the throne room it seemed unlikely the castle would be ready. Of course, that was what Nattiel was staying behind to deal with.

As Maelgyn was saddling his horse, he received word that his father had managed to get out of the throne room alive and was now taking charge of the castle. There was still the coming siege and a serious threat inside the castle to deal with, but Nattiel's immediate survival eased his heart. A platoon of guards and all four court mages, long in knowledge but significantly weaker than Hussack, combined their magical strength to seal Hussack and his son inside the throne room. That would be a significant chunk of Nattiel's resources already expended when the Sho'Curlas siege train arrived, but it would allow him to turn his attention to the castle's defense.

"So," Maelgyn began hesitantly. "Any idea where to go first?"

"There's a post station just twenty minutes hard riding from the castle," Arnach suggested. "It's where most mail from the castle leaves, so they should easily be able to handle notifying everyone."

Maelgyn nodded, realizing he could send a message to Sopan that would likely arrive before he did. "Then we split and go our separate ways?"

"Yes... unless you want to come with one of us?" Arnach asked hopefully. He had been especially close to his father, and now it looked as if Maelgyn would be leaving as well. It wasn't the time for selfishness, but there were sound reasons to keep his friend and cousin nearby while they grieved. "Brode and I could both give you a ship which would get you to Sopan faster than any chance you'd have to get there overland."

Maelgyn shook his head. "No. I'll head to Largo and may ship out from there. The winds are wrong this time of year for an ocean trip from either of your provinces. They know I'll almost certainly have to go by sea to get to Sopan. With a major naval power like the city-state of Oden a part of the 'Alliance,' they're probably going to open their war effort with a blockade of Sviedan ports. Largo has the only fleet large enough to break a blockade on this side of Mar'Tok. A courier might be able to risk trying to get to sea before they get into position, but in my case it would be too reckless – they'll be looking for me."

"Well, be careful," Brode said, joining the other two. "You'll have to travel across the entire kingdom of Svieda to get to either Largo or Sopan, and your Sword and armor will draw a lot of attention. We can't spare you any soldiers for an escort. We aren't taking escorts, ourselves, though we don't have nearly as far to travel."

Maelgyn nodded. "I know. I'll pick up a disguise in the post house. My face is not too well known outside of the Royal Province, so I should be able to move about with relative anonymity."

Brode looked doubtful, but held back any arguments he might have had. "Well, then, off we go."

The trio rode out, driving their horses mercilessly. Each bore a grim face. It was the first time that Brode and Arnach had the chance to reflect on their father's death, and Maelgyn likewise knew he would probably never see his own father again. If the loss of their fathers was not enough to drive them all into fits of depression, they knew their chances in the coming war were grim at best. Sycanth was literally the gold mine of the nation, and without it the funds to raise an army would be hard to come by. Sopan would pretty much have to bankroll the war effort on its own, and there was no land route between Sopan and the rest of Svieda. More importantly, an army from Sho'Curlas would be sweeping through the royal province and probably the neighboring areas before anyone could muster a defense or a counterstrike.

The three young men arrived at the post station even faster than Arnach had estimated, and quickly dismounted their horses to run inside. Brode took charge, barking orders and demanding that letters be sent at once informing the other Swords of the situation. Arnach started dictating what each letter would say as various people inside the facility scurried about as they were directed.

Maelgyn, however, went about his business quietly, sitting down with a piece of paper to compose his own letter. He had a hard time deciding what to say – after all, using a letter to tell *his* people that they were at war seemed much too cold and impersonal. He should be there and tell them in person, but he knew it was unlikely he would arrive in Sopan as fast as the courier – not if he wanted to keep his passage secret. When he finally managed to put pen to paper, he wrote:

"To Duke Valfarn, Regent of the Province of Sopan

"I have just come from Svieda Castle, and the news is grave. The King has been assassinated by agents of the Sho'Curlas Alliance, and an invasion force may have already swept through Sycanth. Sopan, like all the provinces of Svieda, must prepare herself for invasion. The Law of Swords will soon be in effect.

Prepare our seaward defenses, but also look out for opportunistic attacks from the Imperial Republic of Oregal or one of the neighboring border-states. I do not yet know by which route I will take to Sopan Province at this time, but rest assured I will make all haste."

"By my hand and signet,

"Sword Prince Maelgyn, Duke of Sopan."

Maelgyn considered the letter for a moment. He wanted to say more, to describe exactly what he wanted done and how to do it. To describe the different routes he might take to get there. To explain why he was not arriving with this letter. Sighing, he folded it up and, using sealing wax and the Ducal signet ring of Sopan Province, marked it as his own. He couldn't afford to mention any of those things for the very reason he had to send this letter instead of going, himself – there was too much risk of the courier ship being captured and the letter falling into the wrong hands. Addressing the envelope to Regent Valfarn, he nodded and handed it to a waiting postman.

He went over to his cousins, waiting until they noticed him.

"Maelgyn?" Brode asked, acknowledging his presence. Arnach also stopped to look.

"You two have everything taken care of, here, and I just sent off my letter. I must leave quickly."

"What about your disguise?" Arnach asked, gesturing to his fairly obvious sword and dragonhide armor.

"Good point," Maelgyn hesitated. He'd actually forgotten about that part of the plan, but glancing around gave him inspiration. All of the couriers wore the identifying uniform of an oilskin riding cloak when on duty, but several of them who lived outside of the station wore heavier cloaks for travel. Spying several cloaks hanging on wall pegs he said, "I'll buy one of those off of a postman. That should be enough to hide what I'm wearing."

"Aye, if you're careful," Brode agreed doubtfully. "I can't really think of anything better, anyway. I guess there's nothing left but to wish you Godspeed, cousin."

Maelgyn clasped arms with both his cousins, and then he went to talk to one of the couriers about buying said cloak. Deal quickly made, he was off.

He was heading out alone, to the province he officially ruled, for the first time. He was fairly certain the war would still be going on when he arrived, but not so certain it would still be winnable. *Not exactly the most auspicious way of assuming lordship over a land, now is it?* He thought to himself bitterly.

By the time Maelgyn crossed the border from the royal province into his father's land of Rubick, the news was spreading. Sycanth province had fallen without even having a chance to put up a serious fight and Svieda Castle was already under siege. So far, the Sho'Curlas army appeared to have halted its advance at the castle, but it wasn't likely to stay still for long. While much of Sho'Curlas' million man army was devoted towards holding its borders and occupying its lesser allies, the attacking force was immense – large enough to divide into several smaller armies – so even if the siege took years they would continue pushing into Svieda.

That the castle was holding off the siege was a small miracle even with Nattiel's leadership. As long as the castle siege occupied Sho'Curlas forces, there was a chance that Svieda could muster an army sufficient to stabilize the borders and hold the remaining Sviedan provinces for a time. A vigorous defense, in this war of attrition, might be enough: If the cost of taking Svieda was made too dear, Sho'Curlas might be persuaded to abandon the war and sue for peace. At least, that was the hope.

Following a practice recommended by the post couriers, Maelgyn had traded his original steed for two fresher horses. They explained he would be able to ride longer and faster by periodically changing between them to allow the other horse to freshen up. Unfortunately, one horse had been killed by a dreadful fall, stumbling on a hole in the road and impaling itself on a signpost. Maelgyn had been horrified by the accident, but was otherwise unharmed himself. Nonetheless, the loss of a horse was significantly delaying his progress.

He was two weeks into Rubick before he heard anything more on the war. He was just sitting down to eat at a traveler's lodge when a rider from the messenger's service stormed inside, demanding food.

"It's been a long ride," the messenger snapped. "And I bring vital information on the war."

"Tell us," the innkeeper demanded.

"Well... we're holding our own, so far," the messenger

explained. "We feared the castle would have fallen by now, but so far it has held its own. Nattiel's defense has been such a thorn in Sho'Curlas' side that they've yet to divert any portion of their armies to securing the rest of the countryside."

"So they haven't done anything since taking Sycanth and besieging the castle?" the innkeeper asked incredulously.

"There have been some raids on farming villages, all within a few hours of Svieda Castle. Probably just setting up supply lines while they buckle down for a long siege," the messenger replied.

"Are we going to be able to save the castle?" another traveler asked.

The messenger shrugged. "Swords Arnach and Brode have returned to their provinces, and have rallied the armies of Happaso and Glorest. They may be able to mount some sort of counter strike."

Maelgyn knew that there wasn't much Brode or Arnach could do to lift the siege from Svieda Castle, but with the extra time they could form a defensive line to contain the invasion for a time. Still making his way across Rubick a week later, Maelgyn learned that his father's regent already had made plans and was marching several infantry divisions eastward to join up with Arnach's and Brode's defense. Maelgyn witnessed militia forces drilling in the village greens, preparing to repel any attackers. He knew it would be a futile gesture if any serious effort were made to take such small towns, but the fact that the people of the kingdom were keeping up hope and rising to meet the challenge of this war encouraged him.

With the early successes, there was a quiet confidence building. Speculation came out about which of the Swords would win this war and become the new Sword King: Arnach and Brode the most prominent, or Sword Prince Wybert of Largo who controlled the largest navy. Some even speculated about Sword Princess Idril of Stanget. She had publically sworn revenge when King Gilbereth's sister, the Sword of Sycanth, was captured and publically executed early in the war – as the only two women among the living Swords, they had been especially close. As he continued moving westwards, though, the talk changed. Svieda castle had been taken. It was no longer "Which Sword will win the war for us?" but rather "Will we survive this war?"

Chapter 3

Sullen faces and low voices told Maelgyn something was wrong as soon as he entered the inn. A tavern bard sat at one of the tables, his lute stowed, listening intently to a grim faced merchant rather than plying his trade. Maelgyn caught bits of the conversation as he sought a table in the corner to sit at and order a meal.

"...and the castle has fallen." Maelgyn shook his head silently, thinking of his father. With the fall of the castle, he was likely dead... and the Law of Swords was now in effect.

Following a disastrous war of succession early in Svieda's history, laws were crafted to prevent conflict among those in line for the throne in the event that the king died unexpectedly. Once the Royal Swords had been commissioned. As Troubuxet's fatal final lesson explained, these laws were collectively known as the "Law of Swords." There were many statutes and provisions in the Law of Swords, but the pertinent ones were only to be invoked upon the violent death of the King and the capture of his Sword: Each of Svieda's provinces had equal standing with the others, and their Swords may act on behalf of the entire kingdom. Placement in the line of succession barely mattered – any of the Swords could lay claim the throne by re-taking the Castle of Svieda. The only reason the line of succession still mattered was that, if two or more Swords co-operated to reclaim the throne, whoever was highest would take it. And any infighting between the Swords would result in the violent expulsion of the offender from the Swords. Maelgyn might wind up King, after all.

Probably not, however. Brode seemed the most likely, as it

was his and Arnach's armies which were most likely to reclaim the throne. Maelgyn didn't even want the throne, anyway – he still sometimes felt overwhelmed at the idea that he would be ruling over Sopan.

"What will it be, sir?" a young barmaid asked quietly, showing neither the flirtation nor the impatience he'd come to expect as the two customary options. "We've some stew, or mutton, but the mutton's reheated from yesterday. Two silvers. Brown bread with either, but drink is extra."

"The stew, then, and ale. And such news as is to be had today, if you don't mind sharing it."

The barmaid shook her head. "Word is that Largo's fleets suffered something fierce, with but a few of its hundreds of ships returning from its latest battle with the Oden Navy, but at least some escaped, and Oden's fleet was hit pretty hard as well. Worse news, sir, is that none of our people escaped Svieda castle before the fall – many were killed, and any survivors have, at best, been taken to prisons we don't know the location of. No mistake, sir, the folk here are worried."

"My thanks," he said, adding an extra half-silver to the coins he handed her, before she walked off to gather his meal. The naval battle was old news, but the word – or lack thereof – on survivors from Svieda Castle was distressing. Maelgyn swallowed the fear for his father and glanced thoughtfully around the room, listening to threads of conversation for a distraction.

"Where is Wybert, anyway?" the merchant was saying. "Where was he when the battle took place?" The merchant seemed frustrated, Maelgyn observed, but the bard just shook his head. "Even the folks out at Largo Castle don't seem to know."

Maelgyn had just come from Largo Castle, however, and knew Wybert's disappearance was a false rumor. Wybert had been with the fleet during its battle, but was badly wounded. He had lost one leg and was in danger of losing the other. An enemy catapult had hurled a massive stone at his flagship and took his leg clean off, sending splinters flying all around him. Several imbedded themselves deep into his remaining leg, one giving him a nasty gash on his forehead. Thankfully, Svieda's doctors were far ahead of most of the world when it came to medicine and surgery and his life had been saved. New innovations, such as the cleaning and sterilizing of medical equipment and certain herbal medicines, would prevent most infections. The only real fear was whether his other leg was too damaged to be saved. Nevertheless, it seemed unlikely Wybert would be an active participant in the rest of the war.

Only twelve ships of the once proud First and Second Fleets of Svieda returned to port in salvageable condition. Several others had survived, but would have to be scrapped because the damage was too severe. It was not a total defeat, however – the Oden Navy was ravaged in the battle. Only enough ships remained to blockade the port cities of Largo, Glorest, Stanget, and Leyland. While the capitals of several Sviedan provinces were closed off, some smaller ports remained open.

Maelgyn knew the fleet docked in Sopan Province was actually powerful enough to lift any of the blockades, but he couldn't let them know of the need until he reached his new home. Sword Prince Wybert, who when Maelgyn arrived was conscious and in fairly good health, considering, warned him against attempting a trip by sea. It was possible his earlier message had made it despite the weather and the hostile warships, but there were no longer any courier ships to take him to Sopan. "You might be able to find a fishing boat out of a small town that could get you there," Wybert cautioned. "It's a long trip by sea, though, and most of what you'll find are open boats. That's a fairly long trip for an open boat, especially when we can't be completely sure our enemies don't have a patrol at sea looking for you. You probably wouldn't survive the trip."

Maelgyn looked grimly into his own tankard of ale, thinking about his recent visit with Wybert. Wybert's incapacity was being kept secret, for the moment, and thankfully so was his own presence. Maelgyn was waiting, now, to see if Wybert could provide any intelligence for the trip to Sopan, and a messenger should be arriving soon with the report and a set of maps. With the naval route closed, the only way to Sopan would be overland – either over the treacherous mountains in the Dwarven Kingdom of Mar'Tok or the much longer route around the mountains through the Bandi Republic and down the Orful River.

That messenger arrived just as Maelgyn started thinking about him. Spying the unobtrusive seat on the other side of Maelgyn's table, the messenger hurried over to meet him. Maelgyn winced at the messenger's crisply formal attire, realizing other heads must already be turning to see who in the small inn might be the recipient of a royal courier's attention.

"Well?" Maelgyn asked.

"Here. There's a lot for you to read in there, but I'll sum up what you probably most want to know right now," the messenger said quietly. "Wybert is... somewhat obsessive following his defeat. Brode, Arnach, and whoever it is running Rubick's armies have combined their forces, forming a line that should be able to hold against Sho'Curlas. The two largest armies in recorded history will be meeting before too long, but it'll be a long campaign – they have untapped resources the likes of which we could only dream of. Wybert knows that we'll need every soldier we can get our hands on, and so is unwilling to release even a few soldiers to act as your escort. He will return your horse and give you any other supplies you might want, however."

"That's acceptable," Maelgyn answered diplomatically. "Since I don't have any guards, I've been trying to travel incognito."

He looked pointedly at the messenger's uniform before continuing. "I'm quite capable of protecting myself if the need arises. It's probably best that I not draw men away from where they can actually do some good, and it's easier to travel in secret without a large contingent of soldiers following me."

"You may think differently once you've read that report," the messenger replied. "Normally, I think, your best bet would be to go around the mountains, to travel through the Bandi Republic to the Orful River, and then take the short boat trip down-river. However, the Bandi Republic lost its access to the Orful River in an ongoing border war with one of its neighbors. The fighting on that border is so fierce that Wybert doesn't think you should risk traveling through Bandi at all. Instead, Wybert recommends you cross the Mar'Tok Mountains, going through the Dwarven lands to do so. It'll be dangerous, but probably less so than walking through the front lines in Bandi's little war or trying to make it on an open boat."

Maelgyn sighed. "I was afraid of that. It means at least one, possibly two river crossings and one mountain crossing, but I suppose I can do it." He pulled out a piece of parchment and handed it to the man. "I prepared for this possibility and gave it some thought. I need you to get this list to the castle's quartermaster; that's what I'm going to need for the journey. I'll be there tomorrow to pick it all up."

The messenger glanced over the list briefly and nodded. Maelgyn hadn't put anything Largo wouldn't have in excess on the list, so there shouldn't be any problems. "Very good, Your Highness. I'll see he gets this right away, and good luck."

No sooner had the messenger departed than the barmaid returned with another tankard of ale – now with a significantly friendlier expression. She had also straightened her hair, he observed, and adjusted her bodice to reveal a bit more cleavage.

"Your ale... my lord?"

"Thanks," he said in a resigned voice, this time adding two full silvers to his bill.

Maelgyn had two horses with him once again. The second horse was a simple pack animal, but it would do. Wybert couldn't afford to release a horse that might serve in battle, and Maelgyn wouldn't ask him to. The news of Wybert's injuries had been officially announced just as Maelgyn was leaving, as was the news that he was instituting a draft. Wybert planned to draft a new army, spend three months training it, and then send it and half of the existing Largo army to the front line. The draftees, who were not expected to be fully trained by that point, would be used as a reserve force as they completed their training.

Horses were in high demand throughout Largo by all of the men and women joining the army (either voluntarily or involuntarily). Squeezing a simple pack horse out of Wybert had been quite a feat, but Maelgyn felt the effort was worth it. When he fled Svieda Castle, he was woefully under-prepared: He had taken a blanket to keep him warm at night, a saddlebag full of preserved foods that were long since expended, and the clothes, sword, and armor he wore. This time, he would go out better equipped. Wybert had supplied him with a tent, a mess kit, several changes of clothing (including some cold weather gear for the hike through the mountains), a month's supply of travel food, rope, climbing gear, and a number of other things to make his trip through the Mar'Tok Mountains safer. Not to mention his maps, various papers, and a large sack of mail.

That last item was how Maelgyn had finally wheedled Wybert into giving him the pack horse. He had agreed to take a load of mail addressed to locations in Sopan. It likely would be the only chance the people of Largo would have to send mail to family and friends in Sopan until the sea routes were clear. It was a burden, yes, but one Maelgyn bore gladly.

Before getting far into this trip, Maelgyn knew he would have to cross at least one river that had no bridges. There were, according to the papers Wybert had supplied him, a few small villages which offered ferry services across the river, but those papers didn't identify which villages those were. So far, he'd been to two river-side villages, but no ferry service was offered at either one. He wasn't happy, making no more progress beyond wandering up the river for days with nothing to show for it.

He was just entering the third village, Rocky Run, when he spied a situation that made a little delay crossing the river unimportant. A very attractive but bizarrely dressed young woman was leaning back against a stone fence, smiling as if she knew a big secret. She was wearing battered leather pants that seemed to be partially armored and a hardened leather bustier which also appeared to serve as some kind of light armor. Surrounding her bustier, however, was a brightly colored – and strikingly mismatched – light silk vest. Her darkly colored hair was the strangest part of her appearance. It was a fairly standard length in the back, tied into a ponytail, but her bangs were the truly odd part. Neatly trimmed, the style nevertheless covered her eyes completely from view. The hair was so thick that Maelgyn had no idea how she could see out of it. Finally, there appeared to be an odd dust storm swirling lightly around her feet, spiraling around her in a slow whirlwind.

The girl, however odd-looking, was not what displeased him, however. It was the large number of rough-looking rogues surrounding her.

"Hey, darlin'," the lead thug said, approaching the girl with a swagger. "How 'bout you come with us and show us a good time?"

"Nah," the girl said simply, apparently not caring that the guy was leaning into her.

"I think you should reconsider," he said, reaching a hand up to cup her cheek roughly. "See, either you come with us, or we force you to come with us. And I think you'll enjoy it lots more if you come with us."

She flinched a bit when he touched her, sidestepping his

advance. She refused to say anything, and instead just shook her head carelessly.

"Now what did I just say?" the thug growled. "Let's start by you showing us your eyes..."

He'd moved his hand to her bangs, but the moment he touched her hair one of her hands shot up and grabbed his wrist. "No!" she stated emphatically.

The thug seemed surprised at her inherent strength as his hand was forced away, but he didn't retreat. "Okay, bitch, I tried being nice. It seems you don't want to play nice."

"It seems to me as if she doesn't want to play at all," Maelgyn said, hopping off of his horse. "So why don't you let her go?"

"And what's it to you?" the lead punk growled, turning his attention away from the girl. "My friends and I were just having a friendly conversation with this girlie here. Haven't you heard it's rude to interfere in another man's business?"

Maelgyn unobtrusively released the catch on his sword, using a hidden thumb to push it out an inch. "As a matter of fact, I have. But what if this just might happen to be my business?"

"What, is it your business to mess with people using a whore?" the man growled crudely.

Maelgyn raised an eyebrow, and glanced at the woman carefully. Allowing a shade of mocking humor into his voice, he asked her, "Hmm... ma'am, forgive me for being indelicate, but I suppose I shouldn't interfere if these people have the right of it. You wouldn't, by any chance, be a professionally licensed courtesan, would you?"

"Nope," she said, grinning. Maelgyn was pleased to see she got the joke, and wasn't offended by the question.

"I see. I didn't think so, since I've always been told Sword Wybert outlawed prostitution in Largo so long ago I doubt either of us had been born. Well, then, gentlemen, I must ask you to refrain from bothering this young lady any more."

"And just how will you stop us? There are five of us, and..." he pulled out a rusty, beaten sword, "we're all armed. There's only one of you, and I don't see a sword on your person."

"No?" Maelgyn brushed aside his messenger's cloak, flashing his sword. One of the thugs gasped, but the others seemed unphased. "I think I've got enough of a blade to handle the lot of you."

"Ah, cut the crap. Kill him!" the lead thug exclaimed, charging in.

Several of his friends joined him, but the one who had gasped cried out, "No, wait!"

Maelgyn's sword sung as he drew it fully. Magically reinforcing both his own and his sword's strength, Maelgyn's first strike shattered the lead thug's sword into pieces. Without magic Maelgyn might have ruined the edge of his own sword with that move, but that was one reason magic was considered so handy on the battlefield. It was almost certain he could cut through all of their weapons with the same technique, but he didn't need to bother – as he had planned, they were intimidated from the very first blow.

Switching gears, he stepped back, using more magic to take the broken sword's shards and send them flying, wounding two of the other thugs and pinning a third to the wall. The last armed thug in the attack, seeing the destruction wrought upon his friends in mere seconds, held back. It didn't help him, however.

Maelgyn had noticed before the fight began that none of the thugs carried any form of lodestone protection... not that he couldn't have worked around such protection. A mage of average strength – third rate or lower – might have difficulty with lodestones, but despite limited training Maelgyn had tremendous magical reserves. It would take something far stronger than a few personal lodestones to bother him.

With a theatrical wave of his hand, he used those tremendous magical reserves to pick up the fourth rogue and throw him down onto the ground, knocking the sword out of his arms in the process.

The one attacker still on his feet, now disarmed, stared in horror at what had happened. "Who are you?" he asked in wonder.

"That's what I was trying to tell you!" the lone thug who'd held back said. "Don't you recognize that weapon? He's one of the Swords! One of the bloody Swords of the Realm!"

"Sword Prince Maelgyn, Duke of Sopan, at your service," he sighed, nodding his head in acknowledgement. He didn't want his presence known, but it was out, now. He considered cutting the men down to silence them, but they were just petty thugs – not foreign enemies – and they just might be useful. "I'm looking for a ferry across the river. None of you boys would happen to know where to find one, would you?"

"I do," the girl, who he'd almost forgotten about in the ten second battle, chirped. With a wave of her hand, all of the thugs weapons – both intact and broken – flew into a pile at her feet and melted, reforming into a set of bracers for her wrists, a knife, and a bag full of rough "magic powder" – the common name for mustard-seed sized pellets of magically reactive metals typically used by mages.

The gang momentarily stopped gawking at the royalty which had suddenly appeared in their midst, and turned their attention back to the girl they had planned to rape. Apparently, she was a bit more than they might have expected as well. "That whore is a mage?" the lead thug exclaimed incredulously.

"Hush," she answered, knocking him unconscious with a (almost certainly magic-enhanced) rap to the forehead as she walked by. Turning to Maelgyn, she smiled even wider than he'd seen from her before. "Coming?" she beckoned, turning down the street. Somehow, that slow whirlwind of dust followed her along.

Maelgyn himself was rather shocked at her casual display of power, but nodded nonetheless. Ignoring the fallen and wounded of the battle, he grabbed the reins of his two horses and started following. *Hmm, seems I blew my cover for nothing.*

Chapter 4

As Maelgyn followed the mysterious girl through the back roads of a surprisingly large fishing village, a number of questions filled his mind. One of them stood above all others, however, and Maelgyn found he couldn't pull his attention from it: *Who is this girl, anyway?*

She hadn't said anything since she almost casually called for him to follow her to the ferry. She was quite in control of herself, and was obviously quite familiar with the area – she didn't seem to be looking where she was going, although the hair over her eyes made that hard to tell. The powerful magic she had displayed earlier seemed to be passive again, yet she walked with the confidence of someone who believed themselves invulnerable to any kind of attack – not normal behavior for someone just accosted by a gang of armed men, regardless of how handily those men were disposed of.

She knew who he was, thanks to those thugs. If she turned out to be a spy of some kind, she might be leading him into some kind of trap. She might be working with Sho'Curlas – a powerful mage sent to capture a vulnerable Sword in some backwater town where he would have no allies.

He very nearly hit himself at that thought. Yes, he revealed his identity, but he'd been fairly careful with it since that incident with the indiscrete messenger. It's not like Sho'Curlas knew he would be in this particular village on this particular day when even he had no idea he would be here. Worrying about her being a spy was blatant paranoia.

He felt he could trust her, although he didn't know why he

felt this way. Perhaps it was because, given the magical strength displayed earlier, she could have already wiped the floor with him easily. Despite many opportunities, she hadn't done anything to him. She had yet to give him her name, however.

Still, he followed her all the way to the ferry without question. She appeared to be planning to join him on the trip across the river. At least, he figured that when she paid both their fares.

"You don't have to do that," he noted, embarrassed. "I've got more than enough money to pay for the trip."

She just shrugged, and then got on board the ferry. He followed her, feeling increasingly unsure of things, and allowing that paranoia to creep back in. After all, she had hardly said anything since he met her. It might help if he knew why she was joining him on the trip across the river, at least. Or even just what to call her.

"So," he began hesitantly. There were so many questions to ask her, but what to ask first? "What's your name?"

She seemed to not hear him at first, holding out her hand. It was then he noticed the whirlwind of dust that had been surrounding her since he'd first seen her was disappearing... or rather, was collecting in her hand. It didn't take him long to realize that what she was collecting was a very fine form of magic powder. It wasn't the usual iron powder, but rather a fine, silvery-colored powder based on nickel – more expensive, less effective, but favored by certain mages because it was easier to conceal. That little act just added to his questions about her.

When she finally collected the last grain of dust, she poured the handful of magic powder into a pouch around her belt – one of several, Maelgyn noticed. He only had one pouch, himself, and he didn't know why someone would need more than one. Perhaps it could be because she had more than one kind of magic powder; he had noticed that the iron powder she had made from the thug's weapons had been poured into a different pouch. However, there seemed to be more pouches than there were commonly available types of magic powder. That question, like many others, could wait, however... at least until he got her name.

"Euleilla," she answered finally, sitting back on their bench. Even though she was just sitting, every move she made now seemed hesitant and uncertain, whereas before it was nonchalant and confident.

"Okay," Maelgyn replied. "That answers one of the questions that have been burning in my mind for the past half hour. I suppose the next would be... are you following me, or did you just coincidentally need to cross the river yourself?"

"Following," she said, smiling. Well, 'smiling' perhaps wasn't the right word – she always seemed to be smiling. However, her lips twitched a bit to make him think she was smiling more honestly, like she was just joking with him. He didn't get the joke, however.

"Er, I see. Why?"

She shook her head. "No questions, now. Napping. Wake me when we're across."

That, he realized, was the longest sentence he had yet heard her speak. At least it showed him, finally, that she could say more than one word at a time. Still, it was a rather... frustrating answer considering all of the questions he had.

"Now just hold on, h-" Maelgyn suddenly found his jaw magically clamped shut, unable to say anything.

"Shh," she hushed, 'smiling' once again. "Later. Nap, now."

His jaw was released from whatever hold she had over it, but he didn't say anything. After all, it was pretty obvious she wasn't going to answer any more questions – or let him say much of anything else, either – until they were on the other side of the river.

He looked at her and shrugged. He wouldn't have thought a ferry across this small river would take long enough to have a decent nap, but she wasn't the only one who seemed to be settling in for a lengthy trip.

Oh, well, Maelgyn thought. *I suppose I could use the break.*

Despite taking more time than Maelgyn had expected, the trip across the river went a lot smoother than he feared. Even the animals were content, and it was notoriously difficult to keep horses, or animals of any kind, happy on a river trip. Maelgyn vaguely wondered if the girl, whose magic impressed him more and more as he watched her use it, had anything to do with the boat's ease of motion. He doubted she'd give him a straight answer – or any answer – but he wouldn't have been surprised either way.

When they were finally anchored on the other side of the river, she couldn't seem to leave the boat fast enough. She seemed to be stumbling quite a bit as she went, but once she was ashore her balance was restored and she relaxed. Finally, she opened the same pouch she had collected the nickel dust in earlier, and released it into another magical whirlwind around her. Nodding at Maelgyn as he left the boat, himself, she proceeded to follow him as he collected his horses and made his way through town.

"Have you ever been here, before?" he asked.

"Once or twice," she answered, smirking as if she'd just told the most amusing joke she could imagine.

"Know where a good inn is? It'll be dark before too long, and I'd like a good meal to go with my room."

"Yeah," she said, and then started walking. He shrugged, and started following her. She seemed to be doing well as a guide, so far, although she was still a bit of a curiosity.

"Um, Euleilla, can I ask you something?" Maelgyn finally said. "Or rather, several somethings? There are a lot of things I'd like an answer on."

She shrugged. "Sure."

"Well," he hesitated. Which question to ask her first? "I guess to start with I'd like to know how you got so powerful in magic. I've never seen the like! Who trained you, may I ask?"

"Mmm, not saying," she said after some consideration.

That threw Maelgyn off his train of thought. "What? Why not?"

"Bad memories," she explained, not going into detail.

That threw him off. "Right. Then... um, hm." *If she won't answer that,* Maelgyn wondered, *what will she answer?* "Where'd you get all the armor? Not many women outside of noble families wear armor, and most noble families in Svieda supply their children with something heavier than leather."

"Pants were papa's," she explained. "Had 'em altered. Made the top."

Again, that didn't answer the question he really wanted to know. "Why? Are you planning to be a soldier or something?"

At that, she broke out laughing. There was no explanation given for her laughter, but obviously the suggestion of her as a soldier was what caused it. Finally, when she caught her breath, she answered, "No."

This, Maelgyn realized, *is getting me absolutely nowhere. Oh, well, I have more important things to worry about than this madwoman, and I'd better start thinking about them. Maybe, when this war is over, I'll come back here and see if I can ever get a straight answer from this Euleilla girl. Like just who she really is....*

"How far away is this inn?" he asked instead.

"Close," she answered, the 'smile' back on her face. She gestured ahead with her thumb.

He blinked, and then looked around at the buildings lining the street. Sure enough, about a hundred yards away, a building advertising itself as the "Left Foot Inn" stood.

"Left Foot Inn," Maelgyn mused. "Weird name."

"The owner lost his right foot in the Borden Isle War," Euleilla explained, startling Maelgyn.

"Did he, now?" He was more surprised that the girl gave him a complete answer – and to an unasked question – then he was that the owner had lost his foot in the wars. That would have been interesting in itself. Most wounded veterans of that war were given a pension and some simple job, not left to fend for themselves at some inn in the middle of nowhere. A few people had managed to slip through the cracks, of course, but in general Svieda kept track even of those who refused employment. There was no mention in the papers Wybert had given him of any innkeepers along this river who were veterans of a former war.

Nevertheless, a hot meal was his goal, not sorting out people who were pretending they were war heroes or mysterious girls who wouldn't give a straight answer unless it was to an unasked question. Following the girl in question, he handed his horse's reins to a young man taking the role of the inn's porter and stepped inside. To his surprise, the owner of the place greeted the two of them quite enthusiastically.

"Euly! I didn't know you were going to be back today," he cried, getting up on a peg leg.

The old man threw his arms around her in a fatherly hug. "You could stand to put some meat on those bones, but you look healthy enough for a girl that's been out of town for a few months. Did you ever find a guide for crossing the mountains?"

"Him," she said, jerking her thumb at Maelgyn. That startled him, for he hadn't agreed to anything as far as he knew. In fact, he hadn't thought he would be seeing her after getting to the ferry. Apparently, however, when she said she was following

Maelgyn she wasn't kidding.

The old soldier looked Maelgyn up and down. "Well, I guess you'll do, sonny."

It was then Maelgyn knew the man was exactly the veteran Euleilla claimed. Maelgyn had seen a portrait in Largo Castle dedicated to him. It had been commissioned as an apology, of sorts, for the actions of a previous, particularly boorish Sword of the realm. That Sword had unceremoniously dismissed four heroes from the early stages of the war, claiming their war injuries made them "unusable" whatever their past actions. When that Sword was later deposed, three of these heroes had been found, their pensions restored and their status acknowledged with peerages and similar rewards. The fourth was believed to have been dead, but that had never been confirmed.

"Admiral Ruznak?"

The old man's eyes widened. "It's been a long time since anyone recognized me for my military service, boy, but I was never more than a captain."

"I'm afraid you're mistaken there, sir," Maelgyn noted. "Sword Prince Alphor, Prince Wybert's father and predecessor, promoted you, uh, 'posthumously' after a search of the kingdom turned up no trace of you. That was almost fifty years ago, sir."

"Heh," Ruznak snorted. "I ain't dead, yet."

"They thought you were," Maelgyn replied. "But the promotion is valid, nonetheless. What Sword Pennyweaver did to you and the other veterans in the war was a travesty, sir, but upon his death his successors and the other Swords in the kingdom did everything they could to make it up to you."

"Bygones, sir, just bygones," Ruznak laughed bitterly. "Pennyweaver was a louse, but I knew most of the rest of his kin were good enough folk. That's why I fought for them in the first place." The old soldier's stare became even more penetrating. "So, what can an old innkeeper like me be doing for a Sword of the Realm, my boy?"

Maelgyn blinked in surprise. "How did you..."

Once again, Ruznak laughed – this time a much happier sound. "Let's just say you strongly resemble a certain ancestor of yours I was once proud to call a friend and leave it at that. Now, on to business. Since my little Euly here says you're going to take her to Sopan, I'm guessing you're young Maelgyn. I've heard a few rumors about a new war here and there, but I'm afraid this sleepy little town doesn't get much more than rumors. What say, while my cook fixes you both a meal, you tell me a bit about what's been happening?"

"Certainly, sir!" Maelgyn stammered. Somehow, Ruznak seemed to have been a step ahead of him from the moment he walked in the door... a trait the man seemed to share with Euleilla, although in a decidedly different way. Ruznak was startlingly up-front, while the girl was astoundingly evasive. Which made something Ruznak said pop into his mind. "Is Euleilla your daughter... or, rather, granddaughter, sir?"

"My daughter?" Ruznak repeated, sounding just mildly surprised. "Why, no. That is to say, I've sired no children of my own. However, there are quite a few orphans who I've helped on their way, and she's one of them. When my late wife proved to be barren, raising some of the less fortunate children made her feel better. I haven't been too distressed at the idea of continuing that tradition now that she's passed. Most of the other orphans – or their children, since we've been doing this for almost thirty years, now – work here as waitresses, maids, cooks, etc. Euleilla, though, was always a special one. She went out on her own a few months ago, like many children do when leaving their parents, to sell some of her trinkets for the journey ahead. I'm not quite sure what that makes me, though... what am I to you, anyway, girl?"

"Gramps," she chirped cheekily.

"Gramps, eh?" he laughed. "Well, I suppose that fits. I'm old enough, that's for sure. Okay, Euly, why don't you head on back to your room and freshen up while I deal with your 'guide,' here."

"'Kay," she said, 'smiling,' and quickly swooped into one of the back rooms.

"Now, Sword Maelgyn, how about that talk?" Ruznak said, narrowing his eyes at the young man.

There was something dangerous in that stare, and Maelgyn began to understand just why he'd been so successful as a naval captain. "Yes, I suppose we'll just have it."

"Now, why are you taking this land route to Sopan, unescorted even, and not traveling by ship?" Ruznak asked, leading them to a table. Moments later a young maid, probably one of Ruznak's other adopted children, showed up with two cups of some steaming beverage, which she promptly set down in front of the two men before leaving.

"The journey by sea is too dangerous. I'm leaving behind the escorts to make my journey more low-key." Maelgyn took a sip of his drink, and widened his eyes in surprise. "That's pretty good. What is this?"

"A sweet tea sold by the Dwarves. If you stop at any of the Dwarven settlements on your trip through Mar'Tok, you'll probably want to order that over anything else they'll have. It's called Mo'kah tea. It's the only non-alcoholic drink I think they've got, and their liquors are too strong for most humans."

The young prince tried to remember if there was any note of that in his papers, but couldn't think of any. "I'll keep that in mind, even if this tastes like no tea I've ever had, but on to business. What do you know about the war so far?"

"A few rumors and little else. I know the king was assassinated, and that it appears we're at war with our former 'allies,'" Ruznak spat. "I never liked the Sho'Curlas. I always suspected they were the ones who convinced Sword Prince Elaneth to take the Borden Isles into rebellion, and were the ones who provided the rebels with the funds and arms to fight us."

"Well, your guess is probably correct, and so is what you know," Maelgyn said. "Prince Hussack and his son, Prince Mussack, killed Gilbereth right before my eyes, demanding the surrender of my province in order to prevent an invasion. Gilbereth had refused, and so... well, none of us knew Hussack was a mage, and a powerful one at that. Even guardian-sized Lodestones didn't seem to matter, and he actually took the throne room and it seems he held it until the Sho'Curlas army showed up to rescue him."

"You should still have been able to leave by ship, though... unless they've already swept the coast? They had no navy, as I recall."

"Until recently they didn't. Lots of factors, including the weather, made sea travel too risky for me to leave from Happaso or Glorest. By the time I got to Largo, it became obvious that I couldn't leave by sea. Sho'Curlas has essentially annexed the City-State of Oden by 'treaty,' which means its entire navy was made available to our enemies. They've already wiped out the fleet in Largo and established a blockade around our major ports. The naval detachment at Sopan should be enough to break them, once it can be mobilized, but until then naval travel is unsafe."

"Hm," Ruznak frowned. "What other information about the tactical situation do we have?"

"Well, we know that Sho'Curlas fully secured its eastern border in the months before this invasion. Sycanth was taken before they could put up any kind of advance, and Svieda castle fell not too long ago. Our enemy's armies hadn't moved on after taking Svieda Castle, last I heard, and likely will be met by the combined Glorest-Rubick-Happaso army when they do. Gilbereth implied we had some intelligence suggesting that Sho'Curlas instigated the rebellions of Abindol and the Borden Isle, but I don't know what it was."

"I knew it!" Ruznak crowed. "I've said it for decades, but no-one believed me. Now, we know for sure... and I have to wonder if it matters, since we're already at war with them."

"Perhaps not, but we shall see," Maelgyn said. "I've been too concerned with getting to Sopan to think about it much."

"Aye, that's another thing I wanted to talk with you about," Ruznak growled, once more focusing his stare on Maelgyn. "I want you to take care of my little girl on your trip through the mountains, boy. Sword Prince or not, me with one leg or not, if you let something happen to her I *will* hunt you down and kill you."

Maelgyn swallowed nervously. Even in his nineties and with one leg, the old Admiral cut an imposing figure. "I... well, I'll do what I can. To be honest, I never agreed to 'guide' her through the mountains. I've got a lot of questions for her, to be sure, but... well, she never talked about coming with me. In fact, all I expected her to do when she said to follow her was for her to lead me to the ferry."

A dark grin spread out on Ruznak's face. "Well, that sounds like her, all right. You don't mind helping, though, do you?"

"Of course not," Maelgyn said. "I don't know what I'm helping her do, exactly, but I'll assist her in any way I can, as long as it doesn't interfere with the war effort. I'm not sure why she needs my help, though – she seems an impressive enough mage to handle any brigands she runs across. I stopped a pack of them who were surrounding her when I got into town across the river, but from the way she reacted to the whole affair I'm pretty sure she knows she could have handled them, herself."

"She could have," Ruznak agreed. "She's not afraid of being attacked. All she needs is what she asked for – a guide, someone to help her find the right trail."

"I've got a spare map of the area, if she needs it," Maelgyn suggested. "I'm making this trip the first time, myself, though, so I'm not sure how good of a guide I would be."

"No," the old man hesitated. "I don't think a map would work."

"Can't she read maps?" Maelgyn asked. "I mean, I don't know what she needs to go into Sopan for, but I'm going to have to leave in the morning... surely she's going to want more time to get ready to go."

"She's been ready to go," Ruznak explained. "She's been looking for a guide for a while, now, and had recently been trying to raise the money to hire one. She, uh, really isn't able to read a map, but she needs to get to Sopan as soon as possible. A private organization which manufactures mage-produced tools and metalwork agreed to hire her, but only if she can get there before they can otherwise fill the position. Her bags have been packed so that she could leave right away, if necessary."

Maelgyn grinned. "Well, I can guarantee her employment in Sopan. If she's too late to get that job I'll hire her into the Sword's Service as a court mage. No one that talented should be unemployed long."

"If she's willing," Ruznak agreed, although his tone suggested he doubted Euleilla would be. "At any rate, you will take care of her, right?"

"Of course," Maelgyn nodded.

"Good," Ruznak enthusiastically bellowed. "In that case..." He clapped his hands, and immediately three more waitresses showed up carrying platters full of food. "Let's eat. You've got a big journey ahead of you, and you should start it fresh and well fed."

Chapter 5

Despite the rain, slow whirlwinds of magic dust continued to surround Euleilla. As they made their way through the mountains, however, a tendril of that dust had moved forward and wrapped itself around Maelgyn's ankle as well. He still had no idea what purpose it served, or why she had decided to encircle him with it, but he'd given up getting a straight answer from her before she'd even taken him to the Left Foot Inn. He'd tried asking Ruznak some of the questions surrounding the girl before they parted, but the old sailor only shook his head, saying, "She'll tell you if she wants you to know."

It seemed she didn't want him to know anything. He hoped, in the event of a crisis, she would answer questions that needed answering, but he was willing to allow her privacy until then. Still, the fact that she 'leashed' him with her superfine magic dust disturbed him a bit.

She wasn't walking with the same self-assurance she had shown in Rocky Run. Her steps were more cautious and the rain had slowed her more than he was expecting. It had been raining for four days straight and both he and Euleilla were soaked to the bone. She didn't complain, exactly, but she did stop smiling for all of one minute when they set up their camp one night. That had been when her tent tore under the weight of the rain water. Maelgyn had given her his tent, and now he was the one sleeping in the rain at nights.

Those wet nights left him tired, cranky, a little sick, and frustrated – especially when they had to head right back to the start of the trail after a mudslide closed the pass he initially planned to take. That had set him back a full day, and he was fairly certain that wouldn't be the only setback they would have... particularly if it continued to rain like it was.

He turned his head around to watch how his charge was doing, and saw, to his astonishment, her walk head-first into an overhanging tree-limb weighed down with rain.

"Euleilla!" he called, quickly stepping over to her. "Are you all right?"

"Yeah," she said, apparently unconcerned about her injury. He could see a tiny bit of blood trickling down her cheek from somewhere above her abnormal hairline.

"No, you're not. You're bleeding... didn't you see the tree limb?"

"Nope," she answered, reaching a finger up to touch her cheek, and seemingly noticing the blood for the first time.

"Why not? It was right in front of you!"

She froze, not answering for a moment. For the first time that he'd known her, Euleilla actually looked... afraid. There had been times on their journey when she'd looked uncomfortable or hesitant, but he had never seen her afraid. Her smile completely left its face, and Maelgyn knew that there was something seriously wrong. Finally, she sighed, and lifted her hand to raise the hair that covered her eyes. There, he could see, were two eyes which had been scarred over – one scar jagged, the other a perfectly straight line. Both scars, however, covered eyes which would never open again.

"I... I can't see anything," was all she said.

"What happened to you?" Maelgyn couldn't help but ask. He was still astonished that the person who had been his guide all across Rocky Run couldn't see. She had never shown any sign that she was blind... well, no obvious signs. Suddenly, the whirlwind of magic powder around her made sense: That was how she "saw." And the "leash" around him wasn't a leash at all. It was a lifeline.

"My father – my *real* father – was a failed mage and alchemist," she began. Maelgyn nodded. Failed mages frequently went on to become alchemists. With few exceptions, mage training had to begin at birth or you could never quite grasp the technique needed to access magical abilities. Sometimes a person would be trained as a mage but discovered as they aged that they weren't powerful enough to use magic effectively. The rate of failure was partly why parents were so reluctant to have their children learn magic.

In Svieda, only about one out of every ten students failed. Those numbers rose and fell depending on family background, where one lived, how they were instructed, and several similar factors, and Svieda had an atypically high success rate. There were only two fields of magic use open to a failed mage: Teachers (failed mages frequently gave the best magical instruction as they would have tried everything to learn magic, themselves) and alchemists (who, unlike the chemists who studied medicines and poisons, typically studied elemental change and magically reactive substances). Alchemy really was the ideal career for a failed mage, who might still have enough magical strength for alchemy, even if they couldn't use magic for other practical applications.

"Go on," He said softly, placing a comforting hand on her shoulder.

Euleilla spoke again, haltingly at first, and then the words came faster and faster. After the long, silent journey this far, the sudden avalanche of words was all the more striking. "He was able to teach me the basics of magic. I proved to be quite talented at it, so he arranged for me to apprentice under a mage named Cawnpore. Cawnpore was a harsh but effective teacher, who also happened to be a rather violent drunkard. Still, while my father was alive, he made sure he was sober around me – my father had earned his respect, somehow, and so he did nothing which might anger him.

"My father was working on developing a potion for a mining company in Sycanth – something which would dissolve quartz but leave gold unharmed. Unfortunately, a rival company wanted to stop him. At first they tried hiring away my father, but he refused. Then they tried intimidating him. We left town, moving from place to place all the way across Svieda, until we finally settled in Rocky Run. I was eight years old, I think, and it wasn't until much later I understood what was going on.

"My father kept working on his research while in hiding. He hoped that we would be able to live our normal lives again if he could just finish that potion. Any gain for the mining companies at his death would then be moot. And finish it he did. He knew it was risky, but he sent for his old friend, and my old teacher, Cawnpore – he wanted someone to guard him when we returned to our old home and sold the new formula. This may have been how they found out where we were, since before Cawnpore arrived we were attacked by an assassin. My father tried to fight him off, but while my father killed the assassin the damage had been done. He had been poisoned, and died less than a week later. What happened to me, though, was much worse in his eyes."

She pointed to her own eye – the one with the jagged scar. "That was where I got this. One of my father's chemicals exploded, sending a wooden splinter right into my eye. A surgeon managed to remove the splinter with very little damage, but I will never see out of that eye again."

Maelgyn swallowed hard – not just because the story disturbed him, but also because he felt a rage building inside of him the more he heard of her story. How dare one of Svieda's own mining factions harm another citizen of Svieda? It was an outrage... and one which should have been dealt with long ago. "Was any investigation made? Did anyone look for the assassin's employer? Did anyone look for an antidote to the poison your father was given? Did anyone do *anything*?"

"No," Euleilla repeated softly, bitterly. "The assassin was so badly burned he could not be identified, so there was no investigation. And my father didn't bother looking for an antidote. Before he married my late mother, he apprenticed under the man who developed it, and knew there was no way one could be made before he died."

"Who developed the poison, then?" Maelgyn asked, clenching his fists tighter. Perhaps it wasn't too late to find the killers, if they could figure out who developed the poison.

"Delbruck."

Delbruck. Maelgyn bit his lip to hide his disappointment. The most well-respected master of his craft in a century, Delbruck had developed several important medicines... and many more of the most dangerous poisons in existence. He combined magic, alchemy, and chemistry to revolutionize medicine in Svieda... but then he'd been arrested and imprisoned as a traitor for selling poisons to the Borden Isle rebels. He was found guilty of treason and summarily executed, but it made little difference to his reputation as an alchemist. He had many apprentices, and many of them had built on what he had theorized following his death. Apparently, Euleilla's father had been one of them. If it was a Delbruck poison, there would have been no way to trace it to a particular source.

"Damn," Maelgyn softly cursed. "So what happened?"

"My father spent his last days reconstructing his mining formula. He wrote it down and gave it to me, telling me to use the money he was supposed to be paid to continue my studies as a mage, and to live a good life. Then, as his last act, he wrote a letter to Cawnpore, asking him to raise me and complete my study of magic.

"I don't know what my father meant to old Cawnpore, but when I showed him my father's letter, he broke down and wept. He took the money my father had willed to me from his formula and bought us a house in Rocky Run.

"He continued to teach me for about a year following my father's death, but as time wore on something about him changed. He had taken to drinking himself into a stupor on a daily basis, and I had to study on my own more and more. I eventually learned the final lesson on my own – the secret of why lodestones work against magic, and how magic relates to lodestones. I assume you're aware of it?"

Maelgyn nodded. "My own magic tutor had to leave when I was sixteen, but he wanted me to keep up the study and so explained the secret to me."

"Sixteen?" Euleilla mused. "I was twelve when I learned it. Ah, but I realize that was rather unusual... and it was my downfall. Cawnpore got drunk one night, and he tried to use my position as his apprentice to order me to do some things that weren't quite legal. I knew he was drunk and would never have ordered that were he sober, and so I refused, but he warned me that he would throw me on the streets if I refused.

"I responded quite... vociferously. I told him I didn't need him anymore – that I'd figured out the secret, and that all he was doing was holding me back. I told him that I only stayed with him because my father had wanted me to, but if he continued to treat me like a slave I would leave.

"He flew into a rage when I said that, and attacked me. He said some horrible things to me; how he hated me, how he blamed me for father 'letting' himself die instead of researching a cure, how he found my scarred face too ugly for words, and that I'd be lucky to ever receive a 'good offer' from anyone but him without my eye.

"I think his exact words, as he cut my good eye, went something like this – 'If you intend to go out on your own, you're going to need to improve your appearance. Maybe if I make both sides of your face match, you'll get a few looks from the boys.'"

Maelgyn winced. He saw a few tears going down her cheeks, and he wiped them off of her face with his thumb. Somehow, as she'd continued telling her story, he'd pulled her into a comforting hug without realizing it. They just sat there while she cried for a bit, but once she had collected herself she continued her story.

"Cawnpore was a lot stronger than I was in those days, and I couldn't get into the mindset to access my magic. I don't know what Cawnpore would have done to me, but I wasn't able to stop him. Thankfully, Ruznak saved me. He heard my screams from out in the street. Cawnpore declared he was going to kill me just like he killed my mother, which I still don't understand – mother died of a disease, she wasn't murdered. Ruznak heard the shouting and broke into the house.

"I didn't see the fight, obviously. Ruznak never explained what he did, exactly, but it must have been pretty bloody considering he was alone fighting an experienced mage. In the end, however, Cawnpore was dead and Ruznak had a new foster daughter.

"Ruznak didn't just adopt me however, he helped me learn magic. Considering he didn't know any himself, it was an impressive feat, but he was determined to help me. He found books on magic and read them to me, he figured out a method of 'seeing' for me, and he developed 'tests' for me to practice my magic with. Eventually, when I was ready for it, he even introduced me to another mage who could refine what I knew into practical use. I'll never be able to thank Gramps enough for that."

Maelgyn continued to hold and comfort her, his face taught with conflicting emotions. He was horrified at Euleilla's plight and wanted to help ease her pain, but he was also angry – angry at Cawnpore for doing this to her, angry at her father for entrusting her to such a man, angry at the assassin who killed that father, angry at the mining company which hired that assassin, even angry at Ruznak for taking away his own chance at vengeance against the drunken mage.

"When this war is all over," he said, his voice barely under control, "I'll see to it that all of those people who did this to you and your family have paid the price for it. I swear to you I will, even if I have to raze Sycanth province to do it."

"No," she protested, shaking her head against his shoulders. Her tears continued to make her body tremble, but her voice was steady. "I won't have you taking revenge for me... if you do, someone else will take revenge on you, and then someone else will take revenge for that, and it will keep going in a never-ending cycle. Better that I be the one to suffer and not allow it to reach that point than have others die in my name."

"You're wrong there," Maelgyn said. "If someone gets away with doing something like this to you, then they think they can get away with anything. When they believe that, they grow more corrupt... and as that gets more entrenched in your society, it makes it harder and harder to combat that corruption when someone finally does stand up to them. Do you honestly think you're the only one they've hurt? No. They went too far, and they must be made to realize that."

"But..."

"Shh," he whispered, pulling her into an even tighter embrace. "Relax. We'll talk about it later." Releasing her, he backed up a bit. It was hard to tell what were tear streaks and what was rain on her face, and there was a trail of blood still running down her face from where she'd hit the tree, so that had to be dealt with first.

"Let's get you patched up and we'll talk some more, okay?"

She sniffed slightly, but nodded – the smile back on her face, although it was weaker than it had been.

The questions had been answered for Maelgyn. As he pulled out the bandages and medicine to dress her wounded forehead, he wondered what those answers would mean for them.

The one thing he was damned sure of, though, was that he was keeping his promise to her. The people who hurt her would pay... even if he had to win the war by himself to do it.

Maelgyn had set up the tent and led the both of them inside

so that he could finish treating Euleilla's head injury out of the rain, but that was done and now he wanted to talk some more.

"So," Maelgyn said, packing up the extra dressings. "Why didn't you tell me you were blind?"

"I can't see, but thanks to magic I'm not blind," she answered emphatically.

Maelgyn frowned. "That doesn't answer my question. Why didn't you tell me?"

She shrugged, adjusting her damp hair to once again cover her scarred eyes. "Secret," she muttered, looking distinctly embarrassed

Maelgyn supposed he could understand that, but it still bothered him. "You knew it would make a difference in the route we needed to take, right?"

Euleilla shrugged, her enigmatic smile showing itself in full force once again, masking her earlier unhappiness. "Perhaps."

"And you decided not to tell me, anyway?"

"No."

He sighed. "So, back to this 'one word answer' thing again, are we?"

"Yeah," she admitted, letting her smile grow back to what it was before she ran into the branch, starting this whole conversation. Without being able to see the scars thanks to her hair, and with the tear streaks effectively washed off, it was almost possible to forget her as the crying and vulnerable young woman he'd held in his arms just minutes before.

Almost, but not quite. He doubted he'd ever forget that.

"Well, you should have. I wouldn't have taken you here if I'd known."

She coughed deliberately. "That's why."

"What?"

"I want to cross the mountains," she explained emphatically, "And I knew you'd never take me."

"Well, there you were wrong," Maelgyn snapped. "Don't assume things about people, good or bad. If I had been the sort of person who would have left you behind because you were blind – sorry, because you 'can't see' – after having seen you handle yourself in the everyday world, well... then you shouldn't have asked me to guide you in the first place."

"Didn't."

"Didn't?" he started. "Didn't what?"

"Ask."

Maelgyn laughed. "No, you didn't, at that! But you know what I mean."

"Yeah."

"Anyway, I'm fairly certain I still would have taken you... but I wouldn't have taken you by this route, that's for sure." He finished packing his kit, and sighed. "Which might have been the right call, anyway, in this weather. Unfortunately, this may be the only route through the mountains that isn't monitored by the Mar'Tok Dwarves. I've been trying to make this trip in secret, but humans traveling through Dwarven lands inevitably will attract attention. If we don't concern ourselves with Dwarven eyes, however, there are several easier ways across than this route. We just have to develop some sort of cover story for why we're traveling through their lands and we should be all right. Some reason two humans would need to go from Largo to Sopan that wouldn't reveal to them who I am."

"Okay," she agreed simply.

"I'm open to suggestions, by the way," Maelgyn noted dryly.

"Really?" she said, "smiling" again.

"I'm guessing you don't have any," he laughed.

"None."

"Well, we have some time, yet," he said. "We need to get back down the mountain – hopefully before it kills us – and then hike up north for a day or two. There's a small village where we can stay for a bit and sort things out. I believe it's called Elm Knoll." He looked outside the tent, and grinned. "The rain's finally stopped. Let's break camp and try to get off of this ridge before it starts again."

She stood up and left the tent, Maelgyn following behind her briskly. With a wave of her hand, the tent came down and folded itself up, the iron tent stakes wrapping themselves around until the tent was ready to be packed up.

"Ready," she said.

Still shaking his head at her casual use of magic, Maelgyn loaded the tent onto his pack horse. He hadn't been able to ride his war horse through the mountains and so left it with Ruznak in the Left Foot Inn stable, but there was no better substitute for a pack horse available in the area. A Dwarven settlement might contain llamas – the main beast of burden in the region and a central component of the Dwarven heavy cavalry – and over in the mountains near Sycanth mules and donkeys were heavily relied on, but the only human-trained animals in Largo that could handle the mountains were pack horses.

There had been times on the journey that Maelgyn considered dumping that pack horse, even if it meant having fewer supplies. Traveling through the muck and mud would have been considerably easier without having to worry about it. Now, Maelgyn was glad he hadn't – if he wound up heading over the mountains by way of the Dwarven roads, a pack horse would be quite useful. Considering how muddy his pack horse had gotten, though, he would need to pay a stablehand to groom the travel-worn animal once they got to Elm Knoll.

Maelgyn would have liked a hot bath, too, but he had to wonder if a village as small as Elm Knoll could support an inn large enough for such an amenity. He knew they almost certainly wouldn't have running water – few places in Svieda outside of a Sword's capital city would have such a thing – but a wash basin, several large kettles, and some labor could become an adequate bath in a pinch... and was a fair bit better than most non-noble families of the land bothered with.

If there was such a service, he figured he'd go ahead and pay for the manager to fill it for both himself and Euleilla. It was unlikely they'd have a hot bath at all, but he hoped they did nonetheless. His skin itched from the mud and sweat of the journey.

He vaguely wondered what the people at the inn would think when he arrived. It wasn't often that a young man and a young woman who were not related would go traveling alone together unless they were married or about to be. Unmarried young lovers usually managed their rendezvous in their home towns, unattached friends were usually accompanied by a chaperone, and most women in need of bodyguards either hired one woman or several people of either sex.

Occasionally, a professionally licensed courtesan would become the 'camp follower' of a nobleman, accompanying him everywhere he went, even when he was unaccompanied by others. In Largo, however, prostitution in all its forms was illegal, so it was unlikely Euleilla would be seen as that.

Maybe they would think of her as Maelgyn's bride, however. Married couples – especially on their honeymoon – were known to travel together frequently throughout the land. The idea wasn't entirely unpleasant, to Maelgyn's way of thinking. After all, she was quite attractive, if you could ignore the few peculiarities associated with her "inability to see," as she called it – her odd hairstyle and the strangely colored vests. She was certainly intelligent, given how early on in life she had taken an incomplete study of magic and figured out the trick to mastering it and the way she learned to manage her blindness. She had a fairly strong spirit, given how reasonably sane she appeared to be after such a horrid early life. She was powerful, given that her frequent demonstrations of magic showed her to be as strong, if not stronger, than any other mage he had seen. Not that it mattered in his position: As a Sword Prince, he was expected to marry into nobility and not to marry some orphan girl no matter how powerful of a mage she was.

Still, it was likely that the villagers would assume that they were married when they were seen traveling together. It was a better assumption, in his mind, than the alternative – that she was his courtesan. It would be in their best interests to correct any of these assumptions as quickly as possible.

Or would it?

"I have it!" Maelgyn cried out.

"Oh?" Euleilla answered, unruffled despite his sudden outburst.

"Yes. I know exactly what cover to give people... and it'll be a cover no-one will question, precisely because of who we are," he grinned. "When we get to Elm Knoll, everyone is likely to think we're married. We could explain that we weren't, if anyone asked, but I don't think we should. Rather, we should encourage them to think so. It's the perfect explanation for why you and I are traveling together: A young, newlywed couple traveling to a new home stopping in a small town or taking a Dwarven road is fairly commonplace. No-one will question us about it, which means no-one will ask any other questions I wouldn't be comfortable answering, like 'Who am I?' and 'What am I going to Sopan Province for, anyway?'"

"Newlyweds?" Euleilla repeated, sounding unusually stiff. She was almost holding her breath, in fact, while waiting for him to continue. Maelgyn missed her reaction, though, in his enthusiasm.

"Yeah – we'll have complete privacy if we stick to that story, as no-one will want to intrude on a pair of newlyweds. We'll probably have to start our cover at Elm Knoll, though, to keep from being suspected, since I'm told the Dwarves frequent that village for their trading expeditions."

"Newlyweds?" she once again said.

"Right. Is there a problem?" Maelgyn asked.

He could have sworn she was blushing when she asked, "In Largo? In the inn?"

He frowned. "Yes, in the inn in Largo. In fact, it's partly *because* we're in Largo I'm suggesting this. I'd rather not have you arrested on suspicion of being a prostitute just because you travel with me. Ruznak would not be happy if I let that happen."

Her blush grew further. "Okay," she whispered, her smile ratcheting up several notches for reasons Maelgyn could not figure out. He decided not to bother asking why, however – she probably wouldn't tell him anyway.

Chapter 6

Now that he was aware of her lack of sight, Maelgyn marveled at how well Euleilla held up to a forced march – or rather, a forced hike, since they weren't exactly marching. They were making good time – not as fast as he would have liked, but a respectable pace nonetheless. He figured they'd reach the village by the end of the day, which was only a couple hours off of when he would have arrived traveling alone.

Since hitting the main roads again, the tendril of magic powder which had linked Maelgyn to Euleilla as her lifeline was once more absorbed into her ordinary whirlpool. He'd grown accustomed to it over the period they were in the mountains, and its absence was slightly disturbing – it almost felt like she wasn't there anymore. In order to keep that feeling from creeping over him more than it already had, he hung back slightly, taking position behind her, keeping her in plain sight....which was how he knew something was disturbing her the exact second she did.

"What's wrong?" he asked, noticing her cocking her ear in a particular direction.

"Over there," she said, pointing in the direction her ear was aimed.

He would have asked her how she knew where to point when he could see that the magic dust whirlwind she used to see wasn't extended more than a yard away from her, but he figured he'd better just check it out. He wasn't likely to get a straight answer, anyway.

She followed him off the path, that reassuring tendril of dust once again clinging to his arm. As they went, it became clear what had attracted her attention as the sounds of a battle reached Maelgyn's ears. Moving cautiously, he followed the noise until he came to the edge of another, much older, road. There, in the clearing, stood about a dozen Dwarves – obviously traders given the build of their wagons.

Wandering Dwarves were not an uncommon sight, since other races had long since overtaken most traditionally Dwarven lands. Typically based in Dwarven settlements, Dwarves usually traveled in caravans and moved across borders often closed to other races, providing a marketplace for trade between distant countries. This particular wagon looked to be returning to Mar'Tok, the last of the major Dwarven Powers. Given the wagon's design and decoration, it may have even belonged to one of the Merchant Princes, the "royalty" of the Dwarven kingdoms who gained their power not through right of birth (though, with Dwarven inheritance laws, it often seemed that way) but through massive trading empires.

A large roadblock barred the wagon from continuing its trek to Mar'Tok, however, while a number of rather large looking bandits prevented retreat. All armed to the teeth and wearing personal lodestones, the bandits looked prepared for just about any kind of adversary. If the Dwarves abandoned their wagons, they might have been able to escape, but there was no way a Dwarven Merchant Prince would leave his wagons behind.

The situation was decidedly bad. "Those carts will give the Dwarves some cover, but it won't help them much against the swordsmen," Maelgyn whispered.

Dwarven carts were marvels of engineering, designed to be both transport and defense. They were well-equipped to act as a good cover position from archers, but these bandits had both archers and infantry. The wagons even provided small openings to return fire, but there was no way they would be able to cut down a charge from all of the bandits. Once the bandits reached the Dwarves, well...

"Any archers among the Dwarves?" Euleilla asked.

"Some, and that should help." He shook his head. "But it won't be enough."

Dwarves were stalwart soldiers. They rarely surrendered, even when the battle was hopeless, and fought with all of their strength. Dwarves also made good specialists who complimented human forces nicely: Dwarven archers were among the most accurate in the lands, Dwarven Wolfriders armed with either bows or the sword-spear combination of the naginata could make mincemeat of infantry units before an opposing horse-mounted cavalry could respond, great siege weapons and fortifications operated by Dwarven engineers were far superior to the Human equivalent... but outside of legend, no Dwarven infantry could ever stand up to even a quarter their number of the human equivalent.

But the truth was that Dwarves were just too short to fight well hand to hand, as the Imperial Republic of Oregal found when it attempted to field a Dwarven infantry. Dwarven swords were too short to reach their opponents, and an attempt to resurrect the 'fearsome' Dwarven axemen of myth proved it to be just that – a myth. Dwarves were strong enough to handle axes and handle them well, it was true, but their range remained inadequate.

Dwarven archers and engineering could only do so much, however, and while their wagons were heavily armored they were still quite vulnerable. With merely a dozen Dwarven men, only half of whom were armed with bows and arrows, this particular wagon's vulnerabilities were exposed. Despite superior archery skills, this company of Dwarves was doomed against a large and well-equipped bandit force, such as the one attacking them, unless help arrived from the outside.

Maelgyn sighed. "I suppose I should help them," he whispered. "It wouldn't be good for Svieda to allow one of Mar'Tok's Merchant Princes to be murdered inside our borders."

"We'll win," Euleilla assured him. A portion of her magic dust whirlwind left her and surrounded him, much to Maelgyn's surprise. Apparently, she was planning to help him in the battle – not that he minded the help, but keeping her safe as well would add to his responsibilities and divide his attention.

As Maelgyn surveyed the battlefield, he took a quick moment to evaluate the situation. The battle had apparently been going on for quite a while, judging from the number of spent arrows impaled in the ground. The Dwarves – both the unarmed ones and the archers – were pinned down by a constant sheet of return fire, and the human bandits were starting to send their swordsmen forward. It was an extraordinary number of armed men for a simple pack of bandits. Perhaps, Maelgyn realized, this was actually one of the roaming bands of separatists which had shown up in several Sviedan provinces a few decades before. As he drew his sword, he mused that the separatists were probably yet another part of the Sho'Curlas Alliance's plan to undermine the Sviedan Government. In fact, now that he knew what he did about Sho'Curlas' treachery, that logic applied to a number of mysterious occurrences and obscure political movements Svieda's Swords had been trying to deal with for decades. Yet another reason to stop bandits of this sort when he could.

His sword drawn and his magic at the ready, there was no more time to consider the greater implications of the battle. Charging in, he magically scattered a wave of oncoming arrows, positioning himself in front of the Dwarven wagon. Now that the battle was on, he couldn't tell where Euleilla was. Whatever she was planning on doing, she was staying hidden, at least. Without knowing her plans, he had to consider himself alone, fighting with just his sword and some magic.

Correction: A sword, some magic, and six Dwarven archers. Now that he was providing them some additional cover, the Dwarves were able to make their own move, and their bows sung as they started picking off the lead bandit swordsmen in quick succession.

Unfortunately for Maelgyn, the bandits were already too close for the archers to be of much help before the enemy was upon him. They were closing in, and there was only so much he could do while protecting the Dwarves. Unless the bandits had better weapons than they had shown, he could handle them, but it would be a lot easier if he had more help.

The help he was hoping for turned out to be Euleilla. The whirlwind of her magic powder spread out from Maelgyn, where whenever it found a weapon in an enemy's hands that weapon was taken away and magically melted down. Iron or steel-based armor was given the same treatment. Any pieces of the bandits' magically reactive equipment, including some small pieces of cheap jewelry, were ripped off of the bandits and pulled into a growing pile of magically molten metal.

Maelgyn's respect for Euleilla's skill with magic rose as he realized that her attack was even pushing through the magical disruption the bandits' lodestones provided – not that he hadn't been impressed with her earlier. He doubted she could keep it up since using magic that intense was quite taxing on a person, but it looked like he'd have better odds in this fight than he'd feared. He just hoped it was enough for him to finish the fight without letting anyone through to the Dwarves. He noticed more of the whirlwind around him snake out, and wondered what else she had in mind.

The growing pile of molten metal started reforming itself into armor and weapons suited to Dwarves: Naginata, helmets, Dwarf-sized chainmail, shields, etc. That equipment flew off, attaching itself to each Dwarf. The procedure for magically melting metal left it relatively cool, but even so that couldn't be comfortable... yet they didn't seem to mind, and in fact seemed quite pleased with their weapons. Obviously, Euleilla knew what she was doing when it came to making weapons on the fly. He idly wondered just how much her adopted father taught her about military arms and armor, since she seemed to know not just what to make for everyone but how to make it well enough to please even a Dwarf.

The disarmed bandits fell back, and so did Euleilla's magic powder. Apparently, she had exhausted her magic... although she still had enough strength to forge one last short sword that disappeared somewhere in the direction Maelgyn knew she was hiding. And there was still a little whirlwind around Maelgyn himself, although what its purpose was he couldn't even guess.

Maelgyn grinned. There were still a number of swordsmen armed with non-magically reactive bronze weapons, and a few who managed to withstand her attack long enough to keep hold of their weapons, but most of the bandits were now disarmed. With a bit of his own magic, which was also more than adequate to push through the bandits' lodestone disruption, the remaining bits of steel weaponry on the bandits' side was twisted and bent beyond any chance of salvage.

A few of the bandits fled, but most wouldn't give up quite yet. They still had some bronze weaponry on hand – apparently, they were expecting mages – and they were quick to equip it. Maelgyn decided to charge them before they were ready, but it seemed he wouldn't be going in alone. A half-dozen dwarves armed with the naginata Euleilla had made reached his side, and a hail of arrows started laying down covering fire. Now, believing he had the battle won, Maelgyn advanced forward toward his enemies.

Magic strengthened his arm as Maelgyn slashed down on his first enemy. The unnatural force was enough to slice off his first opponent's entire sword arm from just above the elbow. A backhand with his gloved fist sent the now disabled man flying.

"Arrows!" one of the Dwarves called, and Maelgyn immediately set up a magic barrier against them. He was startled to see them pass through his barrier, eyes widening as he realized the archers had prepared for a mage by bringing stone-tipped arrows in addition to the steel-tipped arrows they used earlier... and that those stone-tipped arrows were going to hit him.

Suddenly, just as the arrow was about to hit him, he felt himself flying. He could sense that magic was holding him up, and as he flew he saw that the arrows passed below, killing one of the Dwarven archers. Obviously, it was Euleilla's handiwork, but he'd never heard of someone able to lift a human being this far up off the ground, before.

It hurt to fly. Those areas where he wasn't covered by dragonhide armor were in real pain – Euleilla must have been picking him up by his own blood, but there wasn't much unprotected area for her to grab onto so it was pulling horribly. Just being up in the air, however, was enough to remind him that he didn't know everything about magic just yet: It would never have occurred to him that you could 'pick up' a person with their own blood. It was also a distinct reminder that arrogantly assuming that his magic would protect him in battle was a big mistake... and one he was very fortunate to have lived through.

The powder fell away from him, and so did her magic. The immediate pain went away instantly, but he found himself falling to the ground. He was going to land hard. He would survive the fall, but he would definitely be hurt in the process.

Many thoughts flashed in his head as he fell and collided with the ground. Euleilla, he realized, must have exhausted all of her magic in that little stunt. He wouldn't survive another volley, and she obviously lacked the ability to help him anymore, so he had to act quickly before something else happened. The only problem was, his hands, his feet, his face... most parts of his body, in fact, were in severe pain. It was hard to concentrate on magic when in pain, and especially hard when you only had seconds in which to work. But magic was the only thing he had which might delay the bandit archers long enough to get himself and the Dwarves under cover, so he had to try.

Grimacing, he pulled himself to his feet. He found one of the still-intact shards of armor plate he'd destroyed after Euleilla's initial strike, and concentrated all of the magic he could bear to summon on it. He sent it flying out behind the line where the bandit archers were shooting from, and mentally forced it to explode. Shrapnel went flying everywhere, some of it hopefully hitting the bandit archers and at the very least forcing them to abandon their attacks to take cover. Straining against the pain in his limbs and exhausted of both strength and magic, Maelgyn fell to his knees. He needed time – time to recover, time to regroup, time to regain his strength... and time for Euleilla to recover, as well.

He needn't have bothered worrying.

The Dwarven archers had been busy while he was distracting the bandits. Dwarven archers couldn't fire with the same speed, power or range of the human longbows, but the Dwarves had always done their best to compensate for their shortcomings by training for superior accuracy. While the bandits' attention was not on the Dwarves but on the suddenly flying Maelgyn, the Dwarven Archers repositioned themselves to better hit their opponents safely. With the sudden explosion driving their enemy out from cover, the bandings were easily picked off in rapid succession. The few who escaped the shrapnel and the arrows were not prepared for the final onslaught as the Dwarven naginata reached them. The last bandit fell without even a cry, and the battle was over. Seeing that the immediate threat had ended, Maelgyn relaxed his magic. With nothing left to support him, he couldn't find the strength to stand any more. He knew Euleilla must have passed out from magical exhaustion after saving him with that little flying trick, and now he would be joining her.

Maelgyn awoke to find Euleilla sitting by him, talking to a Dwarf. The pounding in his head was so loud, he couldn't hear what they were saying, but he knew they were talking softly. He sighed, closing his eyes again. He didn't want to go back to sleep, but he didn't want to move, either.

Euleilla obviously had noticed his movements, however. He felt her lift his head up and hold a cup to his lips. "Drink," she said softly.

He drank. He recognized the bitter taste as willow bark tea – a simple painkiller which had been in use for hundreds of years. There were more effective painkillers which Svieda's chemists and alchemists had since developed, but he'd decided not to take any with him on the journey since he didn't expect to find himself in this situation. He wondered if the tea was made from fresh willows, or whether the Dwarves had some with them.

"Thanks," he whispered.

"I'm sorry," she said. "I've never tried that before, and I think I hurt you."

"You saved my life," Maelgyn said, a trifle more forcefully than he probably should have, since it aggravated his headache. "I've got a headache, and it feels as if all of my exposed skin has been bruised. And yet I think I should be thanking you for it, because all of that is better than being dead."

"And I should be thanking the both of you," another voice broke in. Maelgyn's eyes opened at the new voice, and he saw one of the Dwarves he had rescued now standing over him as well. "If it weren't for you two, we'd all be dead. I suppose you should know who it is who you saved, in return."

"That might be nice," Maelgyn agreed, slowly sitting up. He noticed some red blotches on his hands as he pulled himself to his feet. "How bad do I look?"

"Better than you did before your missy here started treating you," the Dwarf noted wryly. "You looked bloated and red, at first, but now you look fairly normal, with some mild bruising. Good lady, that one."

Maelgyn grinned hesitantly. Clearly, Euleilla had remembered their cover story, because this Dwarf seemed to think they were involved. Still, his reply was an honest one. "Yeah, I must agree."

"Anyway, let me introduce myself. I am El'Athras, Merchant Prince of Mar'Tok. I understand you need to travel through my people's lands." The Dwarf grinned at him. "I may be able to help you with that."

Maelgyn glanced over at Euleilla. Just what had she told the man? "Well, yes."

"Yes," the Dwarf said. "I do know everything, but don't blame her. I recognized you straight away – you look a lot like your great grandfather."

"Ah. Well..."

"Stick to your plan," El'Athras advised, a curious grin on his weathered face. "Go on to Elm Knoll, and give me time to get back to Mar'Tok. When you arrive in our lands, come see me. I have an estate in the city of Nir'Thik." The Dwarf handed Maelgyn a signet ring. "Show that to my people if you need to convince them I asked you to come to me. But whatever you do, don't let anyone else know that you are a Sword Prince! I have important things to discuss with you, and certain of my people may try and stop you from meeting me if they know exactly who you are."

"Right," Maelgyn agreed, not quite understanding.

"I have to hurry. I've told your girl everything you need to know, but if I spend too much time here the rest of my troop is going to wonder what we're talking about. Normally, they'd be willing to wait here long enough to make sure you're okay, since you did save our lives and all, but we're carrying perishables this trip," El'Athras explained. "We Dwarves never let gratitude get in the way of making money, so we have to go as soon as possible. They don't know who you are, or they just might act a bit differently."

With that, he left. Maelgyn suddenly realized they were in a tent – a somewhat larger tent than they'd owned before, and he had to wonder where it had come from. "Euleilla?" he said.

"Yes?"

"Where'd we get the tent?"

"I bought it," she explained.

"Ah. Why?"

"I didn't have one," she reminded him. "Now, you don't, but it's large enough for both of us to be comfortable."

Maelgyn blinked. "You traded away my old tent?"

"Yeah."

"I suppose that's okay," he admitted. Dwarves never gave up something for nothing, not even out of gratitude, and it was not like she had much to bargain with. He decided that it might be best to look around discretely and see if anything else was missing, however – he liked this girl, but he couldn't be certain she was not a thief. Wincing, he stretched out. "Ugh. I suppose I feel better than I have any right to, but that flying trick of yours hurts. And making chainmail on the fly – chainmail! That takes both precision and force. You're quite powerful, you know?"

"In terms of raw power, you're significantly stronger than I am. I've just been forced to improve my skill faster than most people our age," she said, clearly in one of her more verbose moods. "I think, if you trained hard for about a year, you could surpass me in skill, easily. You have a lot more potential magic inside you than I do."

"How do you know that?" Maelgyn asked, watching his hands for any signs of unseen injury as he practiced making a fist a few times.

"You can 'feel' magic, can't you?" she asked.

"Yeah, sort of. I can feel it when I touch it, at least, but I have to be inside of the field of magic to sense it."

Euleilla nodded, and touched him slightly with her own magic – just a gentle nudge, but enough for him to feel it. "I can feel magic, too... only I'm better at it than you. I can feel not just its presence, but its strength. I can see you and other mages because of it... and you are so much brighter than anyone else I have ever met; brighter than my father, brighter than Cawnpore, and even brighter than me. You might not be able to do as much with your magic as I am, but only because you haven't practiced enough to hone your skills properly."

Maelgyn grimaced as a particularly knotted muscle cramped up during his stretches. At least the bruises were already fading. By the time they reached Elm Knoll, there wouldn't be too many outward signs of any injuries. "Well, I haven't had many chances to use my magic much over the past two or three years. I used more magic in that one battle alone than in all the time since I turned sixteen. I'm out of practice."

"And I've had to use magic for every waking moment since I was twelve," she explained, shrugging. "It's just a matter of knowing exactly what I can do."

"By the way... how did you know what was going on? I didn't hear anything happening from the road."

"Simple," Euleilla said. "I can use magic to sense where people are, since all people have a little inherent magic in them whether they learn to use it or not. I felt two large gatherings of people and felt the need to investigate."

"So why did you need to have some magic dust around me when we were up in the mountains?"

"Because I might be able to sense where you are, and how strong you are, but without my dust I can't see what you're doing at any one moment." She 'smiled,' and cocked her head at him. "If you duck, I'd like to know you ducked so I can, too. You didn't duck that tree limb, you know."

"Sorry," Maelgyn apologized, grinning himself. "One last question before you start giving one word answers, again: Just how were you able to make swords and armor so quickly, anyway?"

She looked somewhat offended. "I lived with a battle-hardened veteran for several years, a veteran who taught me how to 'see' by using swords and armor to make dummies. I probably know more about swords and armor than most blacksmiths!" She pulled out another sword – one she'd obviously made from the ruins of one of the bandit swords. It was a longsword, and looked to be custom-fit for him and complete with sheath. "Here. You don't want to be flashing the symbol of your nobility around when you're trying to keep your identity a secret, but the way things have been going you might need to draw a sword again. You might find this one better suited for that."

"Uh, right," he said, taking the weapon uncertainly. It felt comfortable in his hands, though, and he found he liked the weight and balance of it. A quick test of the sharpness told him that it was a very adequate weapon. "Thank you."

She just nodded, grinning. "Enjoy."

"Are you recovered from the battle, yet?" he asked, remembering that she'd drained herself during the fight making him fly.

"Mostly," she answered.

"Well, then, should we go?"

"'Kay." She helped him out of the tent and left him standing to attend to their camp. Maelgyn watched her handle things from there with a small degree of awe.

With a wave of her hand, metal tent poles rose from the ground and pulled the tent closed. Another wave and their supplies were rolled up in a metal-lined canvas drop cloth. A few more handwaves and their entire camp was packed up, loaded on their horse. Maelgyn just shook his head, wondering how in the world she thought he would ever be able to match such a feat. Once more, they were on the road.

Chapter 7

Maelgyn wasn't quite sure what to make of Elm Knoll. For what was such a small village, it seemed to have a large number of travelers. He hadn't been sure it would be possible to find even a cheap hostel or inn to stay at when looking at the maps - he was just hoping for a bit of village green he could set his tent up in. However, Elm Knoll had lots of inns, many of them very high class establishments. In fact, outside of a couple of shops, it seemed as if the entire town consisted of inns and nothing else - no farms (though there'd been several along the road into town, which was apparently where the people of Elm Knoll got their food), few private homes, no blacksmiths, no carpenters, no lumber mills, no production of any kind. He'd never known a place like this. Obviously it was a fairly wealthy town, but he couldn't see what it was that made it so much money. It didn't matter, though: According to the papers Wybert had supplied, this was the best place to rest and resupply before starting on the mountain pass they now intended to take. Euleilla and pack horse in tow, he looked for one of the more unobtrusive inns.

He approached the counter at the inn he chose, the "Savage Bear," with Euleilla in tow. "Excuse me, I'd like a room, please."

The man at the counter smiled pleasantly. "Well, this is your lucky day. We just happen to have a single vacancy for you. Name and number of occupants?"

Maelgyn hadn't thought of a false name to use, and wasn't sure what to say. Then again, his own name was fairly common in some parts of Svieda, and so maybe he could get away with it. "Maelgyn. I'm here with my new wife."

"Ah, newlyweds! Well, it just so happens that we have a private hot spring just for newlyweds! What's her name?"

"Um... Euleilla." Maelgyn wondered just what the man was talking about.

"Good, good," the inn manager said. "Now, I need you to both sign here."

"Sure," Maelgyn said. Unlike most countries in the known world, the people of Svieda were largely literate; therefore, signing one's own name was a common practice. He wasn't sure, however, if Euleilla knew how to write, but he'd deal with that as it came to it. As he wrote down his own name, he asked. "So, what's this about a private hot spring?"

"I thought you knew about our hot springs!" the inn manager exclaimed. "Why else would you stop in Elm Knoll?"

"Last stop before crossing over into Sopan," Maelgyn explained, handing the pen and guestbook over to Euleilla with only a cursory glance of concern. "I'm going home. My family, well, they don't know I'm married yet."

"Ah," the manager nodded sagely. "Well, you chose the right place to stop, especially for a couple of newlyweds. Elm Knoll is the home to the only sizable collection of hot springs in all of Largo! Whether you're an old man trying to soak away the rheumatism in your bones, a road-weary traveler trying to relax, or," he winked lecherously, "a young couple on your honeymoon, our hot springs are for you. And, since you're staying here, you and your lovely young bride will have a chance to experience one together, and without interruption from others. Just make sure to sign up for it in advance, as time slots fill up fast."

"I... don't know if we'll be staying long enough to enjoy that, this time," Maelgyn said, wishing for the first time he hadn't come up with his newlyweds story. If he hadn't, then perhaps he'd have a chance to get a nice hot bath and clean the grime off. Now, though, if he tried to take one *without* having his 'wife' with him, people might start to get a little suspicious. "Perhaps at a later date, though."

Euleilla handed the hotel manager the guest book with a blush visible on her face. Maelgyn caught sight of the register, and noticed with some surprise that she'd actually managed to write her name correctly. It looked a little unsteady, but it was legible and that was what was important. "We'll go."

"Huh?" Maelgyn stuttered. "We'll go where?"

"Silly," she said, grinning at him. "Hot spring. Here. Private. We'll go. Tonight."

The manager laughed. "Well, looks like she's interested, even if you aren't! Just remember to check the chart and mark your time beforehand. I'll get a maid to take you to your rooms."

He left, allowing Maelgyn to quickly turn to Euleilla and whisper harshly, "Just what is that about us going to the hot spring?"

"You want to go, don't you?" she asked.

"Well, yeah, but it... it wouldn't be proper," Maelgyn stuttered.

"Why not?" she asked. "Would you be embarrassed by me? I won't be able to see you, you know."

Sometimes, Maelgyn forgot that about her. Still... "What about you? You are going to have to bathe at the same time, so-"

"Here we go," the manager said, returning with a girl about a year younger than Maelgyn. "Cora, here, will show you to your rooms. Good night, and I hope you have a pleasant stay!"

"This way, please, sir, madam," the maid said, gesturing before she started to lead the way. "Our kitchen is open from dawn 'til dusk. We offer a wide selection of food, although I heartily recommend our *kohitsujikashi* – a lamb and yogurt sauce pastry adapted from a Dwarven delicacy. It's our chef's specialty. We brew our own ale here, or if you prefer to remain sober for the evening we offer a wide variety of fruit juices and flavored milks. I'm afraid we're currently out of stock when it comes to teas, although we're expecting a shipment from Mar'Tok to arrive in time for your breakfast tomorrow. Here is your room, number twenty-four. Will there be anything else?"

Maelgyn surveyed the room, thinking. He turned to Euleilla, and said, "Why don't you unpack here? I've got a few things I have to do before turning in."

"'kay," she said, slipping into their room, taking the bags he had been carrying with her.

Turning to Cora, he said, "First I'd like to talk with your stable master about grooming our pack horse. We got caught in a mudslide on our way here, and I'm afraid the beast is the worse for wear. Also, where would I find the latest news?"

The "latest news" had been fairly unremarkable. There had

been several skirmishes at the front line, but it appeared nobody was willing to launch a full-scale attack just yet. Now that the initial panic was over, Wybert amended his draft laws. There would still be a draft, but most of his army would be formed by activating the militias. Many citizens of the duchy, so far from the front lines, had almost returned to a peacetime state of mind already. There was some concern about the damage that the blockade around Largo's ports was going to do to trade and the economy, but not much else about the war appeared to be in the minds of the locals.

It had been a quiet three weeks since he'd last had word from the outside world, and that disturbed him. Everything he knew from the study of Sho'Curlas' tactics said they should have done more by now... unless they were waiting for something.

Maelgyn was still considering what that something might be as he absently opened the door to his room and walked in. He looked around to survey the room and froze. It took him a few seconds to realize exactly what it was he was seeing, but when he did he gasped in shock.

"Remember to close the door," a half-naked Euleilla called, sending a wave of magic to shut the door behind him. "I don't want strangers looking in here."

Maelgyn immediately closed his eyes. "I'm sorry, milady – I didn't know you were changing! I... I should go back on out."

"S'ok. Stay."

"But–"

"Stay, *husband*," she intoned. "Really, I don't mind."

"I don't think this is right – I mean, we're not really married and..."

For the first time, Maelgyn could feel Euleilla's magic sensing him... it almost felt like she was glaring at him for some reason, but he couldn't imagine why. At any rate, it caused him to shut his mouth real quick. He opened his eyes to look at her, and she seemed quite... tensed.

At least she had covered up – maybe not fully, but she was wearing enough to cover everything important. He found himself relieved... and maybe a bit disappointed. He was a man, after all, and she was quite an attractive woman.

"I thought you understood," she said slowly, interrupting his thoughts. "This is Largo."

"Yeah..." Maelgyn agreed uncertainly, not quite getting the implication.

"Maelgyn... how familiar are you with the civil laws of Largo?" she asked, though it sounded like she thought he should know the answer.

"I know them reasonably well," he replied slowly. "Perhaps not perfectly, but then again I don't live here."

"What about marriage laws?"

"Yes, I'm as familiar with them here as I am anywhere else," he answered.

Euleilla nodded. "Then you should know. Maelgyn, what are the three methods two people can marry, according to the civil laws of Largo?"

"Well, the first is religious marriage," Maelgyn said. "If one wishes to marry, they have a priest perform a ceremony, and the priest will take their oath and declare them married. Most marriages are like this."

"Yes, but not all," Euleilla, with forced patience, noted. "What are the other two methods?"

"A town magistrate, a judge, a captain of a ship, or a Noble of the Province may perform a wedding ceremony. This is much rarer. Usually, they are only performed when a priest is unavailable or the bride and groom are from different religions."

"Go on," she encouraged, obviously hoping that the point would get to him soon.

"Well, the third method was created by Wybert fairly recently to stem the tide of illegal prostitution," Maelgyn explained. "So that no-one could pretend to be married when checking into a room at an inn, he wrote a law which stated that any two unmarried people who check into a room together are... are legally married." He blinked. "Like us. Did... did I just marry you?"

"Yes," she said quietly. "And I thought you knew you were doing it, too. Or at least I hoped you did."

"But... that's... I didn't mean to... I just wanted a good cover story!" he sputtered. "I didn't mean to get married!"

"So, you don't want me as your wife?" she asked softly. Just as he could sense her 'glare' earlier, he could now sense her withdraw from him. It was painful to hear that voice, to hear how fragile she'd suddenly become. He hadn't wanted to hurt her, but what could he say? He really hadn't meant to get married to her, after all.

Then again, she didn't ask him if he'd wanted to get married, did she? Just if he wanted her as his wife... which wasn't *quite* the same thing.

"I don't know," he finally answered, unsure even as he spoke just what he meant by that, or what question he was really answering.

"What?" she said, a tiny edge of hope returning to her voice.

"Well... I mean, did you want me as your husband? I suppose you did, since you thought I knew I was marrying you, but... you don't even know me, so why?"

"I... I don't know, either," Euleilla admitted. "When you first said, 'we could be newlyweds,' I didn't know what to think. And then you followed that by saying you didn't want me thought of as a prostitute, so I... I figured that you wanted the 'benefits' of marrying me, at least. And... I didn't want to say no. I wasn't sure about saying yes, either, but I knew I couldn't say no. I convinced myself that you knew what you were asking." She paused. "I didn't think anyone would ever want to marry me, you see. I never thought anyone would be able to get past my eyes. But you knew about them, and I thought you wanted to really marry me. Well, I hoped you really did, so I... I didn't risk making sure that you knew what you were doing. I'm sorry."

"Don't be. I *should* have known what I was asking," Maelgyn replied softly. "And while I didn't mean to get married to you, I... don't find the idea altogether unpleasant. Just... I barely know you. I met you, what, two, three weeks ago? Earlier today, when we were signing into the hotel register, I didn't even know if you could write. Shouldn't that be the kind of thing you should know about a person before getting married?"

"I can sign my name, if I'm careful," Euleilla said with a sad grin on her face. "I can even read. It just takes a special ink on the parchment for me to be able to see the writing."

"Like I said, I don't know much about you," Maelgyn said. He paused, unsure of how to go on. She looked so sad, and it was all his fault. His fault, because he'd let her believe she was getting a husband, which she never thought she could have. His fault that he couldn't answer 'yes' when asked if he wanted her as a wife. His fault, because he just didn't know her.

In a rush of words, he continued, "I'd love to learn, though. I find you... attractive, even if you look a little unusual with that hairstyle and the oddly colored silk vests you favor. I can't believe you intentionally pick clothes in that color! I'm impressed with your magic, and the intelligence you have shown in dealing with all of your problems. I do like you – you understand that, right? I really enjoy your company, and have since I met you. I think you're a little weird, and not because of your blindness, but I actually like that about you. But I can't say I love you, yet, which is what I'd like to be able to say to my bride, you know?"

"Yeah," she answered, her spirits not improved at all.

"There's another issue to deal with, too." Maelgyn shifted uncomfortably. "I'm royalty. I may even become king one day, although it isn't exactly very likely. You... aren't even a noble. While that's at least *legal* in Svieda, and while it has happened a very few times in the past, it's generally frowned upon. Those few exceptions are usually with the very popular civilians, or the very wealthy, or with some civil leader of great renown. You are not any of those, and that could be a big stress on our marriage."

"Of course," she said stoically. It was hard to tell how she was really feeling, but the slight hitch in her voice was a clue that Maelgyn could easily read. "So, I made a big mistake in thinking that I could be your wife. How are we going to dissolve it?"

Maelgyn grinned. Now that he knew just what he wanted, he was pretty sure she'd be encouraged by this. "Now hold on a minute. Any 'mistake' made was mine, but it isn't necessarily that bad an idea. Like I said, I can't say I love you yet. I didn't say I would never do so. Besides, it'll take a lot of effort to get a marriage dissolved. I'd either have to report to the mayor or local lord, which would ruin the whole point of this fiasco, or I'd have to report to Wybert himself as the Sword of Largo. Now, I expect to make contact with Wybert, again, but not for a few months."

Euleilla was still distressed, but there was a hint of confused hope in her question. "So... we're going to dissolve it, but not yet?"

"Now, I didn't say that, either, did I?" Maelgyn replied gently. "Regardless of what else you'll be to me, Euleilla, you *will* become an important part of my court. And, while I don't think I know you well enough to want you as my wife just yet...

maybe we should consider each other suitors. I don't have any others, right now – to be honest, with the war I didn't think there would be time for me to worry about courtship and marriage and all of that. But, until I see Wybert again, let's just get to know each other better as a courting couple normally would."

Euleilla smiled hesitantly. "Okay."

"And if, at the end of that time, we decide to have the marriage dissolved after all, don't think that means you'll never be married," Maelgyn said. "You are a great catch, Euleilla. I can't promise anything, but I want you to understand that I *know* you're a great catch."

"Thank you," she said, apparently shrugging off all of her concerns and once more becoming the confident woman Maelgyn usually thought of her as. "Now, how about that bath?"

"Bath?" Maelgyn echoed, startled by the sudden change of subject.

"Hot springs? I'd like to see what they're like, and I *know* you want to bathe as well. We have to sign up for a time slot, and I told you to sign up for one. So, when do we have that bath?" she asked.

"Just how are we going to manage that? I mean, I don't think it would be appropriate, considering–"

"You'll wear a blindfold."

"...what?"

A cloth belt of hers floated up and flew over to him. He'd learned, over the course of their journey, that her clothing, her tent canvas, and any other cloth gear had at least some metal sewed into them so that she could find and magically manipulate them. The belt wrapped itself around his eyes, making it impossible for him to see.

"Blindfold. Equal footing and all."

"Um, right." Maelgyn shrugged. It looked like they were taking a bath, after all. Well... it wasn't the best of solutions, but he would accept it. Removing the blindfold for the moment, he said, "Well, I guess I'd better go sign us up for that time slot after all, then, shouldn't I?"

The bath had been very pleasant, but also somewhat awkward. Euleilla had called it "equal footing," but Maelgyn had quickly discovered that it wasn't quite so equal after all. She had been learning ways to deal with her blindness for years, while he had only had, well, seconds to get used to it.

They'd entered the room fully clothed, together, and with him in full possession of his sight. The moment the door was closed and locked behind them, however, a strip of cloth wrapped itself around his head. Getting undressed wasn't too much of a problem – he'd had to undress in the dark, before – but then he stumbled over a bucket and fell face-first into the water.

Euleilla rescued him from his predicament without a word (though he could swear he heard a slight giggle as she did). He settled down into the water, struggling with the soaps and other bathing supplies until he judged himself clean. Once all the necessary scrubbing was accomplished, he relaxed into the water refusing to move any more.

He'd been able to hear her moving around, and could have sworn he heard her laugh at his struggles on occasion, but beyond that he had no idea what Euleilla was doing or where she was in relation to him. She got out first, and then removed his blindfold and beckoned him out.

It was very awkward, being naked around her as he got dressed. Yes, in his mind he knew she couldn't see him... but it was still rather embarrassing, and he found himself trying to cover up certain areas as he dressed, despite knowing the futility of it. It didn't help that he knew she was quietly laughing at him about the whole thing.

He just shook his head at the memory. It was the "morning after," as it were, and things were still quite civil between them at breakfast. Sleeping had posed a bit of a problem, as there was only one small bed. Still, they had managed a decent night... after Maelgyn had agreed to be the one to sleep on the floor. He winced, rubbing the knot which had developed on his back.

"What now?" Euleilla asked, finishing up her tea.

"Now," Maelgyn said. "You should tell me whatever it was El'Athras thought you'd need to explain to me."

"All he said was that he wanted to open negotiations with you," Euleilla explained. "And that these negotiations might not be popular among his fellow Dwarves. He seemed to feel it would help you in your war effort, however."

"Did he, now?" Maelgyn said, frowning. "He said he was a Merchant Prince. That means he's on their leadership council, and probably one of the wealthier Dwarves in Mar'Tok, but I still have to wonder what he could do for me. Especially if the other Dwarves are against him."

Euleilla said nothing, and merely took a bite of her pastry while waiting for him to continue. He didn't say anything, either, until an odd bell started ringing outside the inn. Suddenly, many of the employees of the inn started looking quite nervous, while the guests merely looked confused.

Maelgyn stood up, Euleilla coming with him, and made his way over to someone he recognized – Cora, the maid from the previous night.

"What's going on?" he asked.

"That's the bell to muster the militia," the maid said, her voice wavering slightly. "But that's not the ring for the weekly training session. A constant ringing like that is only supposed to be used if we're under attack. This is only the second time I've ever heard it."

Maelgyn nodded. "My... wife and I could probably be of some service – we're both mages. Where does the militia typically assemble?"

"Right in front of the library," the maid answered automatically. "We don't have a large militia, though – under a hundred men, and we have no fortifications to speak of."

Maelgyn just nodded grimly. "Well, I'll see what I can do. I doubt anyone would expect a village like this to have any mages. In addition to being rather effective warriors on our own, we mages can make an army several times more effective with our talents. My old tutor called us 'force multipliers.'"

"Please hurry, then. Our village militia can muster in minutes, and you need to get there before they march out. Good luck," Cora whispered.

Maelgyn turned to Euleilla as they left the inn. He could see the furious pace at which many of the villagers were locking their doors and windows. It was a futile gesture on their parts, but he supposed it gave the people something to do. "Well, as Sword Prince it's my duty to help fight this battle. I'm assuming you want to come along?"

"Gladly," she answered him.

"Lesson one about being my wife," Maelgyn explained, as he marched through the streets. "There may be times when I go off to battle, and you won't be able to come with me. Also, there could be times when I leave for a battle and you'll have no choice but to come with me. Can you handle that?"

"Yes."

There wasn't even a moment of hesitation in that answer. Maelgyn nodded. "Then let's go. Someone has to keep this village from being wiped out."

Chapter 8

The first thing Maelgyn noticed upon arriving in front of the library was that the militia forces of Elm Knoll were not the best trained soldiers he had ever seen. They were well equipped – one of the benefits of a wealthy town – but beyond that, there wasn't much to recommend them to him. Their captain, however, looked vaguely competent.

"Captain?" he inquired of the only man wearing a proper uniform and rank insignia.

"Yes?" he said, not even looking.

"I'm a traveler, passing through town with my wife, and I thought we might be of assistance."

"Oh, really?" the captain said. "Just who are you? My boys may not be the best soldiers out there, but they work together reasonably well. A new person, though, may disrupt what little sharpness they have."

"My wife and I are both mages," Maelgyn replied, anticipating the question. "Powerful ones. She is a First Rate Mage and I... have yet to be truly tested." He didn't know if Euleilla had actually been tested, either, but he knew she was that powerful nonetheless. The formal test was only needed for certain jobs, and there were plenty of informal ways to determine a mage's rate.

That caused the captain to look up at him. "Is that so? Well, sir, my name is Rykeifer, Captain of the Elm Knoll Militia. I... well, I was going to ask for a demonstration, but I can already pretty much tell there's something about your wife, at least."

Maelgyn turned to see Euleilla, not realizing what the man

was getting at until he realized that he was probably referring to the whirlwind around her. He'd gotten so used to seeing her with it he'd completely forgotten how odd that was.

"So, how about letting me know what it is I'm volunteering to fight?"

"Sho'Curlas raiding party," Rykeifer said. "Apparently, a small force of Sho'Curlas' soldiers positioned itself north of Rubick and is sending raiding parties down from the north. We believe that they took over the tiny nation of Squire's Knot as a staging area. It doesn't appear to be a permanent take-over – the runner bringing me this information said that only two thousand soldiers were in Squire's Knot, which wouldn't hold even that small of a country. They aren't even trying. Those two thousand soldiers have been divided into ten raiding parties that have been sweeping through the more undefended villages along our northern border. The runner passed through a town one of those raiding parties hit – they burned out the entire village before the militia bell could be sounded. That detachment is heading straight for us, and the messenger figures they could be here within two or three hours. I intend to be ready for them."

Maelgyn nodded, glancing over the militia. It wasn't the best drilled army unit in the world, but now that he considered it some more he realized it was probably a typical militia force. It wouldn't be able to handle two hundred well-trained raiders, though. Not without some help.

"I can wield a sword, but Euleilla can't," he explained, nodding to her. Not the truth – he was pretty sure Ruznak would have taught her – but she wouldn't be able to contradict him without blowing their cover. He wanted her out of the thick of the fight. "Where's the best place for her to be? She needs to be near enough to use magic, but still out of harm's way."

Rykeifer considered things for a moment. "What's her range?"

"Long," was all she said.

The militia officer raised an eyebrow, which he turned on Maelgyn. The young Sword Prince just shrugged with a helpless smile.

"Right. Do you need a line of sight to the enemy?"

"No."

"Then probably she could manage from the roof of the library, here."

"Good," Maelgyn replied. Euleilla, apparently able to make her own way, left... again wrapping part of her whirlwind around Maelgyn. "Now, where do you want me?"

"Right by my side," Rykeifer said. "And I'd like to know your name before we go into battle."

"Well," Maelgyn hesitated. "I'm traveling incognito, so before I give you my name you must swear to not tell anyone else, got it?"

"And just why would I agree to that?" the militia captain asked. "Just who are you?"

Maelgyn showed his sword – not the one he was planning to fight with, but rather the symbol of his office. "Sword Prince Maelgyn, Duke of Sopan Province."

Rykeifer's eyes widened. "My Lord, I'm sorry I asked, but-"

"Forget it," Maelgyn said, waving off his apology. "It was your job to ask. Just don't let anyone else know. I'm heading to Sopan Province, and the best chance I have of getting there alive is to not let it be known who I am."

"Understood, My Lord," he acknowledged, stiffening to attention.

"And relax. Euleilla's an incredibly powerful mage, and I'm not half bad if I do say so myself," Maelgyn noted. "We took out a small force of Largo separatists on our way here. That was sixty men assaulting a Dwarven caravan, and there were only six Dwarven archers and six unarmed Dwarves to help us. Here, we may have two hundred enemies to fight, but we've got, what, about eighty people on our side?"

"Something like that – eighty six, if everyone shows."

"See? We've got better odds, this time. And those separatists actually had equipment for fighting mages with them. I don't know if a raiding party formed for attacking small villages will come to the fight similarly equipped."

"If they're smart, they would have brought the necessary equipment, at least," Rykeifer snorted. "Mages aren't exactly common, but there are enough of you around that you could be anywhere."

"Well, Euleilla was able to deal with everything the separatists could throw at me," Maelgyn noted wistfully. "She was just blasting through lodestones like they weren't even there, and she saved my life from some stone-tipped arrows."

Rykeifer regarded him for a moment. "I didn't know you were married, My Lord," he commented knowingly. "Even during events like this war, that sort of news should have reached here by now."

Maelgyn coughed slightly. "Um... it was kind of an accident."

The militia captain raised a single eyebrow. "An accident?"

"I said I was traveling in disguise," Maelgyn explained. "Well, she became part of it. My story was that we were a couple of newlyweds traveling to tell my parents that we had gotten married. Which meant, when I signed into the inn, yesterday, I signed us into a single hotel room...."

Despite the seriousness of the situation, Rykeifer laughed. "Oh, my. Well, now, that'll put you into a fix, now, won't it? So, what are you going to do about it? A peasant marriage isn't exactly going to make you popular, you know."

"Treat her as a suitor, for the moment," Maelgyn explained. "She has enough of a civilian pedigree that she might actually be respected as a candidate. If we decide not to stay married or are still unsure about it by the time I meet up with Wybert again, it won't be too difficult to get it dissolved. If we decide to accept each other's suits by then, however, we'll stay married."

"Well, I don't have any problems with her. I suppose she could be an asset, given her obvious abilities as a mage, and she is nice on the eyes... although that hair is a bit off. Makes me want to move it out of her face."

"No-one touches that hair," Maelgyn growled, hand going to the longsword Euleilla had made for him. "She grows it that way for a reason, and I happen to know why. It... isn't something I want to discuss, however."

Rykeifer looked a bit startled, holding his hands up placatingly. "If you say so, my lord. It does appear you are at least somewhat attached to her, though, so might I say congratulations?"

Maelgyn relaxed, smiling slightly. "Well, it's probably a bit premature, but thank you, anyway. Now, is there anything you want done prior to the battle that I could help you with?"

"As a matter of fact...."

As predicted, it was just over two hours before the raiding party of Sho'Curlas soldiers arrived. It was a light cavalry unit, which is what they had been hoping and preparing for.

"It's not likely there are many archers in a force like that, is it?" Maelgyn asked, watching their approach.

"There may be a few. The standard ratio for our own light cavalry is one horse archer out of every three riders," Rykeifer noted. "How many battles have you fought in?"

"Not many," the Sword Prince acknowledged wryly. "I studied swordplay and magic both from the time I was four until I was fifteen, but I never saw any battles. Then, my father demanded I spend the next three years studying protocol, history, and etiquette, and dismissed my swordplay and magic tutors. While I was still studying swordplay, my tutor took me to witness some of the wargames and training practices of our soldiers in Rubick, and I often witnessed the drills performed by the Royal Guard. I continue to practice whenever I can, just to stay in shape, though my father disapproves... or rather, disapproved." He winced. "As far as real battles, however? Well, I've fought a few gangs of thieves and bandits, and I already told you about that band of separatists Euleilla and I dealt with on our way here. That's about it."

Rykeifer whistled. "So, you're a real greenhorn, eh? Well, at least you've bloodied your sword a little bit, so you should be okay. But keep an eye open. You're going to be leading your own men into battle, one day, so you should see what it's like when two sizable forces meet up. The sights, sounds, and smells are not exactly pleasant. And the larger the armies that meet, the worse it gets."

Maelgyn grimaced. "Trust me, I am not taking this encounter lightly."

"Your regent, Duke Valfarn, is an experienced veteran, widely regarded for his tactical prowess," Rykeifer noted. "You'll probably want him to plan your battles for you, at least until you've got enough experience to know what you're really doing."

"Yes, I had already decided that," Maelgyn noted, watching as the approaching cavalry neared what was the first of the traps he'd helped set up. "I plan on gathering together a good advisory council that I will *actually* listen to, unlike some of my cousins, and I plan on having him on it. I've got a couple other people, in mind, as well." Maelgyn waved his hand dramatically, summoning his magic and setting that trap off.

A number of shallow pits, kept closed by a few easily removed iron clasps, opened up suddenly under the weight of dozens of horses. With a crash, both beast and rider fell into the spiked trench underneath, killing roughly a quarter of the oncoming enemy in one quick move. Thankfully, most of the trenches had been dug over the past several years during militia drills, but filling them with spikes took much of their preparation time. Hopefully, that would be enough when combined with the other things they had planned.

"Now!" Rykeifer called, and at his command the fifty archers (who were usually hunters by trade, and therefore ideal to form the largest and most effective portion of a militia) let loose a volley at the enemy. Unlike the hail of arrows launched as rapidly as possible by professional armies trained in large-scale combat, these militia men instead had been told to do what they did best: Shoot accurately, not quickly. They were using Dwarven-made swallowtail arrowheads – designed not to pierce armor, but instead to kill cavalry horses – and their effect was devastating.

Maelgyn knew the raiders had reached Euleilla's range when he saw weapons, armor, the occasional saddle buckles, and more fly up off the approaching charge. It looked as if this wasn't as effective as it had been against the separatist bandits, as one might expect at that range, but it still was immensely useful. The Sho'Curlas soldiers may have been prepared for magic wielding opponents, carrying secondary weapons made of bronze and other metals impervious to magic, so they were far from disarmed, but the spears she made of their old weapons were quite deadly when the oncoming army rode straight into them.

In a matter of moments, the raiding party was in complete disarray. Expecting to find a sleepy village putting forth some token resistance at best, they instead found themselves riding straight into a trap. Had Maelgyn and Euleilla not been there, the raiding party would have had some trouble, perhaps, but they would most likely have managed to raze the town.

A single arrow went flying in response to the Elm Knoll Militia's strike, but Maelgyn knocked it aside before it reached its target. They may have had bronze weaponry and, from the look of things, a few lodestones, but they weren't truly equipped to handle the devastating effect a powerful mage could have on an army. An average mage likely would have had trouble with this many opponents, but neither Maelgyn nor Euleilla were average mages.

The surviving cavalry, now heavily outnumbered and – thanks to the presence of the two mages – badly outmatched, wheeled around and began a retreat.

The militia almost followed them, but Rykeifer's call stopped their advance.

"Let them run," he called out. "We have better things to do."

Maelgyn frowned. "They could come back, you know. If you strike them down now, they won't have time to regroup."

Rykeifer shook his head. "We can't catch them, and even if we could we'd have a severe disadvantage. Here, in the village, the militia will fight well. This is their home, and their families and livelihoods depend on their ability to stop the enemy. Out there, however, the greater experience and training of the enemy will show itself, and we'd be slaughtered."

"Still, it is a great victory," Euleilla said as she approached them. It seemed that, as the battle had ended, she came back down from the library tower before being told to, but neither man would complain at this point. "They were devastated, while we haven't taken a single casualty."

Rykeifer nodded. "Don't expect most battles to be like this, young Maelgyn," he cautioned. "Even in great victories, there are typically an equally great number of casualties on both sides. And then there is tending to the surviving enemies. Come, we need to go see if there are any wounded, and I believe only you and I can speak Tel'Curlan."

Few people who didn't have trade or negotiate directly with those local to Sho'Curlas bothered to learn their native language of Tel'Curlan, but being a Sword Prince it was expected of Maelgyn. Most Human nations relied upon a language known as "Porosian," after the ancient empire which first spoke it, but the only people of Sho'Curlas who learned this common tongue were the merchants and innkeepers.

"I speak it," Euleilla said.

"Oh?" Rykeifer exclaimed. "How do you know Tel'Curlan?"

"Her adoptive father was a veteran soldier," Maelgyn noted, knowing she wouldn't answer on her own. "And I believe her magic may be able to find the living among the dead better than either of our eyes."

"I've never heard of a mage with such an ability," Rykeifer said, glancing at her in amazement before turning his attention back to Maelgyn. "What about you? Can you do it?"

"No," Euleilla answered for him.

"Why not?"

"Let's just say Euleilla has some special talents and leave it at that," Maelgyn explained. He didn't want too many questions which might reveal her secrets. "You performed brilliantly. That was one of the best organized militias I've ever seen. I would like you to consider joining my advisory council once I've taken power in Sopan." It was an honest request, as Maelgyn had been impressed by the man, but he might not have considered it if he hadn't been trying to think of a distraction.

Rykeifer sighed, looking around. "I don't feel like leaving my militia – especially not after a battle like this. I'll think about it, though."

Maelgyn nodded. "If you decide to take the job, head east. Euleilla's adoptive father runs the 'Left Foot Inn,' in... what was the name of your village again, Euleilla?"

"Rocky Run."

"Right. I'll be stopping back by there, soon, if all goes well," Maelgyn noted.

"Of course. You should tell her family you married her."

"Um... right. I'll get to that eventually." Maelgyn hadn't considered the fact that he'd have to tell Ruznak, at some point, that he'd married the old sailor's favorite 'daughter.' Or tell him that he'd dissolved said marriage, if it came to that. He swallowed nervously and decided to change the subject yet again. "Well, let's get moving. Those wounded aren't likely to get better if we stay here gabbing all day."

It was the first time Maelgyn had ever really walked through a battlefield after the action. Even after the bloody fight with the separatists, he'd been unconscious as the Dwarves went ahead and buried or burned all the dead.

Bloody wounds and broken bones, Maelgyn had seen aplenty in his travels – he'd even caused a few. However, the sights and sounds of the battlefield were much more intense: Bits of bone and cartilage, the smell of feces and vomit and urine and guts, the sounds of his own feet stepping through the viscera that once was living flesh as he tried to hear the moans of the wounded.

He felt ill, knowing he'd had a part in all this chaos, but he didn't regret his actions. These dead were intending to do the same to the people of this village. That knowledge, combined with the memory of what their masters had done to his uncle King Gilbereth, tempered the ugliness of the scene somewhat in his mind. Still, he doubted he would be able to eat comfortably for a week.

It was hard to tell living from dead. As he had guessed, however, Euleilla proved invaluable in that matter. Most of the wounded had been trampled or fallen on by their own horses, suffering severely broken bones and internal injuries. A few needed immediate medical attention, but the worst cases could only be comforted on their way to death.

Maelgyn's own efforts were very limited. Unlike Euleilla, he could not sense the inherent magic in people, and so was unable to tell the living from the dead without checking to see if someone was breathing. This, of course, meant he needed to stick his hands into the pools of blood and guts, just to check for breathing. When he did find someone alive, moving them to where they could be treated took even more time given the limited manpower. It would be a while before they could get to work on burying the dead.

He could only take so much of that. It was one thing to be able to deal with dead bodies after a relatively "clean" battle such as the Dwarves had done with the separatists, it was entirely another to sift through the carnage of a major battle as he was doing. He was finding fewer and fewer survivors as he went and figured he'd done his duty. Even Euleilla's efforts seemed to be slowing, and if she couldn't find someone alive in this muck there was no way he could.

He made his way to the tents, where Rykeifer was translating various discussions between the doctors and the wounded.

"You're lucky it was us you fought," the militia captain was saying to a man being worked on as Maelgyn approached. "In most kingdoms, people who get amputations die more than half the time. In your own, one out of four don't survive. Here in Svieda, however, our doctors have learned techniques that allow nine out of every ten survive."

The wounded man didn't seem to respond. He'd been

given a numbing agent and wasn't entirely aware of his surroundings – some form of opiate, most likely. The doctor had his saw out, and was cutting through the bone.

Maelgyn winced, and tried to shut out his view of the treatment as he made his way over to the captain.

"I'm done here," he said. "I'm not finding anyone else, and it looks like Euleilla's about to give up, too."

"Okay," Rykeifer said. "Just what are you going to do, now?"

"Clean up," Maelgyn sighed. "Go back to the inn I stayed at last night, and soak in the hot springs for a while."

"I wish I could join you," Rykeifer nodded. "But I agree. You've done your part. I'll send your wife to join you when she gets here."

"Thanks." He looked over the wounded. They'd identified almost eighty dead and forty wounded, so far, and likely would find more of the former. He shook his head. "And this is a small battle?"

"Yeah."

"Something's odd about this," Maelgyn said. "Why would Sho'Curlas attack here? What do they hope to gain?"

"Good question," the militia captain snorted angrily. "There was no cause for Sho'Curlas to attack us. I would have bet more on Oregal attacking us, but they never did. I think they just got a reputation for grabbing land by taking some from their enemies each time they were attacked and won. Sho'Curlas was always a more insidious aggressor. They have been conquerors from the shadows – making 'defensive' alliances, and using those alliances to dominate their other allies. A 'one world government' is their goal, and the way they make it sound one would think they were peacemakers. The reality is they just want more land, and frame it in terms of wanting 'peace.'"

"In other words," Maelgyn said, understanding lighting up in his eyes. "They want to use calls for peace as yet another weapon in their war of conquest."

Rykeifer nodded. "'World Peace' is an idealist's goal, isn't it? It sounds so appealing, unless you start to think about what that means. If you think of peace as the absence of conflict, you're forgetting that everything is conflict. Swimming is conflict between you and the water. Standing is conflict between you and the ground. Breathing is conflict between the air and your lungs. The only peace, then, is death. Peace as an end to violence? Sure, that's a laudable ideal... as long as you realize it can only be an ideal. But when you start failing to defend yourself or start harming others to create 'peace,' you've lost sight of what it is you really are looking for. I never trust anyone who says they want 'World Peace,' because they are either too idealistic to be sensible or they are dishonest about what they are really after..."

Maelgyn's face darkened. "'Peace' sure didn't seem to be on Hussack's mind when he slaughtered Gilbereth."

"The kings of Sho'Curlas do remember their goal," Rykeifer cautioned. "It is the real reason they fight. It's just that some only keep to it in name. When we made our initial alliance with them, their king appeared to be a decent man. I believe he was an idealist in the cause of 'peace,' and someone whose heart was in the right place, even if I believe his methods were wrong. I doubt the same could be said for this current crop of royalty, however."

"'Peace' is a hard goal for a nation to set for itself," Maelgyn sighed, "But at least Sho'Curlas has one. If I ever become a king, I don't really know what task to lead Svieda towards. Sho'Curlas desires 'World Peace by any means necessary,' Oregal seeks unification of all of the Major Races under Human control, the Bandi Republic wishes to extend the lives of Humans until they are 'as immortal as the elves,' whatever that means, and the Divided Kingdoms of Poros seem merely to want to reunite humanity's ancestral home... but what should Svieda be for? I'm not sure it has ever had a national goal."

"Intellectual growth," Rykeifer proclaimed. "Stability and security, prosperity, the rights of your people to live life as they desire. Those are noble goals, and those are the goals we Sviedans have shared for our nation's entire existence. We launch few wars of aggression, but we have been known to start a fight when those things have been threatened. It is one of the reasons I feel our nation is worthy of my service."

"Agreed," came Euleilla's voice, coming up from behind Maelgyn. He almost jumped; usually, he could sense her approach. She, however, seemed so weary her usually strong magic aura was quite dimmed. She was stumbling around almost drunkenly, except she wasn't drunk, and didn't look well at all.

"I'm going to go take a bath. Are you coming?" Maelgyn asked, watching her.

"Please," she nodded.

He saw her stagger again, and immediately was at her side holding her up. Nodding farewell to Rykeifer, he half-carried her away. "Come on, let's go."

She sighed. Once they were out of everyone else's hearing distance, she said, "I don't think I can muster the strength to blindfold you this time. Can I trust you not to take too much advantage of the situation?"

"Yeah," he said. "I suspect I'll be too tired to do anything but sleep in the baths, myself."

Chapter 9

Once more, Maelgyn and Euleilla were on the road. Elm Knoll had been busily digging graves as they left, but at least all of the bodies had been sorted. In the end, there were a hundred and thirty four killed with forty-three wounded. Seven of the wounded would likely be dead in a few days, but the rest of them would live... and within a couple of weeks would be marched down to a nearby city that could afford the manpower to imprison them.

The stop at Elm Knoll was probably the last chance Maelgyn would get to hear anything about the war for quite some time, so he hoped to get a last report on the situation along the front before leaving. There was the threat, however, that the raiders would make a second assault on the village. With that in mind, Maelgyn could not afford to risk capture by staying, even if his presence would increase Elm Knoll's chances of surviving an assault.

So, he and Euleilla had discussed the matter as they soaked in their bath after returning from the battlefield. He hadn't exactly kept his eyes closed on that trip into the hot spring, but only because he didn't want to stumble face-first into the water. The way he'd been feeling, he doubted he'd have been able to keep from drowning if he had. He figured she knew, anyway – he could sense she was amused by his embarrassment over the whole thing.

They had talked extensively about whether to stay in town or leave. Or rather, he had talked extensively, and she had offered the occasional encouraging word or bit of advice here and there.

The end result was that the two of them would be moving on towards Sopan even sooner than Maelgyn had originally planned.

He was a bit worried about how Euleilla's presence – and position – would be taken upon reaching Sopan. That she was 'married' to him would probably be excused, given the way it happened – it would be embarrassing how it came about, but he was fairly certain that wouldn't be the big issue. If he decided to *stay* married to her, however, that would be another matter.

Most marriages between royalty and peasantry were unpopular. Why this was so, Maelgyn never understood, but they were. Historically, many of them came about from a romance between a household guard or servant and one of the princes or princesses they protected. On rare occasions, a peasant marriage may mean a marriage between a royal and someone of heroic stature, or of great wealth, and these occasionally were well-thought-of in the public eye. Perhaps the most celebrated peasant-royal marriage was a combination of several of these.

Sword Prince Agaeb, who would later become Sword King Agaeb IV and one of the longest-reigning monarchs in Sviedan history, had in his employ a female guardsman – a rarity in that day, but more common now. That guardsman, the future Queen Amberry, had been the daughter of a wealthy merchant. She had run away from home to join the army, and had worked her way into position in the Royal court as a guardsman after many heroic acts on the battlefield.

Six assassins came, incapacitating all of Sword Prince Agaeb's protectors but her. She fought them all off single-handedly, and nearly died of her wounds in his arms. He nursed her back to health, and by the time she had fully recovered they were betrothed.

Despite the general feeling of goodwill among the citizenry for Queen Amberry, some of the nobility resented her. Over the course of their life together, she had to put up with numerous assassination attempts on herself while still defending her husband's life, much as she had when she was still his guardsman. She outlived her husband by a grand total of one week, for she was killed during his funeral; it was said she hadn't even tried to defend herself, though many believe she could have fought the assassins off even in her old age. That outrage had caused the people of Svieda to riot, and the nobles who had opposed the marriage throughout its duration were deposed, in many cases unfairly, in the belief that they were involved in the assassination.

Most peasant-royal couples didn't have nearly as much popular support as Agaeb and Amberry, however. A little more than a century before Maelgyn was born, Sword Princess Ivari married Merchant Prince Laimoth. In Svieda, unlike among the Dwarves, a 'Merchant Prince' was not a royal title but instead one given to a man with so many funds and assets that he could match the financial power of one of the provincial governments. It was Laimoth's trading empire that sustained the Borden Isles, and Ivari was the Duchess of the Borden Isles Province. She knighted him a peer of the realm and married him. In the Borden Isles, they were quite the popular couple... but Laimoth's pseudo-royalty and sudden peerage was not enough for everyone.

On the mainland, Laimoth was resented for what many people regarded as 'unfair' trade practices. Maelgyn had studied the historical evidence, and saw nothing but a fair businessman who just happened to have a near monopoly over trade with the Borden Isles. Given what he now knew about the Sho'Curlas' influence in the rebellions and unrest throughout Svieda, he wondered if Laimoth's unpopularity was brought about by their malfeasance. It was all too easy to make the less fortunate resent the wealthy just by claiming they weren't doing enough to help the poor, the government, or whatever sympathetic cause the inciter could come up with. Or more insidiously, to manipulate dealings and give the claims of unfairness some hint of truth. Whatever they did worked, for it was Laimoth and Ivari's son, Elaneth, who wound up leading the Borden Isle rebellion, eventually forcing Svieda into the unwanted alliance with Sho'Curlas.

That was an extreme case, but most peasant-royal marriages were treated closer to Ivari and Laimoth's than they were Agaeb and Amberry's. Jealousy and resentment by the citizenry, arrogant bigotry by the nobility, and ambivalence at best from the priests, pages, squires, military officers, and others who were somewhat in-between. Would he be able to stay married to Euleilla, knowing how poorly she would be regarded by so many people who never even saw her? Especially considering how hard a life she already had?

Maybe he should talk to her about it. But not yet... not until he was more certain of his feelings. He wanted to give her the final say, and it was only fair that she know exactly what she was up against.

As far as signs of a growing romance between them was concerned, well... they were there. Even he could see them. They had been walking to the baths, for example, he noticed how her own sweet scent had been obscured by the stench of blood. It was only after he noticed that peculiarity that he realized he'd already memorized her natural scent, and found himself enjoying it and missing it when it wasn't there. Cora, their maid, had remarked something about how she wished she had a man who would look at her the way he'd been looking at Euleilla when they were at breakfast the morning after the battle – the maid hadn't meant to speak loud enough to be heard, but both he and Euleilla had heard her nevertheless.

Still, he believed it was more of a fondness combined with physical attraction than love that he felt. Being battle partners in two separate battles and traveling companions for several weeks, that fondness was bound to exist by now, and the physical attraction had been there since he first saw her. It meant nothing, though; it was too soon for him to be in love. He didn't think he was. Was he? He wondered, vaguely, how he would know.

Perhaps the other question should be did he – or would he – want her as a wife? What were the qualities he wanted in a bride?

He would need someone with a level head. Euleilla had broken down, emotionally, twice that he'd seen her... but both of those times were definitely for just cause: Once because he had learned her secret, and once because he hadn't understood that he'd made their supposedly pretend marriage into a real one. In crisis situations, however, she had proven herself unflappable: She hadn't even flinched when those thugs had cornered her back when they first met. She carried herself brilliantly in battle here and when they intervened to help El'Athras – both times, she was the key to victory and his own survival. Even when searching the dead for survivors, she remained in control and in command. Euleilla qualified, there.

He would need a wife who brought some talent or treasure into his kingdom. Well, there was no doubt Euleilla was both a talent and a treasure, given her magical ability. That, however, was a talent and a treasure he would likely have, at this point, whether she was married to him or not. He felt confident enough in their friendship that she would stay with him, regardless.

As bad as it sounded, he had to make sure his wife wasn't ugly. She would have to be a symbol that his people could look up to, someone they would remember positively, and physical attractiveness went a long way towards that. Maelgyn had not fears on that front, however. Despite the hair, which even he sometimes wanted to shove out of her eyes, she was very striking. Rykeifer had commented on her beauty, as well, so he wasn't alone in thinking that.

He wanted someone he could talk with... and, despite her minimalist form of speech at times, she was actually quite conversational. Initially it was a trifle difficult to relate to her, but now he could figure out her moods enough to know when she wasn't talking because she was hiding something and when she wasn't talking because she found it amusing to keep him in the dark. And, he noticed, the later reason was much more common... which showed that she had another thing he wanted in a wife – a sense of humor.

So, was there really anything he needed in a wife that she didn't provide?

Well... perhaps he needed to think about this some more. He'd barely known her a few weeks, which was much too fast to make a decision of this magnitude. Regardless, they needed to talk. By the time he let her know everything she was going to be in for and let her experience just a touch of what being the wife of a Sword Prince truly was like, perhaps he'd feel a little more confident that keeping her as his bride was the right decision. Or perhaps she'd realize the idea was simply too much for her, which would take the choice out of his hands. At least then he wouldn't be so confused about it all.

"You okay?" Euleilla asked, startling him out of his thoughts.

"Yeah," he answered. "Why?"

"You're quiet," she answered. "Usually, you talk. Or sometimes you hum, or whistle, or... well, usually you make noise when we travel."

"Ah," Maelgyn said. He was a bit surprise at that; he never knew that he hummed or whistled. He'd have to consciously avoid that in the future – it wasn't always safe to hum as you walked, especially in wartime. "Well, I was just thinking."

"What about?"

He grinned, but made sure to keep his voice as casual and natural as possible when he said, "You."

"'kay," she answered, even more naturally and casually. Her persistent smile twitched in amusement, but she said nothing more.

They continued on in silence for a little bit more, before the silence finally got to Maelgyn. "Aren't you curious?"

"Maybe," she said. "But I'd rather you thought about me than explained what you were thinking about me."

Maelgyn laughed. "Right. Well, I'll probably think of you some more, later, but right now I'd like to talk for a bit."

"Sure."

He did want to talk, but at the moment he did not want to talk about their marriage. This wasn't the right setting, nor the right time, to have that talk yet. But he always had other questions for her, so there would always be something to talk about. Come to think of it, that was probably a good reason for staying married to her, too.

"Actually, I was wondering just how you sense the latent magic in people. I know it's something you learned to do because of your eyes, but I was wondering if it was something you could teach, as well?"

"Possibly," she mused. "Gramps use to try playing hide and seek with me. He let me use any method I wanted, so I stuck a few grains of magic powder on him when he wasn't looking. Sometimes, when I was following those grains of magic powder, I found myself losing track of it. I repeated the experiment several times, thinking he was using a lodestone or something to help himself hide, but I eventually realized it wasn't a lodestone obscuring my magic; it was his own body. The human body, itself, generates the same waves of energy as a lodestone does. It's not very clearly focused, and very hard to 'see' unless you realize what you're looking for, but it's there. Tell me, could you find a lodestone if you weren't looking for it?"

"If I wasn't looking for it?" he said, surprised. "I... well, no. Not unless it's a very large one."

Euleilla nodded. "Think of someone untrained in magic as a very tiny lodestone, one which you'd have difficulty finding unless you already knew it was there. You wouldn't 'see' the lodestone if you weren't looking for it. Likewise, you must 'look' for magic in people. If you 'look' at a person with this method, and find they are just so unfocused and dispersed that you can't even see the pattern of magic inside them, they are not a mage. If you can see the pattern... well, then you've found a mage. They become a beacon of intense magic, and from that intensity you start to get a sense of how strong a person is."

"Okay," Maelgyn said slowly, mulling that over.

"And then you need to learn to keep looking for magic of that sort all of the time. Something which may be hard to do, if you aren't a person who has to rely on magic to see," she considered. "But you don't need to do that to sense latent magic. Once you get to the point you can sense people not trained in magic, you can apply the same trick to any trained mage and you'll be able to figure out how much latent magic they have yet to access. Like I said, I believe you've got the potential to be much more powerful than you are now. You have so much more magic you have yet to access."

Maelgyn nodded. "Maybe you could help me practice 'seeing' magic?"

"I don't think I could help you with that," Euleilla answered. "You need to work with someone not trained in magic, first, for this to work. I can help you learn how to use your magic better, though."

"And I could help you, as well, I suspect," Maelgyn noted. "Somehow, I think you haven't had much practice with counter-magic, since you need a partner mage for that."

"No, I don't think I've had much practice with counter-magic," Euleilla admitted uncertainly. "Or rather, I haven't studied any counter-magic. I've never even been aware of such a thing, unless you're referring to lodestones and dragonhide."

"No," Maelgyn answered. He pulled up the memory of a lecture given by Thoniel, his old magic tutor, and recited it as closely as he could. "Counter-magic can only be done with another mage. It works under the same principle as all Human magic – by borrowing on the behaviors of lodestone. Hold two lodestones together one way, and they attract each other. Hold them another way, and they try to push each other away. It's one of the major defensive concepts in magical combat."

"Hmm," she said. Suddenly, he felt a magical force pushing

on him in what was recognizably counter-magic. It wasn't nearly as strong as her usual magical touch, but he matched it back instead of trying to break through.

The "battle" continued for hours as they hiked on. It started becoming an interesting game of magic. In Euleilla's case, she was trying to write her name on his skin using a magical combat training technique – forcing a person's blood to come up and mark their skin in a sort of bruise. Maelgyn was trying something else. He was trying to take control of the muscles in her arm and force her to touch her own nose.

They could have easily burst through each other's defenses if they had applied their full power: Euleilla was still an amateur at counter-magic, and Maelgyn's defensive capabilities were not as strong as Euleilla's regular magic. That wasn't the purpose behind the exercise, however. They were simply practicing their defenses, which would improve all of their magical abilities in the end.

When Euleilla finished writing her name on the back of his hand before Maelgyn could make her touch her nose, the game changed. She started magically tickling him, and he tickled her back – sometimes in places he wouldn't dare touch with his real fingers. By the time they set up camp for the evening, both were laughing so hard they were losing their breath.

Euleilla was gasping in air, the battle over, while Maelgyn built the fire pit for their dinner. Sighing contentedly, she said, "Oh, my, that was fun. We're going to have to do that again."

Maelgyn smiled at her. Her face was flushed with excitement and humor, her chest heaving with the lack of air, and her hair a tangled mess. She was beautiful, but he had known that for a while. Now, however, she was more than beautiful to him. She was vibrant. No, that wasn't the right word – radiant, that was better.

He gave up trying to find the right word and just nodded. "I agree. Anytime you want."

Maybe, just maybe, marrying her was the best mistake he'd ever made.

Chapter 10

It took just one more day before they crossed into the mountain pass. Other than the continuation of their practice duel from the previous day, it passed fairly uneventfully. The pace of that action, however, was fast and furious, and this time didn't dissolve into a tickle battle. Maelgyn, to his own surprise, won the day, making her touch her nose just like he'd intended. Then, just to make up for it, he allowed her to sign her name on the opposite hand. He could have removed the first mark, but he hadn't, and now was rather proud of his matching "tattoos." At the conclusion of their day's frivolity, they made camp at the mouth of the mountain pass, and in the morning crossed over into Mar'Tok Dwarf territory.

It was easy traveling, but extensive. The Dwarven roads were superior in durability and maintenance to the roads in most Human countries (and even, theoretically, most Elven countries, though the last purely Elven country dissolved before the time of Svieda's founding), but that didn't make the trip any shorter. They had to walk down many miles of winding roads, and it was going to be a three day journey to cross the entire mountain range. There weren't very many good places to camp along the pass, however, so they had no choice but to make it to a Dwarven village that night.

They weren't playing their magic games as they walked. A fall in this area could be fatal, so they couldn't afford the distraction. The road was wide, and fairly safe if you could see the cliff-side edge, but there was nothing magically reactive for Euleilla to 'see' on that side, so Maelgyn was being especially careful to make sure she was well away from that ledge. In fact, he was not willing to trust the magical lifeline Euleilla had wrapped around him as a proper guide, so instead was leading her by the hand. Whether she noticed that a tiny part of his own magic was concentrated in making sure that grip wouldn't break, he didn't know, but he wasn't going to take any chances with her life.

For such a well-built and heavily maintained road, there hadn't been much traffic. According to the papers he'd read, even in its busiest time this road only had the occasional merchant train. There were many other, much busier roads in the mountains that the Dwarves maintained, but this one seemed unusually well maintained for so little traffic. There was only one reason Maelgyn could think of to have these roads *this* well kept, and that reason didn't please him at all. There were only two places this road exited – into Largo Province, and into Sopan Province. And there was only one excuse for their level of upkeep – the expectation of an army using them. Of a *large* army using them. Of a large army using them against *Svieda*.

It didn't make any sense for the Dwarves to launch a war against Svieda. Mar'Tok and Svieda had one of the most cordial relationships in Dwarven-Human history. Svieda had never launched a single war against any Dwarven holding and had always traded with them in good faith. And yet, there was this road which was built for no apparent reason other than to make war on Svieda.

Not exactly the most comforting of thoughts for a Sword Prince to have as he was crossing through Mar'Tok territory. He did have the gratitude of one of the Mar'Tok Merchant Princes, but how far that gratitude would stretch he wasn't sure. Especially after that little warning El'Athras had given him about not letting anyone else know who he was – if that wasn't a sign that members of the Svieda Royalty might not be welcome in Mar'Tok, he didn't know what was. However, as long as his cover story held it would remain a fairly safe route. And a cover story which was true was always a good one – even if that story was only half-true.

About an hour away from the village, Euleilla frowned. "Maelgyn, are we near the village?"

"We've still a ways to go," Maelgyn said. "We should reach it before night falls, though."

Euleilla shook her head as if to clear it. "How odd. I'm sensing a great number of Dwarves... only they aren't on the path ahead. They're... next to me."

Maelgyn frowned and looked around before he realizing what it was that she was feeling. "Caves. 'Mar,' in Dwarvish, is 'Cave Kingdom.' The people of Mar'Tok originated in the caves, and in fact this is possibly the oldest Dwarven settlement in the world. The caves go on for miles underground – we must be near a pocket of them."

"I've never felt so many people – Dwarf or human – in one place, before. It's a bit... overwhelming." The distress in her voice was worrisome.

"What's the largest settlement you've been to since you developed your ability to sense a person's presence?" Maelgyn asked.

"I haven't been anywhere much larger than Rocky Run. Even before I moved there, I never lived anywhere larger than the small mining town my father decided to raise me in."

"Ah. Well, when we reach Sopan, you'll find that there are a lot of human settlements much larger than Rocky Run and Elm Knoll. Dwarven cities are tightly packed, however, so maybe it's just that you're sensing," he suggested.

"I hope so," Euleilla answered. "I think that a lot of these people are preparing for a battle, however. I can feel swords and armor near most of them."

Maelgyn grimaced at this apparent confirmation of his worst fears, but didn't let his concern carry over into his voice. "Well, we don't need to worry about that just yet. If they're getting ready for war, it could be against anybody. I know they have poor relations with the Bandi Republic in their north. Even if they're hostile to Svieda, they aren't likely to attack two road weary travelers before war has officially started. Bandits might, but disciplined Dwarven armies won't even look our way until we are truly at war. Since they shouldn't even know we're coming, I doubt we'll be a target."

They continued on until reaching a Dwarf village, which had an unusual design founded on terraced mountainside landscaping. There were a number of disquieting looks sent their way as they walked through its streets, but their innkeeper was pleasant enough to them and the rest of the staff at the inn didn't seem hostile toward the human couple.

Maelgyn had intended to scout around the village for information on the Dwarf they were supposed to meet. El'Athras' name did appear in the papers Wybert had given him, but there was precious little information on him. It did say that the Dwarf was, indeed, a Merchant Prince, and that while he normally lived in the underground capital city of the Dwarves he maintained a household on the above-ground part of the city of Nir'Thik. Maelgyn could not even confirm these bare facts, however, as the uncomfortable feeling Maelgyn had been getting while they approached the inn was prompted him to moved on. The signs they might not be welcome were numerous – for example, the menu handed him by their Dwarven waitress at the inn was in Dwarvish, with no translation provided.

He and Euleilla pushed on down the mountain road after restocking their supplies, but traffic wasn't nearly as quiet as it had been. Apparently, there was a lot of transit going back and forth between the Dwarven villages along this road despite the lack of traffic leading into the mountains. That wasn't all that remarkable, except for the fact that most of the traffic wasn't what you would expect for internal traffic between two Dwarven villages: Humans dressed in the robes of several countries, the cat-like Nekoji from the Orful River, and various lesser races dressed in foreign attire made up the bulk of it. Quite a cosmopolitan atmosphere for a race that, supposedly, preferred a self-reliant isolation from the rest of the world when not engaged in trade.

None of those other travelers were giving them strange looks, at least. Euleilla seemed increasingly uneasy and Maelgyn couldn't tell why, but at least he felt more comfortable on this stretch of road than at any other time in his journey... and he had to admit, it was interesting seeing Nekoji in person. He had heard tales of this ancient race of "cat people" who walked and dressed like Humans but grew flame-proof fur, rich manes, and feline faces. Before this day, he had never seen one – or even a picture of one – but they were easy to identify, nonetheless. The reason they made themselves so hard to find was quite understandable: There was a trade (an illegal trade in most civilized nations) in Nekoji skin. Nekoji were intelligent creatures, far more so than some humans, and very civilized. The flame-retarding properties of their fur, however, led hunters to seek them out, and there had been a number of massacres discovered where whole towns had been wiped out and the populations skinned. Oregal maintained some protection over them, but as an independent people they held fewer lands than even the Dwarves.

Mar'Tok was an unusual place for a Nekoji to travel, but there were plenty of them on these Dwarven roads. Perhaps Mar'Tok gave them sanctuary, which was a rare thing, but Maelgyn wasn't sure. However, they weren't built for cave or mountain life, so the large number of them still seemed unusual. Yet another mystery in Maelgyn's mind – one he doubted he would ever have the time to solve.

Euleilla was shrinking away from some of the Nekoji, much to Maelgyn's confusion. Later, she explained that they had such vast untapped potential for magic that their mere presence was enough to overwhelm her senses. Maelgyn found that, using the ones she pointed out for practice, he could sense them too. By the time they reached the town of Nir'Thik, he was able to even detect people without strong inherent magic, just like Euleilla, though he still had trouble sensing Dwarves unless he got very close. She was still much better at it than he was, but he now knew the technique, and with practice he might even match her.

"Well," Maelgyn began after they reached Nir'Thik's outskirts. "We got here earlier than I thought. Do you want to find an inn, first, or go see this 'El'Athras,' instead?"

Euleilla shook her head. "I'm still adjusting to the sensory overload, and I'm getting a headache. Let's find an inn and see him tomorrow."

Maelgyn nodded. "Okay. Oh, and I'm not going to give this inn our real names, so don't be surprised."

Euleilla just nodded. For the first time, Maelgyn noticed how pale her skin was – a sickly pale, accompanied by what looked like a cold sweat. She seemed to be breathing heavily, and didn't seem as steady on her feet as usual. Her whirlpool of magic dust appeared to have disappeared – not completely, as he found when he looked closer, but it so weak he wasn't able to see it any more. His eyes widened in concern.

"Euleilla! What's wrong?"

"Tired," she said, smiling wanly, trying to pass it off casually. Her voice broke, however, even with the lone word.

"No, it's more than that. Something's been bothering you

since yesterday. I didn't think it was any more than what you told me, but now I can see that you're not well." He picked her up, and started carrying her. When she started weakly struggling, he added, "If you're going to be my wife, you're going to have to stop keeping secrets from me. If I'd known you weren't well, I could have fixed some things and had you riding the pack horse. It is my duty to take care of you, you know. That's what married people do."

She slumped into his chest, her remaining magic powder coming to rest in one outstretched hand. "Okay," she whispered, right before falling limp. Maelgyn almost dropped her in surprise, but then recovered.

"Hell!"

Maelgyn burst into the first inn he saw, not even caring to ensure the groomsman was taking care of his pack horse, and hurried over to the main desk. He was still carrying Euleilla, and he was getting more and more panicked the longer he walked.

"Quick," he ordered. "I need a room, a bed, and a doctor – in that order."

The Dwarf running the inn didn't even look at him. "Rooms are thirty shiels," he answered, referring to the Dwarven currency. "And we don't have a doctor, here. I could send someone out for one, though. Whadya need, Dwarf, Human, Nekoji, or something else?"

Maelgyn's eyes widened in anger. "Well, let me see. I'm carrying my sick, unconscious, pale, *Human* wife. What kind of doctor do you *think* I want?"

Only then did the Dwarf look up. He immediately snapped to attention. "My apologies, sir," he said once he'd taken a quick glance at Euleilla. "Tur'Ba! Front and center!"

A young Dwarf – probably in his twenties or thirties – rushed into the front hall. "Yeah, pops?"

"Hurry to Dr. Wodtke's office, immediately! Tell her we have a plague victim, and she needs to get here right away!"

Maelgyn's blood ran cold. Did the innkeeper just say Euleilla was a victim of some *plague*? He hadn't heard of any plagues hitting the known world in sixty years, and surely he would have. So, where did this plague come from? Was there a cure? And... could it kill her?

"Sure thing, pops!" Tur'Ba said, suddenly becoming serious. With a quick nod to Maelgyn, he ran out the door faster than the Sword Prince had ever seen a Dwarf move.

"And don't call me 'pops!'" the innkeeper bellowed. Shaking his head, the Dwarf immediately stood up. "Again, my apologies, sir. My name is El'Ba, proprietor of this establishment. Let's find your lass, there, a nice warm bed."

Maelgyn just nodded, following the innkeeper to a room where he could put Euleilla down. Once she was lying on the bed, he turned to the Dwarf with a fierce glare.

"Just what kind of 'plague' are we talking about, here?" he snapped.

El'Ba didn't answer, at first. He sighed, found a chair to sit in, and looked down at the ground. It was then he answered.

"Is she a mage?" the innkeeper asked cautiously.

That filled Maelgyn's heart with dread. A disease which only affected mages? He'd never heard of such a thing. If that was the case, though, why didn't he also come down with the same thing?

"We both are," Maelgyn answered softly, the reality of the situation tempering his voice. "She's a strong one, too. Never met a stronger one, in fact."

The Dwarf relaxed. "Good. Then she'll probably live. I don't understand all the details, myself – Dr. Wodtke, who's also something of a mage, will explain when she gets here – but I know that it's something curable with magic. And it's best if the magic comes from inside the patient."

"Well, what *is* the plague?" Maelgyn asked. "I haven't heard any news about one. And just what does the plague do?"

El'Ba snarled. "Some... unnatural construct. It only attacks women of child-bearing age, and only during their menses. I don't understand all of it, but it's some kind of blood poisoning."

"Unnatural?" Maelgyn frowned. "You mean it's a poison? But you called it a plague!"

"It is a plague," El'Ba insisted. "I don't get the details, but because it seems related to human magic, our doctors believe some Elf or maybe a Human alchemist developed it as a weapon. Over a thousand women died in Mar'Tok, alone, before our doctors figured out how to deal with it. Now we at least know how to cure it if it's caught in time. Mages almost universally recover within a day with the proper treatment, while other women require magical assistance and take longer."

"An alchemist came up with this? A *human* alchemist?" Maelgyn growled.

"Probably," El'Ba snapped. "Dwarves usually don't bother studying magic, we're all so weak in it, and the few Nekoji who manage to learn magic are so extremely powerful in it it's unlikely they'd ever try for alchemy as a specialization. And Elves... well, they might manage to produce something like this, I suppose, but how many Elves do you see nowadays?"

Maelgyn nodded. "Do you know who developed it? Is that why Mar'Tok is preparing to invade Svieda?"

"Invasion?" El'Ba laughed. "Us? Not a chance. What in the world makes you think we'd do such a thing? I shouldn't be saying this, but it would be pure folly for us to launch a war. We'd be crushed if we attempted any kind of attack against our neighbors."

Maelgyn was about to confront the man when Tur'Ba returned, a hearty human woman in her mid-to-late thirties in tow. The woman immediately made her way to Euleilla's bedside and frowned.

"I brought Dr. Wodtke, pops," Tur'Ba announced. El'Ba immediately started berating the young Dwarf about showing proper respect to his ancestors. Meanwhile, the doctor was checking Euleilla's fingernails and tongue anxiously.

"How long has she been experiencing symptoms?"

"I don't know," Maelgyn said. "I... can everyone else leave? I need to explain some things to the doctor that Euleilla doesn't want everyone to know."

The doctor raised an eyebrow, but the two Dwarfs just left without question. Maelgyn used his newly developed magical senses to make certain that no-one was listening in before he said anything.

"Okay, we're alone," the doctor said impatiently. "Now, are you going to answer my questions, or are you going to let this girl get worse for no reason?"

Maelgyn nodded. "My wife is a powerful mage – more powerful than anyone else I've ever seen, and she certainly would be rated a First Rate if she was ever formally tested. And it's a good thing she is, because she has a major problem." With one hand, he very gently brushed the hair away from her forehead, revealing her eyes. The doctor, upon seeing the scars which proved Euleilla's blindness, gasped. Maelgyn sighed, restraining the rage he felt for both the deceased Cawnpore and the mining conglomerates who had killed her father, before smoothing her hair back into position. "She's learned how to use magic to compensate for her lack of sight. She uses a cloud of magic dust to see the terrain around her. She can even sense people by their magical aura, whether Human, Dwarf, Nekoji, or something else. The problem is she's also always lived in a small town... so, when she started sensing the thousands of people tightly enclosed in a Dwarven underground city, even through the dirt and stone below, it was overwhelming her."

The doctor nodded uncertainly. "And... just how does that matter?"

"Well, I assumed everything that was happening to her was because she was having trouble with all of those people, so I didn't notice anything was wrong until she nearly collapsed about a half hour ago," Maelgyn sighed. "And damn me for not paying better attention."

The doctor nodded sympathetically. "It's not your fault – these symptoms can show up rather suddenly. She'll be all right. In fact, once I've helped her enough, she should be able to cure herself quite quickly. Mages, for some reason, do a better job of cleaning this disease out of their own blood than they do working on someone else's. Now, can you help me get her undressed? I need direct access to her skin."

"Um," Maelgyn hesitated, embarrassed. "I... that wouldn't be a good idea. We're married, yes, but... we haven't, uh, had our honeymoon, yet. I think she'd want to be awake the first time I undressed her."

The doctor looked surprised, and then laughed. "That sounds like there's a story there. Well, I think I can manage this alone. Don't worry – you'll get that honeymoon, if I have anything to say about it!"

Maelgyn nodded, blushing even more. The story was even more complicated than the doctor was ever likely to know, but explaining would be worse. "Thank you, ma'am"

Turning serious, she said, "In another hour or two, we'd have had severe difficulty, and even now I've got to work quickly.

Which means I need to prepare her for the treatment right away, so get out of here unless you want to see her in the buff!"

Maelgyn hesitated, then nodded and headed out the door. "I do," he admitted quietly, more to himself than to Dr. Wodtke. "But not like this."

Dr. Wodtke came out of the room about an hour later. Nodding to an impatiently pacing Maelgyn and a sympathetic El'Ba, she said, "You were right, she *is* an impressive mage. I think her system's already cleared of the disease, or it will be soon at any rate, but it was so advanced when I started treatment that she'll need more time than usual to fully recover. Keep an eye on her tonight and I'll be by in the morning to check up on her."

"Thank you, doctor," Maelgyn said, slumping in exhaustion. He hadn't realized how tired he was until just then.

Dr. Wodtke looked him over, and shook her head. "On second thought, you get some sleep. Hold your wife – it will help comfort her, which should speed the healing process – but go to sleep. It wouldn't do for you to get sick as well. El'Ba, can you check on them periodically?"

"Aye," El'Ba agreed. "That I can do."

"But-" Maelgyn protested.

"No buts. Go in, hold her, and sleep. Doctor's orders," Wodtke snapped.

Maelgyn looked around for support – not that anyone else would understand. He'd never slept in the same bed as his wife before, but only the smugly smiling Wodtke would know that. After all, Euleilla was his wife, and it was assumed he would have bedded her already.

"Fine," he growled. "But I want something from you, too, doctor."

Dr. Wodtke blinked. "Something from me? For staying in bed?"

"That's right," Maelgyn said, smiling. "I'm a stranger around here. I was thinking I'd be staying up all night, keeping one eye on Euleilla while I used the other eye to look at city maps. Since it seems I won't have my night to study, I'll need a guide if you can provide one."

The doctor laughed. "Well, my office shouldn't be too busy tomorrow, so I should be able to help you. Dwarven medicine is pretty primitive, but most people around here don't trust human doctors, much, unless there's an emergency that gives them no choice. Thankfully we don't have many emergencies now that the plague is under control."

Maelgyn nodded to her and then entered Euleilla's room. To his surprise, she was awake when he entered... although she didn't seem aware of his presence.

"Euleilla?" he said carefully. She jumped anyway, and then looked a little embarrassed.

"Hi," she answered back timidly. "I've exhausted all my magic, so I can't really tell where you are, right now."

"Okay," Maelgyn said, stripping off his dragonhide armor as he approached the bed. "The doctor said you'd be better off if I were to try holding you as we slept, tonight."

"I know," Euleilla answered. "She told me the same thing. I'm sorry. I know you probably don't want to, but..."

"Shh," Maelgyn answered. "Now, whatever gave you that impression? Look, Euleilla, I don't know what our future will ultimately be together, but I do know that I find you quite desirable. Maybe too desirable, given your current condition."

Euleilla smiled, although it was fairly weak. Her strength appeared to be fading fast, although she looked healthy enough thanks to Dr. Wodtke's treatment. Maelgyn slipped under the covers beside her. Much to both of their surprise, he lifted up her hair and kissed her lightly on her forehead, before lowering her hair back over her eyes like she preferred. "Good night."

As he felt Euleilla fall asleep in his arms, he vaguely wondered why he kissed her at all. It just added to the awkwardness of everything, although it had felt right. Euleilla hadn't seemed to mind, thankfully, and he...

Oh. That was why. Well, he had wondered when he would know that he loved her.

Chapter 11

Maelgyn awoke the next morning as something rather pleasantly soft stirred in his arms. It took him a moment to realize that something was Euleilla. It took him another moment to remember just why Euleilla was there. In between those moments, he jumped in such surprise he accidentally woke her.

"What?" she said sleepily. Then, she just nodded. "Oh, right. Maelgyn, I know you're impatient to get moving and all, but I'm still not feeling all that great. I think I need to sleep a touch longer, okay?"

"Sorry," he answered her. "I... forgot you were here."

"S'ok," she muttered, burrowing herself into his shoulder. "Just don't do it again."

"Um," he hesitated. "You don't have to get up, yet, but I do. Could you, uh, let me go?"

"No," she laughed sleepily. "You have to stay right here and be my pillow."

"Euleilla," he replied desperately. "I'm sorry, but I have to go. If I don't, well, let's just say this bed won't be quite so pleasant to sleep in."

"Oh." she gasped, embarrassed, as she realized what he was saying. She quickly let go, bundling the blankets around herself as she sat up part-way. "Sorry."

"Shh..." he answered absently, and kissed her gently on the cheek. "Go back to sleep. The doctor will be here, soon, to check you over. I want you as well rested as possible before then."

"'kay," she answered, burrowing herself back into the real feather pillows that only the best of Dwarven hospitality could provide.

Maelgyn left the room. He was still dressed in his clothes from the previous day except for his armor. He realized, as he walked, that he'd left their supplies and clothes on the pack horse. He was fairly bleary, still, and needed his morning toilette before he'd be awake enough to deal with the stables.

"Ah, sir!" El'Ba exclaimed, seeing him walking around lost. "I see you're awake. Excuse me, but I never got your name."

"Maelgyn," he answered, forgetting that he had intended to give a fake name.

"Maelgyn, then. You look a little lost," the Dwarf said.

"I am," he admitted, laughing slightly. "Where's the privy?"

El'Ba gestured swiftly, and answered, "Down at the end of the hall. There's also a bath available for use."

"Ah," Maelgyn answered. "Well, I'd need to collect a change of clothes, first, but maybe later. I left my bags on my horse, so—"

"I'll handle that for you if you want to have one now," El'Ba offered. "It would be no trouble, since your horse is in our stables."

"If you're willing," Maelgyn said, nodding in both gratitude and relief. "Thank you. You've been quite helpful – so helpful I'm starting to worry about the fees you plan to charge for doing all of this."

"I suppose I forgot to mention the cost of doing all of these extra services in all the excitement last night," El'Ba said, trying to hide an all-too-obvious smile by stroking his beard. "Well, I wouldn't be much of a Dwarf if I didn't make something off of you, now would I? Then again, I am making a commission from Dr. Wodtke for recommending her to you. I suppose that'll be enough. You've got enough to deal with, right now without having to worry about extra fees."

Maelgyn grinned. "Well, while I must agree with you, there, I could afford extra..."

"No, lad. Anyone who's had to deal with someone they love being caught in that plague, whether she recovers from it or not, shouldn't also have to respond to the whims of a Dwarf's greed," El'Ba answered. "Go on, lad – relax. I'll find you a change of clothes while you bathe."

Maelgyn nodded, heading for the privy. He was surprised

to discover the inn had running water – albeit only cold running water. Thankfully, while the posted rules require that he clean himself under the cold sprays, the bath itself was heated by a gas flame piped in underneath, and the fire was controlled so that it wasn't large enough to get the water boiling – just enough to heat it. It was an interesting variation to the design Maelgyn was familiar with, but it reminded him a little too much of making a stew over a campfire for him to feel comfortable with it.

Instructions were over the tub in Dwarvish, Nekoji, and three human languages (including his own). They explained that users could drain and fill their own tubs, if they desired, but to please leave hot water for the next bather. That, too, was a different style of public bath than he was used to – in Svieda, either you only filled the tub once a day (a common practice for those inns without running water that still liked to provide a bath to customers) or you filled and emptied the tub every time you used it. In this case, it appeared as if that was only an option. The sign called this a "Fu'Ro System of Bathing." Maelgyn's knowledge of Dwarvish was very limited, but he believed the suffix 'Ro,' in this case, meant 'family,' and the prefix 'Fu' meant 'Water.' He gathered from that simple translation that the system was designed for each family to use a single tub of water. An interesting idea for an inn, which likely had to pay an exorbitant amount of money just to provide the service of running water.

Maelgyn was so caught up in musing on the bathing system that he failed to notice El'Ba's return. The Dwarf walked over to the tub, carrying several things with him: A change of clothes for Maelgyn, his bag of hair brushes and other assorted toiletries, and...

"Well, Sword Prince Maelgyn," El'Ba said, laying down the royal Sword which Maelgyn typically kept at his side at all times... or had, until he'd hidden it in his saddlebags in favor of the longsword Euleilla had made for him. He'd forgotten he left it there when he allowed the Dwarf to go through his belongings. "It looks as if maybe you could afford to give me a trifle more than the usual fees, after all."

Maelgyn took a sip of his Mo'kah tea and sighed. El'Ba had merely grinned, left Maelgyn's gear, and departed after the revelation of his discovery. He hadn't seen the Dwarf since, and hoped that this didn't mean the man was telling his name to whatever bad elements El'Athras had wanted him shielded from. Maelgyn, not knowing what else to do, just finished his bath and changed into the fresh clothes, then went to the inn's common room where Tur'Ba served him the tea and some lightly toasted pastries.

Dr. Wodtke showed up just as he was finishing his tea, looking fresh and pleased with her lot in the world. "Good morning. So, how is your wife this morning?" she asked.

"She was still asleep when I left our room – that was about an hour or so ago – but she seemed well. Her magic doesn't appear to have recovered, yet."

"That's to be expected," the doctor answered. "She'll be weak magically for a couple days, but she can still use it without fear while she recovers. Physically, she should be perfectly fine. I'll just go and check on her, okay?"

"Fine," Maelgyn agreed, nodding. He smiled slightly at the good news, but that went away after she left. He was still increasingly frustrated with himself over El'Ba's discovery of his identity. He'd been trying to keep it secret throughout his journey, but he had allowed it to be discovered at least four times. He still had no idea what this Dwarf felt for Sviedan royalty – after all, he never got an explanation for the apparent war preparations that he and Euleilla had discovered.

El'Ba showed up only moments after the doctor had left, a grin still on his face. Maelgyn had no clue what that grin meant, but at least there wasn't guilt on the Dwarf's face. Guilt would have worried Maelgyn even more.

"Hello, Maelgyn," El'Ba said, sitting at the table and helping himself to one of the young man's sweetbreads. "Well, now that I know you can actually afford it, I suppose it's time to discuss the fee for the extra services I've been providing."

Oh, so it's a bribe, is it? Maelgyn thought as he nodded cautiously. *I should be able to handle that.*

"I've given it a great deal of thought," the Dwarven innkeeper said, the grin never leaving his face. "Unless I miss my guess, it would be within your power to provide steady employment for young Tur'Ba, over there."

Maelgyn's eyes widened, looking over towards the speedy Dwarf bustling about in the bar area. "Well... yes. I might be able to use him for something in my household. I have no idea what for, at the moment, however. I've yet to see how my regent has set up the court."

El'Ba nodded. "That's alright. I just... my son wants to see the world. Given what I suspect you're heading off to do, I suppose you'd be able to help him do that, right?"

"Yes," Maelgyn answered cautiously. "El'Ba, I acknowledge my debt, but it's not in your son's best interest to send him off with me right now. Svieda is at war. Once I organize my armies in Sopan and find a way to bring them across to Svieda proper, I'll probably wind up on the front lines in some capacity. If I give him the kind of job you seem to want him to have... I can't guarantee his safety."

El'Ba's grin slipped momentarily, but then was back up on his face – albeit with a bit more serious of a fix to it. "I know," he answered. "I know that when I send him off with you, I'll probably never see him again. Either he'll see the outside world, experience it, and never return... or he'll die, and still never return. But he's wanted to leave for ages, and he wants to be a soldier. He doesn't want to join the Mar'Tok army – we haven't fought a war in hundreds of years – but he's grown up on those myths of our unconquerable Dwarven Axemen of ancient times, and he wants to be a part of it. I doubt he'll ever find what he's looking for, but as long as he's still looking I feel he could be happy."

"He clearly has no idea about the realities of war," Maelgyn noted darkly. Fresh memories of the battle at Elm Knoll flashed through his mind. "Best to leave him here, with his happy fantasies of becoming a hero."

"I know," El'Ba sighed, finally letting his grin drop entirely. "But he's thirty-one years old, now. At thirty-two, he'll be able to set out on his own. I already know that. I'd rather he go somewhere that he might be able to get a more... survivable job than that of a common foot soldier. He might not live any longer in your company than he would as a common foot soldier, but in the company of a Sword Prince, maybe..."

"Maybe he'll see what it's really like to be in a war from a relatively safe position," Maelgyn answered, continuing the thought.

"Exactly," El'Ba replied. "And even if he does die, it's better he die fighting for a just cause like defeating Sho'Curlas than wasting his life in one of the pointless border disputes in the Orful River kingdoms or somewhere like that."

Maelgyn raised an eyebrow. He wasn't aware of any Dwarven sentiment against Sho'Curlas, before, and was surprised to hear it expressed now. The war which had taken the city of Sho'Curlas from Dwarven hands ended over a thousand years before, and even for a people with the extended lifespan of the Dwarven race that was a long time for such resentment to continue.

He was about to ask its source when Dr. Wodtke returned, Euleilla in tow. Maelgyn noticed, to his relief, that the storm of magic powder was back around his wife, as usual, and while he could sense her powers were weakened they were still greater than the average mage could boast.

"Hello again, Maelgyn," the doctor bowed. Maelgyn could have sworn he never told her his name, but somehow she knew it anyway. He frowned, wondering just how the doctor knew. "Your wife, here, will be somewhat tired for a few days but is otherwise fine. I understand you have an appointment with a certain someone around here, and you mentioned yesterday you need a guide. Euleilla should be well enough to accompany us, if you want to go now."

Maelgyn turned back towards El'Ba, desperately wanting to continue his conversation and find out just what it was the Dwarves had against Sho'Curlas, but sighed. He did need to see El'Athras, as well, and now was as good a time as any. He could always ask the innkeeper what he meant, later.

"I'm afraid she's right, El'Ba," Maelgyn sighed. "I probably should get this taken care of right away. I'll be back tonight, however, and we can discuss this further."

The innkeeper waved, smiling. "Sure. Business is business, after all."

Maelgyn nodded, and stood up. "Well, then, shall we go?"

"Yes," Euleilla said, stepping up to take Maelgyn's arm. "Let's."

Maelgyn was astounded at the appearance of the mansion as they approached it. It appeared to be carved into the stone face of the mountain, and it extended for quite a ways. In a human settlement, it would be the equivalent of a large town hall or even a minor noble's estate in size... and that was just on the outside.

For a city where level land was so heavily prized, it was positively palatial.

The doctor, he had been surprised to learn, was a confidant of El'Athras'. She described the interior in some detail as they approached, but Maelgyn suspected that she was holding things back. Anything this impressive had to be beyond description inside.

"Hello, Dr. Wodtke," the guard greeted them as they approached. "Nice to see you again. How are you doing, today?"

"Just fine. I was merely escorting these people, who were invited to see El'Athras, to his estate. They met him during one of his trading missions, and they were invited to tea."

The guard immediately became suspicious. "Were they, now? And I suppose you two have proof you've been asked to come?"

Maelgyn's eyes widened for a moment, and then he remembered the ring he'd been given. Fumbling through his pouch, he finally found the emblem he had been given and handed it to the guard.

The Dwarf inspected the ring carefully before grudgingly nodding. "Good enough." He tossed it back to Maelgyn, who just barely caught it. "Go on in. El'Athras is in the Red Room, today, doctor. I'm sure you can escort them there."

"Gladly," Dr. Wodtke answered, bowing slightly. Turning to Maelgyn and Euleilla, she gestured, "Come on. We're lucky – he's in the nearby office. If he'd been in the Green Room, we'd have quite the trek on our hands."

The threesome made their way into the Merchant Prince's household. As they passed through the corridors, Maelgyn was astounded to see paintings he recognized as being from the hands of the best Human, Dwarven, and Nekoji artists the world had to offer. He even saw one ancient-looking painting done by a famous member of the extinct race known as Satyrs. The Royal Castle of Svieda also had such treasures, but not in nearly as great a number, and most were hidden away in vaults hidden even to his eyes. The Royal Art Gallery in Svieda only opened its doors to the public once a year to show the entire collection, and when it was closed not even a Sword could pass their doors without the permission of the Royal Archivist. Maelgyn had only been to the gallery once, and that time hadn't left him nearly as impressed as he was now. He only regretted that Euleilla couldn't see the artwork she was walking past.

They stopped in front of a door protected by two guards armed with naginata. Maelgyn recognized the naginata as two of those Euleilla had made in the battle with the Largo separatists, although the men carrying them were unfamiliar. It was a curious thing for someone to arm their soldiers with, since weapons made by magic – especially when made in the spur of the moment as Euleilla had done – were inherently inferior to a blacksmith-forged product, but nevertheless Maelgyn knew they were quite deadly.

"We're here to see El'Athras," Wodtke explained without being asked.

"Please state your names, so that I may properly announce you," one of them replied.

"Dr. Wodtke. Maelgyn. Euleilla," she answered, pausing between each name to make some gesture Maelgyn failed to recognize.

The guard nodded at the gesture, seemingly ignoring the names, and entered the room. It was quickly apparent that Wodtke had performed some sort of recognition signal, though why she would need one escaped Maelgyn at the moment. The guard returned a moment later and formally lowered his weapon, his companion following suit. "Please, enter."

The trio walked through the door to see El'Athras sitting at a desk, sorting through a large stack of papers almost as tall as the Dwarf, himself. He looked up and smiled.

"Good. You're here. I was expecting you to arrive no earlier than tomorrow, but now's as good a time as any," the Merchant Prince said, dropping his papers and standing up. He scribbled a short note, handed it to the guard who had escorted them in, and then dismissed him. "Come on," he said to the trio, "We've got a lot to discuss."

With that, he took a painting off one of the walls in the office, revealing a secret doorway he promptly walked through. Maelgyn blinked.

"Um... rather abrupt, isn't he?"

"Yes," Wodtke agreed, shrugging. "He's always been that way."

Maelgyn glanced at her as she led them through the secret doorway, herself. "You seem to know him pretty well."

"I should," she replied, and left it at that, making Maelgyn wonder what she meant. Why did all the women he met give him such incomplete answers?

"Do you have any idea why he wants to meet with us?"

"Possibly," she answered. "But I'll let him explain, since I'm not certain. He did, however, know of your arrival yesterday. He was the one who told me to bring you here."

Maelgyn raised an eyebrow. "How did he know I was here?"

She laughed. "He saw you through a window, entering town while carrying your lady in a panic. You were quite the sight, apparently! He warned me I might be called to service when he first saw you, though he didn't explain exactly who I'd be helping until after I got home last night."

Maelgyn nodded as they continued down the stairs. He kept his eye on Euleilla, making sure she wasn't stumbling, given that her magic – and thus her "vision" – wasn't as strong as normal. It bothered him a bit that she'd been completely silent since he left their bed that morning, but he wasn't going to ask her to break that silence, either. Sensing the way she was using her magic, and watching the great care she was taking in simply finding each step, he suspected she was using all of her concentration just keeping herself from falling over. He was beginning to regret having agreed to come that day, and wished he'd given her time to recover her strength a bit more... or at least that she'd stayed at the inn while he went on to the meeting.

They continued down the unusually long staircase for almost ten minutes before the floor finally leveled out. It was only level for a short time, however, before it opened into a natural cave, untouched by Dwarven architects. Maelgyn had to wonder why it existed in the heart of the oldest and largest settlement of Cave Dwarves in the known world.

At first Maelgyn found himself catching a falling Euleilla many times at the start. She was more used to darkness, however, so as the light dimmed to where he could no longer see he started stumbling just as much. The cave was cold and smelled of decay, and there was no way to tell how long it stretched. Maelgyn ran into the stone walls frequently, and banged his head more than once. Whenever he touched a wall, his hand sunk almost an inch into the mud, and small drops of water were constantly dripping on him.

It seemed foolish to travel without a spare light through a naturally-formed cave as they were, but somehow they managed it. Maelgyn, while he understood how the Dwarves (who could see in the dark) managed it, had no idea what allowed Dr. Wodtke to avoid getting lost. As he kept going he continued to sense her right behind them, however, taking surer steps than either he or Euleilla and avoiding any stumbles.

It was not a pleasant trip. By the time they emerged from the natural cave into a newly constructed artificial cave, all four of them were caked in mud. Maelgyn wasn't quite sure what was going on when El'Athras led them that muddy hole into a cleaning room, but one look at their host told him this was not the time to ask.

Spare robes of all sizes lined one wall, and open stalls with showers lined another. The torchlight in the room nearly blinded him as he entered, but once his eyes adjusted the first thing he could focus on was the rather disgusting image of El'Athras stripping off his clothes... making him wish he was still blinded by the torch.

"Clean up," the old Dwarf grumbled, staggering off into the showers. Another Dwarf, coming out of nowhere, scrambled to pick up the discarded clothing and ran off with it.

Without a moment's hesitation, Dr. Wodtke started removing her own mud-covered clothing, as well. Maelgyn blushed and looked away, but that was only a temporary reprieve. As he looked the other way, he saw Euleilla pause only for a moment before shrugging and starting to disrobe, too.

"Ack!" he squawked involuntarily, closing his eyes as he blushed. Maelgyn sighed and figured he might as well get undressed and shower as well. He quickly finished the job before sprinting, in all his glory, to the nearest unoccupied shower. As he ran, he noticed another young Dwarf dash out of the shadows, grab his soiled clothing, and run off somewhere.

This facility, thankfully, had both hot and cold running water even in the showers. Quickly adjusting the controls so that he was comfortable, he stepped under the shower and started rinsing all of the cave mud off.

"Maelgyn?" the hesitant voice of Euleilla called from his right.

"Yeah?"

"Um... can you come over here and help me for a moment?

I... don't know what I'm doing."

Maelgyn blinked. *She doesn't know what she's doing? What does she mean by that?* he asked himself as he rounded the corner, only to see her standing in front of a shower stall, completely naked. She was covering herself up, at least partly, with her arms, but she was still exposing areas of her flesh to him he'd never taken a good look at before.

"Is there supposed to be a bathtub somewhere around here? I can't find one," she said, confused.

"No," Maelgyn replied, trying hard to concentrate on something other than her figure. "There's no tub, it's just a shower."

"A shower?" she repeated, cocking her head questioningly. "I've never used one, before. How does it work?"

"Well," Maelgyn said. "There are two counterweighted chains you can pull. One controls the flow of cold water, the other controls the flow of hot water. You adjust each one until the water is the right temperature and rate of flow for you, and then you stand under the spray of water and scrub until you're clean."

"I see," she said, removing her arm from over her breasts and groping wildly for the knobs he had spoken of. "Which knob is which?"

For a moment, Maelgyn almost fled and called Dr. Wodtke to help her out, but instead he resolved to stick it out and guide Euleilla. *This is the woman who is my wife,* he thought to himself. *I should not be embarrassed to help her, or to see her naked. I should be able to deal with her.*

Tearing his eyes off of her body, he grabbed one of her hands and led her further into the shower stall. He placed that hand on one chain and said, "This controls the hot water." He moved the hand over a bit to the other chain. "This is the cold water. Do you think you can handle it?"

"Yes," Euleilla answered, a touch of humor in her voice.

It was then Maelgyn realized he had been set up. The smile that was usually on her face had twitched just enough for him to realize she was trying not to laugh. She'd known she was exposing herself to him, she'd planned it, and now she was laughing about it.

Well, he supposed as he retreated to his own shower. *She*

*thinks she still needs to convince me to keep her as my wife. And...
I can't say I don't enjoy the view. I just wish she wouldn't test my
patience! This is neither the time nor place.*

Maelgyn shook his head as he scrubbed at his hair. He
needed to talk with her about everything, and soon. Someplace
private, without Dr. Wodtke just a few paces away, and without a
Merchant Prince of Mar'Tok waiting on him for a formal meeting.

Fortunately, the whole situation they were in provided ample
opportunity to think of other things. Maelgyn wondered again
why he'd been lead through a muddy cave from the office of a
Merchant Prince of Mar'Tok to what appeared to be little more
than a shower room. And just what did El'Athras want with
him, anyway?

He finished his shower and donned the yukata El'Athras had
provided – a gold-rimmed dark blue silk robe Maelgyn thought
looked like an odd cross between a thin bathrobe and a formal
state dress *kimono*. The Dwarf in question was just sitting there,
waiting for everyone without saying a word. Euleilla joined him
shortly, a smug grin gracing her features. Finally, Dr. Wodtke
showed up, much more at ease with her surroundings than
Maelgyn felt was appropriate in someone who hadn't been
through this experience before.

"Well, Sword Prince Maelgyn," El'Athras said, standing up
slowly and adjusting his own robe with practiced grace. "I think
it's time we met my other guests."

Chapter 12

Maelgyn stared around him. The room was huge, larger than the castle courtyard of the Svieda Royal palace. It seemed a hybrid of the "manufactured" caves in most Dwarven cities and the natural caves he'd just come from. The grey stone floor was polished like fine marble. The ceiling, too, was covered with a curved piece of smooth white stonework. But the walls were the mud and rock of a natural cave, with water dripping down to drainage trenches in the floor.

There was only one fire to illuminate the whole space, and that was a natural "eternal" flame in the middle of the floor. It would have been enough to light a small room, perhaps, yet its light faded out before reaching the walls. The place felt ancient, and the air seemed stale. Maelgyn had a few suspicious about where they might be, but he had a hard time believing it.

Several other people already were present, but Maelgyn couldn't make out anything about them because they stood in the dimmer shadows around the fire. With what little he could tell by sensing magical potential, two of them were probably Nekoji. He wasn't proficient enough to identify the races of any of the others, but none of them were mages.

"Oh, good," El'Athras said, breaking the silence. "Everyone's here. Let's get started."

The others approached, and for the first time Maelgyn could see their faces as his eyes adjusted to the darkness. Two were the Nekoji as he had sensed earlier. Several Dwarves wore uniforms of the Oregal Republic, while others bore the armor or the banners of various border kingdoms. Four humans were garbed in the

livery of each of the Kingdoms of Poros, while a lone Centaur –
looking distinctly uncomfortable in his surroundings – proudly
displayed the banner of the Bandi Republic. The Bandi Republic
was an otherwise largely human nation led by a "not *entirely*
sane" Elven woman named Lady Phalra.

Even tiny Squire's Knot had a representative Elf – a rarity,
since so few Elves ever left their homes nowadays. His frown
belied the stereotypical serenity of that race.

The final person emerged from the darkness and knelt before
Maelgyn. The cut of the man's clothing and the brooch on his
shoulder confused Maelgyn greatly: The man kneeling before
him was a Baron of Borden Isle.

"What—" Maelgyn started, but he was quickly cut off.

"All right," El'Athras said. "Before you go shooting your
mouth off, a few introductions. Today we'll be explaining
some history you humans may have never learned about – not
exactly my strong suit, so I'll let my allies do it for me. It is my
honor to present Emperor Gyato of Caseificio, the Nekoji nation
which borders your Province of Sopan." The Nekoji stood up
and bowed, shaking his lion-like mane. "At your feet is Prince
Uwelain, a Baron in the Borden Isles."

Maelgyn stared at Uwelain, uncertain how to deal with the
man. He gestured for the man to stand. "Please, you owe me no
fealty; our Kingdoms are no longer united."

Uwelain stood up, looking slightly embarrassed. "My lord,
knowing what Emperor Gyato is about to tell you, I believe that
may soon change."

Maelgyn nodded silently, too startled to do more.

El'Athras continued the introductions, gesturing to the Elf.
"This is Spearmaster Wangdu, who has served many nations in
his millennia of life but of late hails from Squire's Knot." Wangdu
inclined his head. "And next to him is Kazdre of the Bandi
Republic, with which Mar'Tok enjoys relations peaceful enough
to share our intelligence." The Centaur bowed to Maelgyn. "He
is our liaison with their spymasters, and will sit in on this meeting
on their behalf. Emperor Gyato, however, will begin."

The Nekoji stepped forward and shook his mane regally.
"Greetings, Sword Prince Maelgyn. There is much that has gone
on in this world that you humans are not aware of, but the time
has come for that to change."

"In that case, speak on," Maelgyn answered. "But I may have a few questions along the way. The first of which is how is it that you all arrived here without getting muddy walking through that cave?"

"We used the other door," Baron Uwelain said, trying to hide his laughter. "Although, we all have taken that muddy pass to this chamber at least once before."

"This is the King's Hall," El'Athras explained. "None may enter the King's Hall unless they have traveled the Path of the Ancients at least once. It's one of the few Dwarven ceremonies we keep sacred."

"The King's Hall?" Maelgyn was surprised even though he had guessed correctly. He had always believed that the King's Hall was a thing of myth, but it seemed he was mistaken. "So this is where the Dwarven people were born... and where the last King of All Dwarves fell."

"With the scars of that fateful battle preserved for all time. Look around you," Gyato noted. The closer Maelgyn looked, the more he realized that, amid the muck and mud, there were also artifacts of a time the Dwarves were strong: Small tablets with aged Dwarven script, a horned helmet of the now defunct sea-faring Dwarven clans hanging by the fire pit, and sticking in one wall, cracked and rusted....

"Is that a Dwarven battleaxe?" he asked, intrigued.

"Yeah, what of it?" El'Athras snapped back defensively.

"I thought they were a myth," Maelgyn exclaimed. "I loved hearing stories of the Dwarven axemen's valor when I was young, but later my history lessons made me doubt their existence."

"No myth were they," Gyato explained lyrically. "Two millennia ago, when the Dwarves first left their caves to meet the outside world, many were taken as slaves as they tried to cross the plains, and were prized as laborers and engineers. The Dwarves still in their caves were unaware of what their surface brethren were enduring, but then the slavemasters became bolder and sent raiding parties into the Dwarven homeland.

"The Dwarves learned to dig deep, to hide, and to swing an axe in battle. The axe was ideal in cave conditions. Its short range was an advantage rather than a disadvantage, for it could be wielded with enormous power in cramped surroundings.

"They trained in secret, and soon had an impressive army

that massacred every incursion into the caves. They knew how to fight, and fight well... but only when inside the caves. The problems came when they tried fighting outside of those caves.

"After fighting off numerous attacks, including raids from Humans, Elves, and even Nekoji, the Dwarves decided it was time to show the outside world that they weren't going to be pushed around anymore. They struck out first against Humanity... and were promptly trounced. The axes they wielded so effectively in the caves could not defeat the spears and swords of the Porosian hoplites on open ground. The Dwarves retreated to their caves to debate what to do.

"Three groups formed: the Plains Dwarves, Sea Dwarves, Cave Dwarves, each espousing their own philosophy for how to deal with the other races.

"Today, only the Plains Dwarves remain. They survived by their inventiveness, learning techniques and skills to counter the advantages of other races. The Dwarven wolf riders were the first to come from their experiments, and when first formed they were the most effective cavalry on the plains. Only my own people, the Nekoji, could match their wolves for speed, and we could not match an armored wolf rider in battle. The Plains Dwarves then adopted the traditional weapon of the Porosian woman, the naginata. With the reach of a polearm and the flexibility of a sword, it quickly became the weapon of choice among all the warriors of the Plains Dwarves. While neither made the same impression as the Dwarven Axemen of old, these elements have allowed the Plains Dwarves to survive to this day.

"The Sea Dwarves lived as much of their lives as possible aboard ships, and developed a close relationship with the Merfolk – the only race that had never tried to enslave the Dwarves. They were feared and respected for their seamanship and their craft with tools of war and navigation. They invented the compass, the astrolabe, the crossbow, and many other things we use today, but they and many of their other creations are now lost to history. Only a few of their former settlements on the Borden Isles, abandoned and in ruins, remain to prove that they ever truly existed.

"The Cave Dwarves advocated staying in the caves and perfecting their skills with the battle axe. But after the death of Tur'ma, last King of All Dwarves, the Cave Dwarves fell apart, and the Merchant Princes took power. Fewer Cave Dwarves joined their armies, becoming merchants or tradesmen instead, and gradually their armies dwindled to where they could no longer defend their cities. Mar'Tok, the ancestral home of all Dwarves and the center of power for the Cave Dwarves, was sacked, its population slaughtered. The Plains Dwarves spent three decades rescuing those Cave Dwarves who had been enslaved and reclaiming the city, and have held it ever since. A colony of the few surviving Cave Dwarves, most ex-slaves with no military training, left to found the Dwarven Kingdom of Sho'Curlas. They never recovered their numbers, and were finally wiped out by an army of Elves aided Humans. Since then, there have been no true Dwarven Axemen.

"They were fearsome warriors once, of course. Indeed, only one Elf survived the initial battle in Sho'Curlas. But he escaped, and rallied a nearby settlement of Humans to his cause. Together, they defeated those Cave Dwarves who remained.

"That joining of forces led to the founding of the Sho'Curlas Alliance you know now. Since that time, Sho'Curlas has been the greatest enemy of the Dwarves... led by Hrabak, the same immortal Elf who led the war against the last of the Cave Dwarves so long ago."

Maelgyn looked up, surprised. "Sho'Curlas is led by an *Elf?*"

"It is a sad case, it is," the Squire's Knot Elf interrupted, speaking with peculiarly Elvish quirks and accents. "We Elves are immortal, we are, but our minds can be ravaged by time, they can. Hrabak went insane, he did, in the war against the Cave Dwarves. He believes in 'peace,' he does, like most Elves... but he believes that means destroying all nations he does not rule. And he may do it, too, he may, for the High Kings of Sho'Curlas are not truly the ones in power, they aren't. Hrabak is the true power behind the throne, he is, and he has been directing them for the past thousand years, he has. Many other Elves believe he may soon emerge from behind the throne to seize it, we do."

"We have reports that Sho'Curlas has trained at least fifty Black Dragons as beasts of war," El'Athras said. "Not even the Oregal Republic has more than twenty dragon-riders at any one time. It would be expected of Hrabak's tactics, however – employing Dragons as war machines has been an Elven tactic since the earliest records tell."

Maelgyn wasn't alone in not knowing that bit of news, as several of the others at the meeting started talking to one another in dismay, but Gyato quickly motioned them all to silence, with an impatient ruffling of his mane. "We are here because we now know what is really going on, and because we believe Svieda is really the only hope of stopping Hrabak."

With that, everyone went silent. Maelgyn stared in wonder at those around him. As the eclectic mix of peoples here showed, every nation in the world but his had knowledge of what was taking place, and yet his nation was the one which needed this information the most. Yet now that he knew this information, what could he do with it? It took an army to slay any kind of dragon – even the "weaker" Red Dragons from which his dragonhide armor was made. Fifty Black Dragons would cost tens of thousands, possibly hundreds of thousands of soldiers to stop. Svieda may have the capacity to deal with such an assault, but they could not deal with both the dragons and the million armed soldiers of Sho'Curlas' armies.

"Dear God," Maelgyn whispered.

"You have resources you may call upon that might tip the balance in your scale," Uwelain said, drawing everyone's attention to him. The Borden islander shifted uncomfortably. "The Golden Dragons still reside in my home province."

Unlike the untamable Red Dragons (which were prized for their hides) or the semi-domesticated Black Dragons (which could – with some risk – be raised as military mounts), Golden Dragons were intelligent creatures who could speak like any of the Five Great Races could, but they rarely entered into alliances with anyone.

Even before the first Humans arrived on its shores, Borden had boasted a small tribe of Golden Dragons. The Sword Kings of Svieda had negotiated with them when colonizing the island, and while they refused a direct alliance they granted Svieda a boon rarely given in return for preserving their safehaven. The Golden Dragons agreed to come to Svieda's aide whenever another nation employed dragons against it – be those dragons Red, Black, or Gold themselves. Maelgyn's own dragonhide armor was a gift from the first fruits of that agreement, when the Golden Dragons of Borden Isle defeated a nest of red dragons that had been attacking shipping lanes. They had been called upon four times since that alliance began, and met their obligation each time with honor.

Unfortunately for Svieda, that alliance was now dormant thanks to the Borden Isle Rebellion: The Golden Dragons announced they would withhold their protection from both sides until the war between the Borden Isles and its mother country was over.

Maelgyn frowned. "That won't do us much good," he answered. "Whatever you may think, sir, I doubt Borden Isle will rejoin us in time for it to matter."

"You've got some time," El'Athras said. "Sho'Curlas doesn't plan to reveal its dragons until Svieda is defeated, if it can help it. Its dragons are still a secret Hrabak hopes to reserve for a later strike against Oregal."

Maelgyn snorted. "Just how do you know that?"

"That," El'Athras replied, "is a long story for another time. We need to concentrate on the important things, now."

"Like returning the Borden Isles to their proper place," Baron Uwelain added, "As a loyal province of Svieda."

"How?" Maelgyn asked. "We've been warring with Borden for nearly eighty years."

"El'Athras and Gyato have proof that Sho'Curlas instigated the rebellion. Svieda's poor treatment of Sword Ivari at her marriage to Laimoth was staged, and Elaneth was corrupted by Hrabak's lies. Now you are at war with our *true* enemy. I believe my people will want to join that war, once they learn where their anger should truly be directed even though it means ending the rebellion."

Maelgyn frowned. That sounded rather... idealistic, to him. "And the current Sword of Borden Isle? What will he think?"

The baron stood up again. "Well, that's where I come in. Sword Ivari and Lord Laimoth had two sons, Koheil and Elaneth. Elaneth, the presumptive Sword Prince, died leading the rebellion, but Koheil survived the war. He was my grandfather and I am the last of his line. The current Sword Prince, Paljor, is the son of a more distant relative and, to my mind, a usurper. He rules with an iron fist and already is unpopular among the commoners. He will lose the support of the nobility as well, once they see that he is in the pay of Sho'Curlas.

Maelgyn raised an eyebrow. "You're a descendant of Prince

Koheil? I thought he died without having any children."

"Not exactly. The official story was that he passed away while making the journey to be invested as the next Sword following his parents' deaths. At least, that's what everyone outside of the Borden Isles believed.

"The truth was, he never left Borden Isle. Instead, he declined his birthright years before his mother's passing and retired to a barony with his wife. He was a nobleman married to a commoner, himself, and didn't want to cause further tension after the unrest caused by his parents marriage. It was Elaneth who spun the tale of Koheil's death, and none of us were aware of it until after he had already launched the rebellion."

Euleilla shifted slightly. "A royal marrying a commoner caused tension?" she whispered softly.

Maelgyn squeezed her hand reassuringly; that conversation needed to be held in private. "So that means you're-"

"Prince Uwelain, Baron of Swathburg, and currently second in line for the 'throne' of the Borden Isles," he explained, and then hesitated. "I won't mislead you on where I stand. My grandfather renounced his claim to the throne, but not those of his descendents. Since he was the elder child, his son – my father – should have been next in line. In which case I would now be ruling the Borden Isles."

Maelgyn nodded slowly. "With your aid, perhaps we do stand a chance of getting Borden Isle on our side... as long as we have your support."

"Exactly," Uwelain agreed.

"That still leaves the problem of convincing the Golden Dragons that our treaty should be honored once more," Maelgyn mused. "And dealing with the Sho'Curlas army. It's not looking very good."

"I agree," El'Athras said. "So we'll have to see what else we can do to tip the scales in your favor."

Gyato was the one who explained. "Since the dawn of time, there have been five true 'Major' races which made themselves a part of this world: The Elves, Dwarves, Humans, Nekoji, and Merfolk. The Elves are nearly extinct, I'm afraid, but some like Hrabak, Lady Phalra, and Wangdu, here, remain prominent in the affairs of others. The same is true for all the races besides Humans. We are all dying out. Something needs to be done to preserve us, so El'Athras and I decided on a plan."

"You seem to have omitted many races bred by the Elves, including the Centaurs, whose creation many regard as the peak of modern Elven achievement," Kazdre said, laughing. "But I may be a bit biased."

"Regardless, friend Centaur," Gyato said, bowing to him, "Despite the Griffons and Dragons that the Ancient Elves created, and the Modern Elves' attempts to reclaim that former glory with the Centaurs and Dryads, and even the minor intelligent races such as kappa whose existence has nothing to do with the Elves or any other race's intervention, in truth there are only five major races on this world, races which are strong enough, organized enough, plentiful enough, and civilized enough to form societies with governments, laws, and influence on the state of the world. Of those, only the Humans thrive.

"Because of this, I contacted El'Athras some three years ago with a proposition. It was my belief that, if the stone of the Dwarves and the fire of the Nekoji would combine, we might prove to be a greater power ourselves. If my nation and the last Dwarven nation merged, I believed, it would spark the resurgence needed for us to remain important in this world. It was my hope that together we could keep ourselves from dying out.

"To my surprise, El'Athras, who at the time had only just ascended to become the High Merchant Prince of the Mar'Tok Dwarves, had been planning something similar for several years, and our envoys crossed paths with each other."

"I wish you success in the joining of your two nations," Maelgyn replied. "But I'm less clear what that has to do with me?"

El'Athras snorted. "I thought it'd be obvious by now, but there's one more piece to add to what Gyato was saying so let me finish. In the past twenty years, Mar'Tok has made itself a refuge for people of all lands who wish to leave war-torn countrysides or oppressive leadership. We have Centaurs, Dwarves, Nekoji, and even the odd Dryad in our cities and caves. We've been building a unified nation, much like Oregal. But, while a scattered few such as Dr. Wodtke are present, Humans are rare here... and it is Gyato's and my plan to make this a greater nation of *all* races, utilizing each of our strengths. We intend to have both our kingdoms join your own – to unite our banners under your protection. That is what this has to do with you."

Maelgyn's jaw dropped for a moment. "I... must have misheard. Are you offering me the fealty of the last independent kingdoms of the Nekoji and the Dwarves?"

"Indeed, we are," Gyato said. "It is our belief that our survival as independent powers will not last, and we want to be the ones to choose who will claim us."

"And the rest of you – the ones from Oregal, Poros, Squires Knot, Bandi, and so on – what is your role here?"

"We are here merely to assure you that the rest of the world will not contest this claim," Kazdre said. "Provided you take these lands and use them to stop the threat of Sho'Curlas once and for all."

Maelgyn realized with a shock that the conversation had shifted from being a history lesson to being an event that would be taught *in* history lessons for generations to come... and that it was his decision that would determine the outcome. He looked around at the men and women who stood there, staring at them as if burning the moment into memory.

Gyato broke the silence, mistaking Maelgyn's moment of reflection for indecision. "Perhaps you are wondering if you have the authority to conclude this treaty?"

Maelgyn shook his head. "No. With no king in Svieda, the Law of Swords is in effect. Any Sword has the authority to make treaties for their home province as if they were Kings. You would be ceding your countries to Sopan Province directly, and then I would need to designate them as separate provinces so that indirectly they... oh, never mind. That is for the barristers to decide. There are no precedents, so we will have to set our own. Indeed, for Svieda to survive this war, I fear I would need to accept even if I was less sure. But if I am to lead you, then I need to understand. Why choose Svieda?" he asked. "Why not Oregal, which already protects others of your races?"

"Because there, all non-humans are treated as inferiors," one of the Oregal Dwarves explained. "There we are all serfs at birth – in a land where serfdom ended six hundred years ago among Humans – and can rise to be nothing more than second-class citizens. Only those who serve in the army may own property, and the taxes are tripled even for those who do."

"The only way for any of our peoples to not just survive, but thrive," Gyato noted, "is to find a nation that may respect us enough to treat us as equals, and join with them. And we judge Svieda to be such a nation."

"To be honest, we're taking advantage of you," El'Athras admitted. "We were considering forming an alliance with the Bandi Republic instead, as you weren't a possibility while you were allied with the Sho'Curlas, but things have changed. Svieda is the better option, and you need us."

Maelgyn nodded. This was the sort of thing he would have expected his father or his cousins to decide... but he saw no alternative. They had to have this alliance. Without it, Sho'Curlas would wipe out Svieda and the question about authority would be moot. "Draw up the treaty. We have much to do."

Chapter 13

Spearmaster Wangdu, after doffing his Squire's Knot regalia to reveal more traditionally Elven clothing, led them out of the chamber. He was obviously anxious, but even so he did better guiding them on their way out than El'Athras had on the way in. Of course, it helped that he was taking them out through the modern entrance, and not the Dwarven Path of the Ancients.

"Wangdu," Dr. Wodtke said to the Elf, breaking the silence which had endured since Maelgyn had dubbed El'Athras and Gyato Counts of Svieda. "I don't believe we've met before. What is your story?"

"I have been the primary messenger between El'Athras and his spies in Squire's Knot these past four years, I have. And I've done some spying of my own, I have. In fact, if it had not been for me, it hadn't, Elm Knoll would have been lost, it would." he replied. "And while we've never met, we haven't, I've seen all of you from time to time, I have."

It took a moment for Maelgyn to realize just what Wangdu was talking about. "The messenger to Elm Knoll..."

The Elf laughed. "Yes, that was me, it was. I was in such an obvious hurry, I was, that your militia captain never even looked to see that I was an Elf, I was."

"Is Squire's Knot really in Sho'Curlas hands, then?" Maelgyn asked.

Sobering, the Elf nodded. "Yes. And as soon as this council of war is over, it is, I must head back and try to save my country, I must. I fear this will be my last war, I do, and the Elves will be losing another of their kind once again."

"Why bother returning to Squire Knot, Spearmaster?" Euleilla asked hesitantly, unsure if she had the right to actually speak to him. Elves were often superstitiously thought of as being slightly 'above' Humans by the peasantry. She was a peasant by birth, and while Ruznak had worked hard to remove those superstitions she must still have a few. "It is admirable to resist an invasion, but now... it's just suicide."

The Elf paused mid-step, and everyone else stopped around him. He turned to her, and with an appraising eye, asked, "And just what else would you have me do, my Lady, what else? I am a Spearmaster, I am – one of the last wielders of the Elven Spears my Ancient brethren developed, they did. My home has been sacked, it has, and there seems little else for me to do but to fight, it does."

"You could join me," Maelgyn offered. He, too, had reservations dealing with Elves, but only because he knew they were some of the most powerful beings in the world... and some of the most manipulative. Even the strongest of First Class Mages were considered inferior in battle to an Elven child, so gaining a veteran Elven Spearmaster at his service would be a small coup in and of itself. Besides, any Elf involved in this war, on either side, would need close watching, and what better way to watch someone than to have them nearby? "At least as far as Sopan. Once there, we can see what we can do. Depending on how things turn out, I might be able to provide you with enough resources to restore Squire's Knot, if that is still your wish. As it is, one lone man cannot restore a kingdom."

"I am an Elf, I am," Wangdu noted, his eyes glinting fiercely. "You might be surprised at what I could do alone, you might."

"I might," Maelgyn agreed jovially. "But only if you're around to surprise me."

The Elf laughed slightly. "Perhaps," he said. "I'll think it through, I will. El'Athras wants us both to wait for a couple days, he does, before we leave. Perhaps I'll have a decision by then, I will."

Maelgyn raised an eyebrow. "A couple days wait? I'm not so sure about that. I want to get to Sopan as soon as possible."

"As your wife's doctor, I'd strongly advise rest," Wodtke noted. "The poor girl just recovered from a plague, so the least you could do is give her a couple days to get her strength back."

"Right, of course," Maelgyn agreed, berating himself mentally for having forgotten Euleilla's health problems. "Well, I could always see the sites. Never been in a Dwarven cave-city before this trip."

"I could, too," Euleilla added. "I'm having fun."

Maelgyn raised an eyebrow. "'Fun?' We were nearly killed several times by mudslides, we have twice fought in battles to the death, and you contracted some kind of *plague*, yet you find it 'fun?'"

"Yep." She smiled mischievously.

He grinned. "Good."

Wangdu shook his head sadly. "You humans are a strange lot, you are."

"Well?" El'Ba asked as they returned. "What did the old man say?"

"Old man?" Maelgyn asked, surprised. "What old man?"

"El'Athras!" El'Ba exclaimed. "He's the only merchant prince in the city who'd consent to see a human prince. Most of them'd rather kill ya than talk with ya."

Maelgyn blinked. "I suppose that's why he told me not to let anyone know who I was."

El'Ba snorted. "You did a right good job of that, now didn't ya? Ah, well, it don't matter. What'd he say?"

Maelgyn hesitated, and then relented. The news would soon be public, and El'Ba had earned his trust more than most. He had helped arrange for Euleilla's care, and would soon be entrusting his son to Maelgyn's service.

"You deserve the truth, but I'd ask that you keep it to yourself until it is formally announced. El'Athras and Emperor Gyato of Caseificio ceded their nations to me," he explained. "It was as much of a shock to me as I expect it must be to you."

El'Ba blinked. "Oh. Well, that's not as much of a surprise as you might think. It's just what El'Athras' rivals accused him of planning. The only reason most Dwarves have yet to rebel is that they see the sense of it. Mind you, some do care, and very strongly, so be careful who you say that to."

"I imagine the word will come out soon enough," Maelgyn said. "El'Athras is preparing his cavalry and archer corps to join the war effort against Sho'Curlas. There are representatives from several other nations who may let something slip. Oh! And there's an Elf I'm hoping will stop by to discuss some things, later. I trust that won't be a problem?"

"Oh, no!" El'Ba laughed. "More business for me, after all, though I dunno about Elves. Our two peoples have had their differences, that's for sure, and I'm not regretting it that they're dying out. But no, what worries me is what will happen when the other Merchant Princes learn that you're here. I wouldn't be surprised if a couple of *them* came to visit, as well. Only they wouldn't be as good for business, I fear."

"Is there a magic shop or alchemist's apothecary in this area, then?" Euleilla asked. "I'm starting to run low on some forms of my magic powder. That may prove... valuable if any of these people stop by."

"Not much call for one, in these parts," the innkeeper sighed. "Only humans have any significant success in the study of magic, and while a few of them – like Dr. Wodtke – are around, there aren't enough to really justify a shop. I think the only place in the city likely to have your magic powder would be crazy old El'Rasi's shop. He's been the only Dwarven alchemist in Mar'Tok for the past two hundred years. I imagine the good doctor would know better than me. El'Rasi lives pretty deep in the caves, I fear, and it would take a day's trip to get there."

"Wodtke will be around this afternoon to check on you," Maelgyn said to Euleilla. "We can ask her, then. If you want, I can loan you some of mine, though."

Euleilla shook her head. "No, you need yours. And I'm not looking for black magic powder, anyway." Maelgyn carried iron-based magic powder (sometimes called "black magic powder") but not any of the nickel powder he often saw her use for "sight." Or any other variety, for that matter.

"I guess that rules that out. So, when we see Dr. Wodtke, we'll ask about any magic shops," he said.

"Good. Now, I'm tired and hungry." Euleilla said. With that, she stormed into their room, Maelgyn staring at her as she went. He blinked.

"What brought that on?" he asked himself aloud.

"Dunno. Was anything bothering her during your trip, today?" El'Ba suggested.

"Huh? Oh, not that I know of... outside of the fact she was

having trouble walking through... what did you people call it? The 'Path of the Ancients.'"

El'Ba gasped. "Oh. You went that way, did you? That's a secret, you know – only the Dwarves are supposed to know of it."

"Well, there were more than just Dwarves at the meeting, and I was told everyone there had walked the path in the past, so...."

"Wangdu!" El'Ba cried. "That's the only possible Elf you could have met, today, if they'd passed through that. That was his name, wasn't it?"

"Uh, yes, I believe so," Maelgyn replied uncertainly. "Why?"

El'Ba was silent for a moment before nodding. "It was he who helped El'Mar reclaim Mar'Tok from the Elves. He foresaw a time when the Dwarves would be driven out of the plains as more and more humans learned to use stirrups and developed cavalry forces. He convinced El'Mar of the need to reclaim our homeland... and helped us do it by providing valuable intelligence which sealed the deal against the Elves of the time. Him, I would be proud to have here."

Maelgyn raised an eyebrow. "Why did he do that, I wonder?"

"What, help us?" El'Ba asked. "Well, he was a young one, then. Story goes, he had a Dwarven friend who just happened to be one of the other Elves' slaves. One day, after spending time with Wangdu, that friend was executed because he didn't meet his quota mining. Wangdu was outraged, especially since he'd already told the masters just why that Dwarf would be absent." The old innkeeper shuddered. "Nasty business, that. Wangdu believed the way his people were treating the Dwarves went against the set of ethics that their Ancient ancestors had established... and so, he set out to punish his own people the only way he could: By destroying them."

Maelgyn's eyes widened. "But then, doesn't that mean he's a traitor to his own people?"

"Depends on which group of Elves you're talking to," El'Ba replied. "A lot of them agreed with him that it was the only solution. Most of those, however, were the ones who were living in Oregal, a society much closer to the ideals of the Ancient Elves. The Elves who still lived elsewhere, like East Poros, were less happy – especially when they had to deal with the thousands of refugees who were expelled when we reclaimed Mar'Tok." He shrugged. "Not that there are many Elves left anywhere. We Dwarves won't mind when they finally go entirely extinct, but Wangdu proves there are still a few good ones."

At this point, Euleilla returned to the room, an impatient look on her face as she said, "Come. Now. With Food." And she retreated, not waiting for him to reply.

Maelgyn raised an eyebrow. "She's in a rare mood. Well, we need to have long talk about a number of things, anyway. Any chance of getting a meal prepared, quick?"

"I've got a stew ready, and some bread the bakery made this morning," El'Ba noted. "I'll fix you a tray."

"No tea today. At least, not for me; I need something stronger than that after the way this day has gone. Euleilla might want some, but I'd prefer an ale – a milder one. You Dwarves brew some stuff that'd be rank poison for most humans."

El'Ba laughed. "You're a bunch of lightweights. Don't worry, though – we carry some of your watered-down Human brews for travelers such as yourself, and I know what Humans can drink and what they can't. One ale, one tea, two stews, two breads. Coming right up."

Maelgyn swirled the last of his bread in the remnants of his stew and chewed down. The ale was pretty strong, but not quite strong enough to get him drunk from a single stein full. It was enough to relax him, however, and prepare him for the coming conversation.

Relaxed he was, but he was still curious. Euleilla hadn't said anything since they entered their room. In fact, she had been very quiet since Dr. Wodtke had come by that morning to check up on her, and it was starting to worry him. Was it just that she was still ill, or was it something else?

"OK, now that we've had lunch, lets talk," he finally said, breaking the silence.

She didn't say anything for a moment, choosing instead to calmly finish a bite of food and take a sip of tea. "Yes?"

Maelgyn blinked. "Um, well, is something on your mind?"

"History," she answered. Maelgyn noticed that, once again, she was in her "reserved" mode, which worried him. She hadn't really been acting like this since they were in Elm Knoll, and even then it was a bit more... playful than she was acting this time.

"What history? Of who, or what?"

"Ivari."

Maelgyn couldn't contain his surprise. "Your foster father was a former Borden Islander. Surely he's told you something about that history?"

"Nope," she answered flippantly.

He frowned. Why would Ruznak have failed to mention that story? That was the one thing most Borden Isles' refugees agreed with the rebels on – that Svieda's treatment of Sword Princess Ivari and Lord Laimoth was horrendous, especially when they had been so popular in their home province.

"That's odd," Maelgyn said, looking at her for any reaction. "It's the sort of story every child is told at a young age. If your father didn't tell you the story, I expected Ruznak would have."

Euleilla just shrugged. "Sorry."

"OK, I assume you want to talk about how their story relates to Borden Isles rebellion." Maelgyn guessed.

Euleilla nodded. "Did the Borden Isles rebel because a royal married a commoner?"

"Well... sort of," Maelgyn answered. "At least, that's what Sword Prince Elaneth claimed. He said his parents had been so maltreated by mainland Svieda he no longer wanted to be a part of it. And that much, I'll believe of him. But in truth, it was the work of Sho'Curlas that started the rebellion."

"So, if we stay married, there is a chance someone could use that as an excuse for war?" she asked anxiously.

It took him a moment to collect himself before he could reply, since he now had some inkling of what was bothering her. It sobered him up quite a bit to realize she was scared, so his first concern was to reassure her. "Well... that is a possibility no matter who I marry, no matter how royal or how common." he hedged. "Let me point out that Sword King Agaeb IV also married a peasant named Amberry, and she didn't inspire any wars. Also, there have been wars started when a Sword married the wrong noble in some people's eyes. The Duchy of Abindol – now the Grand Duchy of Abindol – rebelled for just such a reason. The truth is simply that there's no way of telling."

She sighed. "I see. Well, if that is the case, I understand why you wouldn't want me as your wife."

Maelgyn's eyes widened. "But...."

"I suppose it's good that I know, now," she continued. "It isn't truly your decision, is it?"

"Hold on!" he sputtered. "It sure as hell is my decision who I choose to marry and who I don't. If it weren't my decision, then I would have told you from the start! And, damn it, if you're willing, my decision is to stay married to you!"

Euleilla gasped, and it was only after that Maelgyn realized what he'd just said. He hadn't meant to tell her like that.

Euleilla shook her head, unable to bring herself to believe him. "You're just drunk. You haven't had time to make your decision, yet, or—"

"I'm not drunk," Maelgyn stated firmly. It was true. His mind was reasonably clear, though perhaps the strong ale had loosened his tongue a bit. "I'd planned to talk with you when we got to Sopan, but it looks like we'll be having this discussion now. I want to be your husband, Euleilla - for real, not just due to a stupid misunderstanding of local laws on my part. Yes, there may be a few things you need to understand about being a commoner married to one of the Swords, but if you're willing to deal with it all, then so be it."

Euleilla sighed. "Why?"

"Well, you are everything I would ask for in a wife," Maelgyn noted softly. "You're intelligent, and strong, and beautiful...."

"And?" she asked softly.

"And when I heard you had contracted some sort of plague, I was more terrified than I had ever been in my life," Maelgyn admitted. "I don't know what I would have done if you hadn't recovered. Frankly, the possibility of you dying scared me enough that I now know I can't stand the thought of living without you. Though I'm still going to visit my wrath on the idiot who created that stupid plague and damn him to hell...."

"Oh," she said sadly. "I thought there might be something else."

"You mean, do I love you?" he said, realizing what she was getting at. She didn't answer, so he continued, "I would think the simple fact that I've said I want you for my wife would have answered that question."

She smiled hesitantly. "Could you say it? Please?"

A knocking came from the other side of the door, and they both jumped in surprise. "Hello?" Dr. Wodtke's voice called in.

"Are you all decent?"

"Later," he whispered, knowing she'd heard him as he darted to the door. "I'll say it later. But we still need to talk of certain things first. You need to know what you're in for, and it would hurt too much to say the words and then never be able to act on them if you decide you can't handle it."

"I can handle it," she answered with a true smile. "And I'll hold you to it."

"Well," Dr. Wodtke said as she magically studied Euleilla. "You seem mostly recovered. You're probably a little below your normal magical strength, but you should recover the remainder with a good night's sleep."

"Thank you," she answered.

"I hope I won't need to see you again during your stay here," Wodtke noted. "As much as I'd appreciate the business, I'd rather most of the people I've treated stayed healthy."

"Actually," Maelgyn said, "If you're willing to keep up your role as tour guide, we might still need your help."

She hesitated. "I have some business I need to take care of over the next couple of days, but I might be able to squeeze in an hour or two if it's something nearby. What do you need?"

"Magic powder," Euleilla said. "I use it to see, and I'm running low. My technique works well, but I tend to lose a lot of magic powder when I'm in damp places... like muddy caves."

Wodtke blinked, then shook her head. "Oh, right – I had forgotten about your eyes. Well, if you want commercial-grade powder, you'll have to go to old El'Rasi at the other side of town. He's a bit crazy, though, so I don't like dealing with him."

"What do you do, then?" Maelgyn asked.

"I'm pretty close to the only mage on this side of Nir'Thik," she answered. "There are only about two hundred humans in town, and only three of us have any magical talent at all."

"Can't Nekoji also become mages?" Euleilla asked. "There are thousands around us, and they're all potentially quite strong...."

"Oh, yes," Wodtke laughed sharply. "Nekoji make powerful mages. But not many of them can become a mage. Tell me, what is the first thing a mage must learn?"

When Euleilla hesitated, Maelgyn answered for her. "Meditation. A difficult thing for any child to learn, especially one only four years old."

"I didn't remember" Euleilla sighed. "It's been so long."

"The Nekoji can't meditate," Wodtke explained. "They're too alert and have trouble tuning out the rest of the world. I'd almost say it's the cat in them, but whatever it is they just lack the ability. Over the past two thousand years, their Winter Counts record only two dozen mages. There are no living Nekoji mages, right now, and there aren't any attempting to learn, either."

"I think you're wrong," Euleilla said, frowning. "I could have sworn I felt a Nekoji mage while we were traveling. I thought I sensed it again at the meeting yesterday, as well. Not from the Emperor, but there was someone else in the room...."

"Not possible," Wodtke snapped. "Gyato would know if one of his people were a mage, and he'd have told me."

"But..."

"You were still adjusting to the large numbers of people around you when you first felt it, right?" Maelgyn asked, magically nudging her. Arguing with the doctor would do neither of them any good.

"Well," she hesitated. "Perhaps. I *still* haven't really adjusted to being around that many people."

"It was probably just the confusion, then. At any rate, you still need your magic powder. I take it you don't have the time to help us find El'Rasi's shop, do you, Dr. Wodtke?"

"Nor the desire," the doctor admitted. "Sorry. But, if you're willing to take it pre-processed like I am, you could always try one of the local blacksmiths. There's one, Tur'Ne, not two minutes walk away from my office. We could go there right now; he'll be open quite late."

"A blacksmith?" Euleilla repeated.

"Sure. Iron filings are just a normal byproduct of his line of work. It won't have the rust-proofing you're probably used to, but it's cheap and it should help until you're somewhere you can get the commercial stuff," Wodtke noted.

"I actually need white magic powder, not black," Euleilla pointed out. "A less reactive magical powder allows me to make more sensitive judgments.

"Not a problem," Wodtke replied. "He calls himself a blacksmith, but he actually works in many different metals. I've had him inlay a piece of furniture with the same metal that is used in many types of white magic powder. He should have something we could use."

Maelgyn shrugged. "Sounds ideal, actually. Shall we try it out?"

He offered his arm to Euleilla, and magically encouraged her to take it. When she realized what he was doing, she acquiesced and nodded. "Yes, let's."

"Then let's hurry," he replied. "We have a lot to talk about."

"And a lot to say, still," she added, curling an arm around his. "Quite a lot, indeed."

Chapter 14

This is turning into a long day, Maelgyn thought as he returned to the inn a few hours later.

It was at the blacksmith's shop that the secret was let out. It was Maelgyn's fault, and he knew it, but he couldn't quite blame himself for having worn his armor when he left the hotel. Maybe he could for failing to cover it properly, however. He should have known that a blacksmith would recognize the armor for what it was, even disguised.

"Is that dragonhide?" Tur'Ne asked, staring in awe at the armor. "Real dragonhide?"

"Well—" Maelgyn started to say. He'd only taken off his cloak because it was so hot in the blacksmith's shop - he hadn't considered that the Dwarf would be so interested in what was underneath. He wasn't sure why Euleilla insisted on spending the time in that stifling building to reform the metal filings into smooth balls. Well, to tell the truth, he did: A person could cut themselves badly on non-commercial magic powder, if they didn't prep it first like she was doing, but at that point he wasn't exactly in the mood to be honest with himself.

"Never mind," Tur'Ne answered for himself. "I can see it for myself it is. That's a well-made set! I don't think I've ever seen its like."

"It's a... family heirloom," Maelgyn noted hesitantly, trying not to give away too much information.

"Yeah, it looks older than you," the Dwarf nodded. "By several hundred years. Red dragon, though. That's different. Most dragonhide I've heard about in this region comes from the black dragons killed in the Fifth Battle of Lake Poros. Nasty piece of work, when all four kingdoms of Poros came flying in with two or three trained dragons each... and all the dragons died. Their bodies were salvaged and turned into armor for the royal guard of East Poros."

"No, it's not Porosian in origin," Maelgyn explained.

"I can see that," Tur'Ne agreed. "It looks better than anything Poros could produce. Red makes stronger armor than Black, but at the cost of weight and comfort. As well made as this is I doubt you've lost much comfort, and that you don't even feel the weight. Best dragonhide – if you can ever find it – is Golden. As flexible and comfortable as soft leather, but if you take a hard whack at it your weapon is more likely to break than its wearer is likely to bruise. No-one hunts Gold Dragons, though, and even when a Golden Dragon carcass is found it's difficult to make proper armor out of it. Whoever made this armor, though, refined it well. That interwoven construction would make it almost as strong as Golden dragonhide. Offhand, I'd say it looks Sviedan." He swallowed, realizing just who he was dealing with. "You're one of the Sword Princes, aren't you?"

"A Sword Prince? Here?" a voice boomed from the store entrance. "Who are you, and what are you doing in Mar'Tok?"

Maelgyn turned to the newcomer, another Dwarf dressed in gaudy robes reeking of decadence. Clearly, this was an important figure in Dwarven society... and probably not one of El'Athras' allies, given the angry scowl on his face.

"Just passing through," he said truthfully.

"Nonsense!" the Dwarf barked. "Now, I am Merchant Prince El'Pless from the Grand Council of Mar'Tok. Any official state visits by a Sword of Svieda should have been reported to me. Since you weren't, it's fairly obvious you're a spy! Now, unless you want to be arrested and hung, you'd better talk, you Human bastard!"

Dr. Wodtke, who had been in the back room with Euleilla helping to prepare the magic powder, came out to investigate the ruckus. Seeing the speaker, she sighed. "Hello, Helpless."

The aristocratic Dwarf stiffened. "I am El'Pless, or Pless the Elder if you must call me by something in your tongue. I'm two hundred and eleven years old, and the second wealthiest Dwarf in the world. You would do well to show me some respect."

Wodtke snorted. "Maybe I will, but only when you show me you deserve it."

El'Pless' eyes narrowed. "You may be under the protection of the High Merchant Prince, but that goodwill only stretches so far. Do not test my patience!"

"Sorry, Helpless, but I'm afraid it stretches farther than you can imagine," Wodtke snorted. "As far as the Sword you were about to arrest as a spy is concerned, he has been given safe passage to his home province of Sopan. While they did meet to discuss some business, this isn't an official state visit. That is why you weren't informed."

"And just how do you know that, Human?" El'Pless spat. "Since when are you privy to the politics of the court?"

"Well, I think I'd know my own lover's business," Wodtke laughed. The room fell silent.

That's why she has such free access to El'Athras' house, Maelgyn thought, *and why she knew her way around the caves so well.*

"Lover?" Maelgyn repeated slowly.

"Not another one," Wodtke groaned. "I figured you would have noticed by now, Maelgyn. According to Euly, you're a smart enough guy."

Maelgyn shook his head in disbelief. Yes, he had noticed a degree of "familiarity," for lack of a better word, between her and El'Athras, but... "I never knew that was even possible. Have a Human and a Dwarf ever produced any offspring?"

"No," she sighed. "Why do you think I haven't married him, yet? You can't marry someone you can't have kids with. That's the law."

"Enough about your abomination with Athras!" El'Pless snarled. "Though believe me, the council will hear of it. The important issue is: Just what is this Sviedan doing here?"

"Well, why didn't you say so?" Wodtke snorted. "Helpless, you really do justice to your nickname, you know that? My lover just did what he's been trying to convince you idiots in the council was the sensible thing to do for years. In the process, he demoted you... Baron Helpless."

"Baron? What..." El'Pless' voice trailed off, as he slowly glanced at Maelgyn standing around shell-shocked. "No. Tell me that old fool didn't—"

"Cede Mar'Tok to Svieda? Yep. And you know he can do

it, too. A Sviedan Royal is present, my Athy has been High Merchant Prince for more than a year, and a third national ruler - Emperor Gyato of Caseificio – signed as one of the principle witnesses. Athy signed the treaty, was promptly dubbed Count El'Athras, High Merchant Lord of the Autonomous County of Mar'Tok in Svieda, and that was it – the deal was done. And just so you don't go worrying your beard bald, Mar'Tok was not the only nation to sign the treaty. Emperor Gyato was made Count of the Autonomous County of Caseificio, so he's no longer royalty either. It's all legal. We followed every procedure to the letter, compliant for all of Sviedan, Nekoji, and Dwarven legal systems. And, by Sviedan law, your former title has been converted to their closest equivalent – Merchant Lord Helpless, Baron of the Pathways Mining Company. And that 'Sviedan' you're sneering at is now your royal liege. You might just want to apologize for calling him a 'Human bastard.'"

El'Pless backed away in horror, mouth agape but moving as if he was trying to talk but couldn't quite form the words. Finally, he collected himself, and glared at the two Humans. "The Council will hear about this, you can rest assured. It may be too late to stop this horrible travesty Athras is leading us on, but we can still punish him for it... and you can tell your 'lover' that we'll be expecting him tomorrow morning in the council hall!"

With that, El'Pless stormed out of the building. Euleilla chose that moment to swoop in silently, attaching herself to Maelgyn's side.

"I heard," she said simply. Turning to Wodtke, she asked, "You okay?"

"Yeah. I'm not worried. He can't do anything, not really." Wodtke shrugged. "The worst thing they can do is strip Athy of his clan leadership, and since he is the ruling Count of Mar'Tok regardless of clan that won't matter much. He may lose the 'Merchant' from his title, I suppose, but that's a small price to pay."

"Good," Euleilla nodded emphatically.

Maelgyn glared at his wife playfully. "You knew about her and El'Athras, didn't you?"

"Yes," Euleilla said, smiling enigmatically.

He laughed. "Ah, well. Better I find out here and now than in some other, even more embarrassing way. But the secret of my presence is out, it seems." He turned to the doctor. "And yours is, too. Is that going to cause any problems?"

Wodtke shrugged. "Why should it? I can't marry him, and he is allowed to choose his lovers at will. And he will marry someone – just not me. I can never be anything more than his concubine, but that's all right. Dwarves permit that kind of thing among their royalty and nobility. They know that the person they love isn't always the one who can give them a healthy child, and since they are required to produce heirs..."

Tur'Ne coughed slightly. "Begging your pardon, my lady, but that won't matter. The concubine laws may permit you to be his lover, even if he were to marry, but you won't be a popular person here even so. Your average Dwarf isn't exactly happy to hear that their fellow Dwarf might care for a Human more than one of his own kind."

"Yes, but Athy isn't exactly the most popular Dwarf alive at the moment, anyway," she said. "Yet you Dwarves are loyal to a fault. He'll survive this politically intact, you'll forgive him, and life will go on."

"Forgive me again, my lady," Tur'Ne said humbly. "But while we Dwarves will forgive him, not all Dwarves will forgive you. In fact, they'll probably try to kill you. You might want to look into asking your lover for some protection."

"And you, Tur'Ne?" Maelgyn intervened. "How do you feel about her? You say the average Dwarf won't like this news... What about you?"

Tur'Ne smiled. "Well, my lady Wodtke saved my wife's life when the plague hit, and often treats me after I burn myself on the job. I figure if she does that for me, the least I can do is wish her happiness in her affairs."

"Well, then," Maelgyn turned serious. "Thanks for your warning. I had hoped anonymity would be some protection for us until certain announcements were prepared, but it looks as if that plan has fallen by the wayside. I hadn't considered that some of us were already well-known in these parts. So, doctor, it looks as if you're going to need some protection for a while. Maybe you should head over to El'Athras' mansion, where I'm pretty sure he can guard you until things blow over."

Wodtke shook her head. "I need to get back to my office. I've got two people who need treatment coming in soon, and I have to be there."

"Then we'll have to protect you until you *can* go to safety," Euleilla suggested in a tone that brooked no argument. "Excuse me, Tur'Ne, but could you please head over to the El'Athras' estate and let him know that we'll need some armed guards?"

Tur'Ne hesitated, but nodded. "Since it's for a good cause, yeah, I suppose I can. I'll have to close up my shop for a bit. I might have problems getting *into* the mansion, though – Those guards don't let just anybody in."

"Here," Wodtke said, tossing him a small necklace she had been wearing. "Show the guard this, and he'll let you in."

"Thank you again, Tur'Ne," Euleilla said to him as well, casually tossing him several coins... which was actually easier for her than handing them to him would have been, Maelgyn realized. He was beginning to see where some of her quirky personality came from. Some of it, at least, was to play off the effects of her blindness. "Payment for the metal filings, plus a little extra for your troubles."

Tur'Ne grinned, catching the coins. "And thank you, my lady, for remembering I'm a Dwarf and need to be paid, whether I like you or not." With that, he was ushering them out the door. "Now, I need to lock up, so you better get going. Time is money."

"We'd better move quickly," Maelgyn said as the door slammed behind them. "With luck and speed, we may be able to get out of sight before word spreads. Which way is your office, Doctor?"

"Please, just call me Wodtke," she answered him. "And we're not far at all. Follow me, if you want – though I have no idea how you think you'll be able to protect me. There are just two of you, and if an angry mob wants my head I doubt you'll be able to stop them."

"Well, hopefully we won't have to worry about that, but if we do get into a fight you might be surprised," Maelgyn smirked, falling in behind her. "I'm wearing dragonhide armor and carrying a pair of good swords. Euleilla is a First Rate mage, and I'm a decent mage as well, if I do say so myself. Even you should be able to take care of yourself to some degree, since you are also a mage. A good sized force of well-prepared troops, equipped for combating mages, would be a serious threat. Against a mob of unarmed or lightly armed peasants, I'm more concerned about not hurting them too badly."

"I'm not that good with combat magic," the doctor warned him. "I can use magic to enhance my strength and hold down a single patient when I'm performing surgery, and I suppose I could apply that same technique for battle, but I'm not especially powerful – I was tested at a Fourth Rate mage some years back. I'm strong enough to do my job, and I do it pretty well, but…"

"You've improved some," Euleilla said. "Low-level Third Rate, I would say. I haven't felt anyone with stronger magic than yours around here besides Maelgyn and I… except perhaps that Nekoji mage I thought I sensed."

"Still," Wodtke continued, ignoring for a time Euleilla's mention of a Nekoji mage. "I'm not likely to be much use if it comes down to a fight. And there are just two of you…."

"You've never seen a mage in combat, have you?" Maelgyn asked.

"No, but that's beside the point," Wodtke answered. "The Dwarves have been fighting mages for over two thousand years they've somehow managed to stay competitive. I may not know what it's like to fight someone like you two, but they will… and they probably will expect it."

Maelgyn shook his head. "Armies can compensate for a mage if they go into battle prepared. A simple set of lodestones in strategic places around your armor will deflect the worst of what your average mage can do. Bronze blades, archers with stone-tipped arrows, and cavalry charges which strike so fast nothing magical can be done to stop them are all effective anti-mage tactics – which is why we've come to respect the Dwarven wolf-riders even if they don't stand up well against a real cavalry. Powerful mages, like Euleilla and myself, can generally do a lot more to stop such attacks… but we'd be on the defensive quite a bit and would have to rely on others to do the main bit of fighting for us. That's how the dwarves can survive battles with mages.

"However, protective lodestones for fighting mages aren't exactly common among civilians. Neither are bronze blades or stone-tipped arrows – they have little use outside of military applications. Iron and steel weaponry is cheaper, sharper, lighter, and more durable, and therefore much more common in civilian practice. Unless I completely misunderstood something, your El'Athras is in control of the military right now, is he not?"

"He controls the national armies, yes," Wodtke agreed. "And his clan's army. But if the other clan lords decide to incite a riot, they can easily bring out their own clan armies to support it."

Maelgyn hadn't thought about it, but in his mind that only added fractionally to the danger. "Maybe they'd add to the manpower, but surely no clan lord or Merchant Prince would authorize the use of special military equipment that could be traced back to them. Not for assassinating their ruler's lover, no matter how unpopular he may be."

"The clan lords may or may not be behind it," Euleilla interrupted with a slightly strained lilt in her voice. "But there are an awfully large number of Dwarves up ahead... and they are talking in rather angry tones."

Maelgyn tuned in his senses, and saw that she was right. "Yes.... It feels like it may be a few hundred of them, coming this way, but they're still pretty far off. I can't hear them yet, myself."

"Yes, but you don't have Euleilla's experience relying on your ears instead of your eyes," Wodtke noted. "She can probably hear better than either of us can."

Maelgyn shook his head. "I don't understand – how could there be a riot of this size, already? Doesn't it take time to assemble and arouse this many Dwarves?"

Wodtke grimaced. "Not if the crowd has already been assembled and primed to start it. You may have been trying to keep your visit low-key, but you didn't exactly have the quietest of arrivals. I bet that El'Pless figured your appearance presented him with a good opportunity to usurp Athy's position. He got the rioters together, but he wanted a better pretext to send them out. He must have been looking for us so he could blame the riot on us."

"It doesn't matter why they're rioting," Euleilla pointed out. "That can be figured out later. It only matters that they're here."

"In any case," Maelgyn said, "I'm afraid they're blocking the way to your clinic. It's probably not a good idea to head there. As a matter of fact, maybe we should go back to our inn. When El'Athras gets our message, he'll probably send out the guard and that should make it safe... but I don't think it's a good idea, just now, to return to your clinic. I doubt your patients will be trying to make their way through that mob, anyway."

"Well," Wodtke sighed. "I suppose it won't be possible to do my job if there's an angry mob outside the door. In that case, we should probably just head for Athy's place and wait there for him to assemble a guard."

"No," Euleilla said. "That's not possible, either. The mob is between us and the mansion as well. And if we don't move quickly, I fear they could get between us and the inn."

Wodtke looked alarmed for the first time, and said, "They're trying to surround us?"

"No," Maelgyn replied after studying the mob's movements for a few seconds. "They're just trying to converge on your clinic, I think, and we're still pretty close to your clinic. If we move fast enough, we can evade them... but we need to lie low, and the inn is the best place to do that."

The threesome successfully made it back to the inn, believing themselves to be unrecognized. They hurried indoors, where El'Ba and Tur'Ba met them with arrows on string and bows drawn. They were alone, however; apparently all other guests had left in haste.

"Oh," El'Ba said, lowering his weapon. "'Tis you. I was worried it was one of those lunatic rioters. You, doctor, caused quite the stir – did you have to rile El'Pless up like that?"

Wodtke snorted. "It's the other Merchant Princes trying to give Athy a black eye. I doubt most of the Dwarves out there would have cared if it hadn't been for their clan heads stirring the pot for them."

"Regardless of what started it," El'Ba snorted, "It's going across the city like wildfire. I imagine your boy's already started trying to clean it up, by now, but it'll take him hours to clear a path here."

"Thankfully," another voice said from behind the two Dwarves, "The rioters haven't yet learned that any of the people they're rioting against are here, they haven't. I suspect we'll have to deal with them on our own, we will, if they manage to find us, they do."

"Spearmaster Wangdu," Maelgyn said, nodding his head in greeting. "What are you doing here?"

"Well, I was coming to talk with you, I was," the Elf replied wryly. "But the rioters distracted me, they did."

Maelgyn sighed, taking a seat at one of the inn's tables. "Talk about a long day. I woke up, was given two kingdoms, had a long talk with my wife about our future together, went to buy some magic powder, blew my 'hidden' identity yet again, got into an argument with a merchant prince, and dodged a mob of rioters. And it's not even dark out, yet."

"It ain't over yet, no," El'Ba noted wryly. "I'm wondering how long it will be before the rioters think to come here. The good doctor is a frequent visitor to many of our inn's guests, and I would expect you've been seen here as well. Surely we'll be thought of as a refuge."

"I believe we'll be okay, I do," Wangdu said. "If they come, they do, we can fight them, we can."

El'Ba snorted. "Master Wangdu, I am well aware of the combat abilities of Elves and mages. One Elf may be better than a thousand foot soldiers, as your reputation suggests, but we Dwarves have become quite innovative when it comes to battling the major mystical powers of our enemies."

"Professional soldiers, yes," Maelgyn agreed. "But these are rioters – just an untrained, ill-equipped mob. It's true that the Dwarves were the first to learn how to fight mages, but much of that relied on having the right tools with which to fight. Civilian rioters won't have such tools."

"But they *will*," El'Ba insisted. "You probably wouldn't know, but all Dwarves – be they soldiers or farmers – are taught to fight those of you who are mystically empowered. Civilians aren't expected to fight opposing armies, but our families are threatened by the very existence of your powers. We have fought enslavement for so long that now even the untrained know how to create weapons against mages, Elves, Nekoji, and any other force you can imagine."

Maelgyn frowned, a crack in his confidence forming. "But the costs for equipping everyone, even with the fabled wealth of the Dwarves, would be enormous. Most peasant-class families couldn't afford it, so how…"

"Peasants may, admittedly, not be able to afford the professional's tools," El'Ba explained. "They don't need them for the tactics we are taught, however. A sling is probably useless on the battlefield, but it can be used to throw rocks, and a smart Dwarf can get pretty good at it in a couple days. It's cheap, too; you can make one out of spare rope ends and worn out clothing or a scrap of leather. And there's not much a mage can do to defend himself – or herself – from a sling, outside of what any normal foot soldier can do with shield and armor."

"They wouldn't have armor or lodestones—"

"Irrelevant," the old Dwarf sighed. "These rioters wouldn't be able to use armor properly, anyway. It obstructs movement too much if you aren't used to it. We're Dwarves, so we're essentially armored already just in our skins, after all. Magic doesn't work too well on our bodies, so all we need to worry about is what magic can do to the things around us. And for those Dwarves who might feel that isn't enough... well, you know you can turn any old iron pan into a lodestone if you bang it with a hammer properly, right? And there are a lot of Dwarven families out there with iron pans and hammers."

Wangdu stepped forward. "And may I ask what your common folk have found effective against my kind, may I?"

El'Ba raised an eyebrow. "Well... truthfully, we're even better prepared for you than we are for mages. Mages are powerful people, true, but we haven't faced nearly as many of them as we have faced of your people. Humans never took as much of an interest in us as the Elves did."

"Yes, but there are not as many convenient ways to stop or divert an Elf's powers, there aren't," Wangdu noted. "There are not many things that can stop the trees and plants, there aren't, and we Elves control those, we do."

"Only if there's still a spark of life left in the tree or plant, Spearmaster," El'Ba noted. "And look around you: What plants and trees do you see around here? Even our houses are made without wood, living or dead, save my door – which I doubt you'll be able to use. What do you have to work with?"

Wangdu grinned. "I have a few things which just might be useful, I have. That, and I keep the wood in my spear alive, I do."

"Yes, but our chemists have spent a thousand years preparing poisons for your plants, Elf," El'Ba noted. "Poisons which work faster than you do."

Wangdu grimaced. "Well, that is a matter to contend with, it is. But a race it shall be, it shall, to see if I can grow my plants before you can release your poisons, I can."

"It might come to that," Euleilla warned. "I think the rioters are headed in this direction."

El'Ba turned a skeptical eye on her, but the expression on Maelgyn and Wodtke's faces told him that she probably had the right of it. "How far away are they?"

"I can sense for quite a ways away," Euleilla noted, "It's tiring to 'look' that far out, but I wanted to keep track of them. They are moving slowly, but even so we only have ten to fifteen minutes at most."

"Massacring a horde of civilians would not exactly be the most auspicious beginnings for the alliance I just negotiated. We have to get out of here," Maelgyn sighed, "We need to stay on the move until El'Athras can get the guard moving... and I'd rather not wreck your inn."

"Bah!" El'Ba snorted. "Stay. Any who reside in my walls shall receive my protection. My wife and those too young to fight are away – and the rioters will likely strike whether you're here or not. They know how close we are to the doctor, and they may even have learned that you're staying here for now. It's best for all of us to fight here, together... and to hope that 'Athy,' as the Doc likes to call him, will able to save us before it goes too far."

Maelgyn nodded, lifting his hand and magically summoning his katana. Since he was no longer hiding his identity, he could afford to use the better blade. "We'll meet them together, then."

"And if El'Athras is a bit tardy," El'Ba growled, "We'll just have to make sure these idiots know just what it's like to attack those in my care. Don't worry, Doc, we'll keep you safe."

Wodtke looked vaguely reassured after that statement, but Maelgyn, sensing the same group of Dwarves Euleilla had reported, definitely was not. This was not going to be like the easy battles he'd been in, to date. He was going to have to fight off a horde of angry Dwarves, and he couldn't afford to kill his enemy.

Maelgyn changed his mind. It wasn't just a long day – it was an *extremely* long day.

Chapter 15

The six inhabitants of El'Ba's inn used the scant few minutes they had to fortify the building before the rioters arrived. Tables were overturned to become shields against stone and arrow, chairs were used to prop doors and windows closed, a few very simple traps like trip ropes were set... but even with all of the ingenuity, magic and mysticism two Dwarves, three mages, and one Elf were able to produce, they knew they lacked the resources to hold their attackers off for more than a few short minutes.

"Euleilla," Maelgyn asked when the rioters got close enough for everyone to hear, "Can you tell if Tur'Ne is anywhere near El'Athras' mansion?"

"I've been tracking him," she said. "He was allowed inside about twenty minutes ago, but I can't tell you more than that. They have lodestones throughout the place, which makes it hard to see inside – especially from a distance."

"The guard is probably already assembling," Maelgyn mused. "They'll head to the clinic, first... but what will happen when they find that we never showed up?"

"Probably they'll come straight here." Wodtke suggested. "It wouldn't be hard to figure out where you were staying. At least Athy knows that this is where I'd come if I couldn't get to my clinic."

"Worst case," El'Ba said, "It'll take him another half-hour to assemble the guard. Which means he won't be here for an hour, so we've gotta somehow stall these brainless sheep attacking my inn for that long."

"And we can't kill them. If we kill them, El'Athras' political opposition will be able to use that to completely destabilize his government. 'See,' they'll say. 'He's allied our country with those who think nothing of slaughtering our people!'" Maelgyn shook his head in disgust. "We can only use enough force to drive them off, unless we want the rioters to return ten-fold."

"No killing?" Tur'Ba snorted. "You don't like to make this easy, do you?"

A crash signaled the first attack upon the doors. Apparently, the crowd had already pieced together a makeshift battering ram, and the door, though sturdy, was not built to deal with that kind of attack. It was built with a complex lock no thief would ever manage to pick, but the crowd wasn't interested in dealing with a lock. It was much more interested in destroying the door.

"Well," El'Ba snorted when the second crash echoed through the inn's common room. "It'll take them about ten more strikes like that to break down the door. At the speed they're moving, that means we've got about two minutes until they're in here."

Euleilla grimaced, removing her home-made steel bracers. Magically, she sent them flying across the room, forming them into solid bars as they went. They attached themselves to the door, reducing the noise and apparent effectiveness as the third strike hit. "I'll help keep them closed as much as I can."

Maelgyn sighed. "It won't work for long. That buys us maybe... five minutes. Not enough time, I fear."

"Ten minutes," El'Ba said, taking a good look at the door. "Good woman you've got there, Maelgyn. Those bars look pretty strong."

"Ten minutes, then," he replied, grimacing. "Not nearly long enough, anyway."

"Don't worry, do not," Wangdu said. "I've got a few things I can do, myself, I do. I should be able to buy us more time once they're through the door, I should."

"Until they get the poisons out, that is," El'Ba snorted. "I know you're good, Master Wangdu, but my people are more prepared for your tricks than you'd think. The Elves haven't faced us in battle for almost five hundred years, but if they ever do they'll find we're a lot better prepared for them than anyone else they've ever faced before."

"Debate a theoretical Elf-Dwarf war later," Maelgyn snapped. "We need to think of something else we can try, should Wangdu's methods fail us."

"Hand to hand, of course," Tur'Ba snorted. "You can only delay a riot so long unless you've got an army to disperse it."

"I was hoping for something a bit less... lethal," Maelgyn said. "Besides, Euleilla wouldn't be very effective fighting in close combat. Bows and arrows like you and your father have wouldn't exactly be useful that close in, either, and are even more lethal. Doctor Wodtke isn't a fighter at all, and likely will have serious problems in battle. No, Tur'Ba. We may have to fight as a last resort, but it would be best to avoid that, if possible."

"I can hold Dwarven patients down with magic during surgery," Wodtke noted. "Perhaps we could hold back the attackers with magic, as well?"

"If El'Ba is to be believed – and I trust his judgment in these matters – then they'll likely have lodestones," Maelgyn warned. "I don't think you're strong enough to push through one like Euleilla and I. Even we can only manage it for a short time, with this many people around."

"It's the only other thing we can do," Euleilla sighed. "So we shall do it."

The door started splintering, and Maelgyn nodded. "It'll have to be enough. There's not much else we can do. At least we won't have to worry about them burning down the building – Dwarven stone construction is going to save us that much worry."

The next crash of the battering ram was accompanied by the first crack in the door. A second blow about ten seconds later sent some small splinters flying.

"Either you or El'Athras better pay me for that door," El'Ba sighed, looking at Maelgyn. "I spent a fortune importing it."

With the battering ram pounding on the door to the inn, the only noises the six people trapped in the inn allowed themselves came in the form of El'Ba's groans and moans over his damaged property. Euleilla was using some of her magical strength to keep her reinforcing bars intact, but Maelgyn kept a close eye on her. They knew that, when the door was breeched and Wangdu's diversions were overcome, it would be up to the two of them to prevent the intrusion of the rioters. She had to conserve her strength, and she still hadn't recovered fully from her illness. Maelgyn knew she'd tire much faster than she expected to.

"Enough," he finally said to her. "If you stress yourself out too much, you won't be able to recover before it's too late."

With a sigh, Euleilla released her hold on the door's iron bars. "Okay," she whispered without a protest, leaning back to relax and recover her strength.

It only took one more blow of the battering ram to shatter the doors. Euleilla, with a last bit of magical effort before completely relaxing, recovered the iron bars and reformed them into her bracers. She did not put them on, however, before collapsing in exhaustion.

Maelgyn sighed. She had overtired herself, but she might be able to recover most of her strength with just a few minutes rest. He was so concerned for her that he almost overlooked Wangdu leaping over the makeshift barrier of overturned tables to go on the offensive.

He had to take care of Euleilla while also keeping one eye on the ongoing battle. First, he strapped her bracers on for her – he still wasn't quite sure why she wore them, since they weren't likely to be useful for her, but she seemed to think they were important. He still didn't know enough about her magical practices to know whether they were worn for decoration or for some other reason. That done, he pulled her against his shoulder to comfort her while he watched the ongoing battle.

And it was a remarkable battle. No-one in the room had ever seen an Elf fight: not Maelgyn, not Wodtke, not even the Dwarves. While several centuries old – no-one knew his exact age – Wangdu was counted a younger, less experienced Elf. If this was young and inexperienced, Maelgyn dreaded the day he might face a veteran Elven warrior.

Mages were the elite of the Human fighting force. They could make themselves stronger and faster than any normal human, and had abilities no non-mage could dream of, no matter what tools they had with them. Powerful mages, like Euleilla and Maelgyn, were the central reason humans held such a strong position in the world. Alone, the average mage could fight regular humans and foot soldiers – and expect a reasonable chance at winning – at almost twenty to one odds. An army could face exponentially larger numbers and win when accompanied by a strong mage. That said, *no one* fought like an Elven soldier. From his history lessons at the Svieda castle, Maelgyn knew of a single Elf who held a mountain pass against ten thousand Human enemies for three days before he was killed, slaughtering nearly a tenth of his enemy's forces as they tried to approach. He always had thought that story was a legend... until he saw Wangdu's battle with the rioters.

True to his word, Wangdu wasn't killing anybody... but that didn't mean the rioters were going to escape unscathed. The vines he had planted while Maelgyn was taking care of Euleilla were now growing wildly, tying up many rioters and tossing them into walls, bloodying many a Dwarven forehead. It was a remarkable feat, given the Dwarves notorious durability, that he was knocking so many of them unconscious. Meanwhile, the blunt end of the Elf's spear was thrusting into the bellies and cracking over the heads of the few who managed to slip past the wily plant. As the number of Dwarven bodies lying in the inn grew, Maelgyn started to hope that he and Euleilla wouldn't be needed.

Sadly, Wangdu's efforts proved insufficient to permanently stem the tide. As those who had been knocked out gradually awakened, he was finding himself more and more penned in. His tactic was slightly flawed for this kind of battle – while there would have been no problem if he'd been allowed to kill his opponents, the need to only stun them gave them a chance to recover... and as they recovered, to outflank him. Furthermore, his vines were slowly being beaten back, as someone started deploying Dwarven-made fast-acting plant poisons. The vines were literally melting as the poison touched, and the plants were being killed at a faster rate than Wangdu could regrow them. His spear lengthened and shortened as needed, but after a while he no longer risked it to the crowd that was deploying their poisons so liberally. Instead, he concentrated on the ones trying to outflank him, but gradually they drove him back.

Maelgyn saw he didn't have long before he'd have to act... but then was shocked to sense Doctor Wodtke entering the battle, using her limited skills in magic to hold off some of the Dwarves from attacking Wangdu. Her efforts would give them a few precious seconds more for Euleilla to recover, but he wasn't sure it would be enough. Wangdu was losing ground faster, now, and it wouldn't be long before he'd have to either awaken Euleilla or battle the entire force of rioters alone.

He motioned for Tur'Ba to come closer. "Slowly count to a hundred and then wake her up," he said. "She can't fight in her condition, but give her just another minute or two more rest and she'll be a great help."

Tur'Ba nodded. "Yes, sir!" he snapped, giving him a Sviedan salute... although not properly. He would need to learn which hand to salute with if he was going to stay in Maelgyn's service.

Maelgyn shook his head at the errant thought. If they got out of this situation alive, Tur'Ba would have earned a spot in his service, regardless of his limited knowledge of Sviedan formalities.

Maelgyn stepped out from behind their makeshift barricade, gathering magic in his legs to boost his speed and strength and collecting a nearby strand of rope that had been laced with iron powder. Ready for the battle, he jumped over the tables and into the fray. Startling the nearby Dwarves, he used his magically reactive rope to bind a half-dozen of the rioters together, effectively taking them out of the battle for a time. He assessed the situation closely as he marched forward towards Wangdu, intending to relieve the embattled Elf, and found that El'Ba had been right. Many of the attackers held frying pans converted into lodestones... and a few of them had military-grade lodestones and wore proper bronze armor. Professional soldiers, in fact, seemed well interspersed throughout the crowd – something to take note of and look out for as the battle continued.

Not all of the attackers had lodestones. Maelgyn left as many of those as he could for Wodtke. As completely untrained in battle as she was, her efforts were almost negligible, but with her as a distraction he could concentrate on the better equipped Dwarves.

For someone of his power, weak lodestones such as these were merely targets – iron weapons he could use to fight his enemies. True, it would take a great deal more effort than he would have liked, but he was strong enough to push aside the influence of a lodestone and work on its core of iron. If he had the time, which he didn't, he could even remove their magical properties altogether. As it was, considering the natural magical resistance of the Dwarves, it was actually easier to use his magic on the lodestones than it would be to try anything on the Dwarves themselves.

With a dramatic gesture, he knocked back all of the Dwarves attacking Wangdu's left flank using the rioting Dwarves' own pots and pans. It required more effort than he expected, but he managed it nevertheless. He continued pushing that wave of Dwarves back, until they were once again behind the dying vines concocted by Wangdu.

The effort cost him a tremendous amount of energy, however, and Maelgyn was tiring fast. He realized that his best bet was to help Wangdu regain control of the battle, and then return it into the Elf's hands. Splitting his effort between the attacking Dwarves at the door and the remaining Dwarves on the right flank, he tried to give the Elf enough time to re-establish his defenses.

It was proving too much for him, however, and he started to feel himself get lightheaded. Help arrived in the nick of time as Euleilla, obviously reawakened by Tur'Ba as per his instructions, began to ease the burden of holding the door away from him. No longer having to divide his attention in two places, he concentrated on the Dwarves who had already broken through.

Maelgyn found himself too weakened to effectively magic them away. Instead he resolved to use cruder methods, and drew his sword. Only able to slightly enhance his normal strength and speed in his exhausted state, he nevertheless rushed forward to battle the angry Dwarves at close range. Aiding Wangdu to the best of his abilities, Maelgyn worked towards disarming the Dwarves and then using the flat of his blade to knock them out. The "knock them out" part of the plan wasn't going so well – another testament to Dwarven physique – but at least he was able to disarm several of them without killing them.

He heard a soft twang, and saw to his surprise one Dwarf fall at his side, clutching at an arrow in his arm. Several other Dwarves, also surprised by the sudden appearance of an archer, also backed off behind the line of vines Wangdu was regrowing while Euleilla held the other Dwarves off... but many still remained. And of those that still remained, all of them were carrying the bronze armor and lodestones of the Dwarven military. These were the people who Maelgyn knew he really had to watch out for: These were the professional soldiers. In his weakened state, he was going to have serious difficulties with them, and he knew it. However, the sudden appearance of arrows into the conflict left both sides at a standoff, assessing the situation.

El'Ba, bow in hand and arrow notched, came to stand at Maelgyn's side. "Lower your weapons," he cried. "Your clan lords stand in rebellion and will be named traitors if you do not surrender!"

The leading soldier snorted. "The only traitor among the clan lords is El'Athras, sir. He sold our kingdom for the price of a human whore, and we'll have none of that."

"Is that what you think?" El'Ba snapped back. "I'll have you know, boy, that El'Athras would have allied us with any power he felt was strong enough to support us, Human, Nekoji, Dwarven, even Elven. And do you want to know why?"

"Not really," the soldier answered. "I'm unlikely to believe the propaganda and lies told me by an Athras sympathizer. It is quite apparent that you have El'Athras' Human lover sheltered here, and her mere presence stinks."

"Fine," El'Ba snorted. "Then believe your own reasoning, instead. Be honest – are we capable of fighting Sho'Curlas alone?"

The soldier looked at El'Ba as if he'd gone crazy. "Sho'Curlas? What does that have to do with anything?"

"Because the alliance was made in order to survive Sho'Curlas' plans for conquering us all, you idiot!" El'Ba snorted. "The doctor has had nothing to do with it. El'Athras has been trying to negotiate a merger between our kingdom and other surrounding powers for years – since long before he even met the human woman! Hell, you know the clan chiefs have been complaining about his plans for seven years, now. She hasn't been in the city for more than five! Ever ask yourself why?"

The lead soldier looked a little stunned at that revelation, but continued to argue. "It doesn't matter why he did it. Athras has sold our country to another. That is treachery!"

"Yes," Maelgyn said, intervening. "I suppose you could say he 'sold' it, if you insist on discussing our treaty as a mere business deal like you Dwarves are apt to do. He sold it to me. And at a heavy price, too. Do you want to know what price I'm paying?" The Dwarf just snorted, more angered than calmed by his matter-of-fact admission. It was a calculated risk to explain away the treaty as if he had "bought" Mar'Tok, which would confirm some of the Dwarves worst fears, but it would be easier to make a Dwarf understand everyone's motives if he put it in more commercial terms. "The price is – your lands become the equal of my own. Your people gain my protection. And together, we'll work towards preserving the autonomy of Dwarven and Nekoji people. If we were wiped out, Sho'Curlas would storm your country and take it by force. Your only choice in that event would be to either join us on less favorable terms, when it was too late to do you any good, or to join another major power like Oregal."

"An alliance would have been one thing," another Dwarf snarled. "But Athras went too far!"

"No, he didn't," El'Ba stated slowly. "To be blunt, the Humans are becoming the only independent force left among the races of the world. The Elves are dying out, the Nekoji have been driven from their homelands and are being hunted for their fur, the Dragons have never been plentiful, and we... we cannot face any of the others alone in a modern war. Horse-mounted cavalry has doomed us, as has our pride. We can no longer even defend the caves properly without a proper guild of axemen.

"Just look at this battle, here. My son and I have done almost nothing, but three humans and an Elf are holding off hundreds of our own. We have spent hundreds of years readying our kind for battling them, but even at our best it's not enough.

"My friend... the time has come when we Dwarves must accept the fact we cannot exert any influence on the world by force of arms alone."

"But as a part of Svieda, you can," Maelgyn added. "Mar'Tok has been made a County in Svieda, in most respects the equal of any of the duchies... which means you will have a say in the affairs of the third largest nation in the world. And Mar'Tok? It will retain autonomy, just as all of the other provinces of the kingdom do. You Dwarves will have just as much of a say in anything that happens here as you always have, maybe more of one. All that joining our kingdom means in the long run is that you allow safe passage through your kingdom for all Sviedans – which you do anyway, or used to; that you agree to a common defense with Svieda – which is the only way either of us can possibly survive the coming wars; and that you gain a voice in our national government. If you waited until the Sho'Curlas conquered you instead, all you could look forward to would be a lifetime of slavery."

The Dwarven soldier looked to be trying to muster up new arguments, better ones, but it quickly became clear he wouldn't have time to do so as the rioters at his rear started dispersing.

"The guard!" came the call, alerting those still inside the inn that El'Athras' men had finally arrived. "The guard! Get the hell out of here! The guard's arrived"

The men Maelgyn and El'Ba had been debating with ran off without another word, bypassing the now-dead vines Wangdu had formed and out the door. In only a couple of minutes, El'Athras and his personal guard replaced them, marching into the common room with a definite look of concern on their faces.

"Key?" El'Athras called. Or at least, that's what Maelgyn thought he was saying.

"Here, Athy," Wodtke said, leaving the protection of the tabletop barricade to run over to him and embrace him. "Right on time. I don't know how much longer we could have held those idiots."

"Now, now," El'Athras rebuked lightheartedly. "They're hard-headed money grubbing louts, it's true, but that's because they're Dwarves – *not* because they're idiots." He turned to Maelgyn. "And you – I thought I told you to not let anybody know who you were!"

"Sorry about that," the Sword apologized wryly, shrugging his shoulders. "I did the best I could. It was just a case of bad timing, I fear."

"Well, no matter," the Dwarven lord sighed. "It just gave my men a little rehearsal before we go to war."

Chapter 16

Maelgyn was a bit surprised at how quickly everything fell into place following the riot. He, Euleilla, Dr. Wodtke, and El'Ba's family were "invited" to room at El'Athras' mansion until an appropriate force could be assembled to escort them all to Svieda. El'Ba and his wife declined the opportunity, but Tur'Ba joined them, as did Wangdu in the end.

El'Athras summoned the Dwarven infantry to keep peace in the streets, and they quickly ended the riots. El'Pless and the other former Merchant Princes of the Mar'Tok Council formally censured El'Athras in the wake of the treaty Maelgyn had signed, but that had little effect as far as Maelgyn could see. Possibly it meant more to a Dwarf, but none of the ones he'd talked to could sufficiently explain why this mattered. In the end, Maelgyn merely shrugged and decided to let internal Dwarven politics remain a mystery only the Dwarves themselves could understand, and settled down to enjoy his lodgings.

A couple of days later, the arrest and trial of certain clan heads involved in the riot quickly bolstered the strength of El'Athras' political reach. The verdict was sealed when a soldier – the same soldier who had been debating with El'Ba and Maelgyn during the end of the riot – came forth to testify to something most Dwarves already knew. He and several other guardsmen, he had said, were encouraged not just to join the riots, but to spark them. Accusations of treason were leveled at many: At El'Athras, at the clan heads, even at the guardsman who presented his testimony. The end result, Maelgyn learned, was that the censure El'Pless had organized against El'Athras was rendered politically meaningless.

Euleilla took most of their time in El'Athras' mansion to rest and recover. The remnants of the plague in her system and the stress of using so much magic in battle had her on the verge of collapse.

Doctor Wodtke had examined Euleilla and confirmed that there was no relapse of the plague. Nonetheless, Euleilla was bedridden for days from the magical stress. Even Maelgyn was rendered ill from the excessive use of his magic, and he hadn't strained as much as she had. Maelgyn only needed one night of rest before he had recovered, and afterwards hovered around Euleilla nervously, seeing to her needs. He was frequently called upon to deal with one aspect or another of Sviedan law that needed clarifying to help the Dwarves adjust to their new government, and sometimes Euleilla herself would insist he leave her alone when his overabundant attentions started to get on her nerves, but whenever he was allowed he was by her side.

He was starting to get annoyed at the frequent demands on his time by the Dwarven lawmakers. Eventually he promised to send an envoy from Sopan who could answer all of the Dwarves' legal questions, but he was still called upon to help the Dwarves establish an 'interim government' to rule until all of the legal requirements set forth by Sviedan Law could be met. As that interim government would likely become a legitimate government once they were certain of Sviedan law, they continued harassing him for his input.

But finally, three days after he drove the rioters away from El'Ba's inn and saved its residents, El'Athras called him into his office to discuss more important matters.

"How's your wife?" El'Athras began abruptly after the guards had announced his name and escorted Maelgyn into the Dwarf lord's office.

"Fine," Maelgyn replied questioningly. He had not expected the usually blunt Dwarf to engage in small talk.

"Does 'fine' mean well enough to travel?"

"You would be better off asking Wodtke her opinion, but I believe so," Maelgyn answered hesitantly.

"Good. Then we've got to discuss our travel plans."

"Our travel plans?"

"Yes," El'Athras said, nodding. "You *are* trying to make it to

Sopan Province, are you not?"

Maelgyn nodded uncertainly. "Yes...."

"That's what I thought," the Dwarven lord said, then turned his attention to some papers on his desk. "We've signed a treaty with you that binds our nations together, and I feel it is our duty to help you win your war with the Sho'Curlas. Which means supplying you with equipment, goods, arms, engineers, funding, and whatever military force I can assemble."

Maelgyn coughed uncomfortably, almost embarrassed with the need to bring in that sort of help from his new allies. "Thank you, I appreciate that. Some of the details will have to be sorted out later, of course. "

Ignoring him, El'Athras continued, "The riots will force us to leave a large portion of our infantry at home; they'll be needed to keep the public in line. I doubt this will be a great loss, however, as your average Dwarven infantry is badly outmatched against an organized human army. However, many other components are ready to move, and move we shall."

"Well," Maelgyn sighed in frustration, "I suppose a review of what you have available will be useful when the time comes to deploy them."

El'Athras shoved a paper into Maelgyn's hands. "Here's a breakdown of our current forces, but you'll need me to summarize a few things. Our forces are organized slightly differently from your own: Humans, since the ancient days when the first Human kingdom of Poros wrote the standards, tend to work in groups of five – a squadron of men is five strong, a platoon is five squadrons, a company is five platoons, a battalion is five companies, a regiment is five battalions, and a division is five regiments. We divide ourselves into units of ten, but we have fewer organizational tiers. We have ten Dwarves in a platoon, ten platoons in a company, ten companies in a battalion, and ten battalions in a division. We also have an additional battalion of specialists in each division: Medics, combat engineers, logistics officers, and so forth. That comes to about eleven thousand Dwarves per division, compared to about 15,000 men in the Sviedan equivalent. We have six divisions of infantry, which all total are about equal in numbers to the armies of a typical Sviedan province, but our infantry is unlikely to be of vital importance in this war. It is the other units you're most likely to be interested in.

"There are two divisions of wolf riders, but they are organized differently: Spearmen (a misnomer – as with our infantry, they wield naginata), of whom there are ten battalions in each division; archers, who add five battalions to those ten, and a reserve force of mixed units and specialists totaling about another thousand Dwarves for each division.

"We have just two divisions outside of the infantry and the wolf riders: A division of engineers, archers and artillery officers, and the recently created Llama Riders corps."

Maelgyn, who'd been a bit surprised at the complexity of El'Athras' "summary," looked a little startled at that. "I've heard you were experimenting with Llamas as cavalry, but a whole division?"

"The Llama Riders are still untested," El'Athras admitted. "The Wolf Riders are our elite forces, but finding Dwarves who are strong enough and disciplined enough to be proper warriors, but still small enough to ride our wolves, makes finding sufficient numbers difficult. Our new program didn't have the same size requirements, so it filled out quickly. It requires less skill with your mount, but I fear it will not prove to be as effective as we might have wished.

"At any rate, the Archer and Llama Rider divisions are quite similar to each other. The Archers are organized more like the Infantry, only with some battalions replaced by medical, logistic, and heavy artillery units. The Llama Riders are just like the Infantry, but they have a set of twelve battalions as their base instead, plus their specialists. They have the only mounted engineering company in the world, and that brings them to thirteen thousand strong.

"The result is that we're actually quite a decent standing army of a little more than one hundred and twenty thousand Dwarves," El'Athras concluded. "Which means my 'province' controls the largest army in Svieda right now, at least in terms of sheer numbers. Those numbers don't tell the whole story, though, since not all of our troops are really useful in this war. I figure we have maybe sixty thousand Dwarves of any value to the Sviedan cause, at best, and all sixty thousand of them are specialty forces."

Maelgyn nodded slowly, trying to grasp what he was told.

He'd need to refer to the papers in order to recall all of that, however. "Even that is more than I expected. But how does this affect my travel plans?"

"I am assembling a force to send off to the war," El'Athras explained. "Mar'Tok's borders are essentially secure now. We are protected on the South by the ocean, on the North by mountains that are impassible to any not of Dwarven blood, and on the West and East by Svieda, so I judge that the infantry I must leave behind to maintain order will also be sufficient to guard our homeland here. They will also have the support of the Clan Guards, our version of your militia, who number about five thousand soldiers in total.

"With that in mind, I intend to send both divisions of Wolf Riders, the Llama Rider division, the Artillery, Engineers, and Archer's division, and four of the specialist brigades from the infantry out to fight Sho'Curlas: Two for combat engineering and one each for logistics and medical. And I believe that Gyato also intends to send the battalion of infantry he brought with him – another twelve hundred Nekoji – with my armies, while he only takes his personal guard into Sopan. Most of his remaining forces are required to defend his homeland, but he may be able to send for another battalion of his soldiers, if you think it necessary. With that in mind, I was wondering how many of my men you want in Sopan, and where I should send the rest."

Maelgyn raised his eyebrows. "I don't think it's a good idea to send a large force with me. It might be mistaken for an invasion."

"We'll be traveling under a flag of truce," El'Athras reassured him. "And we'll be very careful. So, how many of us can you use in Sopan?"

"I'm not sure," Maelgyn said, considering. "Before I decide, I could use whatever intelligence you have about Sopan's own forces. My last few years of education have kept me away from my duchy or even from meeting my generals firsthand."

El'Athras frowned. "Do you need me to breakdown what's in your own army?"

"As much as I hate to admit it, you probably know better than I," Maelgyn grumbled. It wasn't exactly politic to rely on El'Athras' spies for an assessment of his own military abilities, but he really had no choice. "My father kept me away from learning much of anything about my own duchy. He believed I had 'more important things to learn,' first, and that I'd find out everything I needed to know when I got there. I'm aware we've got a significantly larger army than the other provinces. We've five and a half divisions of regulars, plus another division and a half of specialists. Also, the eighty ships of the Third Fleet are in ports in Sopan, and I've been hoping to use them to break the blockade of our major coastal ports."

The Dwarf lord nodded. "Aye, all that's true."

"That said, I don't know the breakdown of each division, I don't know who most of my generals are. On the civilian side, I don't know what my regent is like, and I haven't even met the Baron's Council or seen what the Senate in Sopan is like."

El'Athras shrugged, shuffling some papers on his desk to find the right one. "As far as we know, your generals are untested. Your regent has been ruling ably in the years since the old regent retired, and your Baron's Council is as good as any other in Svieda – it has its good leaders and its awful ones. The senators in your province are elected diplomatically every ten years, and so tend to reflect how things are going in Svieda during the period they were elected. The last election was two years ago, and things were moving along well then, so mostly they just maintain the status quo. As far as the breakdown of your armies go, well, they're pretty standard for Svieda."

"In other words," Maelgyn said, "Sopan is pretty average, right?"

"Not quite," El'Athras noted. "Sopan is the only Sviedan province which has had potential enemies on all sides, so it maintains a much more rigid state of alert and a more diverse training regimen than most. And while your generals lack experience in large campaigns, most of the Sopan standing army has seen battle at one point or another. Nothing major – skirmishes with smugglers, Merfolk mercenaries, and 'resistance' fighters of defeated border kingdoms who have turned brigand, for the most part – but most of the army has seen small action in that way. It won't compare to the sheer fury of a pitch battle between roughly equal sides – which, unless I miss my guess, you have yet to experience yourself – but it has served to give them some taste of battle."

"Well, given my lack of experience, what do you suggest I take with me into Sopan?" the Sword Prince asked petulantly.

"Don't take that tone with me, boy," El'Athras warned. "You may now, technically, rank higher than me, but I've got nearly two hundred years more fighting experience than you've had, so I've got the right to call it as I see it."

Maelgyn drew back, abashed. "My apologies. I suppose that having two centuries of fighting experience would make any Human's seem insignificant. With that in mind, for now I'll look to you as my key military advisor. But then why ask me to make the decision? Why not make it yourself, or at the very least just give me some options to decide from?"

"Because you need to learn, somehow," the Dwarf said, "And the best way to do that is through experience."

Maelgyn quickly studied the papers in his hands. He discovered the true numbers of each unit in both the Dwarven and Sviedan armies broken down in even more detail than the brief "summary" El'Athras had given. In the end, he came to the conclusion that he didn't really need any additional soldiers in Sopan. In fact, he had more there than was really needed, since the Mar'Tok and Caseificio borders were now reasonably safe. He'd thought that might be the truth even before he'd started reading the papers, but now it was confirmed.

The end result was that instead of moving new forces in, it would be his job to take Sopan's armies to the front. It would take quite some time to organize and march them even as far as Largo, traveling overland. The sea may not be pleasant, even with the advances in navigation and ship construction the Sea Dwarves had evolved and passed down to the rest of the world, but at least traveling by sea took less time than marching over a difficult mountain pass like Mar'Tok. However, every Dwarf or Nekoji with him would increase the difficulty of shipping armies back into Svieda.

"Actually," Maelgyn said, "I think I'd like it if you instructed most of your and Gyato's armies to set up a rally point nearer the front lines, but which can be reached by ship. Take them east, to... to... oh! How about to a small riverfront town called 'Rocky Run.' My wife's foster father is there, and possibly another military officer I wanted to meet with, as well. I suspect that, under a flag of truce and with a letter of introduction from myself and my wife, your armies could wait there for a few days while I determine how many of Sopan's own forces can be spared to join them. Rocky Run will not be able to support the army alone, but the time your forces are waiting could be spent in building the town up as a military encampment, perhaps establishing a bridge to speed the transport of soldiers and equipment eastward. Take the time to establish supply lines, a temporary headquarters, and whatever else might be needed for when Sopan's contribution to the war effort arrives. We probably need some time to adjust our formations to best incorporate my Human and your Dwarven armies together before sending them to the front, and that would make an excellent staging area."

"But—" El'Athras started, though stopped when Maelgyn raised his hand.

"I need no reinforcements in Sopan, but I would nevertheless take representatives from both your and Gyato's armies as an honor guard, and I'd like you to accompany me. Large enough to be impressive, but not so large that my people will view it as a threat before they learn of the new treaties. Say... about a score of Gyato's infantry. From you, I think three packs of Wolf Riders, one each from the three different brigades. I'll also want two platoons each of combat engineers, Llama Riders, and Archers. And... I think I'll take Spearmaster Wangdu, yourself, Doctor Wodtke, my wife, and El'Ba's son Tur'Ba as well. I'd prefer Gyato accompanied me as well, but someone needs to lead the bulk of the army – meaning the rest of his regiment and whatever you've determined Mar'Tok can spare – to Rocky Run, and set up camp there."

The Dwarf grimaced. "Gyato will be displeased. He wanted to be with you when you arrive in Sopan."

"I'll talk to him about it. I need someone I can trust with the leadership of the main force," Maelgyn noted, "And someone who can handle any diplomatic incidents which may occur. That leaves either him or you. Gyato's not military, but he has been raised to rule and probably knows a thing or two about leadership and diplomacy. He's also a Nekoji, and therefore will almost certainly have the ability to keep up with any army without additional training. I'll take his second, the female Nekoji with him at our earlier meeting, into Sopan as his representative."

El'Athras sighed, but nodded. "I wanted a show of strength from Gyato and myself to allow the people of Sopan to see how valuable an ally we are, but your plan has its merits. Very well,

I will make the arrangements. Even with the army already mustered, it will take us a day to get everything set up, but by morning your escort should be ready to leave. I'll have llamas prepared for you and your wife."

"Thank you, El'Athras," Maelgyn said, then hesitated. "May I ask you an entirely unrelated question, sir?"

"You're my boss now – don't call me sir," El'Athras shot back sharply. "And of course you can ask a question. I just reserve the right not to answer."

"Euleilla is a commoner," the Sword Prince began, "And commoner-royal marriages, as I'm sure you're aware from your association with Uwelain, generally aren't very popular in Svieda. There's a chance that, when the news gets out about our marriage, we'll have riots in the streets."

El'Athras raised an eyebrow. "Aye, that's possible. My read on things is that it's unlikely, given the current crisis with Sho'Curlas, but I wouldn't call it an impossibility."

"Well," Maelgyn sighed. "How do you deal with it? I mean, you had to expect that your relationship wasn't going to be very well liked when it comes out to the public. Euleilla and I are going to have to learn to deal with this same kind of trouble, as well. I just want to know... how do you manage to keep it from being too much of a stress on your relationship?"

"I'm still not quite sure," the Dwarf said wistfully. "The best advice I can give is to ignore what you can, and laugh at the rest. Truth be told, you'll have that same stress no matter who you marry or take as a lover – you'll always have to worry about whether the public will like them or not. So what if your wife has the additional disadvantage of being born a commoner? I'm honestly not sure why that would make any difference, anyway."

Maelgyn frowned. El'Athras made it sound so simple, but he knew better than that. If he didn't defend himself in the court of public opinion, the chances were that his enemies would paint a picture of him to the uneducated masses that could lead to rebellion.

"I was hoping for a bit more," he finally said.

"I can't give you more," the Dwarf said. "There's no advice I can give which will be of any help to you. You'll have to try and solve some of these issues on your own, friend Maelgyn, but I believe you are up to the task."

"Well, thanks for the vote of confidence. I'm not as convinced as you seem to be," Maelgyn sighed. "I'm not sure if the people of my province would have given me an easy welcome even if I *wasn't* showing up married to a commoner. I can only guess how they'll react now."

"Relax," El'Athras said. "At this point, it's really out of your control. I gather you're wondering if divorcing or dissolving your marriage would help things?"

"No!" Maelgyn snapped. "I wouldn't do that. Not just for my sake, at any rate, but if things are too hard for Euleilla...."

"Trust me," El'Athras sighed, understanding. "It's already too late for you to do anything to make it 'easier' on her or 'safer' for her... or for you. Yes, some people might hate her for marrying you, but dissolve your marriage and the scandal will likely result in her being persecuted for the rest of her life. On your end, the very people who might hate her will still hate you for abandoning her, and the people who might have supported you in your decision to marry her will be disappointed in you."

"Even if the... unusual circumstances of our marriage were explained?"

"Even then," El'Athras said. Then he smiled toothily. "I'm afraid you're stuck with her."

Maelgyn laughed, half in relief and half in nervousness. "Well, good. I think she'll make me a fine wife, despite the 'problems' of her birth. Being 'stuck with her' isn't that bad. When Arnach or Brode become king – for I'm sure it'll be one of them – I think I'll retire to Sopan province, and hopefully get her accepted there."

"Oh, I'm sure you can manage that, should you be able to retire to Sopan," El'Athras said. "But I'm still hoping you'll wind up the Sword King of Svieda. After all, I'm investing quite a lot of effort in giving you the tools needed to win the war in Sho'Curlas, and I suspect you'd be good at employing them."

Maelgyn shook his head. "Brode and Arnach are both much better at tactics and strategy than I, at least if our relative skills at games of strategy are any indication. They would know how to lead you properly, rest assured of that."

El'Athras shrugged. "I suppose. I still feel you will treat my fellow Dwarves better, in the long run, than either of those two. After all," he grinned, "You're asking me for advice. That's more than most in your position would do."

"Well, don't start making plans for my coronation yet," Maelgyn said. "To be honest, I fully expect that by the time I get my armies to the front of battle, one of my cousins will already be king." He considered for a moment before nodding, "Probably Arnach. Arnach VII, Sword King of Svieda. Or maybe Brode IX. But I seriously doubt there'll ever be a Maelgyn I."

"You never know," the Dwarf said. "I never believed that I would be named a Merchant Prince, much less that I would ever become the leader of the Free Dwarves. Or that I would use that power to become a Count of Svieda."

"The first Count of Svieda, as a matter of fact," Maelgyn laughed. "But you're going to have to name a choice for another Count, to leave as your regent while you're gone. And you'll have to do it before we leave – you don't happen to have anyone in mind, do you?"

"No," El'Athras said. "I hadn't even thought of it, to be honest. Who's eligible under Sviedan law?"

"Anyone who lives within the borders of your province, unless otherwise ineligible by the local laws. Once he is named, however, the title remains in his line, and his descendents will be your regents as well. If he dies, it will be your responsibility to locate his heir or, should he not have an heir, to designate a new regent."

"Well, I've yet to establish a set of local laws that would make anyone ineligible," El'Athras laughed. "Hmm... maybe I should name that innkeeper – El'Ba, I believe Wodtke said his name was – to the position. He seems to have a good head on his shoulders in a crisis, and it might tweak the noses of those idiot clan heads, now wouldn't it?"

"Probably," Maelgyn agreed. "If he'll take the job."

"Oh, he'll take the job," the Dwarf snorted. "I'll make sure of it."

Chapter 17

"I can't believe you managed to rope me into this," El'Ba sighed. It was his final meeting with the "royal entourage" which was being assembled around Maelgyn: Wangdu, Euleilla, Doctor Wodtke, Tur'Ba, and, of course, El'Athras. "I'm just an innkeeper, after all, and you're sticking me with the job of rebuilding the entire Dwarven government from scratch!"

"Not from scratch," El'Athras laughed. "After all, you've got Sviedan Code to consider."

"Oh, right," El'Ba snorted. "A multi-tiered system. Under the lord of the province is the lord regent, who rules in the lord's absence. There must be a court system independent of the nobility. There must be a council of barons, who receive their titles through inheritance. There must be a representative council of civilians, who must be given at least the power to veto legislation. That's a lot to go on."

"Well, given that we Dwarves have managed just fine since the death of King Tur'Ma with a broken government, I figure you'll manage to come up with something that doesn't screw us up too badly," El'Athras noted. "Besides, you'll have help. I have appointed you an aide.... What was his name? That loyal blacksmith who braved the rioters to deliver me Maelgyn's message. Tur'Ne, I think it was? He should be able to give you all the help you need."

"Of all the people you could have appointed to help me with this task, why him? Tur'Ne is loyal, yes, and he's a good friend, but he's just a blacksmith, and barely out of his childhood," El'Ba growled. "What does he know about politics?"

"Exactly," the other Dwarf laughed. "He'll have all of the strength, vigor, and impetuousness to implement anything you want done, without all the usual hang-ups from most of the career politicians who I might have otherwise chosen. You've got the wisdom and knowledge gained by running a successful business for over a hundred years on your own. Together, you'll make a great team. Besides, you'll still have my entire advisory staff to help you, as well."

"Bah," the new Regent finally said. "Whatever. Just get out of here before I change my mind and turn down the job."

As El'Ba marched away towards his new home inside the freshly dubbed "Count's Estate," Maelgyn turned to the building's past and future tenant, El'Athras. "Hmm," he considered as he mounted his llama. "How did you convince him to take the job, anyway?"

"I didn't. I told his wife that, if she wanted to live in a nice big mansion with servants at her beck and call rather than live as the cook at a small, drafty inn that will be closed down while the riot damage was repaired, she'd better convince him to take the job for me."

"Good plan, that," Maelgyn said, restraining a smile from appearing on his face while he took the reins of his mount.

"Be warned," El'Athras advised as he climbed onto his own llama. "A wife is a powerful tool as a weapon in politics. The problem is that weapon works both ways. A good woman is a strength in difficult time, yes, but they can also be a weakness."

"Athy, dear," Wodtke chirped sweetly. "Don't fill the young prince's head with nonsense, okay?"

"But I was just telling him the truth!" El'Athras protested. "I was just saying that women are a very effective weapon against their men. Not always because they're being used, mind you, but if they, for whatever reason, decided they wanted something... well, any woman can be a danger to their lover, even the most loyal of them."

"Indeed," Euleilla agreed. "I could be, although I assure you I'll be a most loyal danger."

Maelgyn raised an eyebrow. "And just how could you be a weapon against me?" he asked.

Euleilla stared at him pointedly. Her smile, which Maelgyn had long missed during her period of illness, tweaked up on her face.

"Oh," said Maelgyn, his cheeks burning.The journey to the border of Sopan was significantly shorter than Maelgyn had anticipated, though it did take some time. The llamas, while they lacked the burst speed of a horse, definitely showed themselves to be at least as fast over the long haul. A journey he had anticipated lasting a week on foot took less than a day, and Maelgyn had a hard time believing he could have done that even on a horse. Overall, he was rather glad to have won the support of the Dwarves.

He was significantly less pleased with the Sopan Province Army that now surrounded him. Since crossing the border, they had been gradually travelling to Sopan castle using well-travelled roads, and any passing travelers were informed of his coming, but it seemed his armies had yet to hear of his arrival. Maelgyn had expected that his "escort" might be taken as a threat, but that didn't make him any happier to be right.

"Show the sign of truce," Maelgyn ordered. "They don't know who we are, yet."

As the order passed from man to man, tall leafy branches painted white – the ancient symbol of a parley request – rose above the heads of Dwarf and Nekoji warrior alike. The Sopan forces surrounding them came to a halt, and after a few minutes three men on horseback, each in well-crafted armor, came forward to meet the parley.

Maelgyn eyed their armor critically, assessing it for signs of their rank. Some types of armor were generally inexpensive in Human lands – thanks to the relative abundance of magic, iron or steel armor could be mass produced for little more than the cost of the raw materials. That armor, however, was not the best available. Magic might be able to enhance some qualities of steel, but magical mass production typically lacked the quality of workmanship which custom smithing could produce. Furthermore, mages could not fashion cheap armor out of the materials often used *against* mages, such as bronze plate. The armor the three men were wearing did not have any magical enhancements to improve the quality of steel or the fit of the joints, but it was some of the best that could be produced without blending both magic and true smithing skills. It was steel armor, however, which suggested that it had not been purchased to prevent magical attacks, but rather to demonstrate affluence.

Maelgyn noted that they showed other signs of great wealth as well. Obviously, he was being greeted by some of the barony, or at least members of the wealthier set of the aristocracy. There were no obvious symbols to indicate which barony they ruled on their coats, and for that Maelgyn was grateful.

In Svieda, unlike some of the older Human kingdoms such as Poros or Squire's Knot, the provincial governments issued relatively inexpensive armor to any member of the army as required: Leather armor (better against mages and more mobile, but less effective against swords and arrows) for the foot soldiers and steel (poor against mages, but otherwise significantly better defensively) for the officers. However, many of the wealthier officers, especially those in the barony, purchased their own custom-built armor instead. Maelgyn had mixed emotions about the practice. True, it relieved some burden on his own treasury, and it provided officers with more safety and a better fit, but usually the nobles Maelgyn had seen with their own armor eschewed Svieda's colors in favor of their own crests. He always felt the Barons should have to wear the same colors as their men, and he was glad to see that at least these three did.

"Greetings," one of the three barons said, addressing El'Athras. "To what do we owe the pleasure of your, shall we say, unexpected visit?"

"Well, we're merely escorting a member of the royalty for our new allies," the Dwarf explained, looking a little amused.

"Allies?" the Baron snorted. "Who? Is some member of the Caseificio Imperial Family in your company?"

"While the Caseificio is also part of the alliance and some of their representatives are a part of this party, none of the Imperial family are with us," El'Athras chuckled. "However, His Highness, the Sword Prince Maelgyn, Duke of Sopan – your liege lord – is. I should add that, thanks to His Highness, you are now addressing the Count of the Sviedan Province of Mar'Tok. Caseificio is now a County of Svieda as well, and therefore there is no more Imperial family for Caseificio. Our alliance was more of a merger of our kingdoms, you see, and I figured it would be best if we provided an armed escort for our new Prince."

The Baron's eyes widened. "Sword Prince Maelgyn? Here?"

"Um, greetings," Maelgyn said, finally making his presence

known. Realizing how awkward that overly casual greeting sounded, he drew the heirloom sword of his rank, and presented it in a formal salute. "I'm afraid I'm a bit unfamiliar with my own Council of Barons. May I ask who I'm addressing?"

"We knew you were coming, my lord, but we never expected... that is, we didn't know you had been in talks with the Dwarves," the nobleman answered, looking suddenly out of his element when he recognized the katana. He looked in askance at El'Athras, but then collected himself to make formal introductions. "Please, My Lord, let us escort you – and the, uh, new Count – to your capital. I am Baron Yergwain, Colonel in charge of the First Infantry Regiment and acting as the General of your First Division. My companions are Baron Mathrid, Colonel of the First Cavalry, and the Honorable Sir Leno, my brother, who is also the Colonel in charge of the First Archers."

"They may not need our aid, brother," the one Yergwain had introduced as Sir Leno said. "My lord, am I correct in thinking you are a mage? And one of significant power, too, if what I have heard is true."

"No, you aren't mistaken," Maelgyn laughed. "Although power is a relative term."

"Yes, indeed," Leno agreed, nodding. Then he noticed Euleilla and her ever-present cloud of magic powder. "You seem to have another in your company, as well. A powerful one, from that display."

Maelgyn coughed slightly. "Yes, well... that would be my wife."

All three barons froze. "Wife?" Mathrid finally blurted out. "I had not heard you were married, nor even courting, my lord."

"I wasn't," the prince sighed wryly, shaking his head. "At least, not as of the last time a courier was able to pass here. Which reminds me – I have what is probably the latest batch of mail from Largo and eastwards. We may not get another shipment for some time, thanks to the war closing our sea lanes."

"Mathrid," Yergwain snapped. "Arrange for the mail to be distributed as soon as possible. Now, my lord, I'm afraid I don't understand. Our last message from you arrived less than two months ago. How is it possible that you've gone from 'not courting' to 'married' in such a short space of time?"

Maelgyn fumbled for an answer, but Euleilla responded

before he could. "It was... unintentional," she said. "Maelgyn had need to travel incognito, and I was to be part of a cover story. Unfortunately, he was unfamiliar with the Largo law which states that, when two people register in the same room as one another, they are married by common law."

"My lady?" Yergwain said, shifting uncomfortably on his saddle. "If what you say is true, then your marriage is merely a legal technicality. Surely you can get it annulled, if you so wish...."

"Following that event," Maelgyn said, now that the ice was broken. "We began courting, since it would take some time to make the arrangements if we decided to dissolve the marriage. It seemed churlish to do less, given the awkward situation I had placed her in. Since then she has won a place in my heart, and so I will not request an annulment."

Mathrid was the one looking most uncomfortable at that statement. "Er... is she a noble, my lord?"

Maelgyn frowned, allowing his displeasure to show through at the question. "Does it really matter? She has stood by me through hardship and mortal peril, lending me her strength and her love. I trust you will forgive me if I find the nobility of my wife's birth a less momentous concern for our nation than I might have before Svieda's king was assassinated and our castle overrun."

"In any other nation," Mathrid snapped, "this would not be tolerated at all. In a time of war like this, even we cannot afford to have the distraction of your marrying a commoner to add to our problems. The nobility, myself included, are... uncomfortable about those of the royal blood marrying outside of their class. The diplomatic consequences could be substantial, as well."

"What's all this about marriages between royalty and commoners not being tolerated outside of Svieda?" El'Athras snorted. "I would never have protested such a thing. Nor would the former Emperor Gyato."

Mathrid frowned. "You... are not a foreign power, any more. But Oregal, Bandi, Poros, Squire's Knot – none of those nations would accept the legitimacy of such a marriage."

Wangdu laughed. "Well, I'm from Squire's Knot, I am, and I accept it, I do. I think you're mistaken, I do. And I am rather well acquainted with Lady Phalra of the Bandi Republic, I am, and she would be rather hypocritical to protest such a thing, she would."

"Well, that is to say—"

"I find nothing wrong with it," Leno broke in. "Anyone who is as powerful a mage as this woman is would be an asset to any throne, and Maelgyn will do well to keep her."

"Thank you," Euleilla interjected at last, acknowledging the young man. "Your own skill in magic is an asset to your barony, as well."

Leno laughed, though he looked uncomfortable at the mention. "Milady is much too kind. I don't hold a candle to yourself or your husband."

"But—" Mathrid protested.

"Enough!" Yergwain snapped. "Lord Mathrid, remember your place. Is it your intent to make your liege lord and these dignitaries stand here all afternoon in the dirt while you lambast them? There are channels for such protests, but this most assuredly is not one of them. Now, gather those letters and parcels so we may distribute them properly, as I asked you to earlier!"

Mathrid stiffened. "Very well, milord. I will see to it right away."

As he left to tend to the mail, Yergwain sighed. "I am sorry, my Lord Maelgyn, but he is a strict traditionalist. I shall see to it he does not continue to bother you."

Maelgyn sighed. "Thank you, Lord Yergwain, but don't worry – I was expecting some of this. To be honest, I don't have time to worry about everyone who might be upset at my choice of wife. Svieda has been invaded, our navy has been shattered at sea, and we must act. I will need to talk to Lord Valfarn at once. It's taken me far too long to get here, even if it was faster than I feared, and I'm afraid I'm not as familiar with the tactical situation here as I should be."

"Of course, my lord. Leno, inform Lord Mathrid that we must move as soon as possible. I want us to be in Sopan Castle by nightfall."

"Of course, brother," Leno nodded, turning in the direction Mathrid had fled.

"If you'll excuse me, My Prince," Yergwain said, bowing his head in Maelgyn's direction, "I must ready my own force to move."

The baron rode off, leaving the men and women who had

accompanied Maelgyn staring off after him.

"That went better than I hoped," Maelgyn sighed.

"Better?" Doctor Wodtke scoffed incredulously. "One of them insulted your wife and damn near said she belonged at the same level as dirt. Another seemed to regard the Dwarves as worse than dirt! How is that better than you thought?"

"To start with, I was worried that they might think me an imposter and Mar'Tok's presence an act of war," Maelgyn noted. "Just being the man who holds the Sword is hardly enough for some. At least Sir Leno appeared... comfortable with everything."

"True," Wodtke agreed reluctantly. "I suppose I was just expecting a more pleasant greeting. This is my first time in the Human world in several years."

"Eh, don't judge them too harshly, love," El'Athras sighed. "These are just underlings. Wait until we see what kind of greeting Lord Valfarn gives us – it's his job to be the hospitable one. These boys were all military, and their job isn't to make pleasant greetings. Rather, it was to see if we deserved a pleasant greeting, or an... unpleasant one."

Euleilla frowned in thought, but it had nothing to do with concerns about their reception. "Like you, Maelgyn, Sir Leno's more powerful than he thinks," she warned. "Let us hope he, at least, continues to think we deserve pleasant greetings."

"A man shouldn't be kept waiting to enter his own Royal Hall," Maelgyn complained, fussing with his shirt. It was the first time since the days before Gilbereth was assassinated that he had worn formalwear, and he had grown rather accustomed to the simple garb he had used to travel in.

"It's just a bloody ceremony," El'Athras pointed out, though he didn't look any happier about it. He and Wangdu, both waiting to accompany Maelgyn to his introduction to the Ducal Court, had also been dressed in some rather uncomfortable formalwear by the castle steward for the ceremony. "You'll have to get used to them. Once this shindig's complete, you'll be too involved in the war for anyone to worry about formal affairs like this. Besides, it's giving your wife time to dress for the occasion."

"Hah!" Maelgyn snorted. "And that's another thing. Back in the royal court, I had a wardrobe full of clothing that may have been formal, but at least was comfortable to wear. Why do I have to wear this... this... mat of thistles!"

"It was the best we could find that fit you on short notice, your highness," one of the attending guards suggested cautiously. "It's not that bad."

Maelgyn sent him a dark glare before once again fidgeting with his shirt. He was so absorbed in the uncomfortable cut of his clothes that he didn't notice that the girls had returned until he heard several men - El'Athras and Wangdu among them - gasp.

He turned to look, and was stunned into silence at what he saw. For the first time since he'd met her, Euleilla was wearing something other than her leather armor and oddly colored vest. He figured there was no way she could have picked the dress she was wearing alone, in fact, since the color complemented her hair and skin tone perfectly. It was a deep burgundy, cut to expose a hint of cleavage without being improper, with a few gold accents drawing attention to the plunging neckline. It was very... regal, and for the first time Maelgyn realized just how well she was going to fit into her new role as a Princess Consort.

It took him a moment to notice, however, that she looked quite uncertain about where she was, and that she didn't seem to have her usual cloud of magic dust around her. He frowned.

"Milady," he said with a regal air, walking over to her. "Do you need an escort?"

Euleilla smiled at him, curtseying daintily. "Thank you, husband. I'd love one." As he took her arm, she whispered to him, "I'm okay for eating dinner at the banquet after the ceremony, but I'm going to have a little trouble maneuvering the table in this thing without my magic dust until then. Dr. Wodtke assured me you could help, however."

"Don't worry," he answered. "We'll manage." With a gentle tug, Maelgyn lead her to a nearby bench and sat her down. "What's bothering me is the wait. But I suppose you might be able to help me stave off boredom until Valfarn is ready to see us."

Euleilla smiled at him. "Maybe."

When he realized that was all she was going to say, Maelgyn chuckled. "Back to your usual self, huh?"

"Yeah," she answered.

"Well, that's fine. I can enjoy silence, too."

"Really?" she replied, sounding amused.

"Yes," Maelgyn answered. "Though I'd rather have something to distract me from my uncomfortable formal outfit, in this case. Silence is most enjoyable when there's nothing else to worry about."

Euleilla laughed good-naturedly. "Very well. Perhaps, if you were to explain to me just how this ceremony we are about to participate in works, it may help distract you."

"I'm a trifle curious about that, myself," El'Athras, a formally-dressed Dr. Wodtke on his arm, agreed. "I mean, I'm not sure where I fit in on all this."

"You don't," Maelgyn said to the Dwarf. "Provided I manage to hold my end of the ceremony, that is. If I fail, you will be received as any visiting Sword would – assuming your Countship is recognized – and invited to a formal dinner by the Regent. If I succeed, well, then I will formally invite you to the dinner myself."

"Either way, I get to eat," El'Athras laughed. "Well, that doesn't sound too bad."

"But you, Euleilla, may have a bit more of a role," he said, turning his attention to his wife. "This ceremony is mandated by the Law of Swords. Specifically the Fourth Law of Ascension, which was written to limit the powers a Sword may have should he prove to be... unsatisfactory. It says that when a Sword first takes his seat in his Duchy, he is required to obtain the approval of either his Regent, his Council of Barons, or of the peasantry. If he fails to receive the approval of at least one of those three, he may never rule the Duchy and must appeal to the other Swords to remain in the line of Royal Ascension.

"To comply with this law, Sopan Province created three formal ceremonies – the Introduction to the Regent, the Introduction to the Barons, and the Introduction to the Peasantry. Should the Introduction to the Regent fail to go well, we will then have to move on to first the Introduction to the Barons and then the Introduction to the Peasantry. I think only three Swords of Sopan have failed to receive the Regent's approval, but all three of them also failed the other Introductions as well."

"And my role would be?" Euleilla asked.

"The Regent will ask me a set of questions designed to determine my fitness," Maelgyn explained. "As you are my wife, he may also ask questions of you. If he is unhappy with the answers, he will either request that we correct any problem he finds and then submit to his Introduction again, or he may direct us to attend the Introduction to the Barons. While it's important to give honest answers to Valfarn, it would be... unwise... to say something which may upset him."

Euleilla cocked her head at him. "I never deliberately insult anyone, but I will be myself. If he finds what I say upsetting, then it is his fault."

Maelgyn sighed. "I would never ask you any more than that, but you need to know —"

Another guard came out of the double doors leading into the throne room. "Milord Valfarn is ready to see you, now."

Maelgyn winced. There were several things which he still needed to explain to Euleilla. This was something he should have discussed with her earlier, but it hadn't occured to him until he was already there waiting for Valfarn's summons. She didn't know how to act in front of a lord: She had never acted properly in front of him despite knowing that he was one of the Swords, and from the moment she had met him she treated him as one commoner might another. He had never cared before, first because he had been trying to maintain a low profile and then because, well, he'd married her and that level of informality was expected, but now she was being presented before a peer of the realm who likely wouldn't disregard improper behavior.

Well, there wasn't time to explain things, now.

He stood up, once more laced his arm with Euleilla's, and nodded. "It's time."

Chapter 18

To Maelgyn's surprise, the room Valfarn received them in was a fairly ordinary room. It was worthy of the title 'Great Hall' thanks to its size, that was certain, but it wasn't nearly as artistically or functionally constructed as the ones in his father's castle in Rubick or in Svieda Castle. It looked as if it would get cold in the winter months, and Maelgyn could already tell that it was getting to be stuffy as summer approached. Sopan Castle, overall, actually looked older than any of the Sviedan-built castles Maelgyn could remember. As he continued to survey the room out of the corner of his eyes, Maelgyn quickly discovered why. Porosian artistic reliefs in the stonework told of the age of the castle – at least sixteen hundred years, given his knowledge of history. Likely older, given how many centuries it had been since Poros had dominated the region now known as Sopan.

Valfarn was an older lord, well past his prime. There was still strength in him, however, and Maelgyn approved of him at first glance. The old Duke reminded him of his swordmaster back in Svieda Castle, a pleasant man who had a hidden ferocity when the need arose. However, those similarities were no proof that Valfarn would treat Maelgyn the same way.

Along each wall, several members of the Council of Barons stood from their ceremonial seats, flanked by their personal armsmen. Even though Maelgyn had been told that some of the barons were unable to attend, the room still felt overly full. Especially with Euleilla, El'Athras, Dr. Wodtke, Tur'Ba, Wangdu, and a Nekoji woman by the name of Onayari representing Gyato's forces accompanying him.

Onayari had been present during the signing of the treaty in Mar'Tok, showing up at El'Athras' estate off and on since the riots had been quelled. She and Euleilla had quickly become friends, but there was something odd about her that disturbed Maelgyn. Euleilla agreed that Onayari felt odd, but didn't elaborate as to why. Nevertheless, Onayari was the perfect Nekoji to represent her people before the Sopan court, as she had been an ambassador to several Human countries during her life.

When everyone else was standing, Valfarn nodded to the new arrivals. "My lord, before I rise from this seat and offer it to you, I have questions which must be answered," he intoned ceremonially.

Maelgyn replied somewhat stiffly, barely remembering the proper wording. "I stand here to offer proof of my abilities for that seat. I will answer any inquiries and perform any tasks you deem required of a lord, swearing on my honor to speak and act truthfully."

Valfarn nodded slightly. "Very well. First, I must ask – do you truly carry the Sword?"

In answer, Maelgyn drew the antique katana that symbolized his station, bringing it into a formal salute. "I carry the blade forged for the founders of Our Kingdom, the symbol of our strength and the proof of my birthright."

"Do you know our laws in Sopan and Svieda, and are you willing to answer the call to enforce them?"

This was a tricky question, for there were several answers and Sword could give. It was one thing Maelgyn knew might prove a problem for him, because he could not truthfully give the strongest answer. Instead he gave one which he knew could delay his seating as the Duke, if Valfarn so chose.

"The laws of Svieda are well known to me," Maelgyn acknowledged. "But the laws of Sopan are not. My dominion over this province may require your continued aid."

Valfarn nodded. "This is no surprise, and should you take this seat I will remain to aide you in those matters. Will you defend our borders against all invaders, to the best of your ability?"

Again, there were several answers Maelgyn could give that would allow him to continue the ceremony, but he had the right to use the strongest answer this time.

"This Sword has already tasted blood by my hand in the

defense of Svieda. I will continue to use it in the defense of Sopan Province while I still rule," he stated.

"Very well," Valfarn replied, then sat back in his chair and steepled his fingertips in front of him. The required questions had been asked, but a regent was entitled to three more that Maelgyn could neither anticipate nor refuse to answer. To Maelgyn's surprise, his marriage was not the first topic of discussion.

"On whose authority did you enter into treaty with the nations of Caseificio and Mar'Tok?"

"On my own," the Sword Prince replied. "In a time where there is no living king, any Sword may act in his place in foreign affairs. I am sure you are aware of Sword King Gilbereth II's death, and to the best of my knowledge the Law of Swords is still in effect."

"Very well," Valfarn nodded. "Now, I may ask two more questions, but I choose to ask them of your wife. I have heard of your unexpected marriage, which was unsanctioned by the King or any other Sword. I wish to determine her fitness, so I ask her to step forward now."

If Euleilla was surprised at being called upon, she didn't show it. With a somewhat awkward curtsey, she presented herself before the raised dais upon which the Ducal Seat resided.

"My lord?" she prompted.

"My lady," he replied. "While the laws allow a Sword to marry whomever he wills, all tradition goes against the marriage between a Sword and a commoner. There are always exceptions to these unwritten rules, however. You are not a noblewoman by birth, my lady, but I ask if there are any men or women of note in your bloodline?"

"No," she stated proudly.

Maelgyn hesitated, and then stepped up beside her. "My lord, while my wife may not be aware of any notables in her bloodline, I would like to remind the peerage that blood isn't everything. She has, since the age of twelve, been fostered by a man who would surely have been made a peer of the realm had the crown not incorrectly believed him dead."

"Oh?" Valfarn said, surprised. That was news not just to the Duke, but also to all present in the chamber. Even Euleilla looked a little surprised at that. "I'm afraid, my Lord, that statement on her behalf will require more information."

Maelgyn nodded. "Certainly, Milord Valfarn. The Hero of the Flight of Borden Isle, Admiral Ruznak, is alive, and has been the foster father for my wife for the last several years."

Murmurs arose from the Barony, clearly surprised at this news. Euleilla had regained her composure, but Maelgyn was able to feel a certain tenseness in her muscles which was not normally there.

"That, milord," Valfarn acknowledged, "is indeed a pedigree worth noting, and sufficient in my opinion. Now I only have one remaining question for your wife: Please, milady... let me see your eyes."

There was a pause, but Maelgyn knew right away that this would be a disaster. Anger showed on Euleilla's face – an expression she had never demonstrated in his presence, before – and her magic was practically crackling around her. Thankfully, there was no way of seeing that force unless you were also a mage, but its presence told Maelgyn enough to realize that he was in trouble.

"No," she answered coldly, and the entire Barony gasped.

Valfarn raised an eyebrow. "Did you say... no?"

Maelgyn swallowed, and finally recovered his voice. "Forgive her, my lord," he said, trembling slightly. "I am aware of why she has declined, and it is understandable. She is not from Sopan Province, and is unaware of the protocol for this ceremony. Please, allow me to explain it to her."

Valfarn merely nodded.

"Maelgyn," Euleilla whispered, "I won't do it. He has no right—"

"He has every right," Maelgyn sighed. "In this case, you must answer his questions."

"But—"

"Do you want to be my wife?" he asked desperately.

That brought her up short. Slowly, she nodded. "Yes, I do."

"Then you have to show him," Maelgyn explained. When Euleilla did nothing to protest, he smiled sadly at her. She would have to show her eyes, but maybe he could make it more comfortable for her. "Milord Valfarn," he called.

"Yes, Milord Maelgyn?"

Maelgyn straightened his stance, and in his most commanding tone, ordered, "Clear the room."

Baron Mathrid, unable to restrain himself, stepped forward. "What is the point of this? All Lord Valfarn wants is to see the eyes of the girl. Why is that such an issue?"

Maelgyn raised an eyebrow. "Baron Mathrid, the right to protect a secret has customarily been granted in these inquiries. In order to show her eyes, my wife will have to also display something she would rather be kept hidden."

"Like what?" Mathrid protested. "A tattoo on her forehead, perhaps?"

Maelgyn stiffened at that, although Euleilla didn't seem to know what he was talking about. A certain tattoo on someone's forehead could indicate any number of crimes, and the implication that she was a criminal disgusted him.

"Never," he snapped. "There are no tattoos on my wife's forehead – this I swear."

"Mathrid," Valfarn warned, looking thoughtful. "Leave us. The rest of you, as well. If what she is hiding is something I feel should be explained, trust me, I will explain it."

"Milord!" Mathrid exclaimed.

"Mathrid!" Maelgyn barked, his voice frosty. "If you continue to impugn the honor of my wife, then I assure you things will not be pleasant for you should my claim to the Dukedom of Sopan be upheld."

Mathrid opened his mouth to reply, and then closed it. "My apologies, my lord," he finally said. "I do not mean to offend you, or your wife. I merely wish to know that the ones who are put into lordship over me and my people are truly the ones who should lead us."

"That, Mathrid, is why I am here," Valfarn said. "Now, if you'll excuse us."

One by one, the barons slowly filed out of the room. Mathrid was the last to leave, sending a fierce glare back over his shoulder, but he left as well.

Maelgyn glanced over his shoulder, noticing El'Athras and the remaining representatives of the new alliance were still present. "Gentlemen, I asked for the room to be cleared. That includes you, my friends."

"We respect your privacy, we do," Wangdu agreed. "And never let it be said otherwise."

The Elf led the others back out of the Great Hall, taking

Onayari on his arm courteously. Finally, the doors closed behind them, leaving Maelgyn and Euleilla alone in the large chamber with Valfarn. The older lord leaned back in the chair and smiled darkly.

"All right, so what was such an important secret that even your own friends may not know it? After all, they are only eyes, aren't they?"

"Why?" Euleilla asked, voice trembling – with fear or anger, Maelgyn couldn't tell.

"Why what?"

"Why do you want to see them?"

Valfarn shrugged. "Originally, I had no other real questions. Your hair, however, irritates me – I want to push it aside, and see what's beneath. Now, however, I am quite curious about this secret."

Euleilla laughed sadly. "I'm afraid the secret is that I cannot show you my eyes."

"What? But you agreed—"

"Because I no longer have eyes," she explained, lifting her hair.

Valfarn stared at the scars, looking momentarily ill. "Dear god... what happened to you?"

"I was attacked," she explained. "Twice. Once for each eye, by two different individuals."

"Who?" he exclaimed.

When she didn't answer after a minute, Maelgyn answered for her. "An assassin for a mining conglomerate attacked her father, an alchemist working for a rival business. There was an explosion, and the blast... well, let's just say that took care of the first eye."

"And the second?"

Maelgyn winced. "I said her foster father was Admiral Ruznak, and that, milord, is true. However... he is her second foster father. Her first, an old friend of her father's, was a violent drunk on a fairly regular basis after the news of her father's passing. One night... if an approximately ninety-year old Admiral Ruznak hadn't still been in fighting shape, she might have had worse injuries than blindness."

Valfarn nodded. "I can see why you might want to hide your scars, milady Euleilla, but you cannot keep it hidden forever.

Soon, someone will notice that you are not able to see."

"I can keep it hidden," she said. "For, even without eyes, I am not blind."

"How?" the elder lord exclaimed doubtfully.

Maelgyn sighed, and pulled from a hidden pocket in his robes a bag full of magic powder. "Here," he said. "Show him."

"Fine," she said, dumping out the contents of the pouch. Around her a slow spiraling stream of the iron dust formed.

Valfarn's eyes widened. "You're a mage!"

"Indeed," she said, smiling enigmatically.

"A powerful one," Maelgyn noted. "Not certified, but I will attest that she is a First Rate. I've only encountered one mage who might have been more powerful, and that was that accursed Prince Hussack of Sho'Curlas – who held off the entire Svieda Castle Guard, singlehanded."

"But... how can magic help her see?" he asked, confused. "I understood it could only be used to affect metallic elements, and only some of those."

"I do not see," she answered. "I am merely not blind."

"She can sense latent magic," Maelgyn explained. "And anything else magic might effect. Also, through the use of magic powder, she can feel most of the area around her. She has... problems... in some situations, such as heavy wind or rain. It takes more of her concentration to 'see' when something is blowing against or tamping down her magic powder. In most cases, however, she can 'see' better than you or I can."

Valfarn nodded slowly. "I understand. But still, that doesn't explain why you wish to keep it so secret. Are you truly willing to defy the entire council of barons and myself to do it?"

Maelgyn turned to see Euleilla's answer, himself, not really sure of her mind on this.

"I do not want to be judged on my eyesight or lack thereof," she stated. "The people and barons of this land will grant me whatever respect they have without knowing of my blindness, or that respect will be tainted in my mind."

Valfarn gave an understanding nod. "Then you won't be judged upon it." He stood up, and stepped down from the chair. "Your Highness, please take your Seat. Sopan Province is yours. Milady, none shall find out your secret from me."

The barons slowly filed back in, accompanied by their

armsmen. Maelgyn noticed that Mathrid looked rather defiant despite an attempt to appear contrite once he saw the Sword Prince on the Seat. On the other hand, the people who had accompanied him from Mar'Tok looked pleased in a smug sort of way. He took it as an encouraging sign that at least those who actually knew him were glad that he was now officially the Duke of Sopan.

Valfarn grinned as the last man entered, and stood before them all. "Lords and Ladies, and those of us who are not so ennobled but otherwise present, I am proud to inform you that Sword Prince Maelgyn has earned the right to be our Lord. As far as his wife's secret goes, she keeps it in honor and integrity, not out of malice. It is something personal to her and her alone, and in my judgment no others should seek to learn it."

Mathrid grimaced. "Milord... why shouldn't we? I still have my doubts as to her fitness. It may not be my place to do anything about it, but surely I can act to allay my own fears?"

"Mathrid," Valfarn sighed. "I have no authority to prevent you from trying. Before you do something that incredibly unwise, however, please remember that Sword Prince Maelgyn is now your liege lord, and he can make life quite unpleasant for you if he feels you are harassing his wife unnecessarily."

"Lord Mathrid," Maelgyn intoned from behind Valfarn. "I believe you do deserve to know this much about my wife's secret: It is not in any way dishonorable, it does not endanger Sopan or Svieda, and it does not reflect on her ability to produce healthy heirs. In essence, it does not deal with anything which you should concern yourself with. If you ever do find out what it is, however, you had best keep it a secret yourself. That is, unless you want to face the highest punishment established for the crime of Insolence to the Duke: A long imprisonment and the removal of your tongue." He paused. "If Euleilla leaves anything left of you to be imprisoned, that is. I warn you, milord, that she's a First Rate mage. It's entirely possible that she'd do something... worse... should she find you invading her privacy, and with my blessing."

Chapter 19

"I don't know why you threatened him," Euleilla whispered to Maelgyn. They were slowly processing, arm in arm, from the Great Hall to the Feast Hall for a ceremonial dinner. "In fact, I think you're being a bit too hard on him. I want to keep my eyes a secret, yes, but I don't believe others should be maimed just to maintain it."

"I didn't make the threat to protect your secret," he replied. "Although that's a good side benefit. No, Mathrid doesn't approve of either of us, I believe. I probably wouldn't really cut out his tongue, but it's best to keep him guessing. I don't want him inciting discontent among the others, and I need him to get used to the idea that a directive from his Duke isn't just a suggestion."

"That sounds a bit ruthless," she noted.

"Well, yes, but it's also practical. As long as I don't overdo it and really start removing tongues, I think it'll be all right."

"Perhaps," she answered, not sounding convinced. Then again, Maelgyn wasn't entirely convinced, himself – he just didn't know what else to do.

"For good or ill," he finally said, "That is how I will deal with him. Unless you have of a better plan, perhaps?"

"Perhaps," she answered again, grinning slyly.

Maelgyn decided he wouldn't ask too many questions about that grin. "Let's not worry about him for now. We have a dinner to attend... and I do not believe Mathrid is going to be at our table to concern us."

Valfarn, who had been standing where he could overhear the

whole conversation, cleared his throat. "No, milord, he won't. However, Baron Yergwain, the current head of the Council of Barons, will be joining the head table instead."

Maelgyn nodded. "Yes, I met him when I arrived. While his treatment of Count El'Athras was unfairly disparaging prior to my introduction, I liked the look of him – although I have no idea what he thinks of all this. He knows enough to keep his tongue, however."

The old regent sighed. "I fear, milord, he's a bit of a traditionalist. He likely disapproves of your marriage, and of the alliance with the Dwarves and Nekoji. However, he's also a loyal warrior, and will respect you and the Count as he would any Sword of the Realm. That said, I doubt he will be a very... pleasant companion, tonight. Especially after your words to Lord Mathrid, who is a close friend of his."

"Sir Leno liked us," Euleilla noted airily.

Valfarn nodded. "That is not unexpected, but Sir Leno is out of favor with his family. They... disapproved of his mother's decision to let him become a mage, and his own decision to keep up the training after she died. He is only serving under his brother – or rather, his half-brother – because he is such an excellent warrior."

Maelgyn raised an eyebrow. He was just about to ask why Yergwain's family disapproved of the mage training when they arrived in the Dining Hall. It could wait.

The head table where Maelgyn sat was smaller than he expected. There was only room for the most important figures in his government – Euleilla, Valfarn, Yergwain, and a Senior Senator from the commoner's council named Gherald.

Tur'Ba wasn't at the dinner; upon learning that the young Dwarf's father had sent him to essentially to be Maelgyn's personal squire, the Chief Steward of the court – a man named Reltney – immediately corralled him so that he could be taught how to properly perform the duties of servant to a Sword of the realm. Maelgyn wasn't entirely sure that particular trade was what El'Ba had in mind for his son, but it would give Tur'Ba a sense of the world without dirtying his hands in war. Most of the other guests Maelgyn had brought with him, including the officers leading the small detachments El'Athras and Onayari had escorted him into Sopan with, were seated in various places around the room. There was one exception, however, which puzzled him.

"Where's Wangdu?" he accidentally said aloud, thinking to himself.

"Who?" Valfarn asked.

"Wangdu. The Elf I had been traveling with," Maelgyn answered.

"Ah," the older Duke replied. "Well, my lord, he is an Elf. Surely you've noticed he doesn't eat the same foods you or I eat? He must prepare them a special way or they're unhealthy for him. Sadly, our kitchen staff was not equipped to serve him properly on such short notice, so he needed to prepare his own food. I fear he will not be joining us this evening, since his dinner won't be ready until after we all have finished."

Maelgyn raised an eyebrow. "I don't like that. I may make one of my first official acts as lord of this castle an order that any dining eventuality be prepared for. It seems prudent given that we've already gained the support of the Dwarves and Nekoji, and have an Elf in our midst as well."

"It has never been an issue in my time of service," Valfarn mused. "Still, I see the wisdom of such a command. A rather mundane first order for a Sword of Svieda in time of war, however."

Maelgyn shrugged. "We all must start somewhere. Where else would you suggest?"

"Perhaps," Senator Gherald hesitantly answered, "We could discuss about something relevant to the war. I believe I'm not the only person to wonder if his people will be subjected to a draft or not."

"Gherald," Yergwain warned. "Such business is best discussed during an official session of the Council before bringing it to the Duke."

"Please, milord," the senator said. "I am not advocating a policy myself, merely asking what sort of policy the Sword prefers."

"Yergwain and Gherald are rather spirited rivals," Valfarn whispered quietly to Maelgyn. "As the heads of the Council of Barons and the Council of Commons, respectively, they tend to get into vigorous debates."

Maelgyn merely nodded to his regent and turned his attention back to the two bickering men. "Milord Yergwain, I believe that there will be no fault if I answer his question. Although I find it rather disconcerting that I cannot even get through the first bite of my first official state dinner without having to deal with so momentous an issue."

Both of the arguing men flushed. "Sorry, Your Highness," Gherald said, unable to meet anyone else's eyes.

"As far as the draft is concerned," Maelgyn continued. "I do not believe that a general draft is necessary just yet. Perhaps in the future, if other options fall through, but not just yet. I suspect I may need to leave much of the defense of the province to our militia, however, so I am going to order that the militia be expanded and training for it to be increased. I also plan to issue a special draft order for mages – they are always valuable in wartime, and I'm going to want as many as possible in the army. I'd also like to make sure each town has at least one, and hopefully more than one in the larger towns and cities, to aid the militias."

Gherald hesitated. "Your Highness, I'm a Fourth Rate mage, myself. Is there any chance I could be called for this duty?"

Yergwain smirked. "Why, Senator, are you afraid of serving?"

"Milord," Gherald snapped. "I am fifty-six years old. I have fought in more wars than you have, and have the wounds to show for it. My knee doesn't work right, I have trouble breathing in hot weather due to an old chest wound, and after injuring my back I lose feeling in my legs whenever I ride a horse. If I am called upon, I will serve, but I believe I've earned the right to want to retire from the battlefield."

"Relax, Gherald," Maelgyn intervened, smiling. "I have no plans to call the infirm to war duty, even if it comes to a general draft. Besides, you said you were a Fourth Rate mage?"

Gherald nodded. "Barely that," he answered. "I'm so weak a mage I considered going into alchemy, but I lack the patience to learn my numbers well enough for a good alchemist. Instead I joined the army to fight the Borden Islanders when the war broke out again some thirty years ago. My magic is of little use on the battlefield in general, but it was enough to help me through some tight squeezes."

"Well, I don't think we're so desperate we'll be needing Fourth Rate mages who have served honorably in previous wars and have had more than their fair share of wounds to show for it," Maelgyn replied gently. "The orders will only call for the draft of mages who are young enough and strong enough to be effective in battle."

"I guess that rules my brother out, then," Yergwain muttered.

Euleilla, who up until then had been quietly and carefully eating her food (without her magic powder, and using the unfamiliar utensils of a knife, fork, and spoon instead of her usual chopsticks, she was having some trouble with it) nearly choked on a bite of her roast hearing that.

"Milord," she said after a brief coughing fit. Maelgyn looked on at her in concern, but she obviously didn't notice. "Just why do you think Sir Leno's magic would fail to be a help in battle?"

"Oh," Yergwain sighed. "I'm sure it aids him some. But it can't be as useful a tool as a true mage is. He calls *himself* a second-rate mage, so he can't be that good."

"What?" Maelgyn asked, startled. "Don't you even know what that means?"

"What what means?"

Even Valfarn seemed disturbed. "Milord Yergwain, I have no knowledge of magic, yet even I am less ignorant than you are if you believe a Second Rate mage isn't very good."

"I... I'm afraid I don't understand, milord," Yergwain answered.

Gherald smirked. "Indeed. Well, I can explain, if you like."

Yergwain gritted his teeth, but remained courteous. "If you please, Master Gherald. I fear that my, and perhaps my family's, lack of knowledge is doing great injustice to my brother. Enlighten me."

"It's difficult to become a mage," Gherald began. "You must be taught from birth, and it's impossible to tell at that point in a person's life just how much magical potential they might have. It is rare that parents are willing to expose their children to such a burden. However, once they've learned magic and their abilities with it have matured, they can be judged according to a scale established several thousand years ago to 'rate' their magical power. An official certificate can be issued, if you want proof of your magical strength, but any mage is advised how to assess their own power properly if they don't require the paperwork. Most usually they don't bother, instead using those guidelines for self-assessment. There are five rates, according to the standards set by the Porosian Council of Magic —"

"Six," Euleilla corrected.

Gherald raised an eyebrow at her. "That has never been proven possible among Humans. Nekoji mages are aberrations, with only a handful known to history, and the number who have reached that mark can be counted on one hand. No human mage has even come close to that level since the rating system has been established."

"So?" Euleilla asked. The smile Maelgyn remembered her carrying when he met her was on her face – it had disappeared at some point while she was ill, and had only made infrequent reappearances since then. Maelgyn did not know why she had lost it then or why it had returned now, but was glad to see it.

The senator huffed in frustration, but conceded the point. "Very well. While only five rates were established initially by the Porosian Council of Magic, a sixth came into being with the first Nekoji to learn Human magic, for he was well off the scale. But that is not the point.

"The rating a person achieves is important. A Fifth Rate, typically known as a 'failed mage,' is someone whose powers are so weak that they are unable to perform most of the tasks required for a job in magic. They usually have the skill, but little or no power. At most, enough to do minor workings of magic but not enough to truly be considered a mage. Typically, they either teach magic – for their problems with magic do not come from a lack of understanding, but rather a lack of innate talent – or they go into the study of alchemy.

"I am a Fourth Rate mage. While I do have the power to perform most of the tasks required of a professional mage, but performing even one task requiring even average magical strength will strain me to the point of being unable to perform any other magic during the day. Some fourth rate mages are slowly able to build up their skill and endurance to the point where, if they regularly exhaust their magic for years and years, they can reach a third rate."

"Like I did," Wodtke said, walking up to the table. "Forgive me, but I heard what you were talking about and had to join in on this. I was a Fourth Rate mage when I was first evaluated. After using that limited bit of magic for over a decade in my professional capacity as a doctor, I discovered at a re-evaluation that I had increased my endurance to the point of becoming a Third Rate – basically, what the scale considers your average mage. Most mages who succeed as mages achieve the rank of Third Rate, at least, at some point in their lives. Unfortunately, more than half of mages who do not have some magic in their family background are considered Fifth Rate, or 'failed mages.' That is another reason why so few families put their children through magic training."

"Thank you, Doctor," Gherald said, glancing at the woman. "I'd never met someone who managed to achieve a ratings promotion, before."

Wodtke laughed. "To be honest, I haven't found this 'promotion' to be all that important. I use my magic as a Third Rate just as much as I did when I was a Fourth Rate, both in my everyday life and my career. I am a doctor first and foremost, and always shall be one."

Gherald nodded. "Yes. Most Fourth Rate mages typically pick jobs which allow them to use the magic they spent years studying to achieve, but they cannot take jobs where they must rely on it. The medical field is a common one for fourth rates. Teacher is another, but for some reason magic teachers are rarely hired unless they are either Fifth Rate or Third Rate. There's some social stigma over being a Fourth Rate mage and teaching. If you're a Fourth Rate who lacks the math skills to be either an alchemist or a doctor, well, it's unlikely you'll be able to find a job that uses magecraft. Most become soldiers – for even a Fourth Rate mage has some limited advantage in battle, even if he doesn't qualify to be part of the mage corps – or we take jobs where magic is rarely if ever used, such as farmhand, or merchant... or even politician." He grinned ruefully. "Although I've yet to figure out how magic can be useful in elections."

"So, basically," Maelgyn said, drawing the discussing back on topic. "A Third Rate is a mage of average ability. Here's where the ratings get tricky, however, because from here on in everyone has the same skill set, more or less. Being more powerful than a Third Rate is mainly useful only in combat situations, although I'm sure a Second or First Rate could easily manage any number of non-combat feats a Third Rate would find stressful. As far as Sir Leno goes, being a Second Rate he's stronger than nine out of every ten successful mages. As a Second Rate, he's able to work magic despite the presence of a standard-strength lodestone. So, in combat, he can push through lodestone defenses, although it's hard for him.

"First Rates, like Euleilla... and apparently myself, although I have never been formally rated, are really rare in the Human race. Only about one out of thirty successful mages have our power – which makes the meeting of two or more a rather rare occurrence. A marriage between two First Rates like us is even more so. We can push magic through lodestones without significant strain on our magical reserves. There is some, yes, but barely enough for us to even notice."

Yergwain nodded, looking concerned. "I see that we *have* done an injustice to my brother, but our family has always been among the elite. I am still not sure his study of magic is proper in the first place, when it is such a rare occurrence that an elite mage is trained."

"Lord Yergwain," Maelgyn stared. "That statement makes no sense. Aren't you aware that the structure of nobility in Svieda was established to provide for the training and breeding of mages?"

"Surely not!" Yergwain protested. "It would be in our family history – there are no records of a mage in our family before Leno, and our family has been in Sviedan Nobility since the founding!"

"Maelgyn has High Mage potential," Euleilla's voice intervened before anyone could respond to Yergwain's protest.

"There had to have been," Maelgyn said to Yergwain, initially not taking in what his wife had said. "It was required, unless your barony was established more recently... than... err, Euleilla? What did you just say?"

She just smiled at him. "You. High Mage potential."

Maelgyn shook his head in denial. "That's... there hasn't been a Human High Mage in over a thousand years, if ever. You're stronger than I am, in most magical respects. I can't..."

Yergwain frowned, trying to follow the crossed conversations. "My family records would have mentioned mages in the family. And, forgive me, but what is a High Mage?"

Maelgyn was too flustered to answer him, but thankfully Dr. Wodtke was able to explain.

"A High Mage is a rare thing, to put it mildly," she said.

"Nekoji mages are the only ones who we believe have achieved that rating, and some contest even that. Nekoji mages are extremely rare, regardless of rating, and none are alive today as far as we know. Of the few Nekoji mages who succeed in their initial mage training, only one in six have even come close to having the power to be thought of as what we call 'High Mage potentials,' or people who might develop into High Mages. Human High Mages are, well, a thing of legend at best. Which makes me wonder how Euleilla – I mean Her Highness, as I probably should call her now – would know."

"I just know," was all Maelgyn's wife would say.

"That's very interesting, but I'm afraid I still don't understand.... Just what *is* a High Mage?" Yergwain repeated.

"A High Mage," Senator Gherald intervened, finally finding a way back into the conversation, "Is the highest rate there is. It was not on the original Porosian scale, and some argue they are so rare that the scale shouldn't have been changed. A High Mage is believed to be strong enough to punch magic through dragon hide, though even among the Nekoji mages that has never been tested. Untested High Mage potentials may have appeared in the Human Race as many as three times, but only in legend.

"Essentially, a mage achieves the rank of High Mage by being magically strong enough to defeat a dragon in single combat," Maelgyn finally said, regaining his tongue. "Alone. Other tests have been substituted – tests which can be dangerous, but not as dangerous as challenging a dragon singlehandedly – but only a couple of the Nekoji potentials have managed to pass them in the past thousand years. And, Euleilla, you are a stronger mage than I am. If you can't pass those tests, I wouldn't stand a chance."

"Not now, no," Euleilla agreed. "You haven't been trained to use all your power, however. You're still just a Potential. Give it a few years of pushing your limits and you'll be more than capable of handling the standard tests. You're slightly behind me now, but only because of experience, not power. I'm probably at my limit of magical development, but you still have far to go."

Maelgyn shook his head. "I'm not nearly that powerful, but I doubt I'll convince you otherwise. Anyway, back to this whole thing about your family, Yergwain – you say you have family records back to the founding of Svieda?"

Yergwain nodded, slightly startled by the change in topic.

"Yes, Your Highness. I can assure you that we do."

"And your family has been in the Barony the entire time?"

"Indeed. We have an ancient tradition of nobility, I assure you."

"And this line of nobility is of *Sviedan* nobility, correct?" Maelgyn asked, leaning over to the nobleman intently.

"Correct," Yergwain replied, his courteous tone nevertheless hinting at the resentment that the implied insult had upon him.

"Then your family records are either wrong, or incomplete," Maelgyn finally sighed, leaning back. "Because there were no noble families without mages until about three hundred years ago, and Svieda is a lot older than three hundred years."

"Our records are not wrong!" Yergwain finally spat, finally letting his anger get past his civility. "My family has been Sviedan Nobility since the founding."

Lord Valfarn, himself, looked disturbed. "Your highness," he said, swallowing slightly. "I have seen Yergwain's family records, myself. His family really is a noble line, I am sure of it."

"Truthfully, I don't doubt that," Maelgyn agreed. "Sir Leno's abilities with magic tend to make me believe there has been a lot of potential in his bloodline, since most higher ranked mages come from families of noble decent. But what I suspect is that someone destroyed any records that might have existed about mages in your family for some unknown reason. His family could *not* have been a noble family without raising *many* mages until around three hundred years ago, because the law required that all noble families train at least one child in the art of magic."

Yergwain looked disturbed by that. "It did? But the history books don't say —"

"Whose history books?" Maelgyn asked, raising a curious eyebrow. "I have been reading history books at the Royal Castle of Svieda for the past several years of my life, and I assure you I'm correct."

The baron flushed. "Milord, while I'm certain that the Royal Castle had a much more extensive library than any I have had access to, none of the histories in the Sopan Province libraries mention anything like that."

"How odd," Maelgyn commented. "*Every* history of that period in the Royal Castle library mentions it. Even fairly common books I'm sure the libraries of Sopan should have mention it."

"Perhaps," Gherald said, "We could adjourn to the library at some point, and take a look at these books? It might be a better idea than spoiling our dinner arguing the point."

Maelgyn slowly nodded. "Yes... I believe a stop in the library will be in order."

The library was small by Maelgyn's standards, but well filled with books of all kinds. Many of them looked to be well read, but few were of much age. Sopan Province was still young, for Svieda, and nothing in the library was older than the province itself as far as he could tell. Yet it contained many books, both rare and common. He recognized a number of them from his time in the Royal Castle Library, and went to those first.

Maelgyn had left for the library immediately after having finished his dinner while most of the others had retreated to their beds. Only Euleilla, Lord Valfarn, and the curious pair of Senator Gherald and Lord Yergwain had accompanied him. However, he was alone in his search through the texts, as only he knew what he was looking for.

The others glanced through the library as well, however, looking for something to entertain themselves. Valfarn, Gherald, and Yergwain all found something to read on their own. Euleilla, on the other hand, merely took a seat and started magically playing with her metal bracers, dissolving them into geometric oddities with varying degrees of complexity.

Yergwain frowned at her. "Why aren't you reading?" he asked.

Euleilla shrugged. "I need to practice magic at all times."

"In a library?" he persisted.

"Why not?"

A deep frown came upon the baron's face, one which concerned Maelgyn as he noticed it. *What is Yergwain thinking?* he wondered.

"Can you read?" the baron asked disdainfully.

Euleilla twitched, but showed no other outward reaction. Valfarn had stiffened, looking at Yergwain in horror, but the baron took no notice of it. Maelgyn, on the other hand, felt outrage at the accusation. "Excuse me, Lord Yergwain," he growled. "But that is my wife you are talking to. Show her the proper respect."

Yergwain spun on him, showing in his face that he shared

his friend Mathrid's biases, even if it was more subtle. "Your highness, I've given her the respect due her in public, and will continue to do so, but we are not in public. If Valfarn had decided against you, it would have been my responsibility to determine whether this woman was worthy of being the highest ranking Lady in the province. It is not my decision now, but it might have been... and I deserve to know if there is something which would have made me say no."

"You deserve nothing of the sort," Valfarn snapped, recovered. "It was not your choice, it was mine. And it will never be your choice. I—"

"Relax, everyone," Euleilla commanded, restoring her bracers to her forearms. Everyone immediately shut their mouths and spun on her.

"Euleilla?" Maelgyn said quietly.

"I can read," she said softly, but with a power in her voice that made them all pay attention. "But not any of these books."

"Why not? Do you read a different language?" Yergwain demanded, still defiant but less sure.

"No-one here may speak of it out of this room," Euleilla noted.

"Unless you want to lose your tongues," Maelgyn added, suddenly knowing what she was about to do. "This may come out to the public some day, but for the moment we wish it to remain a secret, and I will use whatever authority I have to protect it."

Yergwain nodded his head in acceptance. Gherald, however, smiled. "I, perhaps, should leave. I have no doubts as to her highness' worth."

"Thank you, Gherald" Euleilla nodded thankfully. "My husband and Lord Valfarn may stay, as they already know. Anyone may leave who does not wish to know."

Yergwain hesitated. "Just what kind of secret are we talking about here? Are... are you even human? Or are you some Elven creation? Or... or a Merfolk shapeshifter who—"

The door slammed behind Gherald's departing form, startling him into silence.

"Elven? Merfolk? No," Euleilla laughed. "I am definitely human. A Merfolk or an Elf would be able to heal themselves from this." She lifted her bangs, revealing the scars where her eyes should be. "I do have a difficult time reading for a reason.

However, if you're willing to mix the ink with some magic powder, I can read by 'seeing' the words with my magic. My foster father did that for me a lot, and so I have no problem reading and or writing with the same special inks. But not a single book in this entire library was made in such a way as to allow me to view it, and so I try to find other things to interest me."

Yergwain tensed, seemingly unable to keep his eyes off those scars until she lowered her bangs again. "My lady Euleilla, I will keep your secret. However, if I had known of this, and it had been my decision, I would not have affirmed Prince Maelgyn's choice in wives. A blind peasant, whose only redeeming qualities as far as the nobility is concerned are being the foster-daughter of yet another peasant and a talent for magic? You are hardly the sort of person our nation expects for such a position."

"Then we can be glad," Maelgyn growled, "That it was not your decision. The question is, now that you know, are you willing to serve under me, in the position your rank has bestowed upon you?"

Yergwain stiffened, and then returned to his books. "My family honor is at stake," he said, unable to look at them. "So yes, I will serve."

Valfarn went to the door, and allowed Gherald to return. "Well, it doesn't look like Lord Yergwain was too pleased by the secret," the senator chirped. "Probably means good news for me. Now, how about we get back to our research? I'm immensely curious about those laws you say we had...."

Chapter 20

"This is bizarre," Maelgyn said, looking intensely at the book in his hands. After the tension brought about by Yergwain's outburst, he'd decided to continue searching the texts just as Gherald had suggested. So, he'd pulled out a tall stack of books from the shelves, sat down, and started reading.

"What is?" Gherald said, looking up. Yergwain was looking quite tense, still, and Valfarn hadn't turned the page once in his own open book as he'd opted to glare at the insolent baron instead. Not even the Sword Prince's sudden exclamation was enough to distract his gaze.

"These books," Maelgyn answered. "They... aren't right. They're different from the copies of the same books in the royal library. Some passages are changed, others completely omitted. There are a few things in these books I'd never seen in the royal library. You might expect minor discrepancies in different copies of an illuminated manuscript, which was what I was expecting, but these particular books were produced with a printing press – they should be identical to every other copy of these books. Something is very wrong, here."

That attracted everyone's attention. "What sort of things were changed?" Valfarn asked, curious. "And what were they changed to say?"

"Well," Maelgyn began, "I see alterations to all of the historical texts dealing with issues prior to Sopan Province's induction into Svieda. I'd almost say that it was changed to present a pro-Porosian viewpoint, and in doing so it obscures a number of the things which made Svieda unique. For example, our tradition of training a great number of mages for both military and civilian use, much of the story of our founding, the story of the rebellion of Abindol, and a few things which seem otherwise irrelevant. Even the legend of Sword King Agaeb IV and Queen Amberry is completely removed from the texts. I don't get any of it."

"Agaeb IV and Amberry? Hmm... a few hundred years ago? I don't recall anything particularly interesting in their history...." Gherald muttered.

"Well, I do," Valfarn gaped. "I named my children after them! The Sword King whose peasant bodyguard became his queen is a story which always seemed like a romantic's fantasy! The legend was a favorite of mine growing up – my grandmother told it to me often in my youth, and she said she heard the story from one of the Swords in her youth – but I never believed that Queen Amberry was ever really a peasant. Do you mean to say that story might have some basis in fact?"

"Quite a bit of truth," Maelgyn replied. "At least, if the Royal Library's history texts are correct. Whether they are the correct ones, or these are, I don't know. Given some of the other omissions, I suspect that these are the altered copies, but I can't be sure."

"So the big question is, why did they do it?" Euleilla asked. "Altering common history texts which any learned traveler would know, and so drastically they cannot help but notice it? How did they manage it, and why even bother when it is so easily discovered?"

"You said it was pro-Porosian," Yergwain considered. "What are some of the differences between the Royal accounts and this one, and how are the Porosians featured?"

"I must admit that I am a bit ignorant in this," Gherald sighed. "I am aware that the Porosians are an ancient nation, but why would they even be interested in us? Are they even still around as a significant power?"

Maelgyn sighed. "Well... let's see if I can explain human history in five minutes or less, first, since that'll make explaining the differences easier."

Valfarn looked unhappy, but nodded. "If you believe it necessary, your highness, then please – enlighten us."

Maelgyn took a deep breath. "In the earliest days of recorded history, each race controlled only one nation. The Dwarves ruled

Mar'Tok and later expanded outwards. The Nekoji spread from the western coast of the Orful River through much of what is now Oregal. The Merfolk controlled the sea. The Dragons, created by the Elves, held their homes in various mountain ranges of the island chain now known as the Borden Isles. The Elves have lived throughout the known world, possibly covering all of these lands at one point, but at the time they lived in the mountains to the far north.

"And then there was the Human race, which slowly evolved a civilization around Lake Poros, surrounded by other the other races – south of the Elven lands, north of the Dwarven lands, and east of the Nekoji lands. Poros grew strong in spite of – or perhaps because of – a war between the Elves and the Dwarves in which Poros was the middle ground. As those two nations' powers waned, Poros strengthened its borders in an effort to prevent those two races' incursions. It was during this war the decline of both the Elves and the Dwarves began.

"Eventually the borders of each power converged in a small territory known as 'Squire's Knot.' At that intersection, disaffected Elves, Dwarves, Humans and Nekoji created a small nation that has since been a neutral power – a haven for those of all races who tired of warring against one another.

"This is where the first discrepancy in these historical accounts appears. The books here claim that Poros continued expansion southward, controlling much of what is now Svieda. In the Royal texts, only a small fraction of our territory was ever controlled by Poros: The mouth of the Orful River in Sopan and parts of the Duchy of Largo. All of Svieda's holdings east of Squire's knot, including the Royal Province, were largely uninhabited. Apparently, an ancient enemy of the Elves once held much of Sviedan lands, and no race dared to try and reclaim that territory, but that race has long since vanished from the world.

"Before Svieda's founding, the Nekoji went to war with the Porosians. The reasons given for the war sound unusual, both in the texts here and in the ones I've read in the Royal Castle. Something about a 'trade of skills' that never took place, but the records do not explain what that means. Eventually, the Dwarves joined the war as well, but not until after the Humans had established a fairly large presence on the other side of the Orful River.

"The war with the Nekoji ended quickly once the Dwarves entered the fight. Poros, fighting on two fronts, started drawing back its borders. They were never strong enough to cross the river again... but they left people behind. Those men and women who had settled or who were stationed on the other side of the Orful River started creating a number of city-states, some of which surprisingly still exist today in the disputed region between Oregal and the Orful River.

"Some human settlements on the Porosian side of the river also began to form their own governments and raise their own armies when it became clear Poros had abandoned them. So was born what today is known as the Bandi Republic, as well as the then-Kingdoms of Largo, Stanget, and Rubick, and some of the nations which make up the western half of the Sho'Curlas 'Alliance.'

"Poros itself – or rather, the core of Poros – survived intact. It took the construction of heavy fortifications and the invention of a competitive cavalry force, but eventually Humanity learned how to defend itself against the Dwarves. Poros remained the only human settlement of any great power, despite these fledgling offshoots, but only for a short time. For reasons which are lost to history, a power struggle broke out shortly after the fall of the last of the Elven kingdoms. Dozens of Porosian states, divided by clan, struggled for power over the kingdom.

"As the civil war went on for hundreds of years, many of the clans decided to leave Poros rather than to continue the fight endlessly. Among them were the Six Clans, whose names you might recognize – Glorest, Happaso, Abindol, Leyland, Sycanth, and Svieda. Initially, the Six Clans met in Squire's Knot. By coincidence, they met with a royal member of the Rubick Kingdom – which, by then, had become the largest human power south of Poros. He was there to discuss treaty terms with the nations of Stanget and Largo. Largo, in particular, was in desperate need of assistance as they were in a war on two fronts. The Six Clans, due to their size and strength, were asked to join these negotiations.

"As a treaty of alliance was discussed, the head of Clan Svieda fell in love with and eventually married the Prince of Rubick. A number of additional arranged marriages took place over the next couple of generations binding the Six Clans and the royal

families of Largo, Stanget, and Rubick together. The Six Clans
wanted their own territory, though, and began to colonize the
lands east of Rubick – the first people to stake a claim on the
territory since the Elven Kingdoms fell.

"This is where these texts really start to diverge. The books
from this library claim that the lands of Svieda, Sycanth, Abindol,
Happaso, Glorest, and Leyland were already in Porosian hands,
but this must be false. I've been to some of the places these books
claim were built by Poros and they simply aren't old enough to
be ancient Porosian.

"Eventually, long after the Six Clans had left, Poros settled
down into four separate, relatively stable fragments, all claiming
to be the rightful claimant to the throne of Poros. Their war
hasn't formally ended after millennia of fighting, but most of the
fighting and the continued fragmentation has ended. Most of
the outside world labels these claimants as North, South, East,
and West Poros – names which are now largely misnomers, as
North Poros is now more west than West Poros, and East Poros
is the northernmost fragment, but the names have stuck. All
four have control over part of the coast on Lake Poros and some
plains beyond, but they have been slowly shrinking for hundreds
of years.

"Poros is still a large enough power to halt Sho'Curlas'
westward expansion, at least for those lands north of Squire's
Knot. Oregal rose with the invention of the first cavalry of the
West, and the Sho'Curlas Alliance rose with the same invention
in the northeast. Greyholden I, member of an estranged offshoot
of the Sviedan line, used his powerbase in the Borden Isles to
bring the Six Clans and the Three Kingdoms together formally
as one nation under the Sviedan name, making himself King.
He prepared the Swords as symbols of leadership, blended the
republican and feudal forms of government together in a written
constitution, and established the current laws of succession to
prevent any one province in Svieda from having power over
the others. His dream was for Svieda to be strong enough to
stand up to any of the other major powers. He set up the laws
requiring nobility to train a member of each generation in the art
of magecraft. Almost none of this is in these books, however,
even though the same books from the Royal Library mention all
of it."

Maelgyn grinned wryly. "The most egregious thing is that these books indicate we were founded as a 'neutral place' for Porosian traditions to continue until the civil war ended, mentioning a treaty which I have never heard of before. We're supposed to 'rejoin Poros when the civil war ends,' according to this nonexistent treaty, no matter the outcome – something I am sure would have been in Greyholden I's papers if it were true. Having read them, I can attest that there is no mention of any treaty with Poros in Greyholden's papers."

"It sounds like someone in Poros is attempting a slow conquest by subterfuge," Valfarn said. "Yet apparently they've only hit here, in Sopan. Would anyone like to venture a guess as to why?"

"Not yet," Maelgyn answered. "But perhaps we could get some ideas from someone who might have actually been alive when Svieda was founded. It's late, but first thing tomorrow we talk to Wangdu."

"Very well," Valfarn agreed. "Tomorrow morning. I'll make the arrangements."

Gherald coughed. "Aren't we all forgetting something? Like the invasion? Sho'Curlas? That is more important than a few changes to our history books, right?"

"No reason we can't investigate this matter while dealing with that one," Maelgyn replied. "I think I'd like to put you in charge of establishing the mages draft, Gherald. Valfarn, you know our forces better than I do. With our new treaties, the soldiers protecting the borders of Mar'Tok and Caseificio can be withdrawn. That should provide sufficient additional manpower to assign at least one combat veteran to each city, village, and township to help drill and train militia forces. I would like you to collect enough of Gherald's drafted mages to ensure one is paired with each of those veterans. Once those defensive measures are established, we'll have a better idea of what we have to work with when we go on the offensive. In the meantime, I can investigate this Porosian issue, myself."

Maelgyn hung up the silk divider to give Euleilla privacy as she changed across the room from him. For the first time since leaving the inn at Elm Knoll she was able to find comfortable nightclothes to wear. She'd packed some when she started the journey, but they had been ruined during their travels. The Dwarves had no such amenities even for their own kind, much less for Humans, so she had been greatly relieved when the Court Seamstress was able to produce a wonderfully tailored nightgown between the time that they had arrived at the castle that morning and the end of dinner that night. It was a bit risqué, considering she had company, but it was appropriate for a married woman to wear around her husband.

Though they had yet to do more than kiss, she and Maelgyn had been sleeping in the same bed (or tent and bedroll, or pallet, or whatever else they were forced to sleep on during their journey) for several weeks, now. At first, it was merely a somewhat awkward, but pleasant, traveling convenience. As that awkwardness vanished, he found himself enjoying it more... even with the sheet between them in the traditional practice of bundling. He still wanted to have at least one more conversation with Euleilla before he suggested removing that sheet, however.

It still felt odd when she walked in on him changing, even though he knew she couldn't see him. What made it worse was that Euleilla found his reactions intensely amusing, and provoked them from him whenever she could. He had been half expecting her to try and catch him changing that night, but it sounded to him as if she were simply readying herself for bed at an unusually slow pace. He wondered if it was the unfamiliar room or something else that was delaying her.

Euleilla was, in fact, taking her time because she needed to think. It had been a long time since she had been able to take stock of her situation, but now that she was in what was likely to be her permanent residence, she needed to before she could go any further.

Things had been moving much too quickly since she met Maelgyn: Joining Maelgyn on a trip across Mar'Tok, rescuing a member of the Dwarven royalty from a group of bandits, getting "accidentally" married, fighting another battle against foreign invaders, falling ill crossing the mountains, meeting with the Dwarven leadership as a political figure in her own right, fighting yet another battle while still recovering from her illness, and then, most recently, finding herself in the position of having to reveal her lack of eyesight to several strangers just so that she could continue in her new role as the Princess Consort of Sopan

Province.

Looking back on it all, it was no wonder she'd never had a chance to lean back and put things in perspective. Now, though, things should be settling down, at least for her. The burden of ruling Sopan (and everything that went with it) would fall on Maelgyn's shoulders, not her own. She was sure she would be helping him along the way, but for the moment she could think about her own concerns.

There was her marriage to consider. She thought that maybe, just maybe, she was in love with Maelgyn. She didn't know why – perhaps it was simply his magical aura – but she had fallen in love with him the very day she met him. Clearly some of Maelgyn's barons were having difficulty accepting her, but she would not be dissuaded from having him as long as he would have her.

She was still a little uncomfortable with the fact that being his wife made her a Princess (or rather a "Princess Consort," but she wasn't entirely sure what the difference was). On the long list of things she thought she might be able to achieve in her life, marrying into the royal family was not something she had considered. Marrying a Sword of the Realm... well, that was just so far out of her plans that she wasn't entirely sure what to think of it.

She enjoyed the way the comfortable silks and fabrics felt on her skin when wearing the gown that evening, but if the 'job' of being Maelgyn's wife required that she dress like that every day she feared she would go insane. She much preferred her leather bustier and lightly armored jeans, accompanied by a nice vest or (in cold weather) jacket. She had specially made those with small iron plates in the lining (or the underarmor, for the pants) to allow her to get dressed easier. The silk gown felt delightful, but she kept thinking she was naked in it without the iron markers letting her 'see' them.

The fact that her position as Maelgyn's wife was also forcing her to show her eyes (or rather, the lack of them) to more and more people also disturbed her. When old Gherald voluntarily left the room before she had to reveal them the last time, she almost kissed him – she didn't like letting anyone see anything other than a smile on her face. She didn't even want Maelgyn to see those eyes too often, though she was more willing to let him see her at her most vulnerable than anyone else.

Oddly enough, the war disrupted her life the least out of everything that had happened, and was the thing she felt most prepared for. Despite her blindness, being raised by a military hero like Ruznak had encouraged her to consider a military career. She had been taught something of the art of tactics, she knew how to apply her magic to combat, and – as even Maelgyn would probably be startled to learn – she could handle hand-to-hand combat about as well as any soldier, if absolutely necessary. Ruznak taught her how to fight both unarmed and with a staff, and she had also taught herself some magical combat. Maelgyn's lessons in counter-magic could readily be adopted into what she already knew, making her quite capable in any fight. Rather surprisingly, she felt more prepared – at least in some ways – to deal with the war than her marriage.

But only if Maelgyn took her with him as he led their armies. If he tried to shield her from the action, and keep her away from those things she was most ready to help him with, then they would have problems. There was also the chance that she would be kept out of all of the decision making even if she were allowed to accompany him. As Princess, or Princess Consort rather, she would be held liable for all of Maelgyn's decisions. If he kept her away from the decision making process when she would have to take that responsibility, then perhaps she would need to have second thoughts about the whole marriage thing. It looked more and more like the success of their union lay in Maelgyn's hands.

"Euleilla, are you there?" Maelgyn asked abruptly.

She felt startled momentarily. He normally refused to talk with her when either of them might be dressing. "Yes," she answered, forcing all trace of surprise out of her voice.

"Are you dressed for bed?"

"Maybe," she teased. Even now, she liked pulling out that little bit of embarrassment still in him. She could feel his eyes rolling.

"Well, when you are, I'd like to get your opinion on something I'm planning for tomorrow. As my wife, you should be given a chance to share in the big decisions, and this could be a big one."

Perhaps, Euleilla thought, her smile coming more naturally than usual, *Maelgyn's hands are a good place for this marriage to be.*

Wangdu frowned as Maelgyn related what he had learned about the changes in the local historical record. As the Elf heard more and more about the changes, and the way the changes were performed, something dark flickered in his eyes.

"This library you speak of, you do," he finally said when Maelgyn was finished. "Just how old are the books inside it, are they?"

"Well, nothing in it would be older than Sopan Province's inclusion into Svieda, but a large number of the books look about that old, and most of the library collection is considerably older than I am. Not many new books at all, come to think of it."

"Hm," the Elf mused. "Not good, not good at all, it isn't. You've got an Elf working against Sopan Province, you do, but this Elf is not the one we know from Sho'Curlas, he isn't."

"Really?" Maelgyn said, surprised. "It sounds a little like what happened with Borden Isle and Abindol. Hrabak is an Elf..."

"It could be any Elf, it could," Wangdu explained. "This has been done before, it has. To this same province, it was. By an Elf as well, it was. Did you really think that Oregal gave Sopan to Svieda out of the goodness of their hearts, did you?"

"An Elf arranged for Oregal to give us Sopan Province?"

Wangdu shook his head. "It was not exactly that simple, it wasn't. An Elf spent centuries convincing the Oregal Republic that Sopan Province was indefensible, he did, and that the only way to keep it out of the hands of Sho'Curlas was to cede it into Svieda, it was."

"What Elf did that?"

Wangdu grinned wryly. "It was me, it was. I have been working to defeat Sho'Curlas for centuries, I have, and I figured strengthening Svieda was a good choice, it was. Svieda was already fairly powerful in its own right, it was, and seemed to be ruled by a succession of fairly decent individuals, it did. Between all the parliaments and councils in Sviedan bureaucracy there are enough checks and balances to withstand a few bad monarchs, there are. But I was merely following a several millennia old plan, I was, which Elves have been using in many wars against other races, they have. We Elves are immortal, we are, so spending hundreds of years slowly seeding propaganda into a nation is not as impractical as it would be for another race, it isn't."

"So, this is a traditional Elven tactic," Maelgyn mused. "And yet you don't seem to think that Hrabak is behind this. I suppose I buy that, since it seems to be of more benefit to Poros than Sho'Curlas, but can you think of any Elves who would work on Poros' behalf?"

"Elves are a very scattered race, we are," Wangdu sighed. "In the past there have been parts of Squire's Knot which were considered Elven communities, there were, but I have not seen another Elf in that city for twenty years, I haven't. The Bandi Republic is openly ruled by an Elf, it is, but she refuses to allow other Elves to establish residence in her borders, she does – we may be allowed to travel through her country, we may, but she rightly thinks we're too dangerous to live there permanently, we are. Some Elves want to hide from politics of the world, they do, and live in the wilderness of the border kingdoms. I'm aware of a few Elven communities in Oregal, I am, but they have very little power, they do. Hrabak is a known madman, he is, and so most Elves steer clear of his holdings, they do. I have not heard of any other Elven stronghold, I haven't, but I would not be surprised if an Elf had decided to take a position of power among one of the Porosian political factions, I wouldn't."

"Okay, now the next question," Maelgyn said. "Why Sopan? We share no border with Poros – in fact, the only way to get from here to there is to cross through both Mar'Tok and the Bandi Republic. It's possible to travel upriver and cross through the border kingdoms, but that would take even longer. What could they gain from us?"

"Svieda shared no border with Sopan, it didn't, when your nation took it, it did. Why would Svieda do that, would it?"

"Money," Maelgyn answered quickly. "It's strategically located to control trade along the Orful River, which is the longest river in the known world. Any traders along that river who wish to conduct business with the outside world must go through Sopan and pay a tribute."

"That is a simple answer, it is, but accurate. So, why would Poros not want it for the same reason, why not?"

"Mar'Tok has never been hostile to Svieda, and even if it was both Sopan and the larger parts of Svieda have enough coastline to communicate by sea, but Poros does not. Mar'Tok, Bandi, and the border kingdoms are all hostile to Poros, and would band together to fight it," Maelgyn reasoned. "No, something doesn't fit here. At least... not if Sopan is the only place targeted. But where else would Poros strike? If it's a classic Elven strategy, I doubt they could employ a similar strategy in Bandi, where the mad Lady Phalra rules. I also haven't seen any evidence of such... historical tampering, as you might call it, in Mar'Tok. There are way too many border kingdoms to even contemplate striking out against them all. No, if this does come from Poros it still doesn't make any sense."

Wangdu sighed. "Perhaps you're right, you are. I suggest we ask El'Athras to see what he can turn up, I do. He has considerable resources when it comes to this sort of thing, he does."

Maelgyn nodded. "Very good. Could you ask him for me? I've got to bring this before the Council of Barons. Countering this will require an action only they can take."

"As you wish, you do," Wangdu nodded. "But what will you be doing, will you?"

Maelgyn grinned wryly. "I'm fixing the damage."

Chapter 21

Yergwain stood in front of the council chambers, looking decidedly unhappy. As the head of the Council of Barons, he was the only one of Sopan's peers who could not avoid this meeting. Maelgyn, waiting for his cue to enter the council chambers, wondered if the man was still upset about their heated discussion the previous day. Regardless, Maelgyn expected that he would be even more upset by what was about to happen. If there was one thing he was starting to learn about Yergwain, it was that he disliked the unexpected. Perhaps, however, Yergwain would be better prepared for his announcement than anyone else. It would definitely test the loyalty of his barons.

"This emergency session of the Council of Barons is called to order," Yergwain announced. "Sword Prince Maelgyn, Duke of this province, has asked to address the Council."

The usual muttering and small talk which happens whenever a large enough group of people were gathered together ended with a suddenness that Maelgyn found surprising. Knowing that this first session with the council would make or break his ability to rule the province as Duke, he took a deep breath to collect his composure. As ready as he was going to get, Maelgyn stepped out into the room and looked out among the nobility of his land.

There was curiosity among the gathering, and perhaps a little bit of resentment emanating from some of the Barons over his marriage. There were also a few hopeful expressions, which Maelgyn felt somewhat reassured by – at least there seemed to be some initial support for him. He just hoped his new announcement wouldn't destroy that.

"My Lords and Ladies," Maelgyn began.   "Something disturbing has come to my attention, and in order to correct this matter I will need to ask hard things of you all. We have two major problems which we have to deal with, and unfortunately we don't have much time to correct either of them.

"The first is the one you are probably all aware of by now: The nation of Svieda is at war, the king is dead, and Sho'Curlas has sent a massive army into our kingdom. We are holding them off, thanks to the combined efforts of several of our fellow provinces, but just barely. Our navy in Largo was destroyed. And, this you may not know, I have had reports that there are several dozen trained Black Dragons in the Sho'Curlas army which are yet to be deployed. We, as a nation, are in mortal danger, ladies and gentlemen. We must act quickly if we want our nation to survive."

At the mention of the Black Dragons, murmurs started rising among the barons. "We are not without hope, however," he continued. "We have begun forging new alliances. So far, we have brought in the Counties of Caseificio and Mar'Tok, as you already know. Their armies are joining ours, and are now assembling in Largo to join the central campaign of this war. I expect Sopan to represent itself well in the coming battles, as we are sworn to do. However, all of this has been complicated by a second major issue I have discovered. I will have to deal with this second issue immediately, in order to remove all possible distractions while we are fighting this war."

The murmurs had quieted down significantly, but there was still a great deal of stress and apprehension on the faces of almost all of the assembled barons. Dragons were definitely not something anyone wanted to deal with, including Maelgyn. The hopefulness he had been so pleased to see in some of the baron's faces was gone, but at least there didn't appear to be any resentment left, either.

"It has come to my attention that Sopan Province has been beset by a ploy traditionally used by the Elves in their wars of conquest. This Elven plot is one of slow, methodical propaganda over the course of several centuries. So far, I have discovered that they have been altering history books, usurping our children's education, altering our traditions, and introducing a multitude of additional social changes in a slow but steady pace that have gone unnoticed – changes which weaken our defenses and break our will to fight against certain foreign intrusions. Hundreds of years have gone into this plot, whereas we have only been investigating it since late last night, so we are not sure of all of the details, but enough has come to light to provide some hints. We believe a faction of Elves in Poros are behind it, but have yet to see which part of Poros they are from or why they have chosen us as a target. Nevertheless, it must be stopped, and I judge that only drastic action will thwart their plans. We must do something which will destroy all of their work to date, and hopefully restore our province's true traditions."

Once again, murmurs broke out among the gathering. This was something his people could never have expected, and his youth and inexperience was bound to make them hesitant about his plans. They were listening, however. That, alone, reassured him. As long as they were willing to trust his word, there was a chance his plans could succeed.

"I have a proposal. One which may inconvenience many of you, or even anger some of you, but it is the only way I can think of to solve this situation. I am creating a new rank of nobility for this province – borrowing from Oregal, I will name this new rank 'Earl.' All current Baronies will be reformed as Earldoms, and all Baronets will be promoted to full Barons. The new Baronies will all add an additional ten Baronets under their holdings. That would be disturbing enough to some of you, I suspect, but there is more."

Maelgyn noticed that most of them actually looked pleased by this news. Something he wasn't surprised to see – he had hoped that the temptation of a higher rank than comparable nobles in Svieda's other Duchies would blunt the steel of the rest of his declaration – but wasn't sure would be enough of a bribe to calm them.

"Now for the difficult part. One goal of this propaganda war was an attempt to diminish the number and prominence of mages in Sopan. When this kingdom was founded, every noble was required by law to have at least one of his line trained to be a mage, in addition to learning some skill in the art of the sword. It was much later decided, when the split between the two disciplines was discovered to be too great for all noble families to master, to allow each noble family the option of choosing one discipline or the other for each successive generation. It was strongly encouraged that, if there were multiple offspring, one child would be trained in magic and the other in the sword. It became tradition that the firstborn son of a noble family would be taught magic, and any further children would be taught the sword, or that training be split between the two disciplines for all children.

"Here in Sopan, that tradition has been abandoned. Centuries of propaganda have succeeded in attaching some stigma to noble families raising mages, and that must change. While it is too late for many of the current generation to learn the art of magecraft, I am hereby reinstating the requirement that at least one member of every future generation in a noble family learn magic. All of the new Baronets must be ranked a Third Rate mage or better, and for good or ill, that will almost certainly mean promoting from among the common folk. Back when the nobility was established, our ancestors wrote these laws to provide for at least one combat mage in a reasonable acreage of land – the very reason Greyholden I the feudal system for Sviedan government. Here in Sopan, that principle has been forgotten... and so it must be restored. Milords and ladies, *we need those mages* if we are to survive."

What had begun as more muttering was starting to reach the status of an uproar. Most of the nobles looked fiercely angry at the pronouncement, though not – Maelgyn was a bit surprised to see – Yergwain. The shouting nearly drowned out the last of his words, which were both the most important and least surprising of the speech.

"And, finally, I will send to the other provinces of Svieda, requesting their printing presses print enough books to replace the forgeries currently in the libraries of this duchy. Typically, I am against the destruction of books or any other source of knowledge, but in this case we are destroying lies, not knowledge. Libel and propaganda, perpetuated by a foreign power with the intent of destroying us as an independent power."

Even more shouts responded, but Maelgyn had reached the end of his speech so that no longer mattered. Now, it was just time to get out of there as gracefully as possible. He had intended on a long closing, but the way things were looking now he figured it would be best to just leave and let the barons cool down. As a newly invested Duke, he had the power to reorganize the nobility, but enforcing his decision required their active support.

Shaking his head to clear his thoughts, Maelgyn finished, "Thank you. As I said, this will likely be a bit painful for some of you, but it is necessary."

With those final words – words he doubted many heard, if anyone did – he turned and swept himself out of the room. With a sureness that surprised even him in this strange castle which he knew was to be his home, he made his way back to the bedchamber he shared with Euleilla. His magic told him she wasn't there, but that was fine with him for the moment.

The nobles weren't the only ones who needed time to think things over, after all.

Euleilla sighed, using her slightly better-than-average hearing to discern all that was being said. The Barons were not taking Maelgyn's announcement well, as she feared, but most appeared willing to go along with it. Their acceptance confirmed just how badly they were shaken by the news on the war, if nothing else. It looked like the new reorganization of the nobility, and the laws requiring mages to be trained in noble families, were likely to be applied by *most* of the Barons, at least in regards to the creation of new magically-trained Baronets. None of them were particularly happy with her husband, however, and she more than once heard her own name cursed alongside his as the source of all their misery.

Well, it was as she had expected. She had talked with Maelgyn about it for quite some time that previous night. She had known they would react this way, and Maelgyn had agreed with her completely. However, despite raising the peerage's ire, Sopan Province would be all the better for it.

Deciding she had heard enough, Euleilla headed for her quarters – not the large bedroom she shared with her husband, but a private office suite he had given her for when she needed time alone. She was in the process of redesigning her office so that she could better make use of it. She already knew she'd have to place a few subtle iron 'markers' to help find her way around the room easier, but beyond that she wasn't sure what changes she wanted. A chair, perhaps, or couch. Something she could relax in, at any rate. Perhaps a small desk with special metallic inks, though most paperwork that needed doing could be done in Maelgyn's office. Most decorations that some ladies would distribute around the room would be lost on her, and really, she didn't need anywhere to store extra clothes save perhaps some extra pieces of armor not fit to be stored in a boudoir. Currently, she only owned a single set of brand new nightclothes, a number of cheap vests, a few sets of her specially-made leather bustiers, and the only pair of armored pants that had not been worn out or damaged during their journey across Mar'Tok. Oh, and the silk gown she had worn the previous night.

She wanted to get some more armored pants in the near future. She would probably also need some sort of court dress that was more fitting of her own style and personality than that silk gown. Come to think of it, being the "Princess Consort" would require that she expand her wardrobe significantly. Or being a Princess: As Maelgyn had explained to her the previous night, only the Sword King who had the right to invest a Princess Consort with the full rank of Princess, allowing her to take her husband's place should he desire to leave her in charge of his province or should he pass away. She had recently learned that, as Princess Consort, she was due all the respect of a Princess, but she nonetheless held no real authority that did not go through her husband. Getting invested as a full Princess was now something she wanted, but she knew it would have to wait until there was a Sword King in Svieda once more.

Actually, what she wanted, more than a new wardrobe, more than a desk, more than a new pair of her armored pants, even more than the "authority" of being a full Princess, was a bath like the ones she had seen and used in the Dwarven village. Those "Fu'Ro" baths were exquisite. Perhaps she could get one installed in that private room of hers. She wasn't sure such a thing was possible without significant renovations to the castle, but since the new treaty would allow easier employment of Dwarven engineers—

Euleilla paused, having reached her private room. There was someone else already there, just behind the door, apparently waiting for her arrival. Four someones, actually. Maelgyn was the only person allowed in her suite without her authorization, and he wasn't any of them.

They all had a peculiar magical "signature," one she felt was vaguely familiar but she couldn't quite place. She tried to think of where she'd felt it before, but to no avail. She considered calling the guards, but it would be pretty difficult to explain if her intruders were little more than castle servants cleaning her room. They didn't seem particularly strong, or magically trained, so she had no fears for her own safety... but she did want privacy. One of the advantages of using her magic in place of sight was that she always knew whether a room would be private or not, so finding a room to rest in shouldn't be too difficult a job.

She was very good at avoiding people, as she was able to sense people around corners, and so managed to stay out of sight from everyone until she ran into that familiar sense again – only now she could identify it.

"Wangdu!" she called. "Is that you?"

"Hello?" the Elf said, startled, coming through what must have been a closed door. "Ah! It's Euleilla, it is! Welcome. How may I serve you, may I?"

"Hm," Euleilla hummed. "I was just about to enter my private chambers when I discovered there were four individuals with the same unusual magical signature as you have. I didn't go in, but I've been trying to identify it ever since."

Wangdu's own magical aura flared at those words, startling Euleilla slightly. She hadn't detected any trace of Human magic in him, but apparently he could wield some... albeit at only a fraction of what she or Maelgyn could manage, and likely even weaker than Wodtke.

"You sensed others like me here, you did?" he said, sounding quite agitated. "You say there were *four* like me, you said?"

Euleilla, still a bit rattled at having never detected his magical abilities before, nodded. "Yes, four."

"You are very lucky you did not go in there, you are," he growled. Euleilla was a bit startled when one of his hands clasped on her arm, and he started dragging her away. "You must come with me at once, you must! You may be a powerful mage in human terms, you may, but even you would be quickly overwhelmed in a fight against just one of my kind, you would."

"Your kind?" Euleilla said, somewhat discomfited as she stumbled along after him. Even as she asked it, however, she realized what he was saying.

"The Elves, girl, the Elves, they are! Even a relatively young, untrained nobody like myself can match a first class mage, I can. If those four Elves are warriors...."

Euleilla pulled to a halt, stopping Wangdu in the process. "They weren't after me," she said.

"Yes they were after you, they were," he answered. "To bargain, to negotiate, to blackmail, perhaps, but they were definitely after you, they were."

"No," she stated firmly. "They were not after me. I'm not important enough. We have got to find Maelgyn. Now!"

"They will not strike at him directly, they w—" Wangdu began.

"Now!" she commanded.

"But—"

Without waiting for him, Euleilla spun and pulled her arm out of his grasp, twisting his arm around and pinning him against the wall until he released her. "Come with me or not, but I am going to find him."

"They will not kill him, they won't," the Elf pleaded desperately, rubbing his bruised wrist. "It would defeat their purpose if he—"

"Maybe not," she answered, storming back down the hall to where she believed Maelgyn to be. "But that's not a chance I'm prepared to take."

She heard him snap an interesting expletive that may have been in Elvish, but he quickly acquiesced and started running after her.

She only hoped they'd arrive before it was too late.

Maelgyn sighed. Wherever he went he could hear the muttering of nobles discussing his recent speech; some supportive, most angry. He really wanted to escape them like Euleilla managed to, but unfortunately he had to remain available for his aides... and consequently for the barons, as well. While the barons were obsessing over the reforms to the nobility, everyone else was working twice as hard to prepare for the war. Which meant, even though he had already assigned people to handle the logistics, he still had to be consulted on several of the major decision.

Which meant he was being constantly bombarded with inane questions by just about everyone.

"You know, when it was just me, or even just Euleilla and me, there weren't these kinds of problems," he muttered to no-one in particular after the fifth person asking about the number of horses he wanted provided for each cavalry officer approached him. "Shortly after I left the Royal Castle, I lost my one spare horse. It didn't stop me, and I got all the way to Largo without another. An army, however, would not be able to deal with all the stops I had to make on the journey. I never trained with the cavalry, yet I'm supposed to make decisions for them? I don't think that's a good idea. Shouldn't there be others helping to direct all of this, as I ordered? Who is the head of our cavalry?"

"Lord Terekalo, your highness. He has been ill, however, and is unable to handle these affairs," the yeoman who had been taking notes from him said.

"Then who is his second?" Maelgyn snapped.

"Lord Mathrid is the highest ranking cavalry officer available. I believe you've met?" The yeoman did not exactly sound thrilled, and Maelgyn couldn't blame him.

Maelgyn sighed. "Yes, I've met him. Hates me, hates my wife, but seems competent nonetheless. Direct all questions on the cavalry to him. If there is anything he cannot handle, tell him to summarize it and include it in a report the day after tomorrow. Issue similar instructions to everyone else, letting them know to go through the heads of the infantry, archers, or whatever other military unit they have questions about."

"Yes, your highness," the yeoman said, stifling a grin as he heard the description of Mathrid. "Anything else?"

"Yes. Anyone who isn't covered by that, explain to them that I'm eating lunch in private and won't be available for another hour," he sighed. "I need a break."

"Very well, your highness."

With that, Maelgyn turned and stormed off. His first stop was to the kitchens, where he quietly snatched some bread, cheese, and a small bottle of wine, leaving a note explaining their absence so that no-one on the cooking staff would be blamed. It was somewhat difficult balancing all three in his hands, as there were no easily accessible platters, but he managed it.

Arms full of his lunch, he quietly made his way down to his suite in the castle. He knew it was silly, childish, and likely impolitic to "escape" like this, but he needed the time to himself. Using the tricks Euleilla had taught him, he managed to avoid meeting anybody until he had the door closed behind him.

Sighing, he removed his sword belt and dragonhide armor, changing his clothes into something more comfortable. Leaving the bedroom, he went to the study of his suite and settled down at a desk to eat.

"Sword Prince Maelgyn," an unexpected voice began a few minutes into his meal. He looked up to see not one, but four people standing between him and the only door out of the study. All four of them wore hooded cloaks, only allowing heavily shadowed faces to peer out at him.

Slowly, Maelgyn stood from his desk and turned to face them. He hadn't thought to use his magic to see if anyone would intrude on him in his private offices, since those were usually off limits except by certain specific individuals at certain times of the day. Now, he was beginning to realize that he should always have his defenses up, regardless of the situation he was in.

"Gentlemen," he replied slowly. He took quick stock of his situation – his sword and armor were behind the now closed door between the study and the bedroom, there were four unknown men standing in between him and the only exit, and there was not much chance of someone else coming in to help him. If these people were planning to attack him, he would be in serious trouble. All he could hope was that they just wanted to talk. "How may I be of service?"

The four lowered their hoods and dropped their cloaks, revealing their faces, pointed ears, and sets of a bizarre armor Maelgyn had never seen the make of before. *Elves!* he thought, alarmed. *What are they doing here?*

"You have discovered something recently, you have," the lead Elf replied. "Others have seen it before, they have, and others will again, they will. Usually we have some warning before the discoverer announces it, we do, and can stop them."

"We had no warning this time, we didn't," a second Elf said sadly. "And so centuries of work are in danger of being unraveled, they are. Your decision to respond so radically cannot easily be repaired, it can't."

"You leave us with little choice, you do," the third sighed. "So we must leave you with little choice as well, we must."

The fourth said nothing, but revealed a very Elven weapon: Two wooden spikes – or rather two foot-long thorns, growing as an extension of his fist out of some unusual vine wrapped around his arm. Other wooden thorns and roots formed some sort of thin, flexible shield, all part of the same thing. Maelgyn realized it was some sort of plant, actually growing around the Elf's arm. He had never seen Wangdu or any other living being wear one, but he'd heard of this elite Elven-bred creature before. It was a *schlipf* plant, a living weapon. Elves were the only beings which could use them effectively without danger, though other races could use them at great cost. If a non-Elf tried to wield one, it could, if they were lucky, just prove to be somewhat uncontrollable... or, if they were unlucky, the *schlipf* could bind its roots deep within the wielder's musculature and prevent any non-elf from controlling it without great pain. Regardless, the *schlipf* severely lowered the life-span of most non-Elves who tried to bind with them, and the binding process often left the wielder in severe pain even in ideal cases, but nevertheless many assassins sought it out for three reasons.

It was powerful, versatile... and immune to both Human and additional Elven magic.

Maelgyn frowned. "Are you planning on killing me?"

"Perhaps," the lead Elf admitted. "However, there is a more effective – and far less intrusive – alternative, there is. And you would not be killed, you wouldn't, if you agree to our demands, you did."

"I appreciate the not being killed part," Maelgyn answered wryly. "Tell me something before I answer you. How is it that you've been able to avoid having this information get out before? I mean, you say this isn't the first time you've been discovered. Surely the public knew about it when it happened... or were all those other discoverers killed?"

"We have only had to kill three of the seventy-four others, we have. Most people see reason, they do, when we explain it."

"And no-one has ever gone back on their word?" Maelgyn asked. "Some might see the honor of revealing a plot like this as greater than the loss of honor involved in breaking an oath."

"Perhaps," the lead Elf agreed, nodding slightly. "Yet none have. We can be quite... convincing, we can."

Maelgyn grinned wryly. "Yes, I bet you can. I suppose the fact that I'm working against Hrabak the Mad Elf doesn't help my stand, does it?"

"You would be surprised, you would," the Elf said, giving a sad smile. "We have no more love for Hrabak than you do, we haven't. But if you are not here, you aren't, your nation will nevertheless fight on, it will. But we are not your enemy, we aren't."

"No?" the Sword Prince snorted. "You're just trying to steal the nation I have sworn to protect out from under me."

"We are not, we aren't," the lead Elf declared. "What we are trying to do, we are, is what should be done. We are trying to unify the Human race under one banner, we are – whether that nation is Poros, or Svieda, or the Oregal Republic, or even Sho'Curlas does not matter, it doesn't. It is unity we are after, we are. Sopan Province is an easy place to start, it is, due to its unusual connection with Svieda. It will be centuries still before we can institute our plan, it will, so you do not have anything to fear, you don't."

Maelgyn's bravado left him as he heard that. "You... what? Unite the Human race? Just how are you planning to do that? And more importantly, *why?*"

"You have already found the how, you have – Poros, which was once the center of Humanity, will be it again, it will," the Elf answered him. "As for why... our reasons are our own, they are, but you may know this much, you may. The Nekoji are only in Caseificio, they are, the Dwarves in Mar'Tok, the Merfolk in the sea, and the Dragons in the air. We Elves are a dying breed, we are, and before we go we wish to see balance restored to the world, we do. Outside of the Ancient Elves' works, our Child races will not survive without us, they won't. We destroyed the Dwarves' great strength, we did, and we were largely responsible for the barbarism against the Nekoji, we were. We have killed more Dragons than any other race, we have, and drove the Merfolk from the few coastal towns where they might meet with the land-borne races, we did. We were the ones who made all the other races vulnerable to Humans, we were, and so we will restore balance to the world, we will."

Maelgyn pressed his lips into a tight line, restraining himself from saying something that might provoke his captors. Picking his words carefully, he finally responded. "So, you decided that part of 'balancing' the world was uniting the Human race. Interesting. But there's a flaw in that, or possibly just a missing part of the plan. When we're all one single happy Human nation, what happens to us? We'll still be the largest, and most dominant, race on the planet. Or is there more to it than that?"

"We Elves live a long time, we do. We shall still be around, we shall, to foster the weaker races and to let them grow again – they will become your equals again, they will."

"Oh, I'm sure you'll try that," Maelgyn said, drawing into the mental state to do magic. He didn't have much to work his magic on other than himself, but he was pretty sure a fight was coming soon and he needed whatever help he could find. "But somehow, I doubt that you'll be able to 'balance' the world, as you claim, without... displacing... the humans who now 'control' it."

"No," the Elf agreed with something of a sigh. "I'm afraid you are right, I am."

Maelgyn braced himself mentally. He could see in the Elves' eyes that they were now resigned to a fight. He likely wouldn't live through it, but in case he did he still needed to find out more. "Just tell me one thing – is it all Elves who are now engaged in this war against humanity, or just you four?"

"We merely represent a faction, we do," the Elf admitted. "A sizable one, it is, but still just a faction. Hrabak acts alone, he does, and Lady Phalra of the Bandi Republic continues her efforts at making Humans more Elven in private, she does. A Foolish woman, she is, determined to breed with one of her Human lovers, she is, despite millennia of Elven lore proving that we cannot. Your ally Wangdu has his own agenda which runs counter to ours, he does. As a race we are quite scattered, we are, and therefore do not communicate with each other very often. But there are hundreds of us in this cause, there are, all devoted to this goal. Such a gathering of Elves may be the largest since the fall of the Last Elven Kingdoms, it may. But we intend no harm on Humanity, we don't, as long as we are unopposed."

"Then consider yourselves opposed," Maelgyn snarled suddenly. Moving as quickly as his magically enhanced muscles would allow, he grabbed the wine bottle he had been drinking from and sent it flying. His hopes to catch the Elves off guard, however, were dashed as the bottle shattered against a suddenly appearing wall of vine. Schlipfs worn by all four Elves expanded into living shields, and shot out to form a barrier between the bottle and the Elves.

"We shall give you one last chance, we shall," the lead Elf snapped, looking completely unphased by the sudden attack. "I would rather not kill you, I wouldn't. Your response to our plans has impressed me, it has, even if it works against us, it does, and I would rather work with you than kill you, I would."

Maelgyn tensed. "I gather this was why no-one else ever betrayed your confidence," he growled, trying to delay the attack while searching for some skill or tool which might help him survive. He was not having much success, however – he had never fought an Elf, but he knew that even being a first rate mage meant little in battle with them. "Elven powers can be quite intimidating when used to threaten. But I refuse to let a threat go unanswered, and your plan is a great threat not just to Svieda but to all of Humanity. Therefore, my answer is to kill me if you can, because I will fight you with everything I have."

Using all of the magical power he had, he strengthened his musculature and skin to where it would act as a light armor. Not that it would do any good – the spikes of a *schlipf* could, in theory, pierce stone with anything more than a glancing blow. Dragonhide armor could, in theory, withstand all but a hard, direct blow from one... which did Maelgyn no good, as his dragonhide armor was in the other room. It was unlikely the magical enhancements would help much, but at least it was something. That, and it would allow him to move faster and hit stronger – which was likely the only thing which gave him any chance in this situation... not that it was much of one.

"And you will fail, you will," the lead Elf replied, bowing his head with what appeared to be genuine sorrow. "Just as all who try and oppose us will, they will."

With that, three of the four *schlipfs* were pointed at him, their thorn-based spikes growing out at remarkable speeds to come at him like javelins. Maelgyn dropped to the floor instinctively, his reflexes just barely keeping him from being pierced in the initial strike. With what magic he could divert to a counterattack, he concentrated and struck out against the very lifeblood of the nearest Elf.

It wasn't enough, and he knew it. For some reason, Elf blood, while still magically reactive, was not as easily manipulated as the blood of Humans. Perhaps Elven blood held no iron, but instead some other metal. Perhaps the same element which prevented magic from piercing a dragon's hide was also present in the skin of an Elf, though not thick enough to stop it completely. Regardless, his magical attack amounted to little more than an irritant. For any magic to be combat effective against them, Maelgyn would have to concentrate everything he had against a single Elf, leaving himself vulnerable to the other three.

Maelgyn grabbed the shaft of one of the three retreating *schlipfs* spear-like thorns, letting it pull him closer to the Elves. The short distance would reduce his reaction time, but without magic or weapons his best chance lay in physically battering them with his fists. The *schlipf* thorn shrunk down to its original one foot length, carrying him within striking of the Elf wielding it.

He spun as quickly as he could, slipping behind the first Elf and delivering an elbow to the back of his head. Reaching out with one hand, he magically called for the closest thing to a weapon he had on hand – the cheese knife he'd brought with him for his lunch.

The Elf he'd struck collapsed, dazed and off balance from the single blow. Truth be told, Maelgyn was somewhat disappointed with the result – he had been hoping his enhanced strength would be enough to knock the Elf out at the very least. However, he had known that Elves were tougher than they looked... much as he was.

He threw the cheese knife at the dazed Elf, using magic to speed its flight and change its shape into a sharper weapon. A *schlipf* vine caught it and pulled it away less than an inch from his target – not the dazed Elf's *schlipf*, but another. In fact, the Elf he'd hit lost control the living weapon entirely. Most *schlipf* were 'bonded' with their wielder, and could not be used by anyone but their owner. A few, however, were never bonded to their Elven masters, and would occasionally abandon them if the Elf ever lost control. In a stroke of fortune, this one had chosen to abandon its Elf at this moment, and Maelgyn decided to take advantage of that.

Maelgyn's magic retrieved the knife, breaking through some of the vines that encased it on the way. It was the only bit of retrievable metal he had in easy reach. Or rather, it was the only weapon he knew how to use. Reaching down, he grabbed the *schlipf* with the hand not using the knife.

He had no idea how to use the living weapon, and he doubted he would be able to figure out how it worked before the Elves had killed him, but at least if he held onto it one less Elf would be armed. Or so he thought.

"That was a mistake, it was," one of the Elves said, nodding to the hand holding the *schlipf* as he grinned fiercely. Within moments, vines started wrapping their way around his arm and up his body.

All four Elves, including the mostly recovered one whose *schlipf* he was holding, backed off and simply watched him as he fought with the living weapon. *Stupid,* he cursed himself. *Elves don't need to hold these things to use them. I knew that. Damn.* Slashing desperately with the tiny knife he held, he tried to cut the vines away from him. It was a losing battle, and he knew it, but he refused to give up. It continued to twist around his arm, tightening as it grew, and tried reaching for his mouth, but he kept cutting it down first. It was only a matter of time, though, before it made it past his defenses and started choking him. Before it had a chance to, however, the *schlipf* stopped moving, and withdrew itself into its base form.

The four Elves looked on in surprise. "What happened?" one of them said, with the first note of genuine surprise Maelgyn had ever heard from an Elf.

"A *schlipf* cannot be controlled by two masters, it can't," another Elven voice declared. Maelgyn looked to see an enraged Wangdu, spear at the ready and Euleilla at his side. He shook his head in disgust. "Fools. I would not have thought you stupid enough to try and kill him, I wouldn't – not after he's alerted us to your plan, he has. It's too late to repair the damage without his cooperation, it is, which you will not have without him alive, you won't."

"He would not co-operate, he wouldn't," one of the Elves declared. "Our best hope is to kill him, it is, and to encourage the Barony to reject his plans."

"His death would make him a martyr, it would," Wangdu answered. "You do not understand anything about humans, you don't.

"Wangdu, you must release your hold on my *schlipf,* you must," the unarmed Elf growled.

"I will not, I won't," Wangdu replied. "And I cannot, I can't."

"We are caught, we are," the Elf replied. "You can counter any move we make, you can, and with these stone floors, our numbers can be balanced out by Human magics. But in turn you cannot harm us, you can't, for we are too powerful for the entire population of this castle, yourself included, to subdue. So if you release the *schlipf*, you do, I will not kill him, I won't, and we all may go our separate ways without any deaths, we may."

"As I said, I did," Wangdu answered. "I cannot release it, I can't. I am not controlling it, I'm not."

"Then who—"

Maelgyn suddenly felt a pain in his arm, and looked down. Apparently, in his rabid defense, he'd managed to cut himself badly in several places... and the *schlipf* had rooted itself into his wounds.

"It seems as if... it's *my schlipf* now," he said uncertainly. Then another wave of pain struck him, and he collapsed unconscious.

Chapter 22

Maelgyn sighed, enjoying the ministrations Euleilla was visiting upon him. He wouldn't have guessed it, but she proved to be a fairly capable nursemaid to aid him in his recovery. At the moment, she was cleaning him with a damp cloth since he couldn't move much during the continued bonding process with the *schlipf*. She had been tender and caring beyond his expectations during the whole week he had been bedridden, with the occasional assistance of Dr. Wodtke's medical expertise.

Well, more than a week, but he had only been awake to notice it for about a week so far. It had taken him several days just to wake up, and even when he did he was barely aware of his surroundings for another day or two.

He was now strong enough to deal with conversation, however. A fortunate thing, considering it allowed Wangdu to alleviate his fears about the Elves that had attacked him and about the dangers of the bonding process. The attack had been stopped, thanks to Wangdu and Euleilla, but there was no way to kill the Elves or incarcerate them – it was far easier to defend yourself from an Elf than to attack them, at least inside castle walls where their feet could not touch the soil of the Earth. Instead, the four Elves had been allowed to return to their masters with a warning: Svieda was aware of them, and would not be vulnerable to their deceptions any more.

As far as the bonding went, there was definite good news. While it was impossible to remove a *schlipf* once it began the bonding process, it could be mentally commanded to exist as little more than a living bracelet around the wrist when not in use. Even better news was that Wangdu was able to aid the bonding process considerably – already, the pain had faded to the point where it was only noticeable when he concentrated on it. Within a day or so, it would go away completely. That was extremely rare among Human bondings with the plant – usually the pain never went away.

Furthermore, it was what Wangdu declared a 'clean bond,' which meant that there was little chance it would drain many years off of Maelgyn's life. In fact, it was entirely possible the schlipf could extend his life some years, given the nature of the bond. According to Wangdu, that only happened if the plant "liked him," whatever that meant. There was a lot about the explanation which didn't make much sense to him, but all Wangdu would say in reply to his questions was, "You'll know in time, you will."

He resolved to worry about it all later. Right now, he was allowing himself a well-deserved rest, and enjoying Euleilla's attentions as she treated him. Valfarn had taken over the logistics of the military expedition, for which Maelgyn was quite thankful. After the attack, the Council of Nobles voted unanimously to endorse his plan for the reformation of Sopan. The Elves' efforts had backfired completely. He was almost grateful that they had attacked.

And it helped me to meet you, something said in his head.

"Who said that?" he exclaimed, startling his wife.

"What?" she answered, looking at him oddly. "No-one said anything that I heard, and I would have heard."

"Must have been my imagination," Maelgyn replied. "Maybe I was drifting off to sleep or something."

No, the voice answered in what seemed to be an exasperated tone. *You merely don't comprehend what's going on. Don't speak, just think – I'm talking in your mind.*

Maelgyn didn't know what was going on – and he wasn't sure he wanted to. Was he going insane? He'd heard that insane people sometimes heard voices in their heads.

Relax, it thought to him once more. *You are not insane. I really am talking to you, and if you think for a moment, you'll realize just what I am.*

Maelgyn wondered at that. He'd never heard of anything, even an Elf, talking in his head. It didn't help that his vision was blurry and his senses addled. He started searching for any possible explanation but came up blank.

Oh, come on. You know *what I am.*

It took him a while before he realized that it was the *schlipf* that was "talking" to him. While he knew it was a so-called "living weapon," he never knew it could, for lack of a better word, speak, but that was the only thing that made sense.

Well, I can. But no, it wouldn't be common knowledge – typically, we don't talk to those we bond with. Or even to the Elves which created us and master us. We are a bit picky about who we talk to, and most who we do talk with keep our secrets. We were born to be weapons, but we were born to be living weapons. We were given intelligence so that we could defend our masters even when they were asleep or unconscious. But as intelligent creatures, we have our own ideas about what causes are worthy and what are not. I'm not exactly all that enthusiastic about my former Elven master's plans, so I believe that keeping you alive is a worthy cause.

Me? Why me? Maelgyn asked, by now realizing how he could talk directly to the plant. *I am no-one special, save by the accident of my birth.*

Ah, but the so-called "accident of your birth" is the reason you require my protection, the schlipf replied. *I may not have discovered it if you hadn't wounded yourself, allowing me to root in your nerves, but once I was connected with you I knew your cause was worthy of my support. And so I now greet you as your servant and protector, Maelgyn, Sword Prince of Svieda. I am Sekhar, Schlipf Volunteer, Junior Class.*

Maelgyn didn't know what to think for a moment. Who even knew that plants had classes? Much less that they could talk in people's minds, or make moral choices about who to help and who not to help. His attention was drawn, however, by the sense that Euleilla was probing him magically, searching for whatever was distressing him. He set his wordless thoughts on this new aspect of his bonding aside to alleviate her fears.

"I'm not in any pain. Not anymore," he noted.

"I know," she answered. "I can tell. But something else is troubling you, distracting you. I might think it was me, but I sensed that your attention was not on me. I can't find what the problem is, however."

He really wanted to explain to her what was going on, but he wasn't sure how to do so without explaining Sekhar, which he wasn't sure he should do right then.

Go ahead, Sekhar thought to him. *Tell her. But tell no-one else without my permission.*

You trust her?

Why not? She is your lifemate, is she not?

Well... yes, Maelgyn thought back after a moment's hesitation. *But things were complicated when we met, and they just get more complicated the closer we get. She's a commoner, not a noble, after all, and while I'm okay with that I don't know if she even knows what all it entails, and there's this war about to happen during which...*

Stop babbling, Sekhar chided. *You cannot lie to me, even if you wish to lie to yourself. The politics of Humanity can do nothing to change the fact that she is your lifemate. She will know about me eventually, and better sooner than later.*

"Right," Maelgyn sighed. "Euleilla, I can tell you what the problem is. It will have to be a secret, however, and it must be kept – Wangdu probably suspected this would happen, but even he shouldn't be told."

She sighed deeply, looking disappointed with him. "Surely you know I can keep a secret, by now?"

"Right," he answered, blushing in embarrassment. "Of course. Yes, I know you can keep a secret. I just needed you to understand that it *was* a secret."

There was a pause, and he still wasn't saying anything. Finally, Euleilla could stand the silence no longer. "Talk. It's the *schlipf,* isn't it?"

"What else would it be?" Maelgyn asked, somehow not surprised that she had guessed. "At this point, my senses both magical and natural are so dulled I can barely tell you are here when you aren't talking. If I'm not thinking about you, or whoever else is around that I'm talking to, my thoughts are going to drift... and they'll likely drift to the *schlipf,* given the newness of it all."

"What about the *schlipf?*" she asked. Obviously, she wasn't going to be distracted.

"It's intelligent," he replied. "And it just started, well, 'talking' to me. Or rather 'thinking' at me, I suppose. It says its name is Sekhar, and that it has bonded with me of its own volition. It feels I am worth protecting, for some reason."

Euleilla didn't say anything for a moment, and in fact did little more than continue swabbing him down with the damp cloth as she had been doing for some time. By this point, Maelgyn was certain she was just going over spots she had done before, but it didn't matter. He enjoyed it anyway, and it kept her presence certain in his mind.

"I am not surprised," she finally answered. "I didn't know how it worked for certain, but I knew the wielder had to be able to give it orders in some way. Nor am I surprised that it finds you worthy – I knew you were from the moment we met. But does it know that it can shorten your lifespan?"

Tell her yes, Sekhar answered. *I do. I also know how to expand it... and to expand hers, if she'll let me. But we'll have to wait until the bonding is complete to begin that, and only if she is willing to stay as your lifemate for such an expanded time.*

Maelgyn blinked, looking down at the plant. During the bonding process, the plant could not fully retreat into its smallest, most concealable size... but it no longer looked like a weapon. Now, it merely looked like vines braided into a long bracer. If there was anything which looked less like a thinking creature, he had yet to see it. Which was not, he cautioned himself (and Sekhar, in case it was listening), an insult – he admired its abilities to camouflage itself to look so harmless.

"It admits it can, yes. It claims to be able to increase my lifespan, as well, however... and yours, too, after the bonding is complete," Maelgyn answered. "Sekhar hasn't said how, yet, but he warns that we must remain 'lifemates,' as he calls it, if he does so."

Euleilla "looked" at him momentarily. Nodding, she answered, "I would enjoy spending more than a lifetime with you, husband."

Maelgyn forced his eyes to focus on Euleilla. It was more difficult than he would have thought, but he needed to see her right then. He needed to see her face – which he was starting to read quite well, despite not being able to ever see her eyes.

"I think I would enjoy it, as well," he said. Both of them still harbored fears over the struggle they faced, but they were willing to try and make their marriage work and that was enough.

Dr. Wodtke suddenly appeared – well, suddenly to Maelgyn. He was having a hard time perceiving his surroundings, still, and had no idea how long she'd been listening in on his conversation with Euleilla.

Not long, Sekhar said. *While you may be asleep and defenseless during the bonding, I can sense the proximity of others. I must, in order to know if you need protection or not. She didn't enter this room until a few seconds ago.*

Thank you, Maelgyn replied. *I can tell you'll be very helpful, with all that you seem to be capable of.*

I am bound to you, the schlipf stated. *I must be helpful, or I have no point in existing. By the way, the good doctor is talking to you.*

"...hear what I'm saying? Hello?" the doctor was saying. "I need to ask you a few questions if you're up to it."

"Sorry, Doctor," Maelgyn sighed. "I must've drifted off for a second."

"That's to be expected," she sighed. "Now, it seems as if you're doing pretty good, save for a lack of focus. I think it's time you started eating again, so I'm going to have someone bring you some soup. Do you think you'll be able to deal with it?"

At the mention of food, he noticed for the first time just how hungry he was. "I think the only thing I wouldn't be able to deal with would be the continued lack of food. I'm starving!"

She grinned at him. "Okay. We'll get you something filling, but easy on your stomach. I'll be right back."

As the doctor left the room, Euleilla re-entered his vision. Tenderly stroking his forehead, she said, "You look tired. Why don't you take a nap? I'll wake you when the soup gets here."

Closing his eyes, he nodded. "Okay. Good night, Euleilla."

He felt her lips on his forehead. "Good night, husband."

The next time Maelgyn awoke, it was not to Euleilla and the Doctor's soup. Rather, it was to a distraught-looking young Dwarf, fretting over his bed. He was dressed in a formal steward's outfit (which looked rather ridiculous on a Dwarf) that didn't quite seem to fit him. A stack of abandoned linens showed he had been coming in to perform a steward's duties, but had long since forgotten why he was here.

"Hello, Tur'Ba," Maelgyn said, greeting his young charge.

Tur'Ba spun to face him, startled. "Master!" he cried. "I'm sorry, Master! I should have been there!"

Maelgyn was bewildered. "Been where? What are you

talking about?"

"When the Elves attacked you, Master," Tur'Ba replied, downtrodden. "I shouldn't be doing these silly lessons on how to pick what you need to wear, or what sort of silverware is appropriate for state dinners. I didn't come with you to be a nameless servant in some stuffy castle – I wanted to fight the war at your side. To be in the middle of the action, defending your flank as my father defended his Lord's flank in his youth, when he was a soldier."

I wouldn't exactly call this reaction unexpected, but he's certainly taking it harder than I thought he would, Maelgyn mused. *I didn't know that Tur'Ba's father was a soldier, however. Perhaps El'Ba sent his son with me for more reasons than just to cure the boy's wanderlust.*

"First of all you could never be with me all the time, no matter the role you take in my court – I need my privacy, and I won't stand for having that privacy interrupted even by the most well-intentioned of people. I was attacked when I was looking for such privacy, and I was attacked by four Elves," Maelgyn noted wryly. "I don't think there's much you would have been able to do."

Tur'Ba frowned. "My ancestors, the Dwarven Axemen, were said to stand up to the Elves on even terms... surely, I—"

"Not true. Not under these circumstances," Maelgyn snapped. "I hate to disappoint you, Tur'Ba, but no-one has ever been able to beat the Elves one-on-one. Even a High Mage shouldn't be able to."

Tur'Ba's eyes narrowed, his mood shifting from self-loathing to anger. "No-one was a better defender than a Dwarven Axeman. Not even the Elves...."

"In a cave carved out of stone, as most of Mar'Tok and other Dwarven kingdoms were at the time, I'd agree," Maelgyn mused. "The Elves' biggest advantage lays in control of their terrain, but in a Dwarven cave there is nothing living for the Elves to control. It's what made the Axemen an elite, and what made the Dwarves a major race. Every major race seems to have its own elite warrior class. Humans have mages, for example. The Merfolk have assassins. And the Dwarves had the Axemen. But they're gone, now, and have been for centuries. Like many others."

That confused Tur'Ba. "What others have disappeared?"

"The Nekoji used to have an order of warriors known as

'Samurai,' soldiers trained to use their race's natural superiority in speed and strength to become better than any ten men. They could shoot heavy longbows with remarkable speed, and could move from place to place so fast that any one of them could appear to be five attackers if you didn't see them. Their swordsmanship was peerless. They were very impressive... but the Nekoji dismantled their order after an unfortunate peace treaty, and when the next war came there was no-one left to train new Samurai.

"Also the Ancient Elves had a class of warrior superior to anyone – even other Elves. They utilized the best aspects of every other major Race, incorporating them into themselves. Nothing could stop them, not even whole armies of Dwarven axemen—"

"But the Dwarven Axemen were able to prevent many Elven incursions from even entering the caves," Tur'Ba argued.

"The Axemen could defend the Dwarven caves from anyone, and en masse were effective against even the Elves. But a lot of what made the Axemen effective is that they could work well together while in tight spaces. Typically, it would be three or even four Axemen against each attacking Elf during those Elven incursions you mentioned... but one on one? A Dwarven Axeman wouldn't stand a chance even inside of his caves."

That seemed to disturb Tur'Ba more than anything else Maelgyn had said. "So... the Axemen weren't really very good? Is that what you're saying?"

Maelgyn laughed. "Hardly! In the few wars between Dwarves and Humans during that age, the Axemen were more effective against Mages than any other race, even the Elves. Human magic can affect Elves' blood – not as well as it can Humans, but at least to a limited degree. Dwarven blood is another matter entirely – even a First Rate mage can't do much of anything to a Dwarf if he's protected by a lodestone. The Axemen took this natural advantage and built on it, becoming true counters to the Human mages. I'm not entirely sure how all it worked – you'd need to talk to someone who was alive when the Dwarven Axemen were still around – but the Axemen were insanely powerful anti-Mages." Maelgyn paused. "Unfortunately, the last true Dwarven Axeman died many centuries ago. And it's a shame... we could use a few thousand of them in this war."

"Centuries ago, huh?" Tur'Ba mused, the wheels in his head

obviously spinning. "Thank you, master! I've got an idea!"

"Wait! What are you..." Maelgyn called, but it was too late. The Dwarf was gone. "Oh well."

Moments later, Euleilla came in, carrying a tray with a steaming bowl of soup. "Where was he going in such a hurry?"

Maelgyn frowned. "I'm not sure...." After thinking about it for a few minutes, he mentally shrugged, putting it out of his head.

Euleilla took a spoonful of the steaming broth and held it out to him - a few inches above where he needed it to be, and unintentionally threatening to spill all over him. "Open wide," she hummed.

I think I've got more important things to worry about than hyperactive Dwarves, anyway, Maelgyn thought, trying his best to keep his wife from spilling his dinner over him.

Euleilla grinned, helping her husband stretch. He had recovered enough to get out of bed just a few days before, and was now engaged in an exercise regimen to rework his muscles. The doctors, Wodtke included, had uniformly disagreed with him about just what kind of exercise regimen he should participate in. He wanted to do some sword practice in order to ready himself for the campaign. They wanted him to go on long walks.

After some work, Euleilla managed to talk both sides into a compromise - if he still felt up to it after engaging in a light workout along the doctors' line of thought, she'd engage him in a little practice with the staff. Maelgyn was a little unsure of engaging her in sparring practice, but he finally agreed as it was the only way the doctors would allow him to do anything but take those walks. The doctors believed that he would not be able to go through with it, though Wodtke wasn't quite as convinced.

Despite their certainty, Maelgyn still wanted to spar after they had returned from their walk. That had surprised Euleilla initially, but then he said that he needed her help before they began. Specifically, he found he couldn't quite fully stretch himself out without having someone help push him - literally. He needed someone to add their weight to his own for some splits and squats. She rather enjoyed draping herself over him as he exercised - their relationship was progressing nicely, and she was well able to use a little flirtation in the session.

Mentally, she was preparing herself for the spar ahead. She familiarized herself with the magical signature of his hands and feet, internally rehearsed all the advice Ruznak had ever given her about combat, and considered everything she might try to surprise him. She wanted to make a good impression.

Maelgyn took an unsteady breath and nodded. "Okay, that's enough I think. Let's get ready."

She 'looked' at him in concern, studying his magical signature. He seemed strong enough, but there was something odd....

"Are you sure? You seem to be breathing kind of... oddly."

She could feel his gaze on her. Curiously, even though she had long ago lost her own sight, she could always sense someone else's eyes on her. "Of course I am," he finally said. "You've been hanging on me for a good fifteen minutes. You are quite attractive, you know, and I am a man... and your husband. I would be concerned if I *wasn't* 'breathing oddly' after that."

She felt herself blush deeply as she realized what he was saying. It was true that she'd been trying for a reaction like that, but she hadn't really been expecting one. It was a... pleasant surprise.

"Then I guess I was doing it right," she answered impudently. "So, are you ready to get started?"

"I am. So, how do you want to do this? Do you know anything about staff fighting?"

Euleilla grinned. She picked up the staff she had prepared for her that morning – the one which had iron nails driven in either end so that she knew where it was. With that, she began a practice exercise her father had called a "kata", a complicated pattern of moves that involved an impressive array of twists and spins. She knew her husband was watching her as she worked, jaw open as he found himself unable to believe exactly what he was seeing.

She grinned at him when she was done. "What, did you really think that Ruznak, one of the greatest military minds of his generation and a hero to Svieda, would allow any foster-daughter of his to grow up without knowing anything about how to fight?"

She could feel the embarrassed grin he wore as he selected his own weapon. It wasn't one she was familiar with – in fact, it was made of wood, so she couldn't sense it even to tell its length, but she could make a fairly accurate guess based on how far apart he kept his hands. It was an escrima stick, not quite a full-length staff like her own. It could be used almost like a sword, though, for someone not trained well with a staff... like Maelgyn.

She nodded. "Ready?"

"Begin," he called, taking what she knew was a defensive position.

She made the first few strikes, probing to see where his strengths and weaknesses were. She was pleased when he responded with an attack of his own – a poorly executed one, resulting from him holding back too much of his strength, but an attack nonetheless. Good – he was taking her seriously, even if he was still treating her too delicately.

They started trading blows – she using his hands to find just where the attacks were coming from, he treating his staff as a sword while defending from her own. She could tell he was tiring faster than normal, however, and decided to end it sooner than she would have liked – she was having fun, but his health was her first priority.

With a quick move, she pinned his escrima stick to the floor to counter a poorly executed attack. Continuing her motion, she brought the other end of her staff up to his shoulder, throwing the entire weight of her body into a cross between a hook motion and a tackle. She landed on top of him, the butt end of her staff right under his chin. "Do you yield, husband?"

Something tapped her on the shoulder. "I think we'd better call this one a draw. I think you forgot about my *schlipf*," Maelgyn replied wryly.

"That, husband, is an unfair advantage, and you know it," she answered, not even acknowledging the vine tapping her shoulder. "By the way, when is your, uh, friend going to do whatever it is he plans for me?"

"My friend? Oh! Sekhar, right – I'd forgotten about that. Let me talk to him for a second."

She waited, noting once again the odd magical fluctuations traveling back and forth along his arm while he communicated with the odd Elven plant. She noticed also that he was getting agitated about something, but finally whatever the problem was resolved itself.

Are you there Sekhar? Maelgyn asked, immediately recognizing it to be a bit of silly question.

Of course - where else would I be? Sekhar responded sarcastically. *I need to ask your lifemate a question. To do so I need to put a root inside her.*

That sound like a big step. She should know what you wish to talk with her about, first. Maelgyn thought about it for a minute. *If you can you tell me what you need to ask her I will relay the question, however.*

It will take longer this way, but I see your point. Maelgyn listened carefully while Sekhar explained his question. When he was done, Maelgyn looked at Euleilla.

"Sekhar has something he wishes to ask you, but he cannot speak to you directly unless he plants one of his roots inside you so I'll relay it for him," Maelgyn explained. "Sekhar says he's about six years old, which is the age his kind starts dropping seeds. He wants to know if he can put a seedling in you. You will have the same benefits I do with him, and as the *schlipf* will be in you from seed to sprout, you won't have any adverse effects from the bonding, and in fact the only discomfort you will have will be a brief weariness and a momentary sharp pain when it sprouts. Sekhar will be able to help the sprout nurture you, ensuring your lifespan will be extended as mine is, and you'll have a *schlipf* of your own to help protect you. He adds that his son may be able to help you in other ways, as well - it might help further compensate for your... uh, eye problem."

"I don't need the help," Euleilla answered defensively, but then bit back the automatic reaction. "But it would be appreciated nonetheless. The added lifespan sounds nice, too, especially since it will be spent with you. Yes, I am willing to accept Sekhar's child."

Euleilla heard Maelgyn's relieved sigh. She felt the pull of the magic, and then noticed a slight pinching sensation on her arm before she started bleeding slightly. "Sorry, but I needed to make a slight cut in order for him to plant the seed. I tried to make it as painless as possible."

"You did a good job. I didn't even notice it was me you were using that magic on until I felt the blood," Euleilla replied as she felt the addition of something new - one of Sekhar's vines entering her wound. That stung a bit, but she was distracted enough that it didn't hurt much.

Indeed, a ghostly voice almost breathed into her mind. *He is more talented than he realizes. My apologies, but I have to make a brief connection with your nerves while I search for a good place to put my offspring.*

Sekhar? she asked mentally. *Is that you?*

Yes. You surprise me – your husband wasn't able to figure out who was talking to him for quite some time, nor how to talk back to me.

Well, he wasn't expecting a plant to talk. There aren't many who do in this world, Euleilla noted. *If I hadn't known of it being possible, I wouldn't have realized it was you, either.*

My son won't be able to talk for some time, Sekhar warned. *It may come as a surprise when he does.*

Will he talk before or after he sprouts? Euleilla asked, wanting to know just what she should expect.

I am not sure. Some of us get that ability before, some after. Rest assured he will talk to you, though – we always talk with our birth host, if we have one. It takes a lot of trust for one of us to be willing to plant our offspring inside a human rather than the ground, Sekhar explained.

I hope I live up to your expectations. I will never intentionally betray that trust, she vowed.

You won't, Sekhar declared. *I can sense the truth in you. A piece of advice, though, before I leave.*

Yes? Euleilla asked.

Do not doubt Maelgyn, the schlipf demanded. *I am aware that you both love each other, but do not know if you can make your lifemating work due to the pressures and expectations upon each of you. You may face difficult problems, but know that I have tasted both your minds, and I am confident that you will succeed. Stay with him always, and you will never regret it.*

Thank you, Euleilla thought back... only to discover that she was thinking to nothing, as Sekhar's roots were no longer in her. "Tell him thank you," she said aloud.

"He heard you," Maelgyn replied. "But what were you thanking him for?"

"Oh, he just gave me a piece of advice," she answered with a mysterious smile, not really wanting to explain. "A piece of advice I think I'll take."

"Ah. Mind getting up, by the way?"

Euleilla grinned, enjoying the fact that she still had him pinned on the ground. "Hmm... I dunno. I seem to have you at my mercy right now – and Sekhar seems to have deserted you in this situation." She sensed what she now knew was a mental conversation between Maelgyn and the *schlipf* before something finally made him snort in laughter.

"Yes, it seems he believes his use in this situation isn't called for. Okay, you've got me. Now, what do you want?"

She thought about it for a moment. She could continue the moment of playful teasing, but she had something serious to discuss.

"You are leaving soon on the campaign, I understand. The army is assembled and organized, the navy is prepared to break the blockade against Largo, and all we're waiting for is the completion of the supply train and word from Mar'Tok that it's safe for the army to cross over."

Maelgyn nodded slowly. Euleilla could feel the smile leaving his face, and was sorry to be the cause of it. "Yes, that's true."

"I will not be separated from you," Euleilla stated. "I want to join you on the journey."

"No," Maelgyn answered softly. "Please, no. It's not your place—"

"Yes, it is," she answered. "You could be gone for years, and I will not be left in this castle for years without my husband. My *place* is by your side – always. It is one of the conditions of our marriage – I will not be left behind."

"But—" he started to object, then stopped. After a few moments, she could tell he was talking once more with Sekhar, and seemed dissatisfied by whatever answers he was getting.

"You talk of my 'place,'" Euleilla quietly added, watching for his reaction. "Where is that? It certainly isn't here – this castle is a fine home as long as you are with me, but it would become oppressive if I were left on my own. Here I'm not even a true Princess but a mere Princess Consort – an emblem with no power. My place isn't back with my foster father – while I would love to stay with him again for a short visit before he dies, I don't think I could live in that town any more. Especially not if anyone else ever learns that I was married to you – I would become as much of a public spectacle there as I am here, and I wouldn't have the protection of these castle walls or your armed guards. I have no 'place' any more, except with you. So please, let me take my place and stay there."

Maelgyn sighed deeply. "I... I'm not sure I can say yes. It's... I'll be so worried for you."

"Surely," she answered him desperately. "Surely, you know I can take care of myself in a fight. We've fought in battles on each other's side three times. I just beat you in a sparring match. Ruznak trained me to fight, trained me to know strategy, and trained me to know everything there is to know about combat! I am ready to fight in a war. Probably just as ready as you are. Possibly more so. Please... let me come with you."

"Okay," he replied somberly after some time lost in thought. Euleilla finally relaxed – he had given in. "I'll let you join me at first. If things get too hot, though, if I think that there's no hope for survival, I may —"

"You'll do nothing," she answered. "I will be at your side through everything. Even death. Do you understand?"

"No," he answered after yet another pause. "I don't understand. But I don't seem to have a choice, do I? You may go where you wish, by my side or not. I just hope I never have cause to regret that."

"You won't," Euleilla promised, squeezing his hands tightly. "I swear you won't."

"Can you help me back to our room?" he asked. "I'm feeling a little tired...."

She noticed he didn't respond to her promise. She didn't say anything, however; it wasn't the time. "Sure," was all she said, standing up and helping him to his feet before surprising him with a deep kiss.

Together, they made their way back to their bedroom. It appeared he wasn't too tired, after all, as she guided him into bed before joining him. The kissing continued, getting more and more intense. Euleilla started tugging on Maelgyn's clothes, and he was all too happy to help her remove hers. Soon they were completely naked before each other, and Maelgyn was starting to take the lead...

And then the "brief weariness" Sekhar had warned them about kicked in, and Euleilla found herself getting lightheaded.

"I... think we need to do this another time," she managed to say... right before passing out.

Chapter 23

Valfarn set the parchment down in front of Maelgyn. "I've made the changes to your address tomorrow, as you requested, Your Highness."

"Very good, thank you." Maelgyn wrinkled his nose. "I'm not fond of public speeches, you know. Oh, my tutors' protocol lessons were thorough enough. But it's not something I look forward to, especially under these grave circumstances. It almost seems, well... frivolous."

"I think perhaps presenting oneself for adoration by the masses is never something a liege lord truly relishes, or at least not those who deserve the honor. But you're their new Duke, and the people will want to see you and judge for themselves what kind of man you are. And your first order to them will send us out to war, which makes it worse." Valfarn grimaced. "You should expect some of the peasants to speak out on that."

"I hope not," Maelgyn said. "We were betrayed and attacked without any provocation, our King slaughtered in brutal fashion and our capital city sacked. This war is a fight for our very survival, and it would be foolish for anyone to complain at this point."

Valfarn tipped his hand in the air thoughtfully. "Some, too, will want to reassure themselves that you've really recovered your health. They're good people, and they've trusted me to lead them for a long time, but some may find it, ahem... alarming, if you were to disappear from public view precipitously after so grave an injury."

Maelgyn nodded thoughtfully. He had no worries on that

score. Euleilla's attentions proved to him that his recovery had gone smoother than expected, and between his magical exercises and Sekhar's guidance he was even stronger than he had been before the incident. Unfortunately, the night she had passed out had been the only opportunity he'd had to consumate his marriage – despite his promise to stay by her side, Wodtke had chased him out of their bedroom the next morning. He had been fine and could resume the business of being a Duke, but Euleilla had now fallen into exhaustion. Not wanting the doctor to know about the still unsprouted *schlipf,* they had allowed Wodtke to believe that Euleilla's incapacity had come about because of the amount of time and energy she had put into treating Maelgyn. That led Wodtke to forbid them from spending their nights together until Euleilla was healthy, as well. Maelgyn sighed with frustration at that thought.

"Something on your mind, milord?" Valfarn looked at Maelgyn curiously.

"A moment," Maelgyn said. "There's another I need to have to join us, for a bit."

He stepped to the door, and spoke quietly with one of the guards, who nodded and dashed off. Maelgyn started to move away, but Sekhar interrupted him.

Don't bother, Sekhar thought to him. *I can already sense your young servant heading here now.* A minute or two later, there was a quiet knock on the door, and Maelgyn opened it again, taking a scroll from a short, squat figure. "Thank you, Tur'Ba," Maelgyn said appreciatively. "Right on time."

"Also, your highness?" Tur'Ba asked hesitantly.

"Yes?"

"Since I'm still being trained by Reltney, I tend to talk with your other servants a lot. Rumor has it that nobody will question your wife's unusual hairstyle – some people seem to think your wife is a powerful sorceress and her hair is part of some ritual. I think people are too scared to ask."

Maelgyn looked at him closely. There was no way anyone who knew anything about magic would ever believe that story... or come up with it. While magical knowledge seemed lacking in Sopan, he found it hard to believe a Human would come up with such a tale. "So what do you know about the origin of this *rumor?*"

"I beg pardon, your highness?" Tur'Ba's innocent expression was uncanny.

"Never mind." Maelgyn shook his head, and waved him away. It wasn't likely to do much good, but he wouldn't dress Tur'Ba down for the effort." These papers seem to be in order. That's all I need for now." Tur'Ba bowed and left as swiftly as he had come. Valfarn raised an eyebrow, a bit amused at the exchange with Maelgyn's Dwarven assistant.

Maelgyn turned back to Valfarn. "I have here," he said, "a proclamation, appointing one Duke Valfarn, Regent, to the position of First Advisor." He smiled. "I thought it wise, on the eve of war, to have that clearly stated."

Opening a drawer, he retrieved a quill, an ink bottle, and a stick of red-brown sealing wax, which he promptly employed while continuing to speak. "I have but to affix my signature and signet, and it's done." Maelgyn re-rolled the scroll carefully into its case, handing it to Valfarn. "And now, Regent Valfarn, I believe you have accumulated yet another duty – arranging for a herald, to read this at the conclusion of my address." Maelgyn extended his arm, and the two men grasped hands.

Maelgyn's speech was largely uneventful. Valfarn's concern about the people being upset at the war wasn't exactly justified – they were angry, yes, but at Sho'Curlas and not at him. If anything, it made the speech easier to give – they were so primed about the war that any time he talked about bringing their armies to face Sho'Curlas, the people erupted into cheers. It was entirely possible his people were more ready for the war than he was.

The speech taken care of, Maelgyn joined with the council of war Valfarn had assembled during his recovery period. His plans to counteract the Elven incursion were proceeding well, although he was sure in time there would be more issues on that front to deal with. One of the interesting effects of his proclamation was that Euleilla was officially made a noble outside of their marriage – the newly promoted Earl Terekalo, to make up for his own illness during the planning stages of his cavalry's movements, had directed one of his also-just-promoted Barons to create a Baronetcy for her. It was a bit of a sop to some of the traditionalist nobles, and it gave Euleilla some authority separate from him. Not that she particularly cared, but they both had appreciated the gesture and wished the man well in his recovery. He would not be a part of the initial stages of Maelgyn's campaign, most likely, but he would resume training new cavalry forces to support the war effort... once his health permitted it, that is.

Maelgyn desperately hoped the Elves wouldn't become an issue again until after the war was over, but it was good to know there would be competent people left in Sopan to help defend it if they made a move. He couldn't deal with them now, however, beyond his initial counterstroke – he felt worried for his family fighting on the front, and they needed his help as soon as possible. Patience, he decided, was not his strong suit. "Honestly, the only significant decision I see remaining is how to divide our military leadership on the journey to the rendezvous point," he noted.

"We intend to split the campaign army in two," Valfarn explained for the newcomers. This was the first full meeting of the council, and he was still the only person to know all of their plans. "We have confiscated as many usable wagons to help transport our soldiers to the war front as possible, but it isn't enough for our entire army. Our cavalry train will be sent over the mountains of Mar'Tok, where they will check in with our new Dwarven allies before moving on. As much of the infantry as possible will be transported by our navy while we attempt to lift the blockade on Largo. Archers, engineers, and other specialists will split themselves between the two groups as space on their respective transports permit. Both will require someone in charge. In time of war the Regent can also act as your top general, so I will travel with whichever force you do not, My Prince."

"You know how I feel," Euleilla said simply.

"I'm infantry, I travel with the infantry," was all Yergwain said.

Leno said. "I'll join you, Your Highness, wherever you lead. I have a feeling you'll have a better appreciation of my magic skill than some."

"That is not a reason for joining an expedition," Yergwain growled.

"Settle down, everyone," Maelgyn snapped, almost losing his temper. The two men had refused to do anything but argue since his proclamation in the council chamber, and that had spilled over into every council meeting he had attended since. "That's fine, Sir Leno."

"I'll go with you wherever you go, I will, just as Sir Leno has chosen to, he has," Wangdu said.

"My choice is clear," declared Onayari, the Nekoji representative. "Most of my race who joined us on the march here will return by way of the Mar'Tok Mountains – we are not exactly happy on the water. Someone, however, must be present at sea who can represent us in this great quest. I will be that." She did not exactly look happy with her own decision, but that was understandable.

"My people would not be pleased to see me right now," El'Athras snorted. "I think I'd better go over the sea."

"I think you all know, by now, that I'm going to be going with El'Athras," Dr. Wodtke noted. "And I think you should come with us, your highness. I'd like to keep an eye on you – your bonding with the *schlipf* went faster than I'd heard possible. Usually, it takes two or three months to recover, and you're back to full health after less than one."

"Hold it," Maelgyn said, raising his hands. "We cannot all go by sea. Lord Valfarn will need some help, even if they don't encounter any action before we are reunited."

"I'll be fine," Valfarn noted, waving him off. "Lord Mathrid is competent – that he doesn't want to be part of your councils of war doesn't make him entirely intransigent. He'll work with me, as will some of the other lords."

"So, basically, most everyone is coming with me?" Maelgyn asked, looking surprised.

"Well, I haven't said anything," Tur'Ba deadpanned. "But of course I'm going with you, too. My father sent me to learn by your side. Hopefully, I'll be able to do that when I escape from the, ah, tutelage of Chief Steward Reltney."

"I'll look after the steward," Gherald said, his eyes glinting humorously. "As the head of the Council of Commons and therefore the highest ranking individual left behind, I'm going to be in charge of Sopan. A commoner, in charge of the whole province? He'll go mad!"

Maelgyn looked around as laughter from that statement erupted across the room, although that laughter seemed rather strained from Yergwain's position. Maelgyn made a note to keep an eye on the man. "So... that's it, then? We're really ready to go?"

"In the morning," Valfarn acknowledged. "At the crack of dawn."

"Then we should get some sleep," Wodtke noted. "Everyone. Best way to prepare for a long journey is a good rest beforehand, I've always thought."

"Then to bed, ladies and gentlemen," Maelgyn commanded. "Tomorrow... well, I guess tomorrow we'll make history."

Most of the lords stood and departed, but Maelgyn stayed for a moment as he looked over their plans. He still wasn't sure of everything. Impatient, Euleilla took his arm, motioning him toward the door, where Wodtke was waiting to ensure everyone left. "That means you, too," she said pointedly.

Wodtke heard that comment and snorted. "Remember, girl – I said sleep. I'm still not happy with your stamina after that collapse last week. I don't want you doing anything that might cause a relapse."

"But—" Euleilla protested.

The healer is right, Sekhar noted. *My child is making it as easy as possible on your lifemate, but she still needs to rest some more. She will become ill if she doesn't rest.*

Damn, Maelgyn cursed. With a sigh, he addressed Wodtke. "Don't worry, Doctor – I'll be sure she gets to sleep and nothing else. I swear it on my word of honor."

Euleilla squawked, but Wodtke saw enough in his eyes to accept his word. "Very well."

Maelgyn took the lead this time, guiding her out the door and towards their room. "Listen to the Doctor," he cautioned. "A certain friend of ours says it's important."

He could see the momentary confusion on her face before the realization took over. "Damn," she cursed.

Maelgyn laughed the rest of the way to their quarters.

Chapter 24

The fleet of ships seemed to stretch for miles and miles. Only those in the front were the warships of Sopan – euphemistically called "triremes," although many ships had more than the three decks of oars from which they got that name – while a long train of transport vessels followed. Needing to transfer such a large number of people, Sopan's infantry required all of the ships they could find, filling the hulls of the triremes to their maximum ability and many, many more ships besides. Other transports carried most of the heavy equipment, supplies, and so forth. Once the blockade was broken and this cargo of men deposited at the rendezvous, the whole fleet would be returning for several more loads of soldiers before all was done.

"The thing you have to remember," Admiral Rudel, commanding Svieda's Third Fleet, said to Maelgyn as they stood on the flagship's deck, surveying the convoy. "Is that naval tactics are quite different from land tactics. You can't exactly turn these boats too quickly – you have to plan your turns far in advance if you want to get anywhere. Ranged combat is always preferred, and any time we use our battering ram – the only decent close-in weapon we've got – you're risking sinking yourself even if you do everything right. Your fancy magics aren't going to be nearly as effective in a battle like this."

Originally the Oden Navy – now under the control of Sho'Curlas – was the largest navy in the world. In one single, titanic battle, it had wiped out Svieda's First and Second fleets, but had in turn been reduced to shreds. Now, it barely had enough ships to maintain a blockade over a half-dozen of the more important ports in Svieda, all east of the Largo River. The Third Fleet, based in Sopan and so far uninvolved in the conflict, now outnumbered the blockading force almost ten to one, and all of Rudel's ships were in better trim. The Admiral had decided it would be a good idea to explain naval tactics to his liege lord before the major maneuvers began. He was a bit amused, however, at some of the suggestions given to him by the Lord of his province.

"Which is why you're in charge of the Navy, and not me," Maelgyn laughed. "I think I'd probably sink half of these ships just trying to organize a simple flanking maneuver."

"Glad you realize that," Rudel snorted, amused at the mere concept of a fleet of triremes even attempting a 'flanking maneuver.' "When I called the captains in for my traditional pre-action dinner last night, the captain of the *Narwhal* complained that Lord... Yergwain, I think it was, had been making trouble. For some reason, that idiot seems to think being born a noble gives him enough knowledge to tell a sea captain of thirty years experience that he doesn't know what he's doing. The Elf and the... what do you call those cat-people? Ah, yeah, Nekoji! The Elf and the Nekoji girl are far better company, he said."

"Not surprising," Maelgyn sighed. "Yergwain's seems a bit stuffy, to me, and I've only known him for a few weeks now. He's competent at what he does, though, and I believe he's willing to look past his biases in order to get a job done. Don't take it too personally – he doesn't exactly like who I've chosen as a bride, either."

Rudel, born in Largo and a world traveler before ending up in charge of Sopan's navy, snorted. "His kind wouldn't. Nobility raised with Porosian traditions and biases – God only knows how no-one figured that out in the past two hundred years – are taught to despise mages and look down on commoners. Porosians believe that royalty should marry other royals or nobles so as to keep to their station, and commoners should marry only other commoners, or at most a lesser noble. Yergwain is a strict traditionalist... which is partly why he's so effective as a leader. He knows what works, he knows his place, and he knows that if he doesn't perform well it will reflect on both him and his family. So, in the confines of what his idea of nobility is supposed to be, he is the best. But unfortunately, his idea of nobility is backwards and inflexible. And it doesn't exactly allow for things outside his norm, like commoners married to royals. Your wife's new title of 'Baronet' isn't exactly going to help improve relations with him, though it might help with some of the less hard-lined nobles."

"Yergwain? He has a hard time accepting commoners married to lesser nobles, much less royals," Leno said, coming up on deck. "The, um... midshipman? Is that the right word? The young lad in charge of the lower deck of rowers?"

"Yes, that's one of my midshipmen," Rudel replied with great patience.

"Right. He said to come up and, well, he had some very formal terminology, but basically he would like you to come down to take a look at some kind of problem."

Rudel snorted. "That's the captain's job, not mine. I'm not in charge of the ship, just the fleet. The captain is on the foredeck, over there," he pointed.

"Actually, sir, he said that it was you he needed to speak to. He was very specific about it," Leno insisted.

The admiral just snorted. "A midshipman ordering an Admiral around? Well, I've got nothing better to do for the next couple hours while we close in enough to even start thinking about real combat maneuvers. Might as well go give him a chewing out. I'll be back in a minute."

Maelgyn didn't bother looking as the Admiral left – he was more concerned about the movements of his wife. Euleilla had discovered that she couldn't sense many of the things stored on a ship like rope and canvas, wooden rails, and even many sailors personal effects. Her magic powder was insufficient in as crowded an area as this warship. She had known sea travel was difficult from her barge trips back when she was living with Ruznak, but it hadn't been nearly as bad there.

The best she could do was find an out-of-the-way place where she could just sit still and avoid running into things. The problem was that there was no such thing as an "out of the way place" on board, and every sailor had noticed her stumbling around like the blind woman she was.

To prevent more questions, Maelgyn had ordered a hammock rigged for her above deck, where she lounged most of the time. Dr. Wodtke had covered for her, declaring that she was suffering from severe seasickness and was bedridden, so nobody questioned it. In the run-up to the battle, however, the sailors had to clear the decks and – somewhat apologetically – deconstruct her hammock.

Euleilla was trying to stay in an area where she could safely remain, but Maelgyn had seen her stagger a few times while he'd been talking to the Admiral. He figured that, just perhaps, she'd be willing to talk with him to get her mind off of the discomfort of not knowing where things were.

"You know," Maelgyn began, approaching her from behind. "I figure the big disadvantage of using magic to find your way around is that you don't know how to deal with it when your magic can't help."

"I've been in this situation before," she snapped, flinching as he put his hand on her arm. Her magical sense was 'off,' since all it did was confuse and deceive her while on board. "I've always managed."

"Yeah," Maelgyn agreed, gently pulling her into his arms and tucking her head under his chin. "But you've never had to deal with sea travel for so long. Here you can't just sit in an out of the way place and wait until it's safe to use your senses again; you have to keep moving to get out of people's way. It's already been almost a week, and it'll likely be another couple of days until you can escape to land. In the meantime, you don't know where anything is, and your magic doesn't help. It must be like it was when you were first blinded."

"Yes," she admitted in a scared voice. "I know I'll be able to use my magic again, but... but right now, it's just like I'm blind again. I discovered the ability to 'see' with magic before I had a chance to learn to really deal without sight, and this isn't exactly the best place to learn."

"You shouldn't have come," he sighed.

"I don't regret my decision," she replied fiercely. "My place is here."

"I understand you wanting to come with me," Maelgyn sighed. "To be honest, I didn't want to be separated from you either. But you could have at least crossed the mountains and met me in Largo instead of coming this way."

"You're going into battle," she replied. "I need to be with you when you do – while my magic confuses more than it helps on a ship like this, I'll still be able to use it when we get into a fight. I want to be here, to help keep you safe."

"I doubt I'll need your help," Maelgyn laughed. "Even if the flagship is engaged, there's not much that magic can do to help in this situation, according to the admiral."

"Well I'm here, nonetheless," she said, snuggling further into his arms. "Let's not argue... this is the first time since we got on this ship that I've enjoyed myself. Let's just stay here for a while and relax."

A throat cleared behind them. Maelgyn's eyes darted over his shoulder to see Admiral Rudel standing there. "Admiral?" he asked formally.

"I'm terribly sorry about interrupting your private time, sir," Rudel said, looking embarrassed. "But this is important. Important enough that I decided not to chew out that midshipman after all."

"All right," Maelgyn said, not releasing Euleilla but instead turning the both of them to face the man. "What is it?"

Rudel gestured to someone Maelgyn had never seen before. He couldn't tell what it was, but there was something very odd about him. "This... gentleman... appeared below. He's a mercenary, but he claims he isn't here to fight."

"Excuse me," Euleilla said. Maelgyn felt her magical senses activate to 'look' at the man, and found himself 'looking' along with her. "But I've never, uh, seen anyone quite like you before. What, exactly, are you?"

"I Merfolk," a throaty gargle answered.

"Shapeshifters!" Maelgyn exclaimed. "Of course! I think you need more training if you really want to pass for a Human, though."

"I not do this much. First assignment. Not see many Humans before."

"I understand," Maelgyn answered diplomatically, just now realizing his surprised exclamation might have insulted the creature. "What is that 'assignment?'"

"Boats there," the Merfolk answered, gesturing. "Send message. They Oden City-State. They no want fight. Want give up. No like Sho'Curlas men. One boat not theirs, force them fight. Boat flee. Now want s... srrr..."

"The blockade fleet wants to surrender?" Maelgyn said in surprise.

"Yes."

Maelgyn looked at the Admiral, who shrugged. "Tell them," the Sword Prince said after a while. "To raise a flag of truce, and sail with us into Largo Harbor. We'll discuss the specifics there... under the threat of fire from the most heavily defended port in the world outside of the Borden Isles."

"Okay," the Merfolk replied. "Must swim now. Will tell."

With that, the human-shaped creature dove into the water. After a few minutes of waiting for it to get out of earshot, Rudel said, "That was odd."

"Odd, how?" Maelgyn asked.

"Ships from the City-State of Oden? Surrendering? Against any odds, for any reason?" The admiral shook his head. "Doesn't make any sense. Oden is famous for always fighting to the last man regardless of the circumstances. Even if they didn't really approve of the actions of their allies, their honor wouldn't allow them to leave so simply. No, something is wrong here."

"I'm afraid I don't really know much about Oden," Maelgyn sighed. "I've heard they were fierce, and had a massive navy, but not much more than that. What are the chances that they'll honor their flags of truce entering the harbor?"

"Pretty good," Rudel said. "Assuming they're really Oden sailors. Something else is odd about all this, though: The reliance on a Merfolk mercenary to deliver their message. Oden and the Merfolk have been at war, off and on, for generations – I have a hard time seeing them trust one with such an important message."

Maelgyn frowned. "What could they gain, being in the harbor? They'll be targeted by every weapon available on the land, and would easily be sunk if they tried anything. There'll be a sizable fleet travelling in their wake, ready to attack the moment they try something odd. I don't know much about naval tactics, that's true, but what advantage might they gain from this kind of ploy?"

"Nothing significant I can think of," Rudel sighed in obvious frustration. "But it still doesn't make any sense."

"So, what do we do about it?"

"Well," the Admiral said, "Not much we can do... except stay ready for battle all the way in."

"Keep us posted," Maelgyn ordered. "We'll be right here."

"Of course, your highness," the Admiral acknowledged,

apparently recognizing a dismissal when he heard one. He quickly disappeared up the foredeck, leaving Maelgyn and Euleilla alone.

Maelgyn tightened his arms around his wife. "We'll stay here for a while, okay?"

"Yeah."

"Maybe until tomorrow," he said. "We just have to wait one more day, and then we'll be able to leave the ship. At least for a while – I'm planning to go to the Borden Isles. That's a longer trip, you know...."

"I'll come with you," she said. "I'm not leaving your side."

"I thought that would be your answer," Maelgyn replied. "But I had to give you the option."

They had no privacy, but that was all right. They stayed together the whole day and well into the night, simply holding each other for comfort until they dropped off to sleep.

Fire! screamed in Maelgyn's mind, waking him up from one of the best sleeps he'd ever had at sea. He opened his eyes, still hearing the screams of Sekhar, to see a piece of flaming debris just barely missing him to land three feet away.

Relax, he thought to the schlipf. *I'll get us away from the fire, but you need to stop screaming.*

Our greatest weakness, Sekhar thought. *Fire. Get us away, get us away!*

"Euleilla," he said calmly, though he didn't exactly feel calm. "You need to wake up. Now."

He felt the magic spike indicating her waking awareness of the world. "Maelgyn?"

"Something's wrong. We need to move, and fast."

"What's going on?"

"The ship's on fire, but beyond that I don't know," he admitted. "Sekhar's terrified, burning cinders are falling from the sky, and it's still dark out. But right now, we need to worry about the fire not more than five feet from us...."

"We're on a ship," she answered, sounding more frightened than he would have expected of her. "Where do we go?"

"Somewhere that isn't burning, and somewhere out of the way of the soldiers fighting the fire," he answered wryly, helping her to her feet. "Come on, it looks like the foredeck's clear."

Moving along carefully, and trying to avoid the sailors running around trying to fight the fire while just as confused as they were, Maelgyn and Euleilla slowly made their way to the bow of the ship. The captain was organizing fire parties, but Rudel looked lost, just standing there. Maelgyn lead the two of them over to the Admiral.

"What happened?" he asked the experienced sailor.

"We're just outside of Largo harbor," Rudel explained. "The Oden fleet – all of it – just destroyed itself. Explosions, big ones, sending flaming debris everywhere. We've already lost six ships to the flames, and almost thirty others are still fighting fires – including this one. Debris is still falling, starting more fires as we work... god only knows what's going on in the harbor itself."

Maelgyn was horrified. "We suspected the surrender was a ruse, but this...."

"I know," Rudel snapped. "And I should have thought of it – but I believed the Oden people were too honorable to try something like this."

"Maybe the ships weren't really controlled by Oden," Euleilla suggested softly.

Rudel looked at her for a moment, before huffing and looking over the side at the water. "It's times like this I wish I weren't an Admiral. There's nothing I can do, right now – all I can do is sit and let the captains and seamen do their job. I can't even organize the fire parties because that's the captain's job. All I can do is look back and see what mistakes I made."

Maelgyn sighed. This was a horrible disaster, but then he'd already braced himself to serious losses such as this long before the mission started. In fact, this unusual tactic his enemies employed resulted in fewer casualties than he expected from this battle. "Well, it's over, anyway. The Oden navy is mostly gone, and there's no way for a single port to rebuild faster than the dozens of ports in Svieda can."

"What was the point?" Euleilla asked.

"What?" her husband asked. "The point of what?"

"Of their attack," she asked. "Of this... firebombing. All the people on those ships died... and they failed to take out more than a dozen ships in the process. So what was the point of this act?"

"Honor," Rudel suggested.

"No," Euleilla disagreed, shaking her head. "That doesn't make sense. If they were doing something for honor, they wouldn't do it under a flag of truce, would they?"

"The point," Maelgyn sighed. "The point is to weaken us as much as possible, so that a later attack may be more effective. If they were truly the Oden sailors, then I might agree with you, Admiral, but I've pretty much decided that these people must not have been from Oden. The false surrender and flag of truce, the deal with the Merfolk, and... well, let's just say, everything about this sounds completely unlike what you've told us about the Oden people. Even if one or two of Oden's commanders approved of it, they would have faced mutinies for attempting such an action under flag of truce. Oden's men were not running those ships, I'm sure of it."

"It may have been an assassination attempt. Or they could have been trying to stop your armies. They could know you are here, and they could know that the infantry of Sopan is with you. If so, it means that someone knew our plans with enough advance warning to set this up," Rudel said. Then he shrugged. "Regardless, while there are a few more blockading fleets to deal with, the naval part of this war is effectively over. And my fleet never even saw any real action."

"Perhaps not," Maelgyn said. "But the navy will still be needed to help win this war. I'm going to head over to the Borden Isles once I've reunited my army and sent it marching towards the front. I'll give you a more complete brief when we enter Largo harbor. I'll also need to go and talk to any Borden Isle refugees who I can still find among the living. Re-opening the agreement with the Golden Dragons of Borden Isle is a major priority in this war."

"The Dragons? Why?" Rudel asked. "The most aid they've ever agreed to offer anyone is to fight other Dragons."

"Exactly," Maelgyn replied. "Sho'Curlas has been training some Black Dragons... possibly over fifty of them."

Rudel's eyes widened. "F... fifty?"

"When I signed the treaty to bring Mar'Tok and Caseificio into Svieda, the Dwarves and Nekoji gave me a lot of intelligence on their activities. Our survival may hinge on re-establishing the alliance with the Golden Dragons. Invading the Borden Isles is pointless, though. We know what it's like fighting them, and at best it would take years to successfully complete a reconquest of the islands. We don't have the time for that, and with the current war against Sho'Curlas we don't have the manpower. So, we went with a somewhat less ambitious plan. When I get to Borden Isle, I intend to talk to the Golden Dragons and see if we can negotiate the return of their protection. There may be an opportunity to reclaim the islands, as well, but that's secondary."

"Unquestionably," Rudel agreed. "So, you need a single ship to make a clandestine trip through hostile waters, huh? You're going to need a good captain for that."

"Any suggestions?"

"Well, Captain Pikob knows the waters better than anyone else I know of..." the Admiral considered.

"What about you?" Maelgyn asked.

There was a momentary sense of surprise on the old man's face before he shook his head negatively. "I'm an Admiral, your highness," he said. "And besides, I don't know the waters that well—"

"My foster father will join us," Euleilla suggested. "I'm sure of it. And he knows those waters better than anyone."

"It's been more than half a century—"

"He doesn't forget," she insisted.

"Well... I suppose. But like I said, I'm an Admiral. I command fleets, not ships...."

"What, you forget how to captain the moment you're promoted to flag rank?" Maelgyn snorted.

"Of course not!" Rudel exclaimed. "But I don't have a ship, and—"

"You'll have one. I need someone I know and can trust on a mission this critical."

Rudel looked at Maelgyn hopelessly for a moment before finally nodding. "I would love to command a ship one last time. It would be an honor to accept this role in your mission, your highness. Thank you."

"Thank me when we're back in Svieda with an army of Golden Dragons at our side," Maelgyn snorted. "Now, let's go meet the locals..."

Sword Prince Wybert braced himself on the rails of the deck of the *Greyholden*, the trireme Maelgyn had selected for the journey to the Borden Isles. They made a slight detour before this all important mission – up one of the Largo River tributaries, all the way to Rocky Run. Wybert once felt as much at home at sea as on land, but since losing his legs – and gaining only a pair of wooden pegs to replace them with – his sense of balance was completely off. He had been seasick several times already, and wasn't exactly happy at being on the ship... especially since this was just a short jaunt up a river to pick up some extra passengers. Euleilla sympathized with him, but there wasn't really anything she could do. Besides, she was having her own problems with the ship.

"Tell me again," Wybert grumbled, swallowing tightly. "Just why are we heading over to some small town practically in the middle of nowhere when we should be heading south, toward the Borden Isles?"

"Because this 'small town practically in the middle of nowhere' is where my foster father, Admiral Ruznak, lives," Euleilla laughed. "And Admiral Ruznak's knowledge of the waters around the Borden Isles is unique among your population." This was the fifth time he'd asked the same question, and the fifth time she'd given the same answer.

"Right," Wybert snorted. "Look, dearie, I think you're a great wife for my cousin and all, despite your lack of noble upbringing and the rather... unusual method by which that marriage began. I know some of our other relatives might be a bit upset about that, but I'm not. However, I sincerely wish Maelgyn had met you somewhere else so he wouldn't have been so tempted to go pick this Ruznak up. Your foster father will be a great asset, I'm sure, but getting him takes a lot of time—"

"I know," Euleilla replied at the point where he'd always stopped every other time he'd said that same speech.

"—and I.... Sorry to be so blunt, milady, but I doubt he'll live through the journey. He's, what, ninety-seven years old right now?"

That was unexpected, and the thought tore through her heart horribly. However, from the moment she started her journey with Maelgyn, she had suspected that if she ever saw her foster father again it would be only to say goodbye as he passed away on his deathbed.

"At least this way I'll see him again before he dies," she said.

"I thought I'd said my final goodbyes to him, already, but I'm so glad to see him one last time."

Wybert sighed. "Yes, well... I suppose I can see that. Still, I hate this boat trip."

"You are not alone in that," Euleilla agreed, grimacing. "You, however, will be taking command of the armies at Rocky Run and leading them overland to Happaso. I, on the other hand, will be staying on the ship for several more weeks while we head on over to the Borden Isles."

"You have my sympathies," Wybert laughed, then swallowed loudly and clutched his stomach. "Ulp! Maybe I'd better not laugh. You know, for someone who's seasick you sure haven't thrown up much."

"I'm not really seasick," Euleilla admitted. "I just... don't function well on boats."

"The foster-daughter of the famous Admiral Ruznak, not good on boats? That's almost more of a scandal than your marriage," Wybert joked.

"Just almost?" Maelgyn's voice broke in, echoing Wybert's humorous tone. Euleilla felt his arms go around her from behind – he had been doing that a lot lately. She had to admit she enjoyed the attention.

"Hello, Maelgyn. Where've you been?" Wybert asked.

"With Admiral Rudel. We'll be pulling into port in about ten minutes – if you can avoid getting sick again for that long, you'll be in the clear."

Wybert sighed. "Yeah. And then I'll be in charge of an army of Dwarven wolf-riders and Nekoji infantry."

"You can ride cavalry-style despite those two twigs you're standing on, right?" Maelgyn asked.

"Of course!"

"Good," Maelgyn laughed. "Nekoji 'march' at about the same speed as a cavalry officer rides a horse, and wolf-riders are even faster. You'll need to ride to keep up."

"I can't believe I'm getting myself into this. I'm taking charge of a host of people whose fighting style is completely foreign to me, yet you're putting *my* armies under the command of *your* regent," Wybert snorted. No-one took his protest seriously, as it had largely been his suggestion to put Valfarn in command.

"If it makes you feel any better," Maelgyn said, "You'll have plenty of time to train with them and learn how they operate." What he didn't say was that, after a long discussion with El'Athras, he had decided to put Wybert in a position where other soldiers would be able to teach the peg-legged Sword Prince the difference between naval tactics and land tactics.

"For all the good it will do us," Wybert sighed. "What good is a mere sixty thousand or so people or so in a battle between millions?"

Wybert would be taking command of his own province's division of cavalry, the Dwarven Wolfriders, and the Nekoji infantry to the front. The remaining Dwarves would wait in Rocky Run for Maelgyn's army coming from Sopan.

"When the armies are as large as they are in this war, the battles rarely use everyone at once," Maelgyn noted. "Sixty thousand people could mean quite a bit. Especially sixty thousand cavalry."

"Most of them aren't cavalry," Wybert disagreed. "Wolf-riders don't even match up well against light horse-mounted cavalry, and Nekoji... well, they aren't mounted at all, are they?"

"No," Maelgyn agreed. "But you'll have a mixed unit of Nekoji infantry, Dwarven wolf-riders and llama riders, and Largo's Human cavalry. That will give you a unit that functions as an infantry, a light cavalry, a heavy cavalry, and – thanks to the mix of a standard Dwarven wolf-riding unit – archers, all in one."

"Doesn't count for much in a prolonged war," Wybert sighed. "But I'll come up with something. I have the whole march to Happaso to learn just how effective they might be. When you get back, you're going to be stuck with just Sopan's cavalry and a fairly large infantry. Your future command will be forming a second line in case there's a breach at the front while you're off in the Borden Isles. You still intend to set it up along the river, I gather?"

"Of course," Maelgyn agreed. "If they break past the front line, the best place to set up a new defense is the Largo River." He started to say something else, but then noticed something. Tightening his arms around Euleilla, he turned her slightly to face the coastline. "Look at the harbor," he whispered in her ear.

She knew he didn't really mean "look," but she turned her head anyway. She pushed out her magic to the coast, probing it to find the harbor like Maelgyn wanted. It was then she sensed him.

"Gramps!" she cried.

"Gramps?" Wybert asked, sounding confused.

"You might know him as Admiral Ruznak," Maelgyn explained with restrained laughter, squeezing his wife as if he somehow shared her happiness. "If it were light enough, you'd probably also be able to make out Count Gyato, former Emperor of Caseificio, and Captain Rykeifer, a highly competent militia officer I met on my travels from the village of Elm Knoll."

Euleilla was so excited about meeting Ruznak again that she didn't even realize what she was doing. It took her a moment to realize she was practically jumping up and down in Maelgyn's arms.

When, exactly, had she become so demonstrative with her emotions? It used to be she'd restrain herself from even saying more than a word or two just to keep from letting anyone know what she was feeling. Now, she couldn't keep her happiness from showing... or keep herself from planting a big kiss on Maelgyn's lips.

Maelgyn's arms tightened around her once again, comforting and understanding. "I'm very happy for you, Euleilla."

Chapter 25

Maelgyn squirmed uncomfortably on what was usually the most comfortable couch in the Left Foot Inn, almost wilting under the piercing gaze of his wife's foster-father. It didn't help matters that she was, right then, lying with her head on his lap, dozing.

"So, boy," Ruznak growled. "You went and married her, did ya?"

"It was... well... uh..." Maelgyn started. When that glare intensified, he figured it wasn't in his best interest to prevaricate – not even just to explain how that marriage came about. "Yes, sir, I suppose I did."

The old admiral grinned. Maelgyn had guessed that Rykeifer explained everything that had happened in Elm Knoll, but Ruznak insisted on a confession from him, anyway. The fact that he hadn't blamed the whole thing on his ignorance of Largo's marriage laws seemed to win him some points. "Good. She needed someone in her life other than me, especially since I'm not likely long for this world any more. I figured you might be it when I first saw you, but the way things are in this world I was far from sure. Now, what is it you need me to do?"

"We're sending an expedition to the Borden Isles," Maelgyn said, absently stroking the now sleeping Euleilla's hair as he relaxed. "A secret mission, one lone ship, so that I can meet with the Golden Dragons. I need a guide, and you're about the only Borden Islander I know of in Svieda."

"I haven't been there for decades," Ruznak said slowly, doubtfully. "I may not be who you're looking for."

"You're the only one I know who can do it," Maelgyn said.

"And I suspect Euleilla would be happy if you came."

There was a long pause, before Ruznak slowly nodded. "Okay. For Euleilla... although I don't think she needs me much, any more. I've never seen her as alive, or as expressive, as I have today. Marriage must agree with her."

Maelgyn grimaced. "So far, perhaps, but I'm worried that with this war it'll get tougher...."

"Tell me," Ruznak said, looking at him challengingly. "When you first met her, how often did she say more than two or three words in a row?"

"Not often," Maelgyn admitted.

"And now?"

Maelgyn nodded slowly. "I know. I agree that she's more open. But you raised her, Admiral. She'll always have need of you."

"I'm not going to be around much longer," Ruznak grumbled. "She'd better be able to get by without me."

"She can. She could get by without either of us, I suspect," Maelgyn replied. "But while you're still 'around,' as you put it, I suspect she'd rather enjoy it if you were with her."

"Maybe," the old man sighed, shifting the knee of his missing leg so that he could scratch the end of his stump. "Golden Dragons, eh? That might get a bit uncomfortable, I'd think. Even if they aren't trying to cook you or eat you, they tend to live in hot areas. Like volcanoes."

"Which is where I might be of some assistance," Gyato said, coming into the room carrying a few rather odd-looking cloaks. After leading the Nekoji and Dwarven armies into Largo, he had since sequestered himself in a cabin on the boat for quite some time without offering any explanation. His sudden re-emergence was a bit of a surprise. "Since my people and I have had nothing better to do since arriving in this town, we have worked to manufacture a few dozen of these."

Maelgyn, careful not to wake Euleilla, took one of the unusual garments and looked at it closely. "I don't think I've ever seen anything like this, before – what is it?"

"A Nekoji-fur cloak, made the right way," the Nekoji man stated. "I admit, it's not as effective as some of those which poachers have skinned off of my kind, but it should make your trip into dragon lands more comfortable. We use the fur we shed from our bodies to make these, and sell them to those powers which help protect our kind from hunting. It won't survive a direct blast from dragon fire unaided, but it will protect you from grazing blows and the burning heat of a Dragon's den. We only have a few dozen available now, but if you desire we can have as many as a hundred others finished in another week."

"A few dozen is all we'll need. We can't stay more than a day or two before leaving, anyway. But I truly appreciate the gift, Emperor Gyato," Maelgyn answered, honestly quite touched by the gift. Despite Gyato's claim that the furs were sold to those who protected them from hunting, he knew that it was a rare thing for the Nekoji to simply gift them to others. That his kind were willing to donate as many as they had to his cause was remarkable. That they would consider donating a hundred more was beyond Maelgyn's comprehension.

"Emperor no more," Gyato said. "I am Count Gyato. My claim to any throne is gone, your highness."

"I suppose we never really discussed that," Maelgyn mused. "I imagine the title of 'Emperor' could be preserved, given the lack of precedents. No province has ever been a part of Svieda for long without a Sword being designated to run it. By virtue of our treaty, Mar'Tok and Caseificio will never have a Sword ruling over them."

"Keeping the title of Emperor could help smooth the transition for my people," Gyato conceded.

"I figure it's worth it," Ruznak huffed. "Emperor Gyato, you and Merchant Prince El'Athras have both gifted Svieda with your nations, but Svieda is not the Sho'Curlas Alliance. While you are now a part of our kingdom, I doubt Maelgyn, nor any of the rest of us, have any intention of usurping your traditions in favor of our own. Your titles, whatever they may be, will never be an issue."

The discussion of titles halted as several others arrived. El'Athras and Dr. Wodtke, Rykeifer, Onayari, Sword Prince Wybert, Wangdu, Valfarn's son Agaeb, and Admiral Rudel streamed into the room for an expected council of war. As they were filing in, Maelgyn paused to nudge his wife awake. "Euleilla? You might want to hear this."

"Hm?" she whispered, and then sat up rather quickly. "Oh, has the meeting started already?"

"Just starting," he answered. He bowed his head to greet the new arrivals. "Ladies and gentlemen, thank you for coming. Before we begin, though – Sir Agaeb, I invited you here to act as Sword Prince Wybert's second on his march, but you will also have to answer to Emperor Gyato, here. If you would prefer to participate in the Borden Isle expedition, I could find someone else to take your place. If not, the two of you will be responsible for demonstrating the legitimacy of our new alliances. With the Sword Prince of Largo and the son of the regent of Sopan verifying each others' stories, the treaty should go unquestioned."

Agaeb nodded. "Thank you, your highness. I will gladly accept any role you have for me, and will be honored to act as both Emperor Gyato's and Sword Prince Wybert's second."

"Very good. Also, Admiral Ruznak has agreed to come with us –" he paused feeling the delighted wave of magic burst from his wife. "Ahem. Ruznak has agreed to come with us, and I'm going to ask you to join us as well, Captain Rykeifer."

"I'll be glad to," Rykeifer said doubtfully. "But I am unsure of what help I can be. You already seem to have a significant number of command staff with you on this expedition. In addition to yourself, Admirals Ruznak and Rudel, Gyato, that Elf I have yet to meet, and El'Athras are all very experienced military leaders. Compared to them, your highness, I am not exactly –"

"Believe it or not, you are the only one of us with any real experience commanding a Human army in battle," Maelgyn noted. "Gyato will be marching with Wybert. Ruznak and Rudel are navy, El'Athras has only ever commanded armies of Dwarves, and Wangdu usually acts alone. As far as I am concerned... well, I have had some training, but most of my common foot soldiers have more experience than I do. Sir Leno also will travel with us as an officer of the army, but he has a special mission and will be at great risk of capture. I don't want him to bear the burden of protecting our plans and secrets, so until that is complete he will be out of the loop. I want you to lead our ground forces until his mission is over, and then act as his second in command afterwards. I witnessed you in action at Elm Knoll, Captain, and believe that you could be a great asset to our mission."

Rykeifer nodded, pleased with the praise but slightly overwhelmed. "Very well, your highness. I will do my best."

"Now, let me bring everyone up to date," Maelgyn said.

"Lord Valfarn is currently leading the Sopan Province cavalry across Mar'Tok, with Lord Mathrid as his second, and will arrive here within a week. Lord Yergwain is taking the Sopan Province Infantry and whatever can be spared of the Largo infantry to prepare new defensive fortifications along this river – including one here in Rocky Run, which will be the headquarters for this secondary defensive line. Emperor Gyato, Sword Prince Wybert, and Sir Agaeb will be commanding the Largo cavalry and the assembled Dwarven and Nekoji forces as they head to the front lines. The navy will be bringing in the rest of Sopan's infantry before attempting to break the remaining blockades. The rest of us, in the *Greyholden*, will head to the Borden Isles. When there, Sir Leno will be taking about five men to meet our contact in the Borden court while the rest of us will head toward the volcanoes and hopefully open negotiations with the Golden Dragons. Any questions so far?"

"I believe we all knew our own roles, already," Wybert said after a short pause. "And we have no questions on anyone else's."

"Good," Maelgyn said. "The thing to remember, for those of us going to the Borden Isles, is that secrecy is paramount. If we are very fortunate, we may find a way to restore those islands to Svieda's control, but we have no idea how realistic those plans are until we receive Sir Leno's report. When I return, I will take control of whatever forces have gathered here and take them out to join Wybert. El'Athras, have you had any opportunity to gather additional intelligence about the front?"

"Not much, your highness. All information about the war I have received is several weeks old, but it appears as if the Sho'Curlas' advance has stalled, with the heaviest fighting actually very close to the Sviedan Royal castle. Sword Prince Brode is in charge of the Sviedan army opposing them, at the moment. Sword Prince Arnach was forced to retreat to Happaso city when his leg was injured severely in battle, though he left a sizable force with Brode and is expected to recover and eventually return to the fight. There is no word regarding your father or the other members of the royal family. We have some suspicions, however: Sho'Curlas may have taken your father prisoner following his surrender of the Royal City, but none of those who were in Sycanth survived the battle. Sycanth city was utterly destroyed, and there were few survivors of any station. Three of the Swords are now in

Sho'Curlas hands: Prince Hussack kept the Royal Sword he stole from the King; Prince Mussack has been seen wearing the Sword of Rubick; and Lord Gandrug, ruler of the Sho'Curlas Grand Duchy of Adrabba, now holds the Sword of Sycanth – we suspect from the body of the Sword Princess herself. There have been no sightings of any Black Dragons so far, but we believe there may be plans to station them in Sycanth's ruins – we've witnessed the construction of what might be dragon stables."

There was a pause among everyone, before Wybert snorted. "'Not much,' he says. That seems rather complete, to me."

Maelgyn frowned. "Just out of curiosity... has anything been heard about the situation in Poros?"

"Poros, your highness?" El'Athras repeated, frowning. "I don't believe anyone mentioned anything, but then we haven't been looking their way recently. I'll make arrangements for a study of them, however."

Maelgyn nodded. "Okay, now – can anyone think of anything else which needs to be discussed before we proceed?" There was silence. "Good. Let's get started."

Euleilla lounged in her hammock, remaining as comfortable as possible while shipbound. They'd not even had a full night on land before they were back on the ship, but there was a chance they'd make it to land some time that day. She certainly hoped so – while both Maelgyn and Ruznak constantly doted upon her, she got the feeling that some of the ship's crew were starting to get annoyed at her intrusion.

However, the journey hadn't been all bad. Spending time with her foster father had been delightful, Maelgyn was always very attentive, and whenever the two of them were busy Sir Leno would try to entertain her by launching into discussions on magic. He was quite eager to learn more about the craft, which he had been forced to learn in secret most of his life, and she was just as interested in his own training regimen.

While there was much she had to teach him, he knew techniques she had never even thought possible – ways to create lightning, or fire, using special alchemy powders; ways to defend yourself from magical attacks she had never contemplated; even ways to cook meals without a fire. She was learning a lot. Unfortunately, no matter how much she learned, or how much her husband and foster father would distract her, she couldn't quite make herself forget she was on a ship.

Admiral Rudel had been by to see her from time to time, as well, but his visits always seemed quite awkward compared to those of the others. He, like most of the sailors, could not understand her inability to operate on a ship. She had heard whispers claiming that even the worst landsman would have developed sea legs in that span of time, but since her problem wasn't really seasickness she could never get over it. She sincerely hoped they made landfall soon.

"Hey," Maelgyn said, coming to her side. "How are you doing?"

She smiled in his direction. "Time for my daily exercise?"

"Yeah," he answered. "Let's go for your walk."

Carefully, she rolled out of the hammock and into his arms. "So," she asked. "How much longer are we going to have to do this?"

"Well, we're at Borden Island now," Maelgyn explained. "So not much longer. We made landfall at the wrong point, so we're going to have to go back out and circle a bit so we can make a proper landing undetected. Rudel thinks we'll find the anchorage this evening, but according to your 'gramps' it looks more like we won't get there until tomorrow morning."

Euleilla restrained a smile from showing on her face – something very unusual for her, as she usually preferred to force a smile at all times. "I don't think my foster father would appreciate it if you called him 'gramps.'"

"Why not?" Maelgyn joked. "You do!"

"Somehow, I suspect he wouldn't tolerate it from anyone but me. It's better for your health if you don't."

They walked along in companionable silence for a while, Maelgyn holding her close and steady as always during these strolls. It was a warm and comfortable way of dealing with her problems shipboard, and she suspected it kept the crew from thinking even worse of her.

Hello, something suddenly whispered in her head. *Can you hear me?*

Euleilla froze for a moment, attracting her husband's attention, but shortly had an idea as to what was going on. *Hello?* she thought back.

Oh, Good, it answered. *I was hoping my voice would be heard, soon. Hello, Euleilla!*

"Euleilla?" Maelgyn asked cautiously.

"I'm okay," she said. "Hold on."

Are you Sekhar's son? she thought.

Daughter, the voice answered. *I suppose – truth be told, we don't have genders. We do tend to assume the gender of whomever we are bonded with, however.*

Do you have a name?

Actually, that's what I was hoping to ask you about – our bonded host typically names us, so I was hoping you would do that for me, the *schlipf* requested.

Hmm, Euleilla considered. *I'll see what I can come up with.*

Could you ask your lifemate to let my father know I'm doing okay? Except for the fact that you haven't been very active, recently – I grow a lot better when my host is moving around.

"Maelgyn, please let Sekhar know his daughter is doing well," Euleilla relayed, before returning her attention back to the *schlipf.*

I'm sorry I haven't been more active, she thought. *I can't help it – when I was young, I lost my eyesight. My magic has compensated, mostly, for this loss... but on a ship it doesn't work effectively. It makes it difficult for me to do things in the environment we're in now.*

Oh! Well, I can't really do my job as a weapon just yet, but I think I can help you there. I warn you that the way this works you'll only be able to walk at your normal pace, at best, if you want to avoid everything. I can see your current surroundings clearly, but there's a bit of a time delay when it comes to 'showing' it to you.

Suddenly, Euleilla felt something new in her senses. She didn't know what it was, but there was some kind of tripping hazard nine paces in front of her. To her right, about three paces away, she could risk getting entangled. Someone who was not a threat stood immediately behind her, holding her, but there were others who did constitute minor threats moving all around.

"Oh... my..." she couldn't help but gasp.

"Euleilla?" Maelgyn asked.

She shook her head. "My *schlipf* just lent me some of her senses so that I can move around... but it's going to take some getting used to." She smiled at him, allowing her magic to flare up and caress him as well. "Interestingly, the *schlipf* doesn't think of you as a threat, though just about everyone else here is."

"Even gram – I mean, even Ruznak?"

She paused, and struck out her new sense, combined with her magic, to determine just where her foster father was and what he felt like. She frowned at the results.

"Actually... yes. Very slightly, but yes. Which makes no sense – I know that gramps is no threat, so-"

He is not, her *schlipf* intervened. *At least, not an intentional threat. But he may do things which could accidentally harm you.*

And Maelgyn? Euleilla asked. *Surely he could also 'accidentally' harm me, but you don't see him as a threat.*

Of course not! the schlipf replied. *He would never harm you by intent, and father would prevent all of us from accidents. There is no threat, there – not even from the unintentional.*

Euleilla wasn't entirely certain she agreed with the *schlipf,* but she didn't have a convincing counter-argument.

So, she began, *when do you think you'll be sprouting?*

Oh, not for some time now. I'll warn you, beforehand – the memories my father gave me tell me that it can be a little painful in the moment it happens.

Your father gave you memories?

Of course! the schlipf exclaimed. *All of our kind are born with some memories from our parents. How else would I be able to talk with you?*

Euleilla was surprised. She hadn't even thought of that, but it made sense. "Hmm... interesting." She said the last bit out loud without realizing it.

"What's interesting?" Maelgyn asked.

"A *schlipf* is born with some memories gifted by its parent," she explained. "Which is how mine can talk to me already."

"Does yours have a name, yet?" Maelgyn asked.

"No... I'll have to think of one." She grinned up at him coyly. "You could help me find a name, you know."

Maelgyn's voice soured. "I'd rather not invite rumors of you being pregnant just yet, which would happen if anyone heard us pick out names together. We're obligated to have children one day, you know, and the public is always anxious for such a 'happy' occurrence to come to pass."

Euleilla considered him curiously. "If it wasn't for the demands of royal life, would you want children?"

Maelgyn paused for a few moments before answering.

"Honestly? I don't know. I don't exactly appreciate the idea of it being a duty, but I'm not so against it that I fear it will become a burden."

"I was never really sure if I wanted children, myself," Euleilla mused. "But, as you said, it's not something that feels like it will be a burden."

"Yes, perhaps," Maelgyn admitted. "I am not in any hurry, however. Anyway, with your new senses do you think you can take your walk without me?"

Euleilla thought about how to answer that for a moment. "Well... perhaps I could. I'd rather have your company, however."

"I would, too," he replied. The smile was obvious in his voice.

Maelgyn finally tore his eyes off his wife as she walked around the deck. She had said, once their normal walk was done, that she wanted to show people that she wasn't "seasick" anymore. She figured the best way to do that was to walk around deck unaided, or at least unaided to all outside appearances. He was still concerned about her, however – he knew the extra senses her *schlipf* was granting her were very new, and that she probably wasn't quite used to it yet. Until she demonstrated she was comfortable with it, he would keep a close eye on her to make sure she didn't hurt herself.

Thankfully, she was being very cautious as she walked. To someone who didn't know better, she'd look like someone who was just getting over their seasickness, which fortunately meant fewer questions about her sudden recovery. However, her tentative movements warned him that at least some of his fears were not unfounded.

So, he kept watch over her even while talking with Rudel about... something he couldn't really recall, as he hadn't been paying attention. A commotion taking place below decks eventually was enough of a distraction for him to break his vigil and try to find out what was going on.

Silently vowing to make this as brief as possible so that he could go back to keeping an eye on his wife, Maelgyn descended to the lower decks of the ship. The sounds sorted themselves out into the clash of heavy steal and the forceful sounds of several people training in swordplay. However, as he discovered when he entered the room all the noise was coming from, much more than swords were being trained with.

"What's going on in here?" he demanded, seeing El'Athras and Tur'Ba wielding absurdly large (for them) battle axes against Rykeifer and Sir Leno, neither of whom were armed. Wangdu and Onayari were standing at the side of the room, looking on with an unusual expression on his face that Maelgyn could not identify. It almost looked like an assassination attempt, though he could hardly believe it.

There was a brief pause as all four men in the center of the room stared each other down before El'Athras stepped back and slung the axe over his shoulders. Tur'Ba followed his lead, and then all five of them turned to the Sword Prince.

"I'm sorry we didn't inform you, your highness," Sir Leno explained. "Tur'Ba, here, was feeling rather bored, or so he says – there's only so much a half-trained Dwarven servant such as he can do for someone like yourself, and... ahem, you were neglecting him a bit."

Maelgyn flushed a bit at the rebuke, but nodded in agreement. The fact that the foursome were no longer actively fighting had allowed him to pause and take stock of the situation, so he figured he could be patient with their answer for the moment. "That's true, I'm afraid. I apologize, Tur'Ba, but I've had other things on my mind, and quite honestly I'm not sure what to do with you. I wasn't sure I'd have a use for you when El'Ba demanded I take you on, but—"

"But the old man can be mighty persuasive when he wants to be," Tur'Ba finished for him. "I understand, your highness – and furthermore I can't really say you've had much of a chance to do many of the things Pops asked of you – but that doesn't mean I'm not going to go looking for something to do when you don't need me."

Maelgyn nodded. "I have no problem with that, but surely you don't think killing my other advisors is an acceptable use of your time?"

Leno laughed at Maelgyn's sarcasm. "I suppose it does look like that, doesn't it?"

"Well, I know that isn't really what you were trying to do," Maelgyn agreed, "But what in the world were you doing? That certainly didn't look like any kind of training exercise I'd ever seen!"

"That is because no human alive has ever seen a Dwarven Axeman train, it is," Wangdu spoke forcefully. "And so when young Tur'Ba said just how bored he was, he did, I decided to teach him the ancient Dwarven art of the war axe, I did, as well as to the only other Dwarf on this ship. I have seen it in my days, I have, and I always wanted to teach it, I did, but it is rare that a Dwarf trusts an Elf enough to ask about such things, it is. Tur'Ba seems to have some talent for it, he does."

"Unlike me," El'Athras admitted ruefully. "Although I suppose I'm a bit old for picking up a new skill like that. Master Wangdu's training, however, may prove useful if it means we can restore Axemen to the Dwarves."

"I thought Oregal had tried that and failed," Maelgyn mused.

"They failed, they did," Wangdu agreed. "But they lack the knowledge I have, they do. I know how to train a Dwarf to fight, I do, and I know when an axe is to be used, I do. A Dwarven axeman does not attack, he doesn't, but rather remains defensive, he does. Something Oregal never realized, they didn't."

"Apparently you need an enclosed environment, like a cave – or, say, the inside of a ship – to properly grasp the skill," Rykeifer added, gesturing around them. "And you need someone with a good military eye on the other end, while you perfect your stances. Tur'Ba seems to have grasped them quite well, and despite whatever he says, El'Athras is doing fine. The two of them will have a reasonable set of rudimentary axe skills fairly soon – at least, they'll have enough so that they aren't a liability in battle. Must be in their blood – no Human could learn those skills this fast."

Maelgyn looked on curiously at all the faces around him. They were still hiding something, he felt, but he didn't know what it was. "And just how long have you been training like this, so far?" he asked, trying to figure out where his suspicions were leading him.

"Since before leaving Sopan," Tur'Ba noted. "While you were injured. Lady Euleilla and your chief steward, Reltney, refused to let me take care of you like a good servant should, and so I started looking for other things to do. I had the axes made at a magic-forging shop – paid a fairly good price for them, too, and I probably don't lose as much of the quality for the cheap manufacture as I would if I had bought, say, a sword, or even a spearhead. Wangdu suggested it all to me. Sir Leno started helping, and Rykeifer decided to join us when he found out about it."

Maelgyn slowly nodded. He recalled his conversation with the Dwarven boy on his sickbed, and realized that this was just a cover story. He didn't know why Tur'Ba was being so secretive about this, but he wouldn't pry too far into it. "I understand. But why haven't you said anything to me about all this?"

"You were too busy, you were," Wangdu replied. "If you had not been, you hadn't, then Tur'Ba would not have needed to look elsewhere to keep busy, he wouldn't."

"Very well," Maelgyn sighed, still convinced they were keeping something from him. He was unable to prove anything, however, and decided he wanted to go back and check on Euleilla again. "I think I'll head back on deck. Keep me informed as to your progress, would you?"

It may have been his imagination, but there was definitely some relief in all of their faces as he left.

Chapter 26

"Well, we are finally where we wanted to be," Maelgyn announced to the assembled officers and crew of the *Greyholden*. "The first expedition ashore will be led by Sir Leno, and he has asked for five volunteers to accompany him. This will be a dangerous mission and there is significant risk of capture. If you are captured, you are not to reveal anything, regardless of what threats they hold over you. Do I have any volunteers?"

There was a pause, and shifting among the crew. Finally, Wangdu stepped forward. "I'll go, I will. After all, I know the land better than anyone here, I do!"

Maelgyn tried not to let his surprise show, but felt he couldn't help it. "Master Wangdu, Sir Leno was not invited to our planning sessions for a reason. We did not want him to have any knowledge which might endanger us upon capture. You have a great deal of knowledge about our plans both here an on the mainland."

"Your highness," Wangdu intoned drolly. "I am an Elf, I am. We do not speak when captured, we don't. You can be assured of that, you can."

Maelgyn paused, then nodded in concession. "Very well, you may join them. Who else?"

Tur'Ba was the next to step forward. "Your highness, I also never attended those meetings. I would like to volunteer as well."

The sword prince considered this for a moment. It was true, the boy had no information to spill if captured, but he hardly had any other skills which would be useful... save perhaps his developing talents with the axe. "Do you truly think you are ready for such a mission?" he asked sharply.

"Yes, your highness," Tur'Ba submitted steadily. "I am."

Maelgyn took a deep breath, but nodded. "Very well. You may go."

Two others from the crew volunteered, but then the volunteers dried up. Maelgyn was about to draft someone from the crew when one last person stepped forward.

"I could go," Euleilla said from his side.

Fear seized his heart, and all sense of formality left him instantly. "Wh— what!?" he exclaimed, spinning on her.

"You know my past. Nothing they could do would be able to make me talk," she calmly explained. "And of everyone here, I am the most likely to ensure this mission will succeed. My magic is strong enough that no-one will be able to sneak up on us without our knowledge. You have seen me in combat, yourself. If we are trapped, Wangdu, Sir Leno and I together will be able to stop a small army... and no matter what happens, I will finally be off this accursed ship."

Maelgyn couldn't believe what he was hearing. "I can't... you can't... look. You can't ask this of me – you can't ask me to send you out into something like this without me. Not after I only agreed to let you come because you didn't want to be separated from me!"

"I agree with his highness, Euly," Ruznak said from the other side, startling the prince. After Euleilla had volunteered, Maelgyn had lost all perception of the others around him, and hadn't noticed the old man approaching them. "It is unfair of you to demand he take you with him when he goes into danger, and then chose to leave him for a danger he cannot follow."

"I know you are both afraid for me," Euleilla intoned, "but this is my choice. Gramps, do you doubt how well you trained me?"

"No," Ruznak answered sharply, taking in a deep breath. "You are more than capable of fighting with your magic and the other skills I have taught you. But if you wish to use those talents, use them to protect your husband. Your husband is going to war, and is the Sword Prince and Duke of Sopan. His protection should be your priority, if you must insist on fighting."

Euleilla stepped back from the both of them. "So I have been training for almost half my life to fight, and the only thing I am supposed to do with these skills is to act as a bodyguard? Is that my role in life?"

"No!" Maelgyn snapped. "Your role in life should be to live. And, I would hope, to live by my side. Perhaps to fight by my side. Perhaps, even, to... to die at my side. But not this. This is not your role. This is more than fighting – this is subterfuge, and secrecy, and —"

"And you think I lack these skills?" she asked softly, stepping towards him. "You believe I cannot be subtle, or keep secrets, or any of the other things this mission requires?"

Maelgyn eyed her closely. He saw her face, her sincerity, and knew – much to his chagrin – the only thing he could say. "No." He swallowed as his voice broke. "No, I don't think you lack any of those things, so...." He almost couldn't believe himself, but she was right. She really was the best person for the job. "I will be afraid for you – very afraid – but if you insist on volunteering I cannot refuse your request. I will ask, one last time, for you to reconsider... but I won't force you either way."

She smiled, sadly, letting him know she understood just how much it hurt to let her go like that in one quick moment. "Thank you, husband. I promise that I will do whatever I can to make it through this unscathed. And I will come back to you, whatever happens."

"Hey, what—" Ruznak protested.

"No, gramps," Euleilla snapped. "Please, respect me enough to let me do what you say I can. Respect me enough to let me prove myself to the others. I won't voluntarily leave my husband again in this war, but I need to do this to prove to the rest of the world that I have the talents needed to be to Maelgyn what Amberry was to Agaeb."

Ruznak hesitated for a long moment, then turned and stormed away without a word. As he left, the assembled crew started making their way below decks.

"He is not happy," she muttered under his breath.

"I'm not, either," Maelgyn agreed, his voice still trembling. "But I accept that you believe you have to do this. And I even know in my heart, damn it, that you will be a valuable asset on this mission. I love you, and I still don't want you to risk yourself like this, but I accept it."

His eyes widened as he realized what he just said. It was

the first time he said those three little words to her, and it was a lot more public of a setting than he'd ever planned to say them. He saw Euleilla tense, but in the end she just smiled – one of the happiest and most sincere smiles he had ever seen – and pulled him into her arms.

"I know. I'm sorry, but I feel I must do this," Euleilla sighed.

Maelgyn returned her embrace and kissed her tenderly. "Now go. Leno's in charge of this one, and he'll need to talk with you and the others before you leave."

"I love you, too," Euleilla whispered, so softly he could barely hear it, before turning to go.

Maelgyn couldn't help but watch her leave, the dread gripping his heart tighter and tighter as she went.

Euleilla struggled under the burden of her pack. Travelling with Sir Leno and the others for these past two days was nothing like traveling with Maelgyn alone. Schedules were more set, the pace of travel was more rigorous, she had to carry more of her gear on her own, and there was little sympathy for her inability to see certain things – like tree branches in her path. She was scratched up, dirty, and exhausted, and she was starting to regret volunteering for this mission.

However, she knew she shouldn't. When Wangdu came to her just an hour before they made the final landfall and asked her to join them for the mission, she couldn't refuse him. He had explained, in no uncertain terms, what was needed to make this mission a success.

Apparently, Maelgyn had almost walked in on them when he, Leno, and Tur'Ba had been discussing the plan to ask her with Rykeifer, Onayari, and El'Athras. They passed it off as one of Tur'Ba's training sessions with his axe, so he was still unaware they were the ones who had convinced her to go. She had agreed, and willingly, but she hated not being able to tell Maelgyn the real reason why: Wangdu had explained that she was essential to the mission's success.

And so she had agreed to it. But now, she was starting to hate that she had. If she was so important to their success, why did they ignore her when she needed to rest? She couldn't move as fast as them, and they should have expected that. But no, apparently they felt she should be able to keep up with them, and that was that.

"My apologies," Wangdu said to her suddenly. "I know we have been inconsiderate of your needs, we have, but there was need, there was. We must move fast, we must, to avoid detection. But it will be over soon, it will."

"How much longer until we're there?" she asked.

"Do you sense anyone nearby, do you?" he asked, side-stepping her question.

She frowned, but stuck out her senses as far as they would go. "There may be a small village or something similar about three miles in front of us, but other than that it seems pretty quiet around here."

There was a pause, and she noticed Wangdu fall behind a bit. He started forward again at a slightly faster pace, catching up in only a moment. "Three miles? You must have stronger magic than I thought, you must... but that is our destination, it is, I believe."

"I've been pushing myself since I came ashore," she admitted. She stumbled slightly over a low hanging branch. "Although I still have problems with sensing things like tree limbs in my path."

"I find the ways you've developed magic to sense things from a distance quite fascinating," Leno said from her other side. "I am a little uncertain as to how you use magic powder around you, however."

Euleilla paused. She could tell that the only people in immediate earshot were Wangdu and Leno, though perhaps Tur'Ba could hear as well if Dwarven ears were better than Human. She trusted all three, and decided that perhaps she could reveal her secret to them. Perhaps then, they would understand her need to slow the pace.

"I'm blind," she admitted, opting not to go into the usual "I'm not blind, I just can't see" routine. She didn't want to spend the effort to be flippant, as tired as she was. "The only thing which lets me 'see' the world around me is my magic. I think I've managed to hide it well."

Leno paused. "That would explain some things. It's said that one learns something best when they need it most, and it seems to me as if your magic falls into that category."

"Yergwain learned of this earlier. He said it would have

prevented him from accepting Maelgyn as Duke while I was his wife, if it had come down to his vote," Euleilla noted sadly.

"Yergwain is an inflexible idiot," Leno snorted. "He nearly threw me out of our family household when he found out I was learning magic, claiming it wasn't something a 'nobleman' should bother with. If it weren't for the fact that my father intervened on my behalf, he would have."

"You are a remarkable girl, you are," Wangdu noted. "I would not have known to act as you did, I wouldn't. But I suspected you were blind, I did – your behavior on the ship gave you away, it did."

"I already knew," Tur'Ba said, coming closer to the bunch. "I noticed it a long time ago, back when we were in Nir'Thik."

"You did?" Euleilla gasped, astonished. "How?"

"During the riot, your hair flipped up once. I saw your eyes. Or what's left of them, that is."

Euleilla didn't say anything for a moment. She really had nothing to say in response to that. Leaving them all in silence seemed inadequate... but she had no idea what to say.

Leno, however, was horrified. "My god... what's *left* of them? I thought you meant you were born blind – what happened to you?"

Euleilla shuddered slightly. "It's... a bit of a long story, and one I am not comfortable telling. Maelgyn knows, of course, as does gramps. Ask one of them to tell you – I don't ever want to relive that again."

They moved the conversation to other, more pleasant things, and chatted for some time while they continued down the path towards the village Euleilla had sensed. If, perhaps, the pace was a little more sympathetic to Euleilla's needs, no-one said anything.

Stopping to check on something, she frowned. "Someone's coming down this path from the village."

"One person, or more than one?" Sir Leno asked.

"At this distance, it's hard to say," Euleilla admitted. "But I think it's only one. It could be two or three if they're gathered close together. I'll be able to tell you with more certainty the closer we get."

"One is good, it is," Wangdu said. "We're looking for one, we are."

"Every day, a 'guide' is supposed to leave from the village and wait for us," Sir Leno explained. "He's supposed to be alone, and he's supposed to wait three hours, but the less time he is exposed the better. How far away is he?"

"About a mile," Euleilla answered after a few seconds of study.

"A mile in three hours, huh? I think we can manage that," one of the two crewmen of the *Greyholden* who she didn't know said.

"If we ran," Tur'Ba pointed out hesitantly, "We'd probably be there in under ten minutes."

Euleilla sighed. She'd just been getting used to a pace which allowed her to avoid the natural hazards of her hike, but if it was important enough she could manage it. "I suppose I could manage the run. The faster we move, however, the less reliable my special senses can be." Some of the others, in particular Leno and the sailors, also looked frustrated, but they recognized the need to move swiftly.

"I hate endurance runs, but if it's just a mile that's practically a sprint for me," Sir Leno said. Euleilla might have almost thought he was bragging, but that didn't seem to fit with the man she was coming to know. "I had to train like that in full plate armor, which is much heavier than this light leather gear we're wearing today. I'll make it easy."

"I am an Elf, I am," Wangdu proclaimed proudly. "We do not tire from such a simple thing as running, we don't."

"Er, hey, wait," one of the two *Greyholden* sailors intervened. "We're navy, not army – we aren't used to such things as long hikes over rough terrain and the like. Running across this? Well... uh... we're not likely to manage it that well."

Euleilla sighed. It was her turn to lead, it seemed. "I'm not likely to 'manage it that well,' either, but I'm going to run anyway. So, are you coming or not?"

With that, she shrank the sphere of her 'sight' down to just over a mile, collected the magic that freed up to enhance her muscles and skin, and started running down the path. She noticed that, while she was the first to leave, Tur'Ba, Wangdu, and Sir Leno (also enhancing himself with magic) quickly caught up with her. The two seamen, in the end, were running as well... although they were exerting themselves far more and were lagging behind quite a bit. She and the others slowed their pace slightly – though not by much – to allow them to stay in sight, but other than that spared them no mercy.

Even at the slower pace, it only took them about eight minutes before Sir Leno caught sight of the person they were looking for. The sailors were gasping for breath quite loudly, but could still safely hide with the others while Leno investigated the messenger.

Leno approached the man casually (after she had confirmed for him that it really was just one person) and began a seemingly innocent conversation about the weather. This was why Wangdu, the only person who really knew all the details behind the planned meeting, needed to pawn the mission off to Sir Leno – Maelgyn was too important to risk, and any Dwarves and Elves would be unable to hold such a casual conversation with someone if it were, in fact, the wrong man.

After a few moments of conversation, Leno waved to the rest of them. Evidently, the right things had been said and it was time for them to meet. Euleilla stepped forward, but as she did she began to get a great sense of danger. She checked around, and found no-one else was present – the sense of danger her *schlipf* was sending to her emanated from the stranger.

What's wrong? Euleilla thought to her.

I don't know, the schlipf replied. *All I know is that there is something really wrong with that man – and I don't know what. I don't think he's going to strike just yet, whatever the problem is, but stay cautious and ready to act.*

I will, she answered. *This is what you sense when he isn't even going to strike? It's almost overwhelming!*

My apologies. I'll try to dull the sensations a bit – otherwise, the warning of an impending attack could disable you before he strikes.

Thank you, she thought to her schlipf.

Slowly, and carefully remaining out of the stranger's reach, she followed Wangdu and the others up to meet their contact. The man seemed to be breathing rather heavily – heavier than even the two sailors who had exhausted themselves running to the meeting site – but from his magical aura she could tell he was still quite strong.

"Come on," the stranger wheezed. "Things should be clear, now, but we've only got a few minutes to get to Iggleton before people start setting up shop in the market and it gets too crowded to be safe. If we take too long, we'll have to wait until nightfall."

"We'll make it," Sir Leno said. "Especially if we run." Even the stalwart Tur'Ba joined in the groans at the suggestion of yet more running, but beyond the grumbles no-one protested.

Euleilla hated running – it really disoriented her – but she managed it the whole way with little more than a few scratches and bruises from being whipped by twigs and branches. They made it to the clearing in which Iggleton had been built and saw the village was, indeed, clear of pedestrians. Her *schlipf*, however, gave her the feeling she was being watched – something she would mention once they were under cover again.

Even more breathless than before, the contact gestured to one of the houses nearest the forest. "Come on – the Baron's inside."

Moving as rapidly as possible, Euleilla and the six men silently crossed the empty ground to the small house, and disappeared inside. When they entered the building, the contact quickly ushered them into a back room where Baron Uwelain stood waiting.

"Good to see you all, here," the Baron began. "I've got great news."

"Really?" Leno answered, sounding surprised.

"Yes. It seems our plans are going forward sooner than expected. Bailack, there, was a great help," Uwelain explained.

"I see," Leno said, and suddenly Euleilla's sense of danger flared – not from the man she now knew was named Bailack, but from Wangdu and Sir Leno. It only took her a split second to recognize, however, that she was not the one endangered.

With an explosion of magically enhanced strength, Leno sent a breath-stealing blow to Bailack's body. A muffled crack came from the wheezing man's chest, and he fell hard. With a quick motion, Wangdu's Elven lance was directed at the man's throat.

"Don't even try to scream, do not, unless you want my spear buried in your brain," the Elf warned dangerously.

Bailack coughed up some blood, and nodded slowly. "Okay."

"What's going on?" Tur'Ba asked, his voice shaking. The two sailors seemed quite distressed as well, but Euleilla had a funny feeling she knew what was going on.

That was confirmed a moment later when Uwelain stepped forward. "Someone gag him, fast – we can't afford to spend all of our time making sure this spy stays quiet. We probably should just kill him and be done with it, but there's some hope he could be used as a bargaining chip."

"He's a spy, then?" Euleilla mused. "That would explain the aura I was getting from him. I also noticed that we were being watched on our way in, but I couldn't say anything at the time without giving my discovery away."

"What's it like outside?" Leno asked, ripping a piece of cloth.

"Let me check," she said, concentrating her senses on looking outside of the walls which enclosed them. "Uh oh."

"Uh oh?" Leno asked with a huff as he gagged Bailack.

"Small groups of people are moving to surround the house. Most of them have swords and knives, a few appear to have spearpoints or arrowheads on them. Everything is of a quality you would expect for professional soldiers."

Uwelain nodded. "A few days ago, 'King' Paljor's men discovered that I was planning to help Sviedan Royalty reclaim the islands. They learned of my initial contact plans, and imprisoned me in this house to set a trap for you. I'd estimate about eighty to a hundred soldiers are waiting in the surrounding households, ready to attack us. Bailack may be of some use as leverage, but I fear we'll have to surrender anyway."

"I am not sure I agree with that assessment, I'm not," Wangdu said, a confident smirk in his voice. "Sir Leno is a Second Class mage, he is. The Lady, here, is a First Class, she is. I am an Elf, I am. You and these two sailors are not half-bad when it comes to hand-to-hand combat, you aren't. And Tur'Ba, here, could be called a Dwarven Axeman, he could."

"A Dwarven Axeman?" Uwelain repeated doubtfully. "I find that hard to believe. But the rest of that sounds impressive. I wouldn't be surprised if they had a few mages on their side, too, though."

"One," Euleilla said, checking the nearby Borden Islanders carefully. "Not powerful – maybe Third Class, at best. He'll be a bit of a problem, but nothing we can't handle." She paused, hearing her *schlipf* tell her something new. "There's something which concerns me a bit more, however. Several of them have torches."

"They're going to burn us out!" Uwelain growled. "I figured we only had three options – surrender, fight, or die. Well, they aren't offering to let us surrender, so it looks like we're down to two. And I don't particularly want to die."

Euleilla sighed, pulling in her magic to prepare for the fight. "We've got a few minutes before they're in position to spring their trap. I should rest before I do anything – I've been steadily draining myself of magic for the past two days straight, trying to keep us from being seen. I suspect the rest of you need a few moments of rest, as well, given all the running it took for us to get here."

Tur'Ba coughed. "I don't understand any of this. Maybe, while we're resting up, you could explain to me just how it is you knew Bailack, here, was a spy?"

"Code words," Sir Leno explained. "Always remember to plan for as many contingencies as you can foresee – and for those you can't. Uwelain set up a series of code words and phrases to mean certain things."

"I almost didn't use them," Uwelain explained. "I don't know who you are... Sir Leno, is it? But I recognized the Elf and the Lady, and figured if they were with you I was speaking to the right people. But where is his highness?"

"Running a separate mission elsewhere on the island, by now – I'm not exactly sure where. I wasn't at the meetings."

Uwelain clucked. "If we survive this battle I'm going to need to get in touch with him. He is now the only chance of reunifying Borden and Svieda." He stepped over to Euleilla and bowed quickly before continuing. "Lady Euleilla, your safety is our top priority. We could win public support if you and Maelgyn present your marriage to my people. Yours is the first of a commoner to a royal since the time of Sword Princess Ivari and her husband, Laimoth. The evidence we have uncovered about Sho'Curlas' complicity in our rebellion might be enough of a tool to get the nobility to decide a return to Sviedan rule is preferable to what we have now. Sword 'King' Paljor has greatly disaffected the ruling nobility, and now there are many among us who have been looking for some way to break his power. We believe there might be enough for the Lords to replace him with Sviedan rule if the civilian Senate showed there was popular support, but you must survive for that to happen. If I fall, your highness, then—"

A loud crash and an explosion interrupted him. "Rest time is over," Sir Leno sighed. "We have to break out of here and cut through their line back to the forest. Then we run to safety."

"I will take the vanguard position, I will," Wangdu declared. "I have certain Elven skills which may be useful in that role, I have."

"Good," Sir Leno said. "Tur'Ba, I want you to stay at her highness' side and keep her safe. She's powerful with magic, and from what I've been told can handle herself well with hand-to-hand, but given how much intense magic can exhaust a person she may need periodic rest and recovery periods. I'll cover the rear. Uwelain, bring the prisoner. Forge, Mogs, protect the flanks. Milady, we're going to be protecting you so that you can unleash whatever magic you have – but don't hesitate to rest if you need a moment to recover. The rest of us should be able to hold them off for a while. It will be much worse if you strain yourself to where you're left defenseless."

"Thank you, Sir Leno," Euleilla said, taking her position in their impromptu formation. She wasn't sure she liked being so far out of the action, but then again she was at a disadvantage at close range despite her skill with the quarterstaff.

With their small party organized, the counter-attack began when Wangdu blew out a wall so that they could ambush the ambush around the door.

Once out of the building, Wangdu continued to lead the counter-attack, using his Elven magic to call forth a growth of vines that surrounded the house. With a great tearing sound, the vines dug into the wall, crushing it and throwing the remaining pieces from the house

"Quickly!" he urged. "The roof cannot hold for long without the wall's support, it cannot!"

They made it about fifty paces before they were swarmed by the attacking soldiers. Euleilla and Leno shielded the others from enemy weapons as best they could with their magic, while Wangdu, Forge, and Mogs attacked.

"Fools!" the person Euleilla recognized as the attackers' mage declared. "What do you hope to accomplish against all of us? Do you actually think you can escape? I am a mage, and can make each of our soldiers as strong as any ten of you! You are nothing against me!"

"So, a First Class mage is nothing against you?" she replied, sending a blast of magic his way using the mage dueling skills Maelgyn had taught her.

"Er, First Class?"

"And an Elf, perhaps?" came the call from Wangdu, who grew vines to secure the attacking mage in place.

"While not as powerful as her ladyship," Sir Leno declared, launching his own magical attack. "I also have some skill in the art of magic, myself, and would formally be rated Second Class."

Their three-pronged attack literally crushed the opposing mage, killing him instantly. Their lone mage gone, the other attackers faltered briefly before redoubling their efforts.

Sir Leno's group had gained the advantage, but Euleilla feared her strike on the mage had tired her prematurely. When she rested, things would be tough for them and she knew it. Still, she knew enough of combat to obey her orders, so when she started to feel herself tire she knew what she had to do.

"My magical defenses are going to collapse in a moment, Tur'Ba," she warned. "Prepare yourself."

"Right," the Dwarf said, clutching his axe tighter and bringing it to a more defensive position. "I'm ready."

With a sigh, Euleilla withdrew her magic to the tightest circle she could. Her *schlipf* senses were so full of dangers that they were useless except for detecting immediate, direct attacks on her person. What little magic she was still expending told her that Leno was still providing enough of a shield to prevent archers from shooting arrows at her, but hand-held weapons were still getting through. However, beyond the sounds of the battle, she couldn't tell what was going on around her.

At one point, someone came close enough that even her withdrawn senses could detect him. She blocked a sword strike with her staff, but her planned counterattack was rendered moot when an axe swung in and nearly chopped the swordsman in half. Blood and other visceral matter splattered on her, but she knew better than to react. It was, she supposed, the first time she was in a battle close enough to feel the blood spill on her as she fought instead of in the aftermath, but she'd dealt with worse.

By the time she had regained her powers enough to return to the battle, it was almost over. To her amazement, there appeared to be a wall of bodies around her. The only loss they had taken was Forge – though she wasn't even sure of his fate, since she couldn't seem to find him alive or dead.

On the other hand, the small remainder of the soldiers who

had been attacking them were routed and fleeing. Euleilla hesitated.

"Is it over?" she asked.

"For now," Uwelain answered. "We need to get out of here, though – I don't know if they have any forces in reserve, and if so how soon they can regroup."

"Right," Leno said. "Come on, people, let's go."

"Where's Forge?" Mogs asked.

"I don't sense him, anywhere," Euleilla sighed. "Although I cannot find his body, either."

"I don't see him around, alive or dead," Uwelain agreed. "Either he ran, or he was killed. Either way, I'm afraid we don't have time to find him. Let's get going." He walked over, pausing at the circle of bodies surrounding Euleilla, then turned to Tur'Ba. "I apologize for my earlier remarks. Your skills as a Dwarven Axeman matched those from the myths of my childhood."

"Thank you, your highness," the Dwarf replied, breathing heavily. "Though I think I need to do some endurance training to really qualify for the title. A true Dwarven Axeman would be able to run all the way back to the ship after a battle like that... I don't think I could go for more than an hour."

Laughter erupted at that comment, and Uwelain clapped him on the back. "Come on, let's get going."

Chapter 27

Maelgyn sighed.   Euleilla was back, thankfully, but was exhausted to the point of collapse. So were most of the others from that aborted mission, although Wangdu professed to be perfectly fine, but the news they brought was not as good as Uwelain tried to make it. Paljor, who styled himself as "Sword King of the Borden Isles," knew they were coming. He would be on the defensive for certain, and that would complicate Maelgyn's plans for dealing with the dragons. Not to mention all hopes of restoring the Borden Isles to Svieda.

Nevertheless, Maelgyn was duty-bound to try. He'd have to leave immediately, before Euleilla even woke up from her rest, and hope that they made it to the Lair of the Golden Dragons before the whole island was alerted. It would be difficult, he was certain, but they'd manage it. He hoped so, anyway.

Donning the Nekoji-fur cloak he'd been given, Maelgyn went out on the ship's deck to meet with the others who would be joining him. Wangdu had declared he would be going, despite having had little rest from the meeting with Uwelain. Maelgyn still hadn't received a full report about the venture, but the fact that the baron was now aboard the *Greyholden* instead of hosting Maelgyn's delegation as planned was telling. Onayari, unafraid of the heat of the caves, also intended to accompany Maelgyn into the lair. Uwelain also would ignore his exhaustion and accompany him as well, representing the Borden Isles and testifying that indeed the rebellion might soon be over. Euleilla had earlier professed a desire to accompany him, as well, but given her current state Maelgyn figured it would be better to let her rest. However, that left him lacking one intended party member – something he wasn't quite sure what to do about.

As he made his way to the deck, he passed by El'Athras. "I understand you're one person short," the Dwarf said.

"Well, sort of," Maelgyn answered. "Truthfully, we'll probably move faster without Euleilla, though I would have loved to have her with me for this one. But there is no set number of people required for these negotiation."

"I would have thought there was," the Dwarf answered. "Isn't there some kind of tradition – every meeting of the Dragons with other races, the two ambassadorial teams consist of five individuals? And aren't Dragons creatures of tradition?"

Maelgyn hesitated. "Well... yes. But I'm sure they will understand."

"Yeah, right, of *course* they will. And perhaps Paljor will simply surrender the Borden Islands because we ask nicely." El'Athras snorted. "How about I come with you, instead? I understand you've got more of those fancy furs, and while they may not quite fit me perfectly I suspect I can manage in it."

"I was under the impression Dwarves and Dragons didn't get along too well."

"We don't," the Dwarf agreed. "But then again, neither do Elves and Dragons. And neither do Nekoji and Dragons. And they don't exactly welcome Humans with open arms, either. So what? Someone's gotta ease the tensions between us. Might as well be me."

"I'm more worried about what the Dragons will think of me for bringing you along," Maelgyn snorted. "But if you want to come, you can. Get your gear – I need to talk to Ruznak."

"Ruznak? I didn't think he was coming along," El'Athras mused.

"He's not, but I have an important job for him."

"What is that?"

"Telling Euleilla that I left without her."

Thankfully, the hike to the Dragon Caves was far shorter and required far less running than the one Sir Leno's expedition had to make – they were close enough that Maelgyn hoped he'd be able to get there and back before Euleilla awoke. It was unlikely, he knew, but she actually needed the rest... and he might be in less trouble with her if he got back before she had time to start worrying about him.

However, as much as he wanted her to rest, he also found her absence disturbing. Maelgyn had grown quite used to having her at his side during his travels, and he missed her even when she went to Iggleton with Leno. Before he could follow that trail of thought further, however, Sekhar began speaking to him.

We're nearing a great source of fire, the plant warned him. *I'm unable to contain all of my fears even though I was aware we were planning for this meeting.*

Maelgyn adjusted his cloak. *Don't worry – thanks to the Nekoji, you'll be better protected from the fires then I am. If you want a way to get your mind off of it, though, perhaps you could come up with something for me to tell Euleilla when I get back.*

Oh, that's an easy one, Sekhar mentally chuckled. *Blame it on me being an overprotective parent. I know my daughter would never be able to stand being this close to Dragonfire without driving the both of them crazy. See? Easy.*

Speak for yourself, Maelgyn thought back, but then shrugged. *Well, maybe it'll work. How are the others doing?*

You're the one with eyesight, Sekhar replied. *I can only sense potential threats. What I can tell you is that none of them are lagging behind, so they're all probably in good shape.*

Maelgyn looked around at the others, trying to see if there was anything more he could see from their appearance. He was not nearly as good at reading or interpreting magical auras as Euleilla, but she had taught him enough to make a few observations which the naked eye wouldn't catch.

For example, Wangdu was laboring more heavily than he was letting on. Maelgyn had been told that some Elves sometimes picked up minor Human magical abilities after centuries of experience, and he seemed to have some, but it didn't quite exceed the strength of a fourth rate wizard. One thing it did do for the Elf, however, was give him a more defined magical signature, which Maelgyn could usually follow... but, at the moment, his energy was so low that it was almost undetectable.

An odd twist he discovered was that Onayari, the Nekoji, was actually growing stronger the closer they got to the heat. In an odd way, it almost seemed to almost refresh her. Maelgyn also noticed that her magical aura would sometimes flicker into being more focused than it should be whenever they did something that required more than the usual amount of exertion – something he had never sensed before. He would have to ask Euleilla if she had encountered this sort of thing before, but that was a puzzle to be solved later.

El'Athras, however, was completely unreadable. Dwarves were not magically inclined in the way Humans were, and El'Athras was no exception, but Maelgyn should still be able to detect the kinds of fluctuations which heavy exertion should induce. There was nothing, despite the sweat pouring from his brow, to indicate that he found the journey to be any hardship at all. Apparently, the reputation the Dwarves had for hardiness was well-founded, especially given that after more than two centuries of life, this particular Dwarf was considered past his prime even for *his* kind.

"Who enters the Lair of the Golden Dragons?" a voice boomed from above them, interrupting Maelgyn's thoughts.

The echoes rattled his bones, but Maelgyn refused to be intimidated. He knew that Dragons of all types sensed fear the same way Sekhar sensed danger, and would not respect someone who could not face them with courage. So, steeling himself for the encounter, he raised his own voice as much as he could.

"I am Sword Prince Maelgyn of Svieda, Duke of Sopan, come to make a request on our treaty of old for this time of war."

The "giant" creature landed in front of the group, only to reveal it wasn't quite so large after all. Despite what Maelgyn had heard about how dragons were larger than some towns, this particular dragon wasn't much larger than a horse – a large horse, admittedly, but a horse nonetheless. Then again, it was the Red Dragons whose fabled size the legends were based on.

"And I am Khumbaya, Keeper of the Gates. Tell me, Sword Prince Maelgyn – have you and the masters of Borden Isle returned to your former state?"

Maelgyn shook his head. "No, we are still in a civil war. That may change soon, however, and when it does we will need your aid immediately. I thought to give warning to you, so that you may discuss this matter among yourselves before we meet again, and to prepare your answer to your summons."

Khumbaya snarled. "We do not heed *any* mortal's beck and call. We refuse to fight for you until the war with Borden Isle is over. We have no reason to listen to you until then."

"Ending the war with Borden will be my task," Uwelain declared, stepping forward. "I am from Borden Isle, and I may have a way to reunite Svieda peacefully. I ask that you grant us this preliminary meeting for all our sakes."

"No," the dragon growled. "You are an ignorant whelp of no consequence, and unless you actually have ended the wars already we care nothing for what you have to say."

"Please," Wangdu intervened. "Your leaders would be well advised to talk with us, they would. You must be informed, you must, of what will be asked of you."

The dragon turned its eye on him. "Is that so? And just why should we trust you, Elf?"

"This Elf is trustworthy," Onayari insisted. "If he were not, would we of the Nekoji grant him – and these others – with coats of our furs?"

"I will also vouch for him," El'Athras snorted. "He's just about the only Elf I've ever met with a real sense of honor any more."

The dragon stepped back slightly, looking as amused as an intelligent scaled beast could look. "A Dwarf respecting an Elf?" he snorted, smoke spewing from his nostrils. "Unheard of! Well, perhaps it may be worth listening to you, Elf! A Dwarf, two Humans, an Elf, and a Nekoji, eh? An odd gathering, to be sure. I will discuss this matter with the elders. Await here for word of our response. Proceed no further, lest we slay thee."

Without even giving them a chance to reply, the dragon leaped into the air. Maelgyn had never seen a Golden Dragon in flight – in fact, the only dragons he had ever seen before were the great beasts which were Red Dragons, and those were from afar. To see one of the Golden Dragons soar into the sky was a different experience altogether. Golden Dragons were smaller, yes, but also a lot sleeker as well. It was very difficult for him to compare a creature like the Red Dragon he had seen in his youth with the magnificent being that had just left. Truthfully, they were so different from one another he had a hard time thinking of them both as even being related races.

Khumbaya did not return quickly. No-one seemed to feel like speaking as they waited, yet the silence dragged on oppressively. After a while, Maelgyn started looking around for something that might ease their discomfort.

"El'Athras," Maelgyn began, finally breaking their silence. "I was informed that my ship's blacksmith, the man who is known by the crew best as 'Forge,' disappeared during the expedition to meet with Lord Uwelain. I understand that even those Dwarves who do not specialize in smithery have some skill in the craft. Do you believe you or Tur'Ba could handle the duty until we find a replacement?"

"We Dwarves are skilled in a limited understanding of mining and metallurgy at birth, much as Elves know the science of plants and Merfolk know the ways of both swimming and walking. However, I would suggest your wife or Sir Leno fill the role, instead. My own skill has greatly diminished in its old age, and Tur'Ba is too impatient to truly understand the art. Your wife or Sir Leno would have their magic to help them." El'Athras fell silent, and for a moment Maelgyn feared the silence would return, but then he seemed to recognize the need for a distraction. "We should have found one of the Merfolk to bring with us instead of you, Baron Uwelain."

"Oh?" Uwelain said.

"Yeah. If we had, then it would have looked like an appeal from the united races," the Dwarf explained. "Though I'm not sure we *could* have brought one with us; I understand the shapeshifting abilities which allow them to function on land – and to impersonate people, at times – will only last them for a few short hours. Then, if they don't return to the water, they transform back into a Merfolk, which cannot walk on land easily."

"It's still possible," Maelgyn said. "My uncle, the late king, once received a Merfolk delegation at the Royal Castle. They had to construct a water-storing wagon to manage the journey, but with one they can travel just about anywhere and remain healthy. They don't usually use up the water as they travel."

"They would not have wanted to come, they wouldn't," Wangdu mused. "Deathly afraid of dragons, they are."

"And with good reason," Khumbaya mused, flying back in. "They cannot bear to be near us, for our inner heat will kill them whether we desire their death or not."

Maelgyn straightened his posture, and turned to address the dragon. "So, will your people see us?"

Khumbaya puffed some smoke out of his nostrils. "They

wish more information. What is it, Elf, that you believe we will be so interested in?"

"The Sho'Curlas Alliance has trained as many as fifty Black Dragons to sweep through all nations, they have," Wangdu answered. "Surely, the assemblage of so many under one power at least deserves the honor of your leaders' attention, it does, whether they take action or not, they do."

"The elders will be informed. However, even so great a force to you is insignificant to us. I doubt they will be interested," the golden dragon proclaimed before once more taking off in flight.

"That was rather abrupt," Onayari mused.

"Dragons are an impatient lot, they are," Wangdu answered. "And that one is also cursed with the affliction of youth, he is – possibly no more than twelve or thirteen centuries old."

"He's older than most of us," Maelgyn pointed out.

"The youngest golden dragon hatched is a thousand years old, it is," Wangdu answered. "Our history tells us that the first Ancient Dragons' eggs took almost a thousand years to grow to maturity, they did. It took another two hundred for them to learn to speak properly, it did. Golden Dragons may be different, they may, but even so he's fairly young, he is. There's a reason there are so few of them, there is."

Maelgyn sighed. "I think we can be glad there are so few of them – they are quite hostile to mortals, even when those mortals are actually immortals like yourself."

"Ah," Wangdu replied darkly. "Well, we Elves have done worse to dragons than most mortals, we have. Before the days that Humans, Dwarves, or Nekoji were anything more than wild animals, they were, the Ancient Elves, our Ancient Enemy, and the Ancient Dragons fought their great three-sided war, they did. While true that no Elves or Dragons from that day are still alive, they aren't, stories of them exist still, they do. Our people were quite vicious, they were."

Maelgyn perked up at that, wondering at several things. That the Ancient Elves fought wars was no surprise – many of their relics and surviving creations were centered around warfare – but he had been unaware their wars went back that far in their history. If Humans, Dwarves, and Nekoji had not been their enemy, than who was?

"Dare I ask what those things your people did to them were?"

El'Athras hesitantly inquired, voicing the other question that rose in Maelgyn's mind.

"Ask the dragons," Khumbaya said, once more appearing silently from above them. "Ask the eldest of the Golden Dragons. Their parents, known to you as the 'Ancient Dragons,' lived through those wars at their worst. They know better than any alive how evil the Elves can be."

"I agree, I do," Wangdu said. "Modern Elves do not understand, they don't, just how horrific our Ancient brethren were. I had to go to Ancient Elven libraries long thought lost to learn the whole story, I did."

"Ancient Elven libraries?" Khumbaya growled out, incidentally throwing a few sparks of fire. "You are Wangdu, then, aren't you?"

Wangdu bowed. "At your service, I am."

The dragon returned the bow, displaying a great deal more respect than he had before. "Perhaps you may actually be able to fulfill the condition that the Elders have demanded of you if Master Wangdu, Savior of the Golden Dragons of the Northern Plains, is on your side."

"Oh?" Maelgyn asked, unaware of what Wangdu may have done in his long past to be named a hero of the Dragons, but set it aside as yet another question for a later date. "And what condition is it that they have imposed?"

Khumbaya shook his whole body like a wet dog, then turned to Maelgyn. "My apologies, your highness, but the Elf distracted me from my message. The Elders have asked me to deliver this proclamation: They will not meet with you now. However, if you kill the human styling himself as Sword King Paljor, whether you end the breach between Svieda and the Borden Islands or not, they will agree to meet with you. And they feel that, while the treaties of old are negated by the breach, they might be willing to negotiate a stronger alliance than before."

Maelgyn's eyes widened. No individual Golden Dragon – much less an entire nation of them – had ever even hinted at an actual alliance before. Perhaps, before the days of recorded history, there was an individual Ancient Dragon or two who had allied themselves with a mortal power against the Elves, but that was only in myth. An entire nation of Dragons doing anything more than fighting with other Dragons on behalf of any other race was unheard of, even in the wildest of those myths. What made it even more incredible was that the Golden Dragons of Borden Isle were the largest nation of Golden Dragons still in existence – and one of the last. The Golden Dragons of the Northern Plains who Wangdu had been the 'savior' of had since left their lands to join them, as had many other Dragon colonies throughout the world. Sviedan scholars had noticed that the past century or two marked a growing Dragon gathering, of sorts. Every Dragon in the world, even those from parts of the world not on Human maps, seemed to be giving up their homes in order to join the den in Borden Isle. There had been some concern about that, but if what Khumbaya was saying was true....

"Why? Your people have *never* desired such an alliance, before."

The dragon seemed to hesitate for a moment, but it was hard to read hesitancy in a dragon. "Our people have decided that Paljor's existence is a plague unto us. We are not afraid of war, but killing him ourselves would start a war where we least want one – our home."

Uwelain spoke up at that, as the only Borden Islander present. "This sounds most peculiar, Gatekeeper. The Swords of Borden Island have not been in your favor since our rebellion against Svieda as you deem us Oathbreakers, but you have always been cordial to us nevertheless. What could any mortal do to be named a 'plague' on the largest dragon nation in the world?"

"The *only* dragon nation," Khumbaya corrected. "We are all here now, or will be soon. The breeding season is approaching – an event during which we, as a race, are at our most vulnerable, so it occurs just once every millennia – and there are now so few of us that we cannot support a breeding season across more than one nation. The season, in mortal terms, is still far from now – fifty years, by your reckoning – but we must prepare ourselves decades in advance. By then, we must be on very good terms with whatever mortal power is in position to protect us... and the Borden Isles are the most defensible home we have ever held. Therefore, whoever rules the Borden Isles can do what they desire with impunity, and we can do nothing in retaliation for fear of offending them."

"But that does not explain what Paljor has done against you," Uwelain pointed out. "It must be something he has done both personal and severe, but I have heard of nothing."

Once again, the dragon hesitated. He seemed quite unwilling to answer, but he hadn't refused to explain altogether yet. Maelgyn decided to press for an answer.

"If we could just make him step down from the kingship, would that be sufficient? Or is his offense so great he would have to be killed, regardless?"

"We would hold him to account," Khumbaya finally answered. "For the murder of Elder Veila, one-time queen of another Dragon colony. She survived wars with horrors the mortals in this part of the world would not be able to imagine, only to meet her end at Paljor's hands."

Maelgyn started. "How many men did he use to kill Elder Veila? Surely our spies would have told us if his armies were on the move, even as poor as our intelligence has been, so—"

"I believe you misunderstand, your highness," Khumbaya replied. "He slaughtered Elder Veila in order to make a suit of dragonhide armor – similar to those we gave your ancestors, one of which I see you now wear. He felt that he deserved the stronger and more flexible material of Golden Dragonhide over the typical Red Dragon's skin. However, he did not ask his armies to do it for him – he defeated Veila alone."

Maelgyn couldn't comprehend what he heard for a moment, and lost his composure slightly. "What are you saying? He... he killed a dragon by *himself*?"

The dragon looked away. "I believe, Sword Prince Maelgyn, that if I said he was the most powerful Human mage we Dragons have ever even heard of, that would be an understatement."

"Paljor's a High Mage," Uwelain summarized, more to express his own disbelief than to convince Maelgyn. "And his own people don't even know...."

Maelgyn's head spun. There was only one way to save the world from whatever menace the Elves of Poros were planning, and that was to save his kingdom. There was only one way to save his kingdom, and that was to bring the Golden Dragons into the war. There was only one way to bring the Golden Dragons into war, and that was to defeat the man known as Paljor. And Paljor was a High Mage. How did one defeat a High Mage?

"Well," he finally said. "I suppose we've got our work cut out for us, don't we?"

Chapter 28

"I suppose I'll accept that explanation," Euleilla said, privately amused at how much her husband cowered. Truthfully, she wasn't too upset with him – she realized, when she joined Sir Leno's expedition, that she'd probably lost her place in the Dragon negotiating team – but she wanted to make him squirm nonetheless. It was best to keep him on his toes. Besides, while she suspected the explanation he gave about Sekhar's child needing protection from the heat was true enough, she questioned whether he'd actually thought about it *before* he left... or after.

"From now on," Maelgyn continued, "I will not leave your side. But I expect you to make the same commitment to me, as well. Otherwise, love, I might be a trifle upset with you, too."

"Don't worry, husband," Euleilla answered him. "I went on that mission only because I believed it was the only way it would be successful. I was somewhat disappointed with my role in that last mission, and it wasn't successful at all. From now on, I will stay by your side."

"What?" Maelgyn said, sounding suspicious. "What role did you think you'd have?"

Euleilla hesitated. She didn't want to get Sir Leno and the others in trouble, but she supposed she would have to tell her husband why she really went on that mission, now. "I had been recruited to volunteer for the mission by Sir Leno and Wangdu. I was told that if I went along, there was a chance that the Borden Island Council would overthrow King Paljor on its own without needing to involve you at all. We hoped that if I met with the council, they would accept the marriage of a commoner to Sviedan royalty as evidence that Sviedan customs were indeed changing. However, I never had a chance to meet with the council, so we have no idea of knowing if it would have worked or not."

Maelgyn took a deep breath. "Well... I wish it *had* worked. You haven't yet heard about what the Dragons told us, have you?"

Euleilla shook her head. "No, what did they say?"

Maelgyn spent the next few minutes relaying everything he had learned from the dragon known as Khumbaya, finishing it up with the explanation of Paljor's offense. When he was done, Euleilla couldn't help but be horrified.

"A High Mage, slaughtering an intelligent Dragon because he wants a new piece of armor? That's... that's..." she stuttered, unable to find the words.

"Quite worrisome," Maelgyn understated. "A High Mage with better dragonhide armor than I've got... and one we have to kill. I don't like the sound of this. When it comes to magical combat... well, I know how it's done in principal, and you tell me I have such a natural talent for it that just might be a match to his, at least in potential... but I'm not ready to face someone of his level, and I'm not sure I will ever be."

"We do have a few advantages, you know," Euleilla noted, reaching out to run her hand up and down his arm comfortingly. She knew just how powerful he was, and believed he could meet the challenge. "If Baron Uwelain is correct and we can get the Borden Isles council to join us in overthrowing him, we have a pretty good chance. Even a High Mage can theoretically be overwhelmed... especially when there are two first rates, a second rate, and an Elf massed against him."

"Even you, me, Leno, and Wangdu couldn't handle him on our own," Maelgyn sighed. "He has dragonhide armor – as do I, but my armor can only protect me. Our magic will be ineffective against him because of that armor, but the strength of his magic has been tested even against Dragons."

"You have Sekhar, as well," Euleilla noted. "Physical attacks will be our best bet, and I think that he'll be a good weapon for you."

"He's just about the *only* effective weapon I've got."

Euleilla huffed. This wasn't right – Maelgyn was giving up, and that was more likely to get him hurt or killed than the odds that had been stacked against him. She had to do something to snap him out of it, or else they really wouldn't have any chance of success.

"Husband," she growled, magically smacking him to bring him to his senses. "Shut up. You are betraying yourself."

Maelgyn choked slightly, coughing and sputtering. "What? Why—"

"Do you want to die?" Euleilla asked furiously. "Are you trying to get yourself killed?"

"No! Of course not!" Maelgyn protested.

"Then stop talking like you do!" Euleilla hissed. "The more you talk about how hopeless this is, the more you convince yourself you cannot win. If you are convinced you cannot win, you will not win. The only chance you have disappears if you assume you will lose. You know how vital confidence is in the use of magic."

"I know," Maelgyn huffed, clutching his head in his hands. No matter how much magical strength a person actually had, they could only use as much as they believed they could, which meant a crisis of confidence could be fatal in a battle of magic. "I know, but I can't help it. I don't see a way to win... and I know if I do not win, I might as well abdicate right now, because Svieda is doomed."

Euleilla pulled him into her arms. "I'm sorry, husband. I know this must be hard for you, but I cannot allow you to collapse on us. We all need to be at our best if we want to keep even the slim chance we have."

"I know that, love," Maelgyn began hoarsely, "I know that. I keep telling myself that, as well, but it's not always easy to act on what you know. I do have one thing to say, however...."

"Yes?" Euleilla said.

He took a deep breath. He knew she wouldn't like this, and anticipated an explosion. "I think it would be best if I fought him alone. His magic is so strong, and that dragonhide armor will help him so much, that you and Leno will be ineffective... and if I fail, well, Wangdu will be needed to cover any sort of retreat you might make."

"You are not leaving me behind," Euleilla snapped.

"No, I'm not," Maelgyn agreed. "But I've got to ask you to do something very hard. If I am killed, I want you to leave me behind – I want you to live, and perhaps make something of yourself. We haven't been married very long, love, and you're still young and beautiful. If something happens to me, well...."

"Then I will be right there, and I will fight for you until I'm sure you're dead. And then I will stay and protect your body, until I, too, am killed," Euleilla firmly announced.

"But—"

"No, Maelgyn," she answered. She couldn't solve his confidence problem herself, but maybe she could motivate him to do it himself. "I need you to realize this. If you insist, I will allow you to fight him alone, but I'm not allowing you to die alone. I will die with you, fighting to avenge you. If you won't fight to win, fight to survive... because if you don't survive, then it's unlikely I will, either."

Maelgyn felt his stomach drop. She was serious, and he knew it, but he had to talk her out of it. "If I fall, someone will have to lead Sopan...."

"That someone won't be me, and you know it," Euleilla sighed. "I am still just Princess Consort, you know. If you die before I have your children, I'm as good as a commoner again, save I'm more of a public spectacle. Lord Valfarn and his family will take over as regent, again, until the throne is secure and the line of succession is re-assessed."

Maelgyn cocked his head. "I'd forgotten about that. If we live through this, remind me to get Wybert to invest you – in the absence of a Sword King, a second Sword Prince should have the power to invest you as a full Princess." He paused. "I guess there's no way to convince you to change your mind, is there?"

She grinned cheekily at him. "No."

"And if I don't beat him myself, you'll really challenge him?" Maelgyn continued in wonder.

"Yep," she answered again, still smiling with a touch of humor but turning serious. While she'd said it to motivate him, she had suddenly realized she would really do it – if he fell, she would stand over Maelgyn until the one who killed him was dead, or she was.

"And if I tried to stop you?" he asked, the fear for her making his voice crack.

"Can't," she replied, shaking her head. She knew it hurt him to take her along, but she knew he wouldn't fight as well without her around. She would be his motivation to stay alive in the coming battle, and there was nothing he nor anyone else could do to stop her from being there.

He paused for a very long time. "Could I at least get you to talk with me like you have been these past few weeks, in complete sentences, rather than just the one-word replies from when I first met you? I think it's cute when you do that, but I want to hear your voice as much as possible until we fight this battle, because if this is my last stand I want to be able to remember it."

Euleilla's heart almost broke at that. "Oh, Maelgyn," she whispered, pulling herself up to him tightly. "I'm sorry, I was just—"

"Your highness!" the sailor Euleilla recognized as Mogs, from her trip ashore, called, unexpectedly bursting into their makeshift ship's quarters. The couple broke apart, although their arms remained entangled. "He's back! He... oh, excuse me, your highness. Your ladyship."

Well, Maelgyn thought. *At least he has the decency to be embarrassed.*

"Never mind," he said aloud. "Just explain what it is you came here for, and be quick about it!"

"He's returned, your highness!" Mogs exclaimed enthusiastically, forgetting his earlier faux pas. "He's alive after all! He made it!"

"Calm down!" Maelgyn snapped. He wasn't particularly happy about being interrupted – although Euleilla seemed to be taking it fairly well, considering – but the seaman's babbling was just getting on his nerves. "Who's returned? From where?"

Euleilla answered for him, now that she had regained her composure enough to extend her senses. "Forge. The sailor we thought we'd lost during my expedition – it seems he survived after all. He doesn't appear to be in very good health, though, from what I can feel of him. He has several broken bones, and some flesh wounds which have gotten infected. He'll need immediate medical treatment. Your friend will live, however, Mogs."

Mogs stared in awe at her. "Milady, I knew you had magical gifts beyond what even most mages could boast, but can you really tell all of that from down here?"

She smiled at the new arrival blandly. Maelgyn wanted her to speak more, it was true, but she could hardly give away all her secrets, could she? "Yes," was the only word of explanation she offered.

Maelgyn laughed. "I suppose I'll forgive you for just the one word that time, love," he said, squeezing her shoulder with the arm still around her. He had almost been able to read her mind on that particular piece of internal dialog, and it made it all the more amusing to confuse the annoying, moment-interrupting sailor by forgiving her like that. Still, he needed to actually take a look at this "Forge." There was a chance he had news. "Lead us to him, Mr. Mogs."

Forge was drinking a cup of Mo'kah tea when Maelgyn and Euleilla arrived, followed by an enthusiastic Mogs. Dr. Wodtke was standing by his bed, accompanied by El'Athras, Uwelain, and a frowning Wangdu. Even Ruznak had made his way down to the surgeon's table to examine the wounded man.

"Your Highness!" Forge exclaimed, startled to see the Sword Prince approaching his sick bed. "I wasn't expecting you to come see me."

Maelgyn grimaced slightly. "Well, I need to know a few things. Like where you've been, and how you came back."

Forge nodded slowly. "I suppose my disappearance was a bit suspicious, wasn't it?" he asked resentfully. "It doesn't matter that I hauled myself here despite cracked ribs, a broken kneecap, a torn muscle in my leg, a—"

"We are quite glad to see you, Forge," Maelgyn interrupted. "But your disappearance was a bit suspicious. I'd like to trust that you haven't betrayed us, but I would also like to hear your story – it might not be that you have knowingly done anything wrong, but you were allowed to make it here for some reason or another."

"You think I didn't realize that was a possibility?" Forge asked, hurt. "Look, they beat me and captured me when we blundered into that stupid trap. I was taken to a castle I think was once Borden City – I was told it was 'Castle Paljor,' but I don't remember anything by that name on our maps."

"Then how did you escape?" Uwelain asked. "It's said that no-one who enters Castle Paljor ever gets out... unless King Paljor *wants* you to get out."

"He probably did," Forge admitted. "It's not like I was even questioned after my capture. Nor were there any guards around my cell. The iron door that was 'locked shut' just sort of fell open when I leaned against it." He paused. "They must think I am a complete idiot to not realize they were letting me go, and there would have to be a reason for them to do so."

Maelgyn frowned. Indeed, they had made it much too easy for Forge to escape. "And so you took them up on their invitation?"

Forge grinned reluctantly. "Of course, Your Highness. It would have been impolite to refuse. Of course, I think they intended to track my movements after I escaped and follow me here. I didn't let them do that, however – instead, I led them to their own harbor and stole a boat. I'd know if they'd been able to track me on a boat, and they tried of course. So, I found an inlet and pretended that was where I was getting off. Of course, they came ashore after me, but I managed to scuttle my stolen boat and took theirs. I know for a fact that I wasn't followed after that, so I came here."

Maelgyn checked with Sekhar. The *schlipf* could detect deception with ease, as that was tantamount to finding danger. Sekhar felt none, not even the tiny amount one would expect from boasting, and so he nodded in satisfaction. "Well, I am glad you managed to return. I would have expected our enemies to be more... competent, however, after their demonstrated skills in the trap which caught you."

The sailor nodded slowly. "I did too, your highness, which is why I thought I had to mention it. I still think they wanted me to escape, of course, but I'm not sure if they really just wanted to follow me or if there might be some other reason for my release."

Maelgyn chewed his lips. "Perhaps they were sending a message to us," he mused. "Did you see anything unusual or unexpected while you were there?"

Forge smirked slightly. "You mean like battle plans which might be the key to defeating them, but in reality are just another trap? No, nothing like that. I thought of that, myself. I actually went looking for them, as I was sure they expected me to, but nothing."

Euleilla cocked her head slightly. "Perhaps they didn't want us to see their plans... but to warn us away by demonstrating just how secure their fortifications are. How difficult would you figure getting into that castle would be?"

Forge frowned. "Pretty difficult, actually. There was only one obvious way in or out, and that entrance would be pretty difficult to get in through. They have guards over that entrance all of the time." He paused. "There's also the servant's entrance that I escaped through. That was unguarded completely. Kind of strange, now that I think about it."

"That's what they were trying to show us," Ruznak said suddenly, snapping his fingers. "They're giving us a way in."

"The question is, who are 'they?'" Uwelain asked. "I wouldn't put it past Paljor to give us an easy entryway that in reality is a trap. However, I also know there are many people in the current Borden Isle Council who would like Paljor removed, and they would also be the sort of people who could arrange for Forge to have such an easy escape. I just don't know."

"I think the fact that they made a token effort to track Forge might mean something," Ruznak suggested. "It could be that someone set this up for us, and disguised it with his superiors by making it seem like a plan to track us down."

Maelgyn considered that for a moment. "I suppose that's a possibility...."

"Then do we take this opportunity to break in?" Uwelain asked. "It sounds like time is of the essence for you, and I would like to be able to go home again – which I probably won't be able to until Paljor is deposed. This sounds like the ideal way to strike."

Maelgyn nodded slowly. "Let me think about it for a bit. We need a day to rest up, anyway. Mr. Forge, you may return to your duties as you see fit."

Forge's grin lit up his face. To him, being told to get back to work personally by his liege lord was the highest award he could possibly receive. "Thank you, your highness."

Maelgyn turned to leave, Euleilla on his arm, but he was followed by El'Athras and Wangdu. The Dwarf stopped him when they were out of earshot.

"Are you sure it's a good idea to put that man back into a position of responsibility?" he asked doubtfully.

Maelgyn frowned at El'Athras. "Why wouldn't it be?"

"Forgive me for saying so, Your Highness," the old Dwarf began, "But I've been a spymaster for over a century, now, and

I can tell when someone's telling fibs. There's something that doesn't ring right in that boy's story, and I wouldn't let him be put in any position where he could either sabotage the ship or hear any secret plans. Which means returning him to duty isn't a good idea."

The Sword Prince nodded slowly, but unconsciously reached over to rub the spot on his wrist which circled the only exposed bit of Sekhar that showed of the *schlipf* in its dormant state. "I believe him. He is not a threat."

That upset the Dwarf even more. "Your Highness, I can understand why you might want to believe that boy, but I don't think —"

"This matter is closed," Maelgyn snapped, but then relented slightly, grasping El'Athras' shoulder. "If you are so worried, you can observe him yourself. However, I know he is no threat."

"If you insist, Your Highness," he sighed.

Rudel watched as Forge made his way up the rope ladder towards the lookout post in the crow's nest. It was a difficult thing for a wounded man to do, and it would go a long way towards seeing how far into his recovery he really was. There was also the hazard of a man falling off the ropes to worry about it. Forge was slow, but he made it up to the top without incident, and so Rudel turned away from the man to deal with other things.

He was talking with the ship's cook about that night's dinner, and wasn't particularly happy about what he was hearing. "And you think we need to have split pea soup again tonight for *what* reason?"

"I thought you liked my pea soup!" the cook protested.

"Well, it is generally regarded as the best quality provision we can store on a ship," Rudel admitted. "But having the same thing to eat for seven meals in a row does get a bit old, no matter how good that food is."

"Well, our cheese is rancid, our salt beef is inedibly bad, the potatoes have rotted, our biscuit flour is infested, and we used up the rice a long time ago," the cook explained. "Not much else to base a meal on is in our stores, except a bunch of pickles – which you're just as tired of. I know some ship's cooks would serve all that stuff, anyway, but I refuse unless it's a choice between that and starving." He paused. "I suppose if you were willing to authorize a fishing and hunting expedition, we could at least have some variety. We didn't take the time to properly stock up before leaving Sopan, sir, so I only had what we kept in storage to prepare meals on in the first place, and so much of that was old to begin with."

Rudel pinched his nose, fighting a dawning headache. He'd forgotten some of the annoyances of single ship command, the minutiae which a captain would have to deal with. He was starting to regret accepting this command, and hoped to go back to the job of being an Admiral pretty soon. "I think land expeditions are out of the question for the moment. Anything you can catch from shipboard, however, is fine – and that includes not just fish but the birds flying around the deck. Just remember to butcher them cleanly, and please remember to pluck the bird before cooking it. I had a cook, once, who nearly sunk my ship because the feathers of a bird he'd caught started turning into floating ash and set the whole ship on fire. You'd better be able to figure that much out or you can expect to lose your job as our cook and move on to something a bit less... pleasant."

"What's less pleasant then being a cook on a ship like this?" the cook muttered as he turned to collect men for the fishing expedition. "Half the ingredients are spoiled, the light is so bad in the kitchen you can't see what you're doing, and the spices! What I wouldn't give for a teaspoon of paprika... or even a single clove of garlic! Garlic! One of the most useful and important spices in all of cooking, and we can't even keep a single clove on hand...."

Rudel shook his head as he watched the man leave. *Figures,* he thought. *I've got the only navy cook in the world who actually cares a damn about what he makes.* It wouldn't be a bad thing, mind, if we were well stocked, but considering the circumstances....

The Admiral sighed as he spotted another problem. More headaches. First, it was the supply dilemma, and now it seemed as if one of his VIPs was intending to throw himself overboard in order to get a look at the crow's nest. "Lord El'Athras," he said, approaching the Dwarf and reaching out to grab him before he overbalanced while standing on the railing. "That is a very dangerous position to be in, and as captain of this ship I must insist you get down from there."

El'Athras glared at him. "Fine, but I'm going to keep an eye on him since it seems none of *you* will."

Rudel looked a bit startled. "What? An eye on who?"

"On him, of course," the Dwarf snorted, pointing to the crow's nest. "He could be signaling the enemy from up there, or... or... I'm not sure what, but I'll catch him when he does it!"

"Forge?" Rudel laughed, realizing what El'Athras was saying. "Oh, come on, Your Lordship. Forge is no spy - I've known him for years. Plus, His Highness has vouched for his honesty. I suppose you can keep an eye on him if you wish, but please, Your Lordship, do it safely! I don't want my men to have to rescue you if you fall overboard."

El'Athras stalked away from the Admiral, disgruntled, while Rudel made his own way down below - he could use a dose of willow bark tea for his headache. The Dwarf was still muttering, not looking where he was going, when he collided with someone else.

"I wasn't going to fall overboard - I knew what I was doing! I have a perfect sense of balance, and he should know that. I'm a Dwarf, after all, and everyone knows that Dwarves are— oof!"

"Friend Athras!" Wangdu said, offering a hand to the said Dwarf with the 'perfect sense of balance,' who had been knocked off his feet by colliding with the lighter Elf who was standing on just one leg while he exercised. "You seem a bit distracted, you do."

"What is it with the bloody Humans?" El'Athras snorted. "They don't seem to have an ounce of sense in them!"

"I'd agree with you, I would, I'm sure," Wangdu said, "If I knew what you were talking about, I did."

El'Athras glared up at the crow's nest. "I don't know how they can continue to trust that man who just returned from 'captivity.' Uh huh, sure. If he was really a captive of Paljor, then I'm an Elf!"

I didn't know El'Athras was my cousin, I didn't, Wangdu mused, forcing both the smile off his face and the laughter out of his voice. "So, you don't believe his story, you don't?"

"It has so many holes I could sail this ship through them!" El'Athras exclaimed. "Now, I could understand Maelgyn believing him, perhaps - he's still just a lad, even among humans, but Rudel is old enough to know better. But no, he takes the word of an eighteen year old boy over the word of a man who's been looking for deception in men for over a century."

"I believe Maelgyn, I do," Wangdu noted. "And his people are right to believe him as well, they are. He is their liege lord, after all, he is."

The Dwarf eyed Wangdu suspiciously. "All right, give. What do you know that I don't?"

"I know how his *schlipf* works, I do," Wangdu explained. "And I know that it would warn him if that man had lied, I do."

The Dwarf looked surprised. "I didn't think *schlipf* did that. I knew they were a living weapon that your people traditionally used. I thought that was the extent of it."

"In a sense, that's true, it is," Wangdu admitted. "The *schlipf* was my people's greatest hand-to-hand weapon, it was, and still is in many ways, it is. But a *schlipf's* powers include the ability to sense danger, deceit, and more, they do. I have never had a *schlipf,* I haven't, and I do not know what all their powers are, I don't. I would have to consult the notes of their makers, I would, and the Ancient Elves' library is very difficult to get to, it is. But I'm sure this *schlipf* likes his host, I am, and so I believe Maelgyn when he says Forge is telling the truth, I do."

El'Athras averted his eyes, suddenly uncomfortable. He didn't exactly have a reply to that, but deep down, he realized that Maelgyn might actually have known what he was talking about. He still would keep a close eye on Forge, however.

Chapter 29

"I have decided," Maelgyn announced. "That we should bypass the 'secret' entrance we have been handed, whether it has been trapped or not."

Euleilla nodded, having extensively discussed the matter with him the previous night, though most of his advisors looked perplexed. Maelgyn and his wife both figured it would be a good idea to find out if it was a trap, using one of their schlipf to determine if it was safe to go through the door. She had wanted to be the one to check, but he had convinced her that – after having fought against some of Paljor's people – she was too recognizable, increasing the risk of discovery during the covert part of their mission. After a brief argument, they eventually came to the conclusion that there wasn't any point to checking at all – they had realized sneaking in wouldn't help them, anyway.

Uwelain was the one who asked the obvious question. "Why?"

"This is the first time a loyal member of Sviedan Royalty will enter a city on the Borden Isles in generations," Maelgyn pointed out. "I will not sneak into that city – indeed, I cannot, not if I hope to ever reclaim the support of its people. Instead, I will enter one of two ways: As a conqueror, with an army at my back... or as a visitor, coming to appeal to the Borden Isle Council for an end to our war. And there aren't enough of us to be an invasion force."

Everyone save Euleilla was startled at this. "You can't possibly mean to do this," Uwelain exclaimed over everyone else's protests. "There may be some people who would support you, but if you intend to go in the front gates you would be killed on sight!"

"Your people would attack someone entering under a flag of truce?" Maelgyn asked, looking at Uwelain curiously.

Uwelain looked abashed for a moment before he hesitantly answered, "Well... I don't think anyone, save Paljor himself, would even consider something like that. The laws and customs of war must be respected on both sides, or there can never be any hope of a resolution, good or ill."

"In that case, I think we should go in the front gates," Maelgyn explained. "Let's try to do this in a way that won't have the Borden Isles rebelling again as soon as I take a step off this island."

In the end, the only people Maelgyn took with him were Euleilla, Ruznak, El'Athras, Wangdu, Onayari, and Baron Uwelain. Rudel and Wodtke would remain on board the Greyholden, while Sir Leno would command a small group of soldiers who would be tasked with rescuing this diplomatic party if things went poorly and they were all imprisoned. The Baron looked rather uncomfortable being part of this entourage, but that was understandable: By entering under Svieda's flag of truce, he was essentially declaring himself a traitor to Paljor. If this didn't work, he would – at best – be exiled from his home for the rest of his life, even if he managed to talk his way out of being executed.

Unlike the branches used when Maelgyn entry into Sopan with a Dwarven escort, this flag of truce his party carried this time was actually a flag. In contrast to the Dwarves, Human societies actually employed cloth flags, and a single plain white flag was all that they needed to show they wanted a parlay. It was a clearer symbol than the white or green branches most non-Human races preferred, and it meant fewer people would have their hands full in the case of treachery.

It might have helped the seven of them if anyone had been watching their approach. Apparently, no one had even bothered to close the castle gates – not that there weren't guards, but they didn't seem to care about anyone just walking on in. It felt kind of silly, marching in a formal procession under the white flag while no-one paid much attention. There were a few guards lounging around on the plaza and a couple of merchants who looked on curiously, but outside of that it was as if they were any normal group of people walking through a peaceful town. The only things which made Maelgyn feel that the appearances were deceiving were the warnings being screamed at him by Sekhar. These people were not as inattentive as it appeared.

The lack of attention was explained when they reached the front door of the Council Hall. A couple of well-armed guards stepped out before they could knock, and bowed sketchily to Maelgyn. The lead guard stepped forward. "Your Highness, we have been expecting you since we saw your ship sail past our lookout point last night. We are pleased to see you come under flag of truce, rather than with steel and battering ram."

Maelgyn was startled. Of all possible reactions the Borden Isle government would have to his arrival, this was not one that he expected. "Well, yes. It doesn't exactly look like you were prepared for a battle, though, had I come offering one."

"We would have been if you were," was all the guard would say. "I assume you're here to petition His Majesty, Sword King Paljor?"

Maelgyn hesitated before replying, nervously rubbing his hand along the cloth band he had been using to hide Sekhar from outside view. "Actually, I hoped to speak before your Council. I'm not sure I could trust a fair hearing before Pa... before His Majesty."

The guard looked privately amused at that. "Perhaps not. Nevertheless, your meeting will be with His Majesty, although the Council will be present as well. And I'm afraid you don't have much choice about it, so if you would follow me?"

While it was easy enough getting into the castle, it would be much harder leaving if things got difficult, Maelgyn realized. The "inattentive" guards who had been mulling about the courtyard were now lined up in formation between the only door into the Council Chambers and the gates leading out of the castle. Said gates were now shut tight, and it would take quite a bit of effort to open them, again. If things went wrong now, there would be no easy escape.

The Council Chambers were plainer and smaller than Maelgyn had expected. There was a moderately sized open floor for petitioners, but there were only twelve chairs for the Council

Seats, arranged in a row on the dais. Each Seat had an alcove behind where three or four pages could take notes, dispense advice in secret, send or receive messages between Seats, and so forth. Only eleven of the chairs were filled at the moment, and the twelfth... well, from Uwelain's wistful expression it was pretty obvious who the twelfth belonged to.

There was also a throne, of course, on an elevated platform down center from the Council. In it sat a powerful-looking man in his mid-thirties with a dark, rich beard. He was wearing dragonhide armor, like Maelgyn himself, but that armor shone with the rich amber color of a Golden Dragon's skin. Laid across his lap was another familiar sight – one of the Ten Swords, the royal treasures of Svieda.

So... this is Paljor, Maelgyn mused, feeling somewhat intimidated. This man was obviously stronger, both in physical and magical ability, than Maelgyn felt he could ever be. He silently prayed that this situation could be resolved without a battle.

Another man stood to the Throne's right, holding a gavel in front of a sturdy podium. He was the first to speak, as he hammered a strike plate at the podium for attention. "Bow before His Majesty, the Sword King Paljor of New Svieda," he called.

Uwelain did so, as did the Council Seats, but none of the other visitors made the move. Maelgyn and Euleilla gave the same simple nod of deference they would to a fellow Sword Prince. Elves, Dwarves, and Nekoji all had their own forms of respect, but none of these involved bowing. Ruznak just snorted, never having respected the line from which Paljor sprang to begin with.

"Come, come," Paljor called, deranged laughter unhidden in his voice. "You are visitors to my Court. Bow, friends... or perhaps you aren't friends after all!"

Maelgyn glared at the so-called Sword King, and shook his head. "Your highness, I do not recognize your crown. I offer you the respect due a Sword Prince, no more." He paused. "I am not here to speak with you, anyway, but rather I wish to discuss our wars with your Council."

Paljor laughed even louder. "Oh, go ahead. Speak with the Council, if you desire. This could be amusing."

That wasn't encouraging, but Maelgyn forged ahead, anyway. "Gentlemen," he said, addressing the Council. Most of the eleven Seats looked uncomfortable, but at least they seemed to be listening with an open mind. He had no idea how Paljor was behaving, however - he could place where the "Sword King" was, being able to sense him with magic, but Maelgyn's back was to him and so his face was hidden. "I have come to appeal for an end to our civil war. I ask you to return your allegiance where it belongs - to Svieda - and to help us in an hour of great need."

Paljor snorted. "And just why would we agree to this?"

Maelgyn paused, considering his answer carefully. He needed to bait Paljor into allowing a fair vote from the Council, at the very least... and there was one thing he could offer as that bait. Something which, theoretically, was true... although Paljor, thanks to the edict of the Golden Dragons, would never have a chance to benefit from it.

"An event has occurred that has happened only once before in Sviedan history. The Sword King of Svieda has been assassinated. While catastrophic for Svieda, the unique circumstances make this an ideal time for Borden Isle to consider rejoining us," Maelgyn replied.

"I think some of you know the Law of the Swords as well as I. If the Sword of Borden Isle rejoins Svieda and reconquers its Castle, the Law of the Swords makes it possible for him to be crowned Sword King of all Svieda."

There was a long pause. Not even his allies had expected him to mention that, but Maelgyn needed a carrot to offer... and the opportunity to rule all of Svieda was a pretty large carrot.

Still, while even Paljor seemed to be considering the offer at that news, there were objections. "Who cares about the rest of Svieda?" one of the Seats snapped. "We have never cared to conquer it, only to be left alone. We didn't leave Svieda because our Sword lacked for opportunity; we left because of how the rest of Svieda treated Ivari and Laimoth! You turned your back on them, and because of that, we turn our backs on you!"

Ruznak stepped up at that. "That was a long time ago, and unless I miss my guess, none of you were even alive back then. I was, however... and I was a Borden Islander." That elicited glares by many on the Council, both from the Seats and their staff. Those who had chosen to support Svieda in the rebellion had always been looked down upon by the other Borden Islanders. "And you know what? I agree with you. Sword Princess Ivari and

Lord Laimoth were treated rottenly by Svieda. I did not think we were right in rebelling against Svieda, but I always felt the cause of the rebellion was just."

The Seat who had spoken before looked both angry and confused, but decided to try and reason with the man. "Then why do you think we will change our minds, traitor? If you agree with us, then why would you even want us to?"

Ruznak straightened as much as his old bones would allow him. "For one, Svieda has changed, and I will speak to that in time. More importantly, I think you should learn what we now know – that Svieda's hatred of Sword Princess Ivari and Laimoth was incited by those who are at war with Svieda right now, seeking to manipulate the conflict to their own ends."

Maelgyn sensed Paljor stiffening behind them. So, Maelgyn thought, He knows something.

"And you expect us to believe that?" the Seat snorted. "Or to believe that Svieda has changed? Will the lineage of our rulers suddenly be treated with the respect due them? Has it suddenly become acceptable for a commoner to marry a Sword? Who was the last commoner to marry a Sviedan royal, anyway?"

Euleilla coughed politely. "Me."

The Seat looked abashed. "Um, well—"

Maelgyn was about to say something, but Euleilla touched his arm lightly. "This is my time to speak, husband."

Maelgyn nodded, understanding. "Go ahead."

Stepping forward, she addressed the council.

"Ivari and Laimoth were treated poorly, we all acknowledge, but their time is past. They were not the last pairing of nobility and commoner. I am of common birth, yet I also am the wife of Sword Prince Maelgyn." She took his hand, and held it aloft. "We stand before you as living proof that Svieda *has* changed."

"I won't say all of the old prejudices are gone," Maelgyn admitted. "We had some difficulty being accepted... but not as much as I feared, and most of it brought on by foreign influences. Svieda treats us more like Agaeb and Amberry than it did Ivari and Laimoth. We have learned since their time – and one of the things we have learned is that the prejudice against Ivari and Laimoth was a careful and deliberate manipulation of our politics by our enemies. The agents of Sho'Curlas sowed the seeds of discord, played to fears, and ultimately incited riots among the populace."

"This we can prove," Ruznak said. "We have the testimony of this Elf, and this Dwarf has the evidence to confirm it."

"And more, besides," Uwelain finally spoke up. "When I was contacted by the Elf, Wangdu, about this matter, I felt as you all did – that there was no way I would ever believe Svieda was innocent in the matter. Svieda has much to answer for in allowing itself to be led astray by propaganda and in making itself vulnerable to rebellion not just once, but many times. However, when I heard their testimony and saw the physical evidence he and El'Athras presented, I knew that a hidden power behind the throne of Sho'Curlas was the real enemy."

"And we are more than willing to show that same evidence to you, we are," Wangdu declared. "If you require more proof than just the words of one of your own Barons, you do."

Several of the Seats looked rather curious until Paljor spoke. "You can show all the 'evidence' you want," he said. "But it will change nothing. These islands will never again be a part of Svieda! We have been running this land on our own for eighty years, now, and my children and I will continue to do so until the end of time!"

Maelgyn cocked his head. "I believe, if we were to check the private family records of the line of Sword Prince Elaneth, who started the rebellion in the first place, we would find that he was also part of the conspiracy against Svieda in the first place. And that the decision to rebel had little to do with 'Ivari and Laimoth,' as he claimed, but rather the bribe paid to his side of the family line by Sho'Curlas, or more specifically the Mad Elf Hrabak who silently rules that Alliance." He was completely guessing, but he felt it very likely that he was right. Paljor's reactions were telling him that he was on the right track, even if the details weren't entirely correct.

Paljor certainly wasn't pleased at the suggestion, at any rate. "Enough! Barons, vote against this proposal now, so that we can end this charade... and so that I can destroy these cowards for their lies!"

The Council looked rather uncomfortable at that declaration. Even the Seat who had objected to the proposal initially found himself saying, "They entered under flag of truce. We can't—"

"I am the Sword King here!" Paljor screamed. The flow of

magic could be felt even by the untrained as he slammed the offending Seat back down into his chair. "My words are law! Which means you have no choice in how you vote. I order you to vote against these liars' proposal, so that I may kill them at my leisure!"

Well, Maelgyn thought to himself, taking a deep breath. *I guess I've got no choice now, do I? I've got to take this step even before the vote. I was hoping to get the Borden Isle Council to agree first, but I suppose it might work out better this way.*

"It seems to me," he said aloud, turning to face Paljor, "That you are violating your own laws, 'Your Majesty.' And even a Sword King is not above his own laws."

And what do you know of our laws?" Paljor snapped.

Maelgyn cocked his head. "Do you take me for a fool? Do you really think I would have come here, and made a proposal like this, knowing nothing of the laws that would govern the Borden Isles? Come, now – you have barely changed the common laws from the time before the rebellion, much less the laws of Governance. I know that you are not allowed to force your Council to vote one way or another. Let them vote without interference, or their vote becomes meaningless... in which case I will have the right to challenge their ruling as being made under duress."

"Which would lead to a duel between us," Paljor laughed. "I am not worried in the least by any threat a simple child such as yourself might present."

Maelgyn raised an eyebrow. "Perhaps not. But I stand ready to fight you if necessary. You would be well advised to allow these Barons to vote their conscience instead of directing how they vote. In all likelihood, they will vote against us, and it won't be a concern for you."

Paljor's eyes narrowed. "And if they *do* vote on your behalf?"

"Well," Maelgyn said slowly. "As the reigning Duke of the Borden Isles, you would be obligated to follow their ruling under both Sviedan law and your own. One minor change in your laws grants you a 'trial by combat' if you desperately want a law overturned. If the vote was unanimous, you could challenge me, as the law's sponsor, to a duel in an effort to veto it, but as long as the vote is not unanimous you could veto it regardless."

Paljor cocked his head slightly. "And in that unlikely event, what happens?"

"Then we are still at war. Or you may allow the vote to stand, and remain a Sword as the Sword Prince and Duke of the Borden Isles," Maelgyn replied, then smiled slowly. "I would even be willing to pardon you and your family line for its treachery, myself, regardless of what your family papers show in regards to any deals with Sho'Curlas, provided you swear to remain faithful to Svieda for the remainder of your days. But I am afraid you would nevertheless be subject to justice, if not under Sviedan laws... for you violated the treaty with the Golden Dragons when you murdered the one from which you made that armor. The law will still require me to deliver you for trial by their Elders."

"Who of course, will sentence me to death," Paljor snorted. "I'm sorry, but I don't exactly see the advantage for me to allowing the vote to stand, in that case."

"Well," Maelgyn considered. "Perhaps there is none to you. But your followers might think different." He paused – the fight was now inevitable, but he could still engage in a little diplomacy for the benefit of the Seats. "If the Borden Isles legally votes to maintain independence after this news, I, as a Sword Prince in a time without a reigning Sword King, will use my authority to formally recognize the Borden Isles' independence and end our war. But I will still be obligated, by treaty with the Golden Dragons, to either bring you before them for trial or kill you myself."

Paljor cocked his head. "It sounds as if there is no way for me to avoid a fight, doesn't it?"

"You could always surrender," Ruznak suggested. "The Golden Dragons won't necessarily kill you if you can justify your actions."

"My only 'justifications' are those I require as the Sword King," Paljor snarled. "The Dragons intrude upon my lands, and as such they forfeit their lives to me to do with as I please... and I desired a set of dragonhide armor, which requires a dead Dragon to make. If they cannot accept that, then I shall destroy them, as well."

"The Council has voted," the Sergeant at Arms called from the podium on Paljor's right. "By a unanimous vote, Baron Uwelain's proposal that Paljor be removed from the office of Sword King – pending the examination of Maelgyn's evidence – is passed."

Paljor's eyes widened. "What is this? When was this bill

proposed? And when was the vote taken?"

"Moments ago for both questions, your majesty," Uwelain explained. He had quietly taken his chair while Maelgyn and Paljor talked, and evidently had been working on a solution of his own. "Your abuse of power in this situation was enough to convince even the most reluctant of the Seats that Maelgyn deserves a fair hearing, at the least. We discussed the matter and voted silently, as the law allows. It was your own right hand man, the Sergeant-at-Arms, who counted the votes for us... and he says it was unanimous."

"Then I will simply challenge you to a duel, Uwelain." Paljor shrugged. "For the right to veto. You cannot stand against me. Or will you, as the bill's sponsor, decline said duel and allow my veto to stand?"

Maelgyn swiftly made his way to within earshot of Uwelain as the Baron paled. Everyone knew that Paljor could easily crush any member of the Seats in a duel, and as the bill's sponsor his only hope to survive was to win the duel or withdraw his bill.

"Accept the challenge," Maelgyn said to him. "But make me your champion. He's right that you cannot fight him, but as a mage I might stand a chance. And if I fail... well, we're both dead anyway, from what Paljor has been saying."

Uwelain was looking even more nervous at those words, but he nodded nonetheless. "I, Baron Uwelain, accept the challenge," he called, causing all of the Seats to look at him in shock. Not a single one of them expected him to agree, even those that heard Maelgyn's plea. The chance of anyone beating Paljor in a duel was so unlikely that it was considered suicide to enter into one with him. "And I name as my champion Maelgyn, Duke of Sopan and Sword Prince of Svieda."

Paljor nodded slowly. "Very well. Sword Prince Maelgyn. Prepare yourself – the duel will begin in ten minutes, and it will happen here – on the floor of the Council Chambers of New Svieda. Here I shall spill the blood of my cousins... and finally teach them never to cross the waters again."

Chapter 30

Uwelain stepped before the Sergeant-at-Arms, negotiating the terms of the duel while acting as his own champion's second. "We believe that Royal treasures such as the Swords should not be used in this duel. They are of too much value to risk in a battle of this nature."

Acting as Paljor's second, the Sergeant-at-Arms nodded. "We shall agree to that – we would have proposed something similar. However, we desire Maelgyn's Sword to be offered up as a trophy. Paljor must give up his Sword should he lose; it is only fair that he has the right to gain another when he wins."

That surprised Uwelain, and he looked over at Maelgyn for instructions. The Sword Prince hesitated briefly before saying, "As long as it is understood that only the weapon itself is offered as trophy. Sopan will remain a province of Svieda, regardless of the outcome."

"As expected," Paljor's second agreed. "Do you have any other terms for this duel?"

"Regardless of who wins," Maelgyn said, not allowing Uwelain to answer for him. "All of those who entered with me under flag of truce will be allowed to depart, unharmed."

"No!" Paljor snapped. "There are two traitors to New Svieda in your party, and both must die."

Both seconds looked momentarily nonplussed at that exchange, before Uwelain sighed and reluctantly conceded the point. "Withdrawn," he said. "But I propose, as a substitution, that the Elf, Dwarf, and Nekoji be allowed to leave. Euleilla has declared she will stay with her husband even after his death, and both I and Ruznak accepted our fates before we volunteered for this. The others, however, came in under flag of truce, and with the expectation that it would be honored."

"That, I think, we can agree with," the Sergeant-at-Arms said uncertainly, glancing at Paljor for confirmation. At the man's impatient nod, he continued, "And now I believe our negotiations are at an end. You will have two minutes to prepare yourselves as the Council Chambers are cleared for the duel, and then we will begin."

The principles of the duel both glared at each other before returning to their corners. Maelgyn closed his eyes, taking a moment to collect himself before the battle, when Euleilla stepped up to kiss him. "Husband," she said. "Remember my vow. I cannot fight alongside you in this duel, but they will have to kill me to stop me from protecting you should you fall."

"I know," Maelgyn sighed, feeling his heart tighten up as he thought of it. "We'll see what I can do." He handed her his Sword, and then pulled out another weapon. "And I shall use the weapon you crafted for me during our first battle together to fight him. You will be well represented, love."

"He isn't really stronger than you, husband," she insisted desperately, her composure breaking. "He may be a High Mage. That is easy to see. But you have powers still untapped, and weapons he knows nothing about. You can be a High Mage, yourself, if you don't hold yourself back too much. You can win this."

"He's crazy, he is," Wangdu noted softly, stepping in to offer his advice. "Even his allies know this, they do. That can be exploited, it can."

Ruznak, though, had the strongest words. "My foster daughter is your wife, and she believes in you. If you make a widow of her, I know I'm dead as well... and I'll be haunting you for the rest of your afterlife, so you had best fight well."

Maelgyn laughed bitterly. "Thanks, 'gramps,'" he said. "If anything will make me want to kill this guy more than saving Svieda and all our lives, it's the thought that your ugly face will be harassing me for all of eternity."

"I ain't your gramps!" Ruznak snarled, but everyone knew he wasn't serious. The tension had been broken, however, and his job was done.

Paljor laughed from across the room. "The time for you to pretend you have a chance is over. The floor is clear. Come here, boy, and let me teach you a final lesson in 'diplomacy!'"

"Perhaps it is I who will be teaching *you* a lesson in humility, Paljor," Maelgyn snapped back with a confidence he did not feel. He was neither an ideal swordsman nor a High Mage, in truth. He was a dabbler in swordsmanship and he had some raw, underdeveloped talent in magic. That combination was usually enough to combat the average soldier or the average mage without a serious strain, but... this was neither an average soldier nor an average mage. This was a High Mage, and one who likely had much more experience as a swordsman than Maelgyn. The only advantages he held were slight: His youth, his enthusiasm, and his *schlipf*. Well, the *schlipf* was more than a "slight" advantage, perhaps, but Maelgyn believed that it would be best to use its offensive capabilities to catch Paljor off guard, but it would also be his coup de grace. That was the totality of his plan, at this point, so he couldn't afford to tip Paljor off by using Sekhar too early in the battle.

Maelgyn threw his magic into his blood, hoping to make his strength and reaction time great enough to match the more experienced man. He then drew the sword Euleilla had made for him, and said a silent prayer that she would somehow survive this even if he did not. "Whenever you are ready, your 'majesty,'" he said, his voice thick with sarcasm.

"Then let us begin," Paljor laughed, casually swinging his own sword a few times as if to loosen up. His sword looked to be a well-forged katana, not quite at the level of one of the Swords of Svieda but certainly a fine piece.

Better equipped, stronger, more powerful, and more experienced, Maelgyn thought in resignation. *Hopefully I at least have luck on my side.*

"Fight!" snapped the Seat refereeing the duel.

It wasn't all a rush of action straight from the get-go, like Maelgyn had been expecting. In his previous "real" combat experience, the moment two swordsmen got close to each other they would start fighting... which was only to be expected when there was the possibility that taking the time to evaluate your opponent could get you killed by his allies. This was a duel, however, which was a very different situation. He wasn't sure when to attack, but thanks to Sekhar he would know when to block. He was relying entirely on that, hoping that he could possibly use a counterattacking style which would utilize his skills, both natural and magical, to the best of their ability.

Left! Sekhar suddenly shouted to him. The living weapon knew of Maelgyn's plans, and while he could have blocked for Maelgyn he opted to follow the plan as it had been set. Fortunately, Sekhar could remain hidden underneath cotton wraps and still sense danger as if he were in the open, or else it would have been too obvious that he was present to even attempt such a plan.

Maelgyn leapt back, barely avoiding the katana as he brought his own sword up to launch a counterattack against Paljor's right side. He pinned together the flats of both blades, forcing his opponent's arm to hyperextend. He used the opportunity to bring his armored knee up into the Borden Islander's arm, hoping to knock the sword out of his hands and end the battle quickly. Even though Paljor's arm was bare, it felt like Maelgyn was kicking armor plating. He heard a crack from his knee, and moments later sharp pains raced up his leg.

Remind me not to try that again, he thought absently to Sekhar, staggering slightly as he magically popped his dislocated kneecap back into place.

Paljor, on the other hand, was unaffected by the blow. However, the action forced both of them to step back and re-evaluate each other. They circled around, each looking for another opening. Not able to find one, Maelgyn again decided to play defense and wait for an opportunity to counterattack.

Parry! Fast! came the warning. It almost came too late, but with a flash of steel and all the magically enhanced speed he was able to muster he deflected a rapid flurry of blows. Maelgyn was forced to retreat, unable to either stand or counterattack under the furious onslaught. His eyes were not able to keep up with the speed of the attack, and only Sekhar's extra senses kept him from being completely overwhelmed.

This isn't working, he thought.

Do you want to change plans? I could help you even more if I could attack, Sekhar asked.

Maelgyn managed to duck under one sword strike and roll away, putting some distance between them again and giving him another chance to re-evaluate the situation. *No,* he told Sekhar.

Not yet. It seems, though, that I am outmatched defensively even with your aid. Let me try mounting some sort of offense and we'll see how things go from there.

I'll watch for counterattacks, Sekhar thought back. *But be careful – he's good.*

I noticed that, Maelgyn replied wryly, preparing to attack. He decided to use as much speed as possible – if he could move fast enough that Paljor's eyes couldn't clearly see his movements, there was a slim chance he could win. After all, while he was only able to stop that last assault with the aid of a *schlipf's* senses, he must have been the equal to Paljor in speed to block it. Without a *schlipf* of his own, Paljor would have to rely exclusively on his eyes to react. That was an advantage Maelgyn realized he might have.

Unfortunately, Maelgyn couldn't change the direction of his attacks fast enough to bring that speed to bear. Each time he launched an attack he only got a single blow in before being knocked back several steps by powerful parries with the flat of Paljor's sword, ruining his chances to follow up with his newly discovered speed. However, those initial attacks were preventing Paljor from renewing his own offensive... although that would only be until Maelgyn was shoved back into a wall by Paljor's defensive pushback.

I have to think of something, he realized. *A new plan... I need a whole new plan....*

He felt the wall coming up behind him, and suddenly had his idea. When he was given the final block that sent him slamming against the stone, he was expecting it. Rebounding off of the wall, he swung a powerful overhand strike. Paljor, of course, defended himself just as he had before – with a hard shove back, but no true counterstrike. Maelgyn's sword tore itself apart cleanly as it hit the katana, slipped through, and reformed seamlessly on the other side. The longsword passed through all of Paljor's defenses and slammed into his armor.

Dragonhide was impervious to pure magic and some types of arrowheads, but it could nevertheless be pierced by a sharp sword or a heavy axe... usually. And Paljor's golden dragonhide was slightly scratched by Maelgyn's blade... but a scratch was all the damage he could manage despite landing a solid blow with all of his weight behind it. Maelgyn hadn't even felt any magic trying to stop him... which meant that the armor, made from the dragonhide of a Golden Dragon instead of the usual Red or Black, could not be pierced with steel, either.

Uh, oh, he thought.

Paljor stepped back, not using the easy opportunity to kill Maelgyn then and there. He checked his blade carefully, and when he saw no defect he smiled slowly. "Oh, good," he said absently. "It seems as if you are a mage, yourself. I was wondering how you were matching my attack." He paused, and then grinned. "I guess that means I can start using my own magic as well."

For the first time, Maelgyn could feel Paljor's magic flaring, slipping into the Borden Islander's blood to strengthen his muscles. More magic came flying his way, shattering the sword Euleilla had made and sending the shards flying into Maelgyn's skin and throwing him to his feet.

I was using all of my magic and Sekhar's senses, yet he was able to outfight me using none of his own magic? This is not a fight I could have ever hoped to win, Maelgyn thought in horror.

"So, just how powerful of a mage are you? Fourth rate, perhaps?"

A magical attack calibrated to throw a Fourth Rate mage into the wall slammed into Maelgyn, but he was easily able to summon the necessary counter-magic to stop him. Fighting at this level was actually to the Sword Prince's advantage – his practice with Euleilla made counter-magic his greatest magical combat skill, and his own dragon armor aided him even further. Paljor's assault was deflected easily, and Maelgyn tried to gather the concentration necessary to both attack and defend.

"Third Rate, perhaps?" Paljor continued. Maelgyn felt the force he was trying to combat start to rise with increasing speed. He was forced to abandon plans of his own offensive just to keep up. "Oh, ho, so you're at least a Second Rate! No, a First! Well, this is a pleasant surprise... it's been a long time since I had the challenge even of a Third Rate, much less a First. Pity you're otherwise such a wimp."

Paljor's attack slowed, or so it seemed. Compartmentalizing his mind, Maelgyn found the mental discipline to be able to defend himself and to finally lay into his enemy with his own magical assault.

Paljor was caught off guard momentarily, and staggered back

before recovering. "Well, well, well. Looks like we have High Mage potential, here. Shame it's still just potential, though – if you had reached that potential before challenging me, we might have had the first duel of High Mages in all of history... and likely the last, considering how few of us there really are. What an amazing amount of talent can be found in the Sviedan royal line, eh?"

Paljor redoubled his magical attack. Despite his best efforts at counter-magic, Maelgyn found himself slammed back against the wall. He could feel shards of his own exploded sword ripping through his skin, but Maelgyn had just enough strength to keep Paljor from damaging anything vital with them. Nevertheless, he was losing blood. Lost blood was an even greater danger to a mage, for as their blood ran out of their body so did some of the power of their magic. With that in mind, he did his best to seal the cuts as quickly as they appeared, but it was hard to concentrate enough to defend himself from multiple angles and heal himself at the same time. He had yet to feel the headache which would let him know that he had reached the limits of what he could get his magic to do, but he feared he would reach that point soon.

"Oh, this is no fun," Paljor sighed. "I had hoped for a real fight from you, but all you're doing is trying to stay alive! I want that berserker rage so many people feel at this point in their lives, where they give up hope of survival and let me destroy them just so that they can try to get in one shot. Why don't you try it? After all, my death is your goal, is it not?"

"You won't goad me into acting foolishly, Paljor," Maelgyn replied, more calmly than he felt.

Paljor shook his head. "It seems I need to give you a little... incentive, before you really push things into that stage of self-destruction I want from you. So, let's see about what we can do to give you that incentive, shall we?"

Without releasing his attack on Maelgyn, Paljor launched a powerful magical wave that slammed each of the observers of the duel into the walls of the circular chamber. Everyone, from the Seats to Maelgyn's party, started struggling against the intensity of Paljor's magic.

Maelgyn, Sekhar thought to him. *His back is to us, so we have the perfect opportunity to attack. Can you point your fist at him?*

What? Maelgyn thought back. *What can you do?*

I can pierce even that grade of dragonhide armor as long as you point me directly at him, Sekhar explained. *I am unaffected by his magic, but my power is too limited unless I am facing him directly.*

Maelgyn tried to move his arm but it wouldn't budge. He was completely pinned by Paljor's assault, and it was all he could to keep from bleeding out. *Sorry,* he thought. *No good.*

Keep trying, Sekhar demanded. *I'm the only thing around here which can pierce that armor!*

Paljor walked around the room. First, his attention was on the Seats. "So, who should I use to anger you, Maelgyn? I doubt you would care much for these turncoats, even if I would enjoy using them. They are complete strangers to you, after all." He walked casually, as if he wasn't fighting a mortal battle against what was now more than a score of enemies, until he came to the final Seat. "Although perhaps this traitor means something to you, hm?"

"No!" Maelgyn cried, but there was nothing he could do as Paljor casually slit the throat of the straining Baron Uwelain. Without a word, without a visible protest of any kind, the idealist nobleman who had brought the hope of an end to the civil war between the Borden Isles and Svieda died.

Paljor considered Maelgyn curiously. "Hm, so that upset you, didn't it? But still you restrain yourself from a sacrificial attempt to destroy me. Perhaps I should move on to your other friends. Surely *one* of them should inspire a futile attack against to save them, don't you think?"

"Your fight is with me!" Maelgyn cried. "Leave my friends out of this. This is no longer a duel, it is treachery!"

Paljor just ignored him, moving on down the line. "Let's see. An Elf? Well, well, well... you do keep interesting company, don't you, your highness? You claim to be a friend of the Dragons, and yet you consort with their greatest enemies. Although I suppose the Dragons aren't alone in that – the Elves are *everyone's* greatest enemies. Those 'papers' you correctly suspect me of having tell me all about that. Still, it's pretty hard to kill an Elf. I can do it, of course – as you can see, even he can't escape the force of my magic – but I think I'll save him for last.

"And you also have in your company a Dwarf! Magic doesn't affect them, of course, so I have to use his own steel axe to hold him against the wall. You know, I've heard you can't injure or kill these creatures by simply bludgeoning them? I think I would like to test that. We don't really have the time, right now, though – you aren't going to last long enough for me to finish him off.

"And then there's the Nekoji girl! There's something odd about this one – it's almost like she's trying to use magic and can't – but I would so love one of those fireproof cloaks you can make from their skins. Who wants to have to wash blood out of such a fine coat, though? I'll wait until we can kill her cleanly."

Maelgyn continued struggling as Paljor went on down the row of people. He found he had just enough counter-magic to spare to make his arm move very slowly without significantly affecting his ability to staunch his bleeding wounds. At the rate he was going, however, Paljor would be through the line before he could point Sekhar at the man. And next on his path....

"So, you're the commoner who married a 'Sword Prince,' are you?" Paljor said, looking Euleilla up and down. "Not bad, I must say. Not the snappiest of dressers, but what does one expect from a commoner, anyway? And that hair is so awful it's embarrassing! Still, I imagine she has her... uses."

Maelgyn felt Euleilla 'flinch' magically as Paljor rubbed a hand along her cheek. The action caused the deranged Sword King to step back in surprise. "Don't you ever touch me, you cretin," she declared, fighting back with all of her own magic. It wasn't enough, of course, but it seemed to make him pause.

"Oh, this won't do at all," Paljor sighed. "I had hoped to spare you for a while and taste your 'charms,' as I am sure many have before me, but you are a mage! I suppose I can still have fun by testing your skills, at least. So, what rate are you, anyway? Fourth? No, you've already demonstrated more power than that. At least a second... no, a first! I'm impressed, Maelgyn – for a commoner, you seem to have picked a powerful one." He laughed. "Of course, that means she's too powerful to play with. Looks like she'll have to die!" His katana raised itself over his head.

"No!" Maelgyn shouted. His magic flared up around him. His subconscious took over his magical efforts to heal himself, as all his concentration focused on saving Euleilla. In his panic, adrenaline rushing through his veins, he found himself drawing upon a well of raw magical power he had never tapped into before. His arm began moving faster.

Too slow too slow too slow too slow... he chanted mentally. Finally, he even started pulling from that magic that kept him from bleeding. Paljor had won, but Maelgyn could still sacrifice himself to stop this madman.

Now!

"Glug!" was all Paljor could say as he his body heaved when Sekhar's blow hit him from behind. The feeling that a fiery icicle had been run through his chest was overwhelming, and he found himself having the hardest time catching his breath. He was also in more pain than he had ever experienced when he tried to breathe, and found himself too distracted to maintain the waves of magic he was using to pin everybody to the walls. Euleilla forced him to drop his sword, but he didn't even pay any attention to that – he was much too concerned about what had happened to him.

Paljor looked down, coughing some bloody foam out of his mouth as he did. That was when he saw it – the green spike of a *schlipf* thorn coming out of his chest, directly through his right lung. It missed his heart, but the wound was immediately crippling. He recognized the implement, however, and stepped forward to get away from it.

"So," Paljor rasped, now requiring all of his magic internally to keep himself alive and functioning. "You are full of surprises, aren't you, your highness? I would never have expected you to sacrifice yourself for a *schlipf.*"

"I didn't sacrifice myself," Maelgyn replied, breathing heavily himself. Now both of them were badly wounded, but Paljor still could win. If Maelgyn showed any weakness, Paljor could launch a fatal attack instantly. "He's a volunteer. Few of the weaknesses and all of the strengths."

Paljor tried to laugh, but it turned into more of a hacking cough as he vomited up some more blood. "I see," he finally said. "An Elf, a Dwarf, a Nekoji, a female Mage, a Sword, and a *schlipf.* But it is not enough." He picked up his katana and started advancing on Maelgyn. "Neither of us is strong enough to fight using our magic at this point, but that is still in my favor. For wounding me like this, you are dead, you –"

That was his last word, as another weapon impaled its way

through his neck. Wangdu's spear twisted before it withdrew, gouging out his throat from behind.

"You forgot something, you did," the Elf said to the dying man. "You violated the code of conduct for a duel, you did... which freed this Elf to fight you, it did. High Mage or not, you may be, but you could never have beaten me in a battle, you couldn't."

Euleilla pulled the sword out of Paljor's failing grip once more with her magic, pulling it into her own hand. "Not just the Elf. Your treachery has freed this Mage to act as well."

"And the Dwarf, and the Nekoji," El'Athras noted. "And your own Barons, who just might take a dim view of your murdering one of their own and threatening their lives."

Paljor could not speak, he could not breathe, but he still had a fractional bit of his magic remaining. He was dead, and he knew it, but at least he could have his revenge. There was one person who was completely unprotected from magic, who was weak, and who would hurt those who killed him... and, his target chosen, he put all his remaining magic into crushing that man.

Ruznak stumbled back as the attack hit him... but that was all the harm he suffered, as Euleilla and Maelgyn both threw up magical defenses around him. Paljor's last attempt at magic had failed.

It was not completely futile, however. Maelgyn had been holding himself together with his magic, but to protect Ruznak he had to pull from the magic keeping him alive. Paljor's last moments saw Euleilla collapse at her husband's side, sobbing, as he also fell.

Epilog

In the aftermath of the duel, the Borden Isle Council was in serious disarray. Maelgyn was only barely alive, and only by virtue of Euleilla's own magic. Their party, Maelgyn included, had been carried into a side room and placed under heavy guard. They had killed the King of the Borden Islands – there was bound to be repercussions, no matter Paljor's mistreatment of the Seats. Still, none of their weapons were being confiscated, which led to some confusion as to their status: Were they being imprisoned, or protected?

Ruznak shifted uncomfortably on a hard stone bench. "Well, now what are we going to do?"

"Do?" El'Athras snorted. "What do you mean?"

"We still don't know if Maelgyn will live or die," Ruznak noted. "We're not being allowed to leave, not even to summon medical aid. Uwelain is dead, and we do not know the sympathies of whoever it is that is now supposed to succeed Paljor. I know that my life hangs by the thread of our parlay agreement, and if Paljor's successor decides that we violated that agreement when we deposed Paljor than I'm as good as dead already. Not that I'll be missing much – I'm so old I might die of old age before they could build the gallows for me – but what do we do if the new 'Sword King' is hostile to us?"

Wangdu grinned, bringing his hand to his staff. "We do what we have to, we do. Not many people can harm an Elf, they can't, and we'll be fine no matter what, we will. But I doubt that an escape will be needed, it won't."

"They'd never have let us keep our weapons if they were

going to harm us," El'Athras pointed out. "Not that it would have been easy for them to take them from us."

"If it comes to a battle, we are well prepared," Onayari pointed out. "I am the greatest warrior of my clan. El'Athras is a master of infiltration, sabotage, and planning. The Elves are the most powerful warriors in the known world. Not to mention all of the mages our company could bring out in a battle with any force the Borden Islanders could muster."

Wangdu's face darkened. "Well, we Elves aren't necessarily the most powerful warriors, we're not. We've lost major battles before, we have – to the Ancient Dragons, to Ancient Enemies whose names we no longer speak, and even to some armies of Dwarves or Humans. Paljor was almost as strong as me, he was. There should be enough mages and soldiers in Borden to counter even me, there should. If it comes to a battle, it does, the numbers say we'll lose, they do." He paused. "But I do not see us being involved in a battle with them, I don't."

"Well, I'm relieved about that," a Borden Islander said from the door. He glared briefly at Ruznak before turning to the Elf. "I presume, in His Highness' absence, you would be the leader of your little party?"

Wangdu wasn't surprised by his silent entry in the least – or at least, didn't look it. He grinned at the newcomer and shook his head. "We never settled that, we didn't. I may be called that, I might, but I am not Sviedan, I'm not. We also have with us the newly made Count El'Athras of Svieda, we do, who has an official position in Sviedan government, he does. My status in the kingdom has not been discussed."

The guard frowned, but then shrugged. "I suppose I'll ask you both to attend, then."

Wangdu considered that for a moment. "I trust you, I do, but my friend Ruznak is a bit anxious, he is. Perhaps he could join us as well, he could?"

"As you please," the man replied, clearly disinterested. "All of you may come, if you so desire, though it looks like the Lady is too busy to attend."

"Then let's go," El'Athras grumbled gruffly, directing the others to the door as quickly as he could make them move. "Never a good thing to keep a Council waiting, is it?"

*

The bloodstains on the floor were a grim reminder that, yes, the room they were standing in was the same in which Maelgyn fought his duel in only a few hours before. The eleven surviving Seats of the Council were in their chairs, looking extremely serious. Resting on the late Paljor's throne was the Borden Isles' Sword. Maelgyn's Sword and the katana Paljor fought with were in Euleilla's possession, the last anyone saw of them, but some of the shards of Maelgyn's lesser sword had been gathered together and placed at the throne's foot. The Seat belonging to Uwelain was shrouded in the black veils of mourning, and all torches and other lights near the chair were extinguished – stark reminders of their fallen fellow conspirator.

"Where is her highness, Princess Euleilla?" one of the Seats asked the escort.

"She was unwilling to leave her husband's side," the guard explained. "So I brought Prince Maelgyn's advisors, including a newly made Count of Svieda."

The councilman nodded as if he had expected that answer. "Very well. Representatives of Svieda, you should know that your actions have left us in a very difficult position."

"We apologize, we do," Wangdu replied. "But our actions were necessary, they were."

"And we understand your actions," the Seat assured them. "Nevertheless, it has caused many complications in our government."

"Such as?" El'Athras asked, not willing to deal with the diplomatic nonsense of floral phrases and formal words.

"The royal family is gone: Paljor had no heirs. Uwelain was the last of his line as well. There are some distant relations, but it would take an extensive effort to track them down." The Seat paused. "Plus, we have taken the evidence you presented into account while evaluating our situation. The Borden Isles are ready to return to Svieda... but, in the process, we will need you to help rebuild our government. The details of this treaty will need to be worked out further once Sword Prince Maelgyn is healthy enough. We have sent word to your ship requesting your best doctor, and sent the call for the best surgeons in the court, but in the meantime... we wish to ask for your help in establishing an interim government."

El'Athras snorted. One of the reasons he left Mar'Tok was to avoid just this kind of thing. "Well, what else do we have to do at the moment?"

"Maelgyn, can you hear me?"

Everything hurt, but he was surprisingly still alive. As consciousness returned to him, Maelgyn felt a gentle magic field bathing him in its energy. He momentarily panicked, his last memory of being involved in a fight to the death with a superior magic-using opponent. He was quickly reassured, however.

Calm yourself, young Prince, Sekhar told him. *This is just the healing touch of your lifemate, under the instructions of several doctors and surgeons. They are trying to help you, but if you move too much you could hurt yourself further.*

Nevertheless, Maelgyn tried to open his eyes. Last he could recall, Euleilla was in mortal peril. His memories were quite jumbled, however. Unable to find the strength to even move the muscles of his eyelids, he realized the only way he would find the answers to his questions would be to, well, ask them.

"We're alone right now," Euleilla's voice whispered softly. "But Dr. Wodtke will be here in a moment. I... I didn't think you were going to make it."

Is she all right? he thought to the living weapon. Her voice was wavering more than he would have thought.

Better than you are, it thought back. *She's probably a bit tired, since she's been keeping you from bleeding to death for almost twenty four hours straight, but you were able to save her from anything worse than getting bloo... uh, dirt on her face. You were awake for that, you know.*

My mind's in a bit of a jumble, Maelgyn admitted. *I don't even remember... did I win?*

Yes. Uwelain was slain, but he was the only casualty among your companions, Sekhar reported. *I hope most of your enemies aren't that strong.*

Maelgyn thought of Hussack, remembering that the Sho'Curlas royal who had assassinated his king was also about Euleilla's equal... which meant they were probably on par with each other until he learned how to access his full potential regularly. Then again, 'on par with Euleilla' was significantly better than what he just faced. *No, I don't think most of our Human enemies will be quite that strong. It does look like there may be a few Elves we'll have to fight in the coming years, however, and you know how hard it is to deal with them. They could be harder to fight than Paljor was.*

Maybe I made a mistake bonding with you, Sekhar mused jokingly. *Oh, well, too late now. Maybe we can rest up a bit before we face the next threat, at least.*

"You know, in all this time we've never consumated our marriage," Euleilla noted. "You were ill. I was ill. I couldn't function on the ship. There was too much danger of someone walking into our camp tent. Despite that, I was more worried about your life than I was my own." She paused. "Right now, I don't care what else happens. I thought you were going to die – that will not happen again, got it? I won't have you scaring me like that again." Another pause. "And when you're healthy again, I don't care if we both really are seasick and it's in broad daylight on board a ship with an audience of hundreds, we are consumating this marriage, got it?" There was a click, and Euleilla stiffened. "Dr. Wodtke's here. Now, hush."

Maelgyn would have laughed if it didn't feel like laughing would kill him. Euleilla had nothing to worry about – he wouldn't say a word.

"Good, good! It's probably not your destiny to become a doctor, but at least it looks like I can teach you to patch up your husband when he gets hurt," the Doctor said.

"Maybe." It sounded like Euleilla was more tired than he'd realized.

"He'll be fine. You've sealed up all the wounds, and as long as he takes the time to heal they won't reopen. Just try to keep him from overexerting himself, okay?"

"I don't think that'll be possible," Maelgyn's wife said. Was she crying? He could only remember one time he had ever heard her cry, before, and the sound made him want to sit up and hold her. He couldn't do it, however.

"What do you mean?" Dr. Wodtke asked.

"Look at what we have left to do!" Euleilla snapped, her nerves obviously on the brink. "The Borden Island Council has voted to end their rebellion and rejoin Svieda, true. But we haven't finished – we still need to set up an interim government, appoint a new line of regents, find a new Sword, and restore the Code of Svieda to the Borden Isles. Uwelain will need to be buried, and so will Paljor. Paljor's papers will need to be investigated, and any agents or spies from Sho'Curlas will have to be found. And even when we have finished with the Borden Isle government, that is not all we came to do here – we still have to return to the Golden Dragons' lair and negotiate with them. Then we have to organize our armies to fight the Sho'Curlas... and *then* we have to deal with those idiot Elves who want to 'balance' the races. Will we be able to 'take the time to heal,' anyway?"

Well, you heard her, Sekhar, Maelgyn sighed mentally. *I think we don't exactly have much time to spare resting. The threat has yet to be lifted.*

A shame, Sekhar replied. *But I believe we can answer it.*

Fennec Fox Press

If you enjoyed this book, feel free to sign up for our electronic mailing list (http://fennecfoxpress.com/social.html) or join our forums (http://www.maelgyn.com/forums/) for discussions, news, and supplemental material for this and all future installments in the Law of Swords series and other fine Fennec Fox Press books.